Also by Sarah Hinlicky Wilson

Fiction

Pearly Gates: Parables from the Final Threshold

Protons and Fleurons: Twenty-Two Elements of Fiction

Nonfiction

Sermon on the Mount: A Poetic Paraphrase

To Baptize or Not to Baptize: A Practical Guide for Clergy

*I Am a Brave Bridge:
An American Girl's Hilarious and Heartbreaking Year
in the Fledgling Republic of Slovakia*

A-TUMBLIN' DOWN

a novel

Sarah Hinlicky Wilson

Thornbush Press

Copyright © 2022 by Sarah Hinlicky Wilson. All rights reserved.

Publisher's Note: This is a work of fiction. Names, characters, places, and incidents are a product of the author's imagination. Locales and public names are sometimes used for atmospheric purposes. Any resemblance to actual people, living or dead, or to businesses, companies, events, institutions, or locales is completely coincidental.

Thornbush Press | www.thornbushpress.com

Cover design and artwork by Laura Shallcrass

Book Layout © 2015 BookDesignTemplates.com

A-Tumblin' Down / Sarah Hinlicky Wilson. -- 1st paperback ed.
ISBN 978-1-7372611-4-8

for all the faithful pastors
and their families

O Thou! whose fancies from afar are brought;
Who of thy words dost make a mock apparel,
And fittest to unutterable thought
The breeze-like motion and the self-born carol;
Thou Faery Voyager! that dost float
In such clear water, that thy Boat
May rather seem
To brood on air than on an earthly stream;
Suspended in a stream as clear as sky,
Where earth and heaven do make one imagery;
O blessed Vision! happy Child!
That art so exquisitely wild,
I think of thee with many fears
For what may be thy lot in future years.

I thought of times when Pain might be thy guest,
Lord of thy house and hospitality;
And grief, uneasy Lover! never rest
But when she sate within the touch of thee.
Oh! too industrious folly!
Oh! vain and causeless melancholy!
Nature will either end thee quite;
Or, lengthening out thy season of delight,
Preserve for thee, by individual right,
A young Lamb's heart among the full-grown flocks.
What hast Thou to do with sorrow,
Or the injuries of tomorrow?
Thou art a Dew-drop, which the morn brings forth,
Not doomed to jostle with unkindly shocks;
Or to be trailed along the soiling earth;
A Gem that glitters while it lives,
And no forewarning gives;
But, at the touch of wrong, without a strife,
Slips in a moment out of life.

—William Wordsworth, "To H. C., Six Years Old"

All chapter epigraphs are taken from John Hector St. John's *Letters from an American Farmer* (1782).

CHAPTER ONE

August 1988

*If they be not elegant,
they will smell of the woods,
and be a little wild.*

Kitty lived in a parsonage with white wooden siding and big green shutters. A strip of gravel bordered by hydrangeas separated the house from the church, which was covered with the same white wooden siding but had no shutters at all; its splash of color was a pair of bright red doors out front. Church and parsonage alike perched at the top of a sharply twisting driveway on the south side of Shibboleth, New York, so high up over the town that Kitty called it their "eyrie," savoring the strange word. On summer nights of slashing rain and violet-tinged lightning she declared it their "eerie eyrie," savoring equally the homophone.

In the meadow behind the house grew a tangle of golden-rod, Queen Anne's lace, and blue chicory. Kitty devoted hours of her waning summer vacation to attacking the milkweed that grew riotously throughout the tangle. "It reproduces like rabbits," she would solemnly inform the teenage girls at church, with no clear notion of what that meant or why it made the girls conceal little smiles. Her weapon for the attack was a sturdy branch of sugar maple. She swung and sliced with the precision of a samurai. Every so often she stopped to split open a pod and let the milk trickle out, stroking the opalescent scales and soft fur, before renewing the attack.

Sometimes, when she was savaging the milkweed, or braiding corn silk the exact same color as her hair, or threading a daisy chain that would inevitably split and fall apart, her mother would stick her head out the pantry door and warn Kitty, for the thousandth time, to stay away from the east edge of meadow. Beyond the parsonage, past the lilac tree, where the curly dock with its rust-red smokestacks of flowers gave way to layers of shattered rock, there was an almost sheer drop to the saddle between the hills below. "You can't see how dangerous it is," Carmichael explained again and again, because the drop-off was obscured from sight by the blackberry canes gripping the rock face all the way down. "I don't want Saul and Asher getting any ideas from seeing you over there."

Kitty always replied irritably, "Yes, I *know*," because she did know, though exactly how well she knew she never mentioned. Within a week of moving into the parsonage three summers before, when Kitty was still only eight, she'd found a low shallow cave just below the lilac and just above the drop-off. No one else in the family knew about it. Whenever she disappeared, they figured she was crawling inside the forsythia tunnel or hiding in the heart of the lilac tree. No one had any idea that in fact she shimmied into a dry mouth of rock to hold her council meetings.

Kitty thought her mom's warning was silly anyway, because the really terrifying thing about their eyrie was not the drop-off but the driveway with its pair of hairpin turns and the sensation of gravel skidding beneath the tires even in hot dry weather. Driving it in winter was enough to make your heart stop, and even Asher didn't complain about putting on his seatbelt for that. The founders of Mt. Moriah Lutheran Church must have chosen their site because the land was cheap. Its location certainly didn't do it any favors through Shibboleth's long snowy season. There are limits to what even feisty old German ladies will endure.

"You know, Pastor," Mrs. Feuerlein would say in her gentle growl, "I vorked in zhe hospital laundry for sheventeen years, I escaped from zhe Stasi, I shlept in barns, I accepted rides from shtrangers, you know zhere is nozhing zhat I am afraid of, but I vill *not* drive up zhat driveway vhen it is icy." Mrs. Kipfmueller would nod in solemn agreement, despite the fact that *her* ancestors had left Germany a century and a half earlier and tarried in Brazil for more than half that period before landing, improbably, in Olutakli County. Then Pastor Donald would assert that they were both remarkable women and surely never stayed away from church unless extreme circumstances required it.

And so at least once a year, when a snowstorm direct from the Great Lakes dumped its payload late on a Saturday night, nobody would come to church at all, because even if the county roads got cleared in time, the church's driveway never did. Then on Sunday morning, Kitty and her little brothers and their mother would tromp across the pristine snow to sing as loudly as they could in the empty sanctuary, but they wouldn't ever have communion. The first time it happened their mom said, "Can't we?" and their dad, faintly shocked, said, "Carmichael, the sacraments are not a private family affair." Kitty was surprised at how easily her mother accepted this, because as far as *she* could tell there was no boundary between church and family at all, especially considering where they lived. But then Kitty didn't much like those pallid little wafers that gummed up on your tongue anyway, so it wasn't that big a deal.

Access to a vacant church where you could sing yourself hoarse was one thing, but Kitty knew that the real goods came from the English department at the college where her mother worked, a promised land with treats far better than milk, honey, or communion wafers: an infinite supply of felt-tip pens in blue, black, red, and sometimes even a luscious brown, highlighters in lurid yellow and pale green, stacks of post-it notes in pastel colors, cute little black-and-white bottles clearly labeled "Liquid Paper" yet unfailingly referred to as "white-out," and composition notebooks colored like cows.

"Did you bring me anything?" Kitty demanded one evening toward the end of milkweed season. She had obliged with a "Whee! Mommy!" and an enthusiastic kiss before settling down to business.

"No," said Carmichael.

"Hmmph," said Kitty.

"Sweetheart, the main job of an English professor is to read, not to collect office supplies. You should shift your focus a bit."

"I read *all the time*," she sassed. "I read more than all the kids in my class put together. They still think 'Alice in Wonderland' is a *movie*. I wanted some more post-its. What are we having for dinner?"

"Roasted post-its," said Carmichael.

The phone rang. "Can I have a snack?" Kitty interposed before her mother took the receiver from its cradle.

"Run into the pantry and get an apple," then, "Hello?"

Kitty did as she was told, bringing the peanut butter along for good measure.

"No, I can't come down just now," Carmichael was saying as she returned. A whispered "Bammy" was sufficient to explain.

Kitty heard the hiss of telephonic reproach.

"Mom, I don't understand why I have to keep explaining this to you. I can't just pop down for a weekend. Donald works on Sundays. I can't leave him alone here with the kids."

"I don't need looking after," said Kitty loudly.

"Plus my classes begin next week, and Asher is starting kindergarten the week after. There's just too much going on right now."

Carmichael's silence witnessed to the objections at the other end of the line.

"Look, even if I could manage, the kids don't want to miss Sunday School," said Carmichael. A sudden warning note sounded in her voice out of all proportion to the words. Kitty checked to see if her mother's teeth were clenched. She'd always wanted to see clenched teeth.

Apparently Kitty was not the only one to detect when a line

had been crossed. Mollifying sounds murmured through the receiver. Carmichael's hunched shoulders dropped an inch or two, almost back to their usual position. Then she said, "Why don't you two come up here for Labor Day?" A pause. "All right, then come later in the month when the traffic won't be so bad. We're always here. Every weekend without fail."

Platitudes crossed the wires and she hung up.

"Bammy and Bampy are coming up for a visit later next month," Carmichael announced with a grand exhalation.

"I know. I heard," said Kitty pertly. "Why we can't go and see them? I like New York. I wouldn't mind missing Sunday School for once. It's boring."

"*I* don't want you to miss Sunday School, and I don't like to leave your father alone on Sundays." Carmichael picked up the apple and scrubbed it in the sink like it was Asher in the bathtub. Asher never let a day go by without ending it grubby.

"We never go to church when we visit them," Kitty remarked. She noticed her mother's shoulders rising again.

"No, we don't," said Carmichael. Her tone was so neutral that it was anything but neutral.

"They don't believe in God, do they?" The thought occurred to Kitty for the first time, but she knew all at once with absolute certainty it was true. The knowledge was tantalizing and horrible.

"No, they don't," said Carmichael. The apple gleamed.

"They're ay-*thee*-sists!" cried Kitty.

"Atheists," corrected Carmichael. "But not really. 'Agnostic' is a better word for them. It's not that they think God doesn't exist. They just don't care."

Kitty crouched on the kitchen stool and dug into the peanut butter jar with a soupspoon. "Have they always been like that? Have they always been agnostic? Wait, does that mean you never went to church or Sunday School at all when you were a kid? What did you *do* on Sundays?" As she glommed peanut butter into her mouth, a whole new prospect opened up to Kitty: a world where Sunday mornings were every bit as free as Saturdays. It staggered the imagination, and Kitty was not deficient in that department.

Carmichael shrugged. She centered the apple cutter over the stem and pushed hard. The apple blossomed like a flower. "I just played, when I was little. Or watched TV. Bammy and Bampy read the paper. Sometimes we had people over for breakfast and I made pancakes or waffles for everyone. That was when I was a little older."

"You knew other agnostic people?"

"Lots of 'em," said Carmichael.

Kitty stopped to digest the revelation that her mother was a foreigner. A refugee from a strange and wondrous place. Horrible, yes. But wondrous all the same.

Carmichael chewed on a piece of apple and stared at nothing. "I could make Chicken Marbella for supper if there are any of the good green olives left," she mused. "No, wait, that recipe needs to marinate overnight. I'll just make something up."

Kitty's mind churned down another unimagined path, then burst out with the demand, "How come *you* believe in God?"

Carmichael pulled her arms out of the cupboard along with a package of prunes and a can of tomatoes. "Things make more sense to me this way," she said. "God explains things. My mom and dad have spent their whole life explaining things one way or another, but I was always suspicious of their explanations. Like they were trying to cover up stuff that didn't make sense to them. Or blocking out a whole big chunk of reality that they didn't want to admit was there. I didn't know any of that when I was little, of course. We never talked about it directly. I had to grow up and find out. Meeting your dad helped."

"Did you believe in God when you and Daddy met?"

"Not by name, but I think I did in my heart. Your daddy told me who God was, and then it was easy." A cutting board emerged, then a knife. Carmichael sharpened it on the steel.

"Do you love God?" Kitty pressed.

"You are just like I was, when I was a little girl," said Carmichael, beeping Kitty on the nose. "Always asking the hardest questions."

Kitty said nothing. She was trying to decide whether she liked being called a little girl. At least it was better than being accused of growing up and becoming such a fine young lady.

"Yes, I love God very much," Carmichael said at last.

"Me too," said Kitty. She shoveled another load of peanut butter into her mouth and slurped it around while Carmichael settled the cast iron skillet on the stove.

Kitty loved God because she had always loved God, as long as she could remember being alive. It didn't feel like much, to be honest. Not like loving her parents or her brothers or the council. But it was a solid sort of thing that was always there.

Suppose it wasn't there, though? That's what it was like for her own mom as a kid. Could you really start to love God when you were already an adult, and already a liar? Kitty knew one thing for sure about adults, and that was their rampant tendency to lie, especially for good causes.

What about Bammy and Bampy? They were adults, but nice ones. Kitty didn't think they were liars. But weren't they lying when they said there was no God?

She'd have to take the question to the council. They'd know better than she did. It was too late to visit anymore tonight, but she could talk with them about it tomorrow.

∾

Donald rose with the sun, whatever the time of year. At the summer solstice that meant quarter to five and by Christmas nearly seven. Late August was a comfortable sort of time with a reasonable wake-up call of six o'clock. He made his own coffee. Carmichael scoffed at the "swill," as she called it, that fueled him, and would not suffer her own coffee, brewed from beans dutifully toted northwards by her discriminating City parents or purchased at no small expense from the Shibboleth Co-op, to be wasted on his tastebuds. He was amused by her snobbery and made a point of smacking his lips on his "ditchwater" (another term of disapprobation) whenever she saw him drink it.

On this particular morning, the pleasure of sunrise, coffee, and quiet vanished the moment Donald flipped open his pastoral agenda to find the next Sunday's lessons.

He should have seen it coming. It's not like he hadn't come across it before. Donald was on his fourth trip through the three-year lectionary, a curiosity that remained unfathomable to his assorted cousins and uncles, for whom there was no preaching but expository preaching, straight through one book of the Bible at a time, one verse at a time. Donald had in fact always taken wary note of this particular Sunday, the Fourteenth after Pentecost in Year B, for its distinction of featuring the one and only passage from the book of Joshua in the whole cycle.

Lucky for Donald, there were four texts in all to choose from any given Sunday, so the first time Joshua reared its ugly head he instead manfully shouldered his way through a fifth consecutive sermon on the bread of life from John 6. Three years later he tackled the almost-as-impossible text on husbands and wives from Ephesians 5; impossible for 1982, anyway, or whichever year that was. Another spin of the cycle brought him to Psalm 34. Only gradually had Donald realized that his fellow Lutheran pastors never preached on the Psalms, however dutifully they forced their congregations to chant through one each and every week. Donald remembered his own childhood pastor giving three solid years to the Psalms, one per week, except for Psalm 119, which got a few extra Sundays.

So now the only passage for the Fourteenth Sunday after Pentecost that Donald had not yet preached on was this very one from Joshua chapter 24. In all honesty, he could recycle a previous sermon on a different lesson and get away with it; he'd been at Mt. Moriah only three years and its members had never heard the other sermons. But Donald's relentless conscience told him he couldn't put it off forever.

Anyway, just the sight of the Joshua lesson set in motion the same old argument in his head, and he was powerless to stop it. He watched it unspool in his mind like a filmstrip.

"Choose this day whom you will serve." Joshua issued the charge to the Israelites on their way into the promised land. And the Israelites, in turn, chose the Lord. Simple enough.

That was the crux, the foundation, the fountainhead of everything Donald's grandfather had believed. Wilkinson Abney: preacher, evangelist, revivalist, convicter of sinners, uplifter of penitents. He was terribly tall, with huge rangy bones nearly poking out of his joints, whiskers like Lincoln's but white. He was powerful and gentle at the same time. As a child Donald never feared him but admired him desperately. He knew by the time he was six years old that he would grow up to be a preacher, too. Grandfather Abney detected the call early on, which made him all the more gentle and loving toward the boy.

Even then Donald had perceived that some of his grandfather's affection served a double purpose, directing barbed arrows at the heart of Grandfather Abney's son, Donald's father. Jimmy Abney grew up with religion but, as far as Donald could tell, got bored with it. He didn't hate it. He didn't tell stories about crazy clergy, hypocritical moralists, or shocking extortions. He just got his lifetime dose of religion a little too soon and spent the rest of his life patiently making good money as a general contractor. Donald's mother Dot grew up among poor and disorderly folks, for whom church was the one slender tether holding them back from total dissolution. Jimmy rescued her from all that and honored his wedded wife like a princess. She took Donald and his two siblings to church most Sundays because her in-laws expected her to. Jimmy brooked no objection and attended with the rest of the family rotely on holidays. But in a family like the Abneys', Jimmy's disengagement was practically to trumpet unbelief.

Donald knew his father had shrugged off *his* father easily, but Grandfather Abney still sat enthroned in Donald's heart.

And this was the one who had said, time and again, "Choose this day whom you will serve."

"I *have* chosen, Grandfather."

"Have you handed it *all* over, Donald? Is it all truly laid down before the Lord? What are you holding back? In what corner of your heart have you not chosen? Think, grandson, before the time runs out for thinking."

The Donald of the present hour sighed. He knew his line in the liturgy. He couldn't turn the argument away, not even in his imagination. He couldn't submit to it, either.

"Grandfather, it doesn't matter that I choose God. It matters that God chose me."

"Is that so?" rejoined Grandfather Abney. He rose up to his full height in Donald's imagination, the ratio the same as in childhood: the man stood eleven feet tall. "Does not Joshua command the Israelites to choose? Are those not his very words? Is Joshua not chosen a model and exemplar for all the Israelites? And yet *you* will not choose! Woe to him who evades the choice."

"But look," Donald said desperately. "So the Israelites chose. They *said* they chose the Lord. But did they cleave to it? Did they abide by their choice?" Something about Grandfather Abney called forth archaic verbs from Donald's deeps. "No. They failed the Lord again and again. They were a stiff-necked and faithless people. What good did it do them to choose?"

Grandfather Abney did not answer the question directly. Donald had never been able to force him to answer it, not even in his own mind. "We must choose again and again, Donald. Every day. Every noon. Every night. Every moment of the day is the Lord's. Choose to whom this minute will be offered in spiritual worship. Does it belong to the Lord? Or to the sinner hankering after the fleshpots of Egypt?"

"Of course we choose every day." Donald was exasperated. "But that's—that's not the good news. Choice is death for us every time."

"'I have set before you life and death, blessing and cursing: therefore choose life, that both thou and thy seed may live.' Donald, if the choice is death, is it not because *you choose death*?"

Donald shook himself free of the scene. He could never win, not even if he pointed out Grandfather Abney's illegitimate switch from Joshua to Deuteronomy to make his point. The old preacher would never concede the objection's relevance anyway. To him it was all the Good Book and all of it spoke the one good Word of God and that was that. A command to choose would not cease to be a command to choose, even if the very next verse demonstrated the choice to be impossible.

The irony of the thing was that Donald actually *had* made a choice, and not a small one. A choice, made with eyes wide open, to which he cleaved like a lifeline.

Donald, Jimmy, and Wilkinson Abney all came of age in a branch of the Holiness movement that had chosen, in addition to the Lord, to be separated from another branch of Holiness whose speciality, to hear it told, was Unholiness. This much and no more Donald had gleaned from his grandfather's passing remarks. Jimmy Abney exited the quarrel, mentally if not denominationally. Donald Abney remained within the fold in his youth, and after finishing college he doubled up on Bible school and ministry at a sister congregation, thereby pleasing one but not both of his forefathers.

During his third year of Bible school, sitting in a quiet corner of the small library, inhaling the sweet scent of mildew, Donald glanced up from his Greek homework and espied *The Journal of John Wesley*. He tugged it off the shelf and, paging through, came across the passage where Wesley described his conversion, how his heart had been strangely warmed. The anecdote was famous enough, a favorite retold from the pulpits of Donald's youth. But in reading Wesley's own account, Donald was surprised to discover that what warmed his heart was not Scripture but Martin Luther—his Preface to Romans, to be exact. Luther, that distant hero of old who got the ball of restoration rolling but failed to see it through. What a curious collision of worlds.

Donald followed the trail through the library till he located a shelf-long sequence of volumes, half in ruby-red, half in sherbet pastels. He tracked down the heartwarming Preface and settled back in his chair to read but promptly found himself unsettled. Luther rang familiar notes when he praised faith as a "living, busy, active, mighty thing," but then undermined his case just a page later with the assertion that, "as no one can give himself faith, neither can he take away his own unbelief." But was that not the very point of prayer and worship and discipleship? To generate and build up and secure one's own faith? To annihilate the whispers of unbelief and quite possibly the unbelievers? That was the very stuff of salvation. What game was Luther playing at?

With fifty-five volumes at hand, Donald did not lack for answers. He all but abandoned his Greek in the weeks ahead. By the end of his unauthorized binge, he discovered God's choice, a choice that lay beyond the vicissitudes of Donald's own slippery, insubstantial choices. Before the year was out, Donald chose to align himself with a tradition where his own choices were no longer of cosmic consequence and to enroll in one of its seminaries. If Grandfather Abney was neither heartbroken nor suspicious, it was only because he was dissonantly confident that Donald would see the error of his ways and return home where he belonged. Choices for God were subject to constant scrutiny; choices for church, by contrast, were supposed to be easy and absolute.

Carmichael slipped into the sunny office facing out over the saddle between the hills. "Morning," she said brightly, rubbing Donald's shoulders and setting her chin atop his head and its thinning mousy blond hair. "Working?"

"Arguing," said Donald. "Same as always."

"What over?" She peered down at his yellow legal pad, the

scriptural citation written boldly, even a little angrily at the top. "Joshua? Really? In a *sermon*?"

Donald nodded.

"Can't you just skip it? There's three others to choose from."

The lightness with which she said it was salve to Donald, but only to treat the symptoms, not to cure the root cause. It was all so easy for her. She'd grown up religionless, then fallen into faith like she fell into love with Donald, and nearly at the same time. The chasms between faith and understanding that threatened to swallow Donald whole were just wrinkles in the linen to her—natural to the subject, useless to try to eliminate, part of the charm.

"It's in the lectionary," Donald said, feeling stubborn and stupid. "It's canonical Scripture. I've always skipped it before. I can't in good conscience do it again."

"I'll leave you to it, then," and she kissed the top of his head.

Once she was gone he looked back at the scrawl on the page. His handwriting was atrocious and he had never learned to type; the clacking of typewriter keys annoyed him. But illegibility posed no problem. His procedure was to write up notes on the lesson, organize an outline for his thoughts, internalize it, and finally preach the message without either paper in front of him or absolute certainty of what he was going to say. He found that his sermons came out dead, lifeless, and unconvincing if he did otherwise.

The parishioners of Mt. Moriah had not realized that about him at first. When they did, they were shocked. A pastor was supposed to come equipped with a manuscript. A *Lutheran* pastor, anyway. Donald grew up with preachers who would no more bring a manuscript into the pulpit than a feather boa. Eventually the congregation became accustomed to its eccentric pastor, though Donald was pretty sure that no one heard a word from the pulpit during the first six months of his pastorate. They'd spent the whole time worrying he'd forget what he had to say.

Commander of his own mind again, Donald flipped open his well-thumbed Revised Standard Version (another shock to his clan, that he had abandoned the King James and even dared to say it contained errors. As if God almighty could make mistakes!). He laid one index finger on the agenda's listed range of verses and another on the corresponding page of the Bible.

"What fresh hell is this?" Donald's gut spoke ahead of the emendations of his brain. The appointed reading cut short just after Israel's pious poppycock, deleting from the record Joshua's sarcastic rejoinder, "You *cannot* serve the Lord!"

Improbably and unbelievably, the Lutherans were in cahoots with the revivalists. Donald settled down to his sermon with a passion, if not quite a message, that would have made his grandfather proud.

∼

Saul and Asher had the run of the parking lot, the strip between the parsonage and the church, and the meadow out back. For all that, every time they went out to play they followed a strictly determined itinerary, devoted to tradition as only the very small can be.

The boys were "Irish twins," a fact of which Kitty informed the church teenagers with the same solemnity and noncomprehension as the rabbit-like milkweed. She knew only that it meant they were born within twelve months of each other and, in their case, even in the same calendar year. For the three weeks between New Year's Eve and late January, during which period Asher caught up to Saul, they could even claim the same number for their age, a fact that pleased the younger Asher far more than the elder Saul.

The two boys lived in a small, rich, self-sufficient world of tractors, swords, and blanket forts. In winter they added snow to their oeuvre; in summer, bugs, sticks, and mud.

Asher, though the younger, always led the way. He had a shock of curls and a fierce gaze. His snuggles were athletic, squirmy, and brief, leaving Carmichael both elated and exhausted. Asher was not quite sure he wasn't one of Max's monsters in *Where the Wild Things Are*, just as he wasn't quite sure whether he was a different person from Saul. The only certain border in his mind was the invisible circle drawn around house, church, and meadow. The steep driveway and the cemetery comprised a fuzzy annex to the circle, the state forest a reassertion of its limits, the eastern edge of the meadow a nebulous mixture of threat and invitation. Asher longed to creep past the forsythias to the edge where Kitty went to play by herself. She possessed the qualities of a fairy to him and Saul: a mystical figure filled with stories, wisdom, lore, advice, and warnings freely dispensed before she poofed out of sight. She became real only when she was to be envied.

On that particular August morning, Asher as usual shot out ahead of Saul and made right for the fire ring. He grabbed one of a stash of sticks and poked at the smoldering remains of the garbage that Carmichael had brought out earlier and burned. Saul caught up and parroted the eternal warning of parents, "Be careful or you'll hurt yourself."

Even at the age of five, Asher was tired of hearing it. He ignored Saul and tried to get the stick to glow red. Then he could wave it in Saul's face, and Saul would run off. Saul was bigger but easily scared. In the short stretch of time when Saul existed but Asher didn't, Saul sickened and spent a month in the hospital. Carmichael's distracted worry over her baby accounted for the contraceptive oversight resulting in a second son before the year was out. The infantile sickness, both parents inferred, explained a good deal of Saul's meekness.

Asher didn't know any of that. What he did know was that something satisfied him beyond all reckoning, beyond even cookies, to see the bigger boy run from him or shy away from doing the things that Asher wanted to do.

The fire, mostly dead already, disappointed. Asher zoomed up to the tree line and Saul duly followed. They had a favorite spot where a copse of sprightly young sugar maples took a stand in front of the threatening shadows of the geometrically planted pine trees of the state forest. Asher shimmied up the tallest of the set. "Come up," he called.

Saul ignored the summons. He squatted down and worked at a sea-green lichen stuck to a rock as if with super glue. Asher yanked off handfuls of leaves and dropped them on Saul's head. "Stop," whined the latter.

"Come *up*," ordered Asher.

Saul slid between the sugar maples and picked his way down a sharp decline. Brambles impeded further downward progress. He spied black raspberries and stuffed them into his mouth even though they were still hard and sour.

"Whatcha eating?" yelled Asher. "Hey, save some for me!" He slid down the tree like it was a fire pole and pelted over. The berries were plentiful but he grabbed at Saul's.

"Get your own," snapped Saul.

"No," retorted Asher. He clawed at Saul's hands. Saul placed his right elbow neatly in Asher's stomach, and Asher toppled over backwards. Other kids, especially at Sunday School, cried and tattled at such treatment, but Asher never resented a physical takedown. He jumped up and tried again, but Saul was ready this time and pushed him into the bramble. Asher tore free his bare arms and pant legs, earning scratches on the former and snags on the latter. "Look at my blood!" he shouted happily. Saul obliged. Asher licked it. "It tastes like a penny," he said.

Saul shrugged with the wisdom of the wise. "I know," he said.

At that, Asher liked his brother again, and the tacit call of the next station lured him on. "Come on," he said. They ran back down the meadow, across the gravel in front of the parsonage and church, and over to the oak tree right at the top of the driveway. Without discussion or quarrel they hopped onto the swing hanging from its thickest limb. Its seat was wide enough to accommodate two little-boy bottoms, Asher as always to the right of Saul. They pumped their legs hard and got it going. Asher tried to go higher than Saul liked. The latter's refusal to cooperate made the swing go all twisty, but not twisty enough to be fun. After that they swung together docilely, engaged in earnest conversation about what it would be like if the kinds of dinosaurs that didn't have wings had superpowers instead that could make them fly.

After the swing they walked the verge between the parking lot and the weedy hillside sloping down toward town. They scoured the gravel for pineapple weed, yanking it up by the roots to get a good sniff. They tried, without any real hope, all the doors of the church. No good. They were always locked, which both boys figured to be against robbers, though in fact they were locked against Saul and Asher themselves. Asher pointed to the ladder leaning on the back wall of the church, resting quietly between summer shingle replacements and winter snows. A well-worn argument about climbing up (Asher) or not (Saul) ensued. Saul won by the simple expedient of running off to the hose at the back of the house. Experiments in varying the pressure with a thumb, soaking each other unawares, and rehydrating their favorite patch of mud saw them through to mid-morning snack.

The brothers sat on the porch deftly devouring a banana apiece when Kitty banged out the pantry door and stepped over their shoulders leaning into each other.

"Where're you going?" shouted Asher after her.

"To my place," she said without turning back. She had a notebook in hand and several pens sticking out her back pocket. One of them was an emerald green ballpoint, an English department special.

Asher shoved the rest of his banana in his mouth and dropped the peel on the porch. "I wanna come with you!"

Kitty turned around. She looked very tall. "You *can't* come with me," she declared. "It's *dangerous*. You could *die*."

"I wanna come," wailed Asher. Saul could be prevailed

upon by brute force, but only sympathy would work on Kitty.

"I can't let you get so close to the edge," said Kitty. Behind the words they both felt the vast, nebulous, unassailable force of all things adult.

"It's not fair!" Asher jumped down the steps and kicked at a patch of grass hard with his rubber boot. He wanted to spray Kitty with dirt but it didn't work. Even the white globes of clover only bent over and bounced back.

"The world isn't fair," Kitty quoted their mother. She turned away and stalked off.

"I wanna come with you!" Asher howled as loud as he could.

Saul finished his banana. He didn't like it when Asher got like he would be soon, if left unchecked. "Come on, let's watch TV," he called over.

"No, no, no," Asher wailed. "I wanna go with Kitty." All of a sudden great big tears were spilling out of his blue-gray eyes. He stood rooted in place.

Saul scratched all over his short dark hair and said, "I'm gonna go watch DuckTales." He went in through the pantry door, then peeped out to see if Asher was following. He wasn't. He was still crying and fussing and stomping his boots on the ground.

It didn't occur to Saul to ask either of their parents for help. Somehow he felt the whole thing was his fault. The situation was grave indeed if TV was insufficient incitement for Asher to relinquish his quixotic cause.

Saul stood in the pantry. One end of it held their mother's collection of African violets under a UV lamp. Saul understood this to mean that they were specimens from another planet. He avoided them carefully because he knew what aliens were capable of. He clambered up onto the built-in counter, balancing on the very short overhanging ledge with a firm grip on the knob of a cupboard, and with his other hand wrenched open the opposite cupboard door. He grabbed two packets of fruit leather, not the good kind that kids at school got but some other kind their mom bought at the Co-op. It was strictly off limits outside maternally designated occasions. He shut the cupboard door as quietly as he could, dropped to his knees, flipped around, and sat down on the counter before slipping off. Asher would've jumped. Saul snuck back out of the house again.

Asher was still wailing in the same place as if planted there. He paused momentarily to observe his brother's reappearance while licking snot and tears off his upper lip.

Saul knew better than to summon him. Instead he dropped to his belly and crawled, alligator-fashion, across the yard in the opposite direction of Kitty and the drop-off.

Asher watched until it became clear that Saul was headed for the church cemetery. Only one equally forbidden realm could break his desire for another. He tore across the lawn and caught up with Saul under a stand of sumac trees, ruddy in anticipation of autumn. He dropped to the ground. One after another they inched under the single-chain fence surrounding the cemetery, a fence that could only suggest but not enforce the rule.

Saul arose into a squat and waddled around the perimeter to the tallest gravestone at the back, affording both shadow and concealment from parental disapproval. The stone face was engraved with a long name the boys could not pronounce but gave Saul the opportunity to display his knowledge of the alphabet: S-C-H-I-C-K-E-D-A-N-Z. Asher liked the A best because, according to Saul, it was the first letter of his own name, too. Asher thought it amazing that he could share something like a letter with a dead person.

But the present occasion required more than alphabetic charms. "Sit down," Saul ordered. Asher obeyed. "Here." He handed over the fruit leather.

"Did Mommy give this to you?" Asher asked in awe.

Saul didn't answer. Asher understood.

They ate together in silence.

∽

Bypassing her brothers, Kitty waded through the goldenrod pawing at her bare legs, followed the hedge of bloomless forsythias to the end, pushed through burs and blackberries, and achieved the lilac tree. A path as faint and narrow as a deer's led a short way over little scuffs and overhangs to a hollow in the hillside about five feet below the meadow. Only a few steps beyond, the rock face turned steep and treacherous, but Kitty never ventured that far. She worked herself backward into the cave. Timothy grass and daisy fleabane grew upside-down from its ceiling. It was always cool inside, even on hot days, because the sun only struck it for a couple hours each morning.

Kitty arranged herself into a cozy spot where she could settle her back against the cave wall and summoned her council.

First came the Fawn from *Alice*. He tripped in delicately, folded his legs underneath himself, and cuddled up next to Kitty. Kitty's parents could see Fawn now and again cavorting in the meadow at daybreak. She was grateful for his willingness to be seen. Kitty's parents accepted her assertions of friendship with the creature in tones of placid unbelief, but at least they granted his existence at all. The rest of the council remained invisible to everyone except Kitty.

Next came Nutcracker, very much nutcracker and not at all prince. He was from Hoffmann's story, not from Tchaikovsky's ballet, which Kitty had watched once and refused to watch again because of its many offensive alterations, not least of all to the name of the female principal. Nutcracker bowed stiffly to Kitty. "Marie sends her greetings," he said in his deep somber voice.

"And I send her mine," Kitty replied. Marie never came. Kitty never asked why.

Rhea the titan arrived in a melodramatic blaze on her chariot drawn by two lions. The two escorts never spoke and therefore did not technically count as council members. They were more like bodyguards, ostensibly for Rhea, though they also warded off impostors, nightmares, liars, and little brothers. Rhea stayed put in her chariot while the lions settled at the cave entrance to surveil with their sleepless eyes.

Riding in on the tail of Rhea's gusts came Ichabod the dog. Back when Asher was still growing inside their mom, Kitty had eavesdropped on her parents' scouring of the Bible for suitable names. Carmichael particularly liked Old Testament names—she was the one who'd chosen "Saul"—but this time around Donald nixed one suggestion after another: Zadok, Abinadab, Hacaliah, Mahershalalhashbaz. For some reason, the proposal of "Ichabod" had made Donald laugh uproariously, so Kitty assumed it was a go. She was so surprised that her new baby brother ended up being Asher instead of Ichabod that it took her a month to remember his real name. When at last she did, that very same afternoon, while she was trying to build an igloo in the backyard—this was back when they lived in North Dakota; Kitty remembered of it mainly the wind and how her father always talked in a bemused way about Norwegians—a dog showed up, a slobbery cheerful golden retriever, equipped with the name her little brother didn't end up getting after all. Ichabod was the only member of the council who hadn't first appeared in a book. Kitty respected him for that.

Last of all came Jo March from *Little Women*. She was Kitty's best friend. Kitty never told Jessica Hodyl about Jo. Jessica thought *she* was Kitty's best friend, and the whole class accepted it as fact. Kitty accepted it for the purposes of school. Jessica listened obediently to Kitty's stories, traded notes in loopy cursive on perforated pages creased and excised from notebooks (though Jessica used wide rule instead of college rule, and apparently without shame), complained about Megan Moravsky on cue, and never got better grades than Kitty. Kitty found Jessica pleasant enough and useful for the hours condemned to school. But she was no Jo. Jessica wouldn't cut off her own hair to do someone else a good turn; she wouldn't even leave the house without hairspraying it halfway to heaven.

Also, she was weak, like Beth March, not tough, like Jo March. Jo you could tell the truth. Not Jessica. She'd probably faint.

When everyone was settled in—Jo at the back of the cave writing verse longhand on a very old-fashioned paper tablet, Rhea dead center in her chariot, the others scattered about—Kitty cleared her throat and said in a very official voice, "I suppose you're all wondering why I've gathered you here today." She had learned, somewhere, that this was the appropriate invocation to a meeting.

Fawn, Nutcracker, and Ichabod nodded, rapt. Rhea stared. Jo kept writing.

"I've been thinking about this problem for a long time," Kitty continued. "It's adults. They're liars. You can't trust them. They say not to do something, but then they go and do it themselves. Or you ask them a question, but they don't want to tell you the real answer, so they make something up instead." She thought about mentioning her grandparents as an example, but somehow she couldn't quite bring herself to do it. And it wasn't just them, after all. All adults were the same.

There were murmurs of assent.

"So here's my problem," said Kitty. "I don't want to become an adult because I'll just end up like one of them. I mean, I don't *really* think I will. But I'm afraid I will, because everyone turns out like that. Maybe I won't be any different, but even if I *am* different, I'll still be an adult, and kids won't trust me anymore. And I'm always on the side of the kids. So I need a way not to grow up."

"Would you rather die?" Rhea asked.

Her stark expression rattled Kitty. "No," she said, eyeing the lions.

"Hmm," said Rhea.

"Wasn't there some boy named Peter Pan who never grew up?" Jo called from the back.

"Yeah, but he was stupid," said Kitty. "He was just immature. There are kids like him at school, and I don't want to be like them, either."

"It is indeed a problem," said Nutcracker gravely.

"Well, we have to figure out an answer, and soon," Kitty replied. "See, I'm already in the double digits." She raised both hands and spread out her fingers, then held up one pointer. "In October I'm twelve. Then only one more year till thirteen. It seems like once you hit thirteen everything goes wrong. Take Michelle from church. She used to be fun, but she isn't anymore. Not since she turned thirteen."

"We have a whole year and a half to solve the problem," Ichabod pointed out cheerfully.

"But we don't know how long it will take. And I just wanna say," she added, glancing sidelong at Rhea, "that I guess I *could* grow up, if I had to, as long as I didn't have to be a liar. It just seems like the two always go together."

"We'll work on it," stated Rhea.

Kitty wasn't entirely sure she wanted Rhea working on it. But it was too late now.

CHAPTER TWO

August 1988

*About one mile farther on the same road,
his next neighbor may be
a good honest plodding German Lutheran,
who addresses himself to the same God, the God of all,
agreeably to the modes he has been educated in,
and believes in consubstantiation;
by so doing he scandalizes nobody.*

Carmichael blinked her way into the dawn diffusing over hills that shrugged and hunched across the horizon. The maples had that tired, late-summer look about them, dusty overgrown leaves just waiting for the first hint of cool to trigger their color change and fall to kindly death. The meadow grass alone remained fresh and lively. Carmichael sauntered through it barefoot, dandelion seeds sticking to her dewy toes.

During daylight hours, the yard and its fraying edges belonged to the children, but before they woke it was hers. She walked straight uphill to the edge of the state forest, tracing unawares the same path as her boys, to nestle in the sugar maple copse and gaze out over the Shibboleth valley, the bottle-green Nekamisto River turning corkscrews through it.

A city kid, Carmichael never tired of the stillness or the greenness. The village was picture-postcard perfect, at least as seen from her perch atop the hillside, what with its colonial covered bridge and vintage twenties theater, and the school and the college and the courthouse all in matching red brick with white trim as if they'd sprung out of the same Playmobil set. Up close, Shibboleth teetered on the edge of run-down: the peeling paint, scrubby lawns, slumping barns, and abandoned machinery of rural deprivation. Still, countryside poverty was charming sheerly on account of not being urban poverty. Carmichael felt affection toward it, however much her professorial mind told her not to romanticize.

A good life. Husband, children, the beginnings of a career, a green and pleasant place.

It was always in these moments of settling into happiness that the alternate Carmichaels began to appear.

The real and original Carmichael allowed herself the rueful thought that, if hers were an actual disorder, some fillip of brain chemistry or neurologically-encoded trauma, she could get help, take medicine, talk it out with a nodding, prodding therapist. But hers were existential hauntings, not psychiatric ones.

California Carmichael came first. She always did. Even her title made the real Carmichael cringe with embarrassment.

This one wore a sleeveless sundress, a garment that was tolerable only about six days out of the whole Shibboleth summer. Her hair was long and dark brown like the original's but streaked with gold and swishy like in a commercial. Her skin was tanned unbrokenly instead of spottily. She looked younger and had no midriff stretch from three children—she'd *had* three children, of course, but something about the smog or a diet of grapefruit and sprouts drove off the lingering lumpiness. She plopped down next to Carmichael.

"Do you remember—?" she began.

"Of course I do."

California Carmichael was never deterred by the real Carmichael's rudeness. "We were fourteen and it was the farthest we'd ever been from home. Mom and Dad were always such East Coast snobs!"

"New York snobs," the real Carmichael corrected her. "No one's more parochial than a New Yorker."

"'Nothing worth seeing west of the Delaware,'" the other quoted. "And Philadelphia marking the near end of the Midwest. But there was that fad among their friends to visit Napa Valley vineyards and L.A. movie studios, so we spent that one July tooling around California. Remember how after we arrived at LAX and were riding in the rental car, we kept saying, 'I know this place, I've been here, it's like coming home,' and Mom and Dad just laughed? We thought it was some kind of mysterious, tremendous intimation of a past life. I think it may have been our first glimmering of religion. But then—"

She laughed. It was just different enough from the real Carmichael's laugh to unnerve her.

"—then we realized it was only TV! We'd been seeing California on TV all our lives and never even knew it. No wonder it felt like home."

"But it sure ruined TV," Carmichael said. "I can't watch anything set anywhere other than California anymore because it's so obviously fake. Like *you*," she added, sharply.

California Carmichael smiled with pacific calm. "Then why do you still wish for me?" she said, rising, and dissipated.

"I don't know," said Carmichael to the orange hawkweed crushed beneath her heel. "Only because you *could* have been."

California Carmichael was the easy, obvious alternate self. She came first because she was easiest to dismiss, and the real Carmichael couldn't take her seriously enough to hold her off. But she was the gateway alternate, and the others followed without fail.

Maybe it was on account of its being Sunday morning, a morning with church, and with church, an anthem from the choir—so this morning they came as a choir. A naggle of alternate Carmichaels singing one song of alternate existence after another, a dissonant orchestra, each trying to lure her to its own version of herself.

One Carmichael had gone into the sciences instead of literature, as a beloved high school teacher had fruitlessly urged. One had gone to a different college, indistinguishable from the one she did attend in its boilerplate prestige, but it sent her down different paths with different companions. One sang of staying on in France after her semester in Montpellier, not to undertake the trite pattern of falling in love with Paris and a Parisian, but to recapitulate her present rural life in the fashion of a paysanne, garlanded with lavender plaits about her head and an orange blossom-scented pompe à l'huile in hand.

A soprano trilled society wife, as so many of her college friends had become despite their erstwhile commitment to busting glass ceilings, too fond as they were of luxuries and low-conflict lunches. A mezzo soprano moved her to Boston and a fine old home with a corner tower and elegant dinner parties that nurtured sophisticated conversations about art and philosophy. Then an irritated alto made her a philanthropist who threw it all away to serve somewhere vaguely exotic and indefinably risky, where she could be helpful, even heroic.

They beckoned to her with her own fingers, in her own voice, inviting her to merge with them. Individually each sang in a thin and wobbly voice, just as Carmichael did in real life. Individually no particular life was more compelling than another.

But all together, in chorus, they posed the insidious question over and over: why *this* life? Out of a hundred or a thousand alternatives, how did you end up with *this* one? Are you, right now, the very best soloist in this whole choir?

Carmichael stuck her fingers in her ears to make the symbolic point, though it didn't silence their noise. Their question was not hers. It was not one she cared to ask. Left alone, she loved her life. The alternates tormented only on account of their sheer possibility.

They didn't take the hint, didn't budge, didn't shut up.

She stood up and ran back down through the wet grass to get ready for church.

∼

Hazel Quinn was busy in the sacristy.

Pastor Donald burst through the door but, as his eyes were on a clutch of hand-scrawled papers, he nearly tripped over her. She watched as he took in her activity, stooping to get a closer look just like he always did, being taller than just about everyone else at church and positively towering over Hazel herself.

Then he reminded her, in a calm and measured tone, that it was *not* her turn to set up for communion.

Hazel agreed, cheerfully. She removed the half-disintegrated faux-leather cover from the chalice and laid a neatly folded doily on the paten.

Faced with the impenetrable wall of her agreement, Pastor Donald said, "Shouldn't you leave it for—" his eyes flickered over to the chart on the wall with its insipid script and garland of cartoony lilies "—Bonnie?"

"Well," said Hazel, "she lives so far away, and I know sometimes it's hard for her to make it on time, so I just thought I'd make things easy for her by getting everything out and ready to go." She smiled at the pastor. He's such a nice boy, she thought, such an innocent still, trusting those who oughtn't be trusted. He means well, trying to get them involved, but if someone doesn't keep hold of the tiller, the whole ship will founder.

She set the bottle of port and the box of wafers stamped with the plus signs that passed for crosses on the very edge of the counter closest to the chancel. This thoughtful arrangement would save Bonnie every second lost to her late start and long drive. Hazel heard Pastor Donald sigh as he passed through the sacristy and headed down the stairs. She interpreted it as the solidarity of the reliable against the unreliable.

George Pohl on his way up the stairs from the basement assailed Pastor Donald on his way down, who said jovially, "Good morning, George!" George reacted to his joviality with suspicion every single time. He could not fathom that the pastor might be genuinely happy to see him in his own right, apart from news or duties.

"Pastor Donald's a very nice man," Hazel always tried to tell George when he voiced his disorientation. "He *likes* people."

"We'll cure him of that," was George's retort.

"I saw the July numbers. They're very good," said Pastor Donald. It sounded like he was congratulating George, and George alone, for the generosity of the congregation at large.

"They're not," pronounced George. He shook his head. This was the problem with Pastor Donald. Far too optimistic.

"Oh no?"

"There were *five* Sundays in July this year," George explained. "It's a distorted statistic. We had twenty-five percent more opportunity for giving than in a normal month. We shouldn't take it as representative. It's a false positive." In addition to being church treasurer, George was a technician at Blackwell Memorial Hospital in Kuhsota, the nearest city, over in Tryon County. George saw a lot of malignant lumps. He was always braced for the worst.

"OK," replied Pastor Donald, "but in any given year there's still the same number of Sundays total, so even if one month happens to have five Sundays instead of four, that's still normal, isn't it? Overall giving for the year is still basically the same."

"But that doesn't make *July* any better," George insisted, blocking Pastor Donald's downward progress. He saw the pastor move a hand to his throat to adjust the tab collar. George always wondered if it was cut out of a bleach bottle. That's what he would have done, anyway, to save money.

"Well, if we divide the month's income by five, we'll get the weekly offering, and then we could compare it to other weeks in other months, couldn't we? That would be more accurate."

"We *could*," said George in doomful tone. "I bet we'll find overall giving goes down in a five-Sunday month."

"Well, you find out and let me know." Pastor Donald marched forward down the steps. George had to give way. He paused a moment more, then dashed up to the sacristy and grabbed the calculator. He punched the numbers and found the quotient to be a bitter disappointment. Weekly giving in July was *higher* than usual.

"What's wrong?" asked Marilyn Gross, the organist.

"Nothing," said George. He stumped out of the office to check the fuse box.

Marilyn waited in the sacristy ignoring Hazel, who was still hovering over the communion ware, until Pastor Donald reappeared with a sheaf of bulletins fresh off the copy machine. "Pastor," she said, "about the hymns for next month."

He said nothing, but Marilyn had the feeling that there were a lot of words in his head that were not coming out of his mouth.

"It's just that they're too hard," she wheedled. She stopped, ashamed that she'd resorted so quickly to that tone of voice, especially with Hazel standing there listening. She cleared her throat and started again. "Not for me, of course." She could have sworn the pastor's lips twitched, but still he said nothing. "I just don't think you can expect the congregation to manage all those old German chorales."

"More than half the congregation is German," said Donald.

"We're all Americans now," said Marilyn loftily. "And also," she pursued, "I really think you should reconsider your ban on the choir singing 'Borning Cry.' Everybody loves it. I *asked*."

This time Pastor Donald's shudder was unmistakable. "I know people like it," he said, "but it assumes that everyone's life follows the same trajectory, and it assumes that everyone makes it to old age, which is demonstrably not true." Marilyn knew he was alluding to a seventeen-year-old boy killed the year before in a drunk driving accident. His wasn't a church family, but Pastor Donald did the funeral anyway and refused to accept payment, which meant that Marilyn also had to refuse payment for playing the organ. Even though they weren't a church family! "And that ending about a surprise—as if God is going to sneak up and say *boo!* and scare you to death to get you into heaven. No. Never again," he finished, in that pastor voice.

"Well, I've talked to everybody and everybody loves it and wants it back," said Marilyn mulishly, as George reappeared.

Pastor Donald said, "Then ask everyone to come speak directly to me about it. By the way," he added, in a different tone, "isn't it your birthday tomorrow?"

"Why, yes," said Marilyn, all aflutter.

"How old are you going to be again?"

"Surely you don't expect me to tell!" She glanced coyly at Hazel and George.

"Surely you can tell your pastor and your fellow Christians, if anyone."

"Forty-eight," Marilyn simpered.

"Is that right, forty-eight?" Pastor Donald repeated vaguely.

Marilyn wasn't quite sure, but she had the feeling he was disappointed.

"Oh, you can't pay any attention to that," Hazel assured her after Pastor Donald left to place the bulletins in the narthex. "He has the kind of face that always looks a little sad, even when he isn't. It took me a couple years to figure it out. But don't take it personal."

"Actually, he's a reckless optimist," put in George.

The shriek of a banshee pierced the air. Moments later Asher came tearing through the sacristy, dressed in a button-down shirt, underpants, and polka-dotted socks full of holes freshly acquired from tearing across the gravel without any shoes on.

"Where's the other one?" asked Hazel as Asher streaked down the stairs.

On cue Saul appeared, fully clad, alternately blowing on a kazoo and bellowing, "*Asher. Martin. Abney!* Get back here right now!" He paused for a fistful of candy corn out of a glass globe.

"Hello there, Saul," said Hazel indulgently.

He nodded, stood still a moment, then tore off down the stairs after his brother.

Third in succession came Carmichael, hair still wet. "I'm so, so sorry," her apology arrived in advance of her. "Asher is just in one of those moods this morning."

"Not to worry," chortled George. He liked a boy to be a boy.

"If you joined the choir it would take your mind off your Sunday morning worries!" Marilyn could not refrain from saying.

"And then who would look after Asher?" Carmichael called back as she, too, disappeared down the stairs.

"Well, I think Lisa or Tammy could do it, or Michelle even, they're all old enough," opined Marilyn. "Even Kitty, for that matter."

"Oh, she doesn't want to sing in the choir, just let her be," said Hazel rebukingly.

"I'm going to get myself a cup of coffee," Marilyn announced to the air. She followed the flux of traffic down to the basement. Carmichael stood at the foot of the stairs, holding a wiggling Asher in a football grip to one side and talking to Sandra Forrad, who led the singing that kicked off Sunday School every week.

"Let! Me! *Go!*" shrieked Asher.

Carmichael flipped him upside-down so she could yank the socks off his feet. "If I set you down, will you run right home and put on new socks and your shoes?"

"I hate shoes!"

"Then you can stay right here."

"LEMME GO!"

Marilyn caught up to them. "If you don't put on shoes, someone can tickle your feet," she teased with outstretched fingers. Asher kicked harder than ever, nearly clipping Sandra in the nose.

"I don't think that's going to help," said Carmichael.

"We're singing a very special song during Sunday School today! Isn't that right, Mrs. Forrad?"

"That's right, Ms. Gross!"

"You're gross! You're gross!" Asher laughed and pinched Carmichael's legs. His curls were spread out in an upside-down halo around his head, making him look like a deranged cherub.

"Asher!" snapped Carmichael. "Enough of that! Daddy is going to have a word with you."

"No, no! OK, I'll put my shoes on!"

He slinked out of her grasp. Sandra just managed to catch him by the ankles before he crashed head-first onto the floor. The moment he righted himself Carmichael gripped his shoulder and said, "You apologize to Ms. Gross."

Asher gave a mutinous look, but Carmichael's glare in turn bespoke vast consequences for misbehavior. "Sorry," he said in a tiny voice.

"Now, shoes!"

Asher vanished quicker than Superman.

"He's a handful, that one," said Marilyn.

"She's a tough lady, this one," said Sandra, pointing an appreciative thumb at Carmichael. "Three kids, full-time job, pastor's wife! She's practically Wonder Woman."

Carmichael blushed and murmured thanks.

Sandra smiled her benevolence. She was good to the pastor and his family. She was always good to the pastor and his family. She, too, was a servant leader, serving on the Board of Directors for the social service agency Hope for Olutakli. She knew better than anyone what hard and underappreciated work it was.

When Donald and Carmichael and their little ones had moved to Shibboleth, it was Sandra and her husband Alan who'd met them in the parking lot of the Grand Union and led their U-Haul and hatchback to the long driveway up to Mt. Moriah Lutheran Church and parsonage. They'd stayed to help unload the truck and distract the children, quietly installing in the fridge two loaves of zucchini bread, three jars of jam made from their own raspberries, and a full bag of corn on the cob. The Forrads were about a decade older than the Abneys and fell neatly into a role halfway between mentors and colleagues. Alan was head of the humanities department at SUNY Shibboleth, instrumental in hiring Carmichael, and now her boss. The Abneys were grateful for all of it, new as they were to this neck of the woods and nearly always overwhelmed by their children.

"Is the new semester off to a good start?" Sandra inquired pleasantly.

"I suppose," Carmichael said. "Much as I love being a professor, I've never quite forgiven college for starting in August and not in September."

"But you're done in early May," Sandra pointed out. "Alan always knuckles down to finishing his overdue journal articles in May the minute he gets his grades in."

"Every year I really believe I'm going to take May to do the same thing, since Kitty and Saul are both still in school, but the truth is I'm always so wiped out by the end of the school year that I just let Asher talk me into watching cartoons all day instead."

Marilyn sniffed and excused herself. She'd never been to college and always had the feeling Carmichael and Sandra looked down on her for it. Here again they were reminding her of her inadequacies. But without an organist, how would the church hold services week after week? There's more than one way to be indispensable.

She went to the kitchen for some of the thin brown liquid that passed for coffee and found Bonnie frowning into a styrofoam cup. "Good morning," Marilyn sang out. "And how are you today?"

Bonnie straightened her skirt and adjusted her glasses as if coming out of a trance. "Oh, fine," she said. She hesitated, then said, "It's just that, when I got here, I found the communion stuff all set up. All there was left to do was put it on the altar, but I thought it was my turn to do everything. I mean, it *is* my turn. I'm on the sign-up sheet for today. I left extra early just in case." She cast an anguished look at Marilyn. "Do you think Pastor Donald decided—well—I mean, I know that I..."

"It wasn't *him*," Marilyn announced. She drew herself up tall, aquiver with righteousness. "It was that Hazel Quinn. She just can't stand to let someone else move in on her territory."

"Oh. Well..." began Bonnie doubtfully.

"We can't let her do this to you," said Marilyn. "Give her an inch and she'll take a mile. Come on, we'll find her and set her straight." She set off. Bonnie followed.

Hazel was to be found in the narthex, fingernailing the crease of each bulletin to crispness. Marilyn bore down on her.

"Hazel, oh, Hazel!" Marilyn rang treble in her authority.

Hazel looked up, spotted Bonnie trailing behind, and arranged her face in a simper. "My goodness, aren't you here early today?"

"Don't you play the innocent, Hazel Quinn," Marilyn said. "You know perfectly well that you stole Bonnie's day to set up for communion and it's not right."

"Well, I was just concerned about having everything ready on time."

"She left *early*, on purpose. She knew it was her day. You had no right to take it away from her."

"It's not that, it's not that at all," Hazel countered with a tremor in her voice. "It's just that, if certain people create certain expectations and then certain things don't get done on time, it makes the altar guild look bad. And the *head* of the altar guild. And the whole church, for that matter."

"You know, it's fine," Bonnie interjected. "I *am* late sometimes, I get it, and I'm sorry if I..."

"Don't you apologize," Marilyn snapped. "Everybody makes mistakes sometimes, but that's no excuse for Hazel here to go stealing your job. She likes to think the church couldn't manage without her..."

"That's the pot calling the kettle black!" said Hazel. "As if you didn't remind us constantly of how you're our one and only organist and we don't have any backup at all! When that poor Holocomb boy wanted to play guitar one Sunday, you just shredded him to pieces—"

This tête-à-tête ended abruptly with the apparition of Pastor Donald swishing along in his white alb and adjusting the point of his green stole at the back of his neck. "Five minutes till start time, Marilyn," he said absent-mindedly.

With a superior glare at Hazel, she swept off down the center aisle.

Pastor Donald looked up. The two remaining women were gazing uneasily near but not at each other's faces. "Something the matter?" he asked.

"No, not at all," said Bonnie.

"Well, then, shall we prepare to worship the Lord?" said Pastor Donald. He smiled mildly at both of them and headed back toward the sacristy.

Hazel drew a deep breath and said, "I'm, um, sorry. About—"

"Don't mention it," said Bonnie quickly.

Hazel handed her a beautifully creased bulletin. "Here you go."

"Thanks."

∼

Sunday afternoons found Donald on the old corduroy sofa, inert, a glass of sweet tea shedding tears of condensation all over a coffee table too wretched to protect with coasters. Most of his parishioners would be in the same position, though alert, not inert, a six-pack near at hand, suffering through the spectacle of the Angels creaming the Yankees with a superstitious attention that reminded Donald of Luther's dictum: if only I could pray the way my dog looks at a piece of meat. He accepted the dictum but not the beer—there are limits to what post-Holiness piety can enjoy in good conscience. Communion wine was his only indulgence on that score, and he suffered no small amount of ribbing from his colleagues for it. Occasionally Donald considered spreading a rumor that he was a recovering alcoholic, as that seemed to be the only acceptable excuse for abstinence. But he couldn't quite bring himself to lie.

As a rule, baseball was just compelling enough to absorb Donald's depleted post-church consciousness, but on this day, by the innocent fault of the Sunday School, he was instead back in the grip of his mental debate with Grandfather Abney.

After the service, Donald had led Bible study for the adults upstairs in the sanctuary while the children trooped downstairs to sing with Mrs. Forrad and Ms. Gross. Afterwards they split up into makeshift classrooms partitioned by dividers hanging from the ceiling. When the education hour was over, Pastor Donald came downstairs to pray everyone safe and healthy through the week ahead before the mass exodus to baseball or football or lunch or shopping in Kuhsota.

But when he arrived downstairs, the children were twitching with excitement, the teachers beaming proudly. Before he could even open his mouth to ask, he was informed that the whole Sunday School had prepared a special treat for him, and wasn't it lucky that he had chosen Joshua out of all the lessons to preach on that morning? The teachers had decided that chapter 24 was a bit abstract for their small charges, but it was a great opportunity to cover the battle of Jericho—a real favorite when they were kids, how come it never came up in the Sunday lessons?—and they had a song to go with it. Maybe Pastor Donald knew the song. Would he like to sing along?

Of course he did, and of course he would.

Joshua fought the battle of Jericho, Jericho, Jericho
Joshua fought the battle of Jericho
and the walls come a-tumblin' down.

You may talk about the king of Gideon
You may talk about the men of Saul

But there's none like good old Joshua
at the battle of Jericho.

Up to the walls of Jericho
He marched with spear in hand
"Go blow them ram horns," Joshua cried,
"'Cause the battle is in my hands."

Then the lamb ram sheep horns began to blow
The trumpets began to sound
Joshua commanded the children to shout
and the walls come a-tumblin' down.

Joshua fought the battle of Jericho, Jericho, Jericho
Joshua fought the battle of Jericho
and the walls come a-tumblin' down.

They loved the line, "Joshua commanded the children to shout." Did they ever shout! They marched and kicked up their knees. Asher climbed on the piano while Marilyn played. Donald wrangled him free and set him on his shoulders. Asher played Donald's head like a bongo. Saul held Kitty's hand and stood proud at the singing of his name. When it was all over, Donald clapped and cheered and blessed them.

Then he came home, turned on the TV, and started stewing about his grandfather all over again.

It had happened at Thanksgiving during his first year of seminary. Donald, already acquitted of a bout at Bible school, knew full well the dangers of the first semester—the danger of knowing everything, or at least far more than the local clergy dulled by so many years on the circuit. He came home determined not to brag or enlighten. Grandfather and uncles and minister friends of the family prodded him, hoping to lure him into a first-year whopper, or at the very least oblige them with a good rousing quarrel over the foolishness that was being stuffed into his head at that "Luth-ern" seminary of his. Donald remained judicious and humble, to everyone's great disappointment. But his resolve weakened before Grandfather Abney.

It being hunting season, and in view of the now-dissected bird lying in state on the table, conversation turned to shotguns the hunters had known and loved, which led to imitations of turkeys gobbling, which led to discussion of box calls, which led to speculation about hunting horns, which led to recollection of the role of horns in the Bible—always an immediate and relevant document in any situation, and none the less when hunting was at issue.

"I don't think they used the horns for hunting," Donald said.

"Is that right now?" said Charlie Abney. He was a nephew of Grandfather Abney and a first cousin of Donald's father, home on furlough from mission work in the jungle lowlands of Peru. He smiled, and Donald knew he was hoping for the youngster to rise and take the bait.

"Horns served a liturgical function," said Donald, in a flat and disinterested tone.

"Fancy vocabulary," said Charlie with a grin.

"Call to worship," Donald translated. He put a placid smile on his face. There were appreciative nods; a call to worship was relatable. "I can go you one better on the vocab. In Hebrew it's called a shofar. Made of ram's horn. But definitely for praise and worship, not hunting and trapping."

"Well, unless you count what they did to Jericho," chuckled Charlie. Various other uncles and cousins chimed in approvingly. Someone mimicked a horn blast and shouted, "Attack!" There was good-natured laughter.

"I'd like a horn that takes out all the bucks in the forest! Just like those walls of Jericho," said Aunt Helen's son Wayne.

"Pay good money for that," said Uncle Mort.

"Well, it didn't really happen that way," said Donald before he could stop himself.

He swore afterwards that everyone fell silent, stopped chewing, and as one rotated their necks in his direction with ominous unanimity.

As if in unspoken deference to his age and authority, no one said anything until Grandfather Abney saw fit to break the silence. "What's that you say now, Donald?"

Donald cursed his big mouth. He considered backpedaling, then cursed his cowardice. The inevitable quarrel would not result in a swift toppling of walls but, at best, a war of attrition. "It's just that. Well. The archaeological evidence suggests that no such thing as Jericho's collapse ever took place. It's just part of Israelite national mythology. Later redactors invented the story. Probably something significant happened at Jericho that they were remembering, but not that. Not the walls tumbling down."

There were no words, at first, just a resumed chewing of turkey. The various implications of Donald's speech were being worked out. Then all at once:

"What do you mean the archaeologists didn't find anything?"

"The Old Testament isn't mythology; it's fact."

"Redactors?"

But Grandfather Abney saw straight into the heart of the problem. He never got distracted by fringe details. "Donald," he said, staring relentlessly into his grandson's heart, "have you lost your faith that God works miracles?"

"I'm not sure you and I define 'miracle' the same way," Donald hedged.

"Nonsense," declared Grandfather Abney.

It *was* nonsense. Donald knew that well enough. He had to divert the old man, who would shake him like a dog shakes a rat till everything came out. "Look, since the nineteenth century extensive research has been done on the biblical texts. What we now call the Old Testament was the work of four different strands, one from the northern kingdom, one from the south, another from a priestly editor interested in cultic ritual, and the fourth from a Deuteronomist concerned to develop a certain understanding of the law. It's a really helpful theory, Grandfather. It explains why there's two creation stories, for instance."

Grandfather Abney was unflapped. "The first speaks to the unity of the human race; the second, its division into male and female."

"There are two Noah stories, too. In the first Noah takes only one male and female of each species, but in the other he takes seven pairs of clean animals and four pairs of unclean animals. Why are they duplicated but with conflicting details?"

"The Lord intends us to probe the meaning of each."

It was a non-answer, but still, Donald felt a little desperate. The minister uncles and cousins and friends were watching him now like vultures preparing for a feast.

Might as well go down for a whale as for a minnow, he thought. "For that matter, all responsible science indicates that the world is much more than six thousand years old. It's actually billions of years old." Oh, Lord, why had he gone for *that*? Wasn't it better to argue about Jericho than the age of the universe? But, strangely, the latter was familiar territory for debate—Donald had come around on matters of biology and physics already in college—and therefore less threatening. The Jericho problem unsettled him far more, for reasons he could not fathom.

"The Scriptures say the world was created six thousand years ago, Donald," Grandfather Abney said softly, like a warning.

"But it wasn't," Donald said flatly. "What of the dinosaurs? The Scriptures say nothing."

"The fossils are a test to see whether we believe God's holy word or our own human devices." Grandfather Abney returned calmly to his green bean casserole.

"But would the God of truth and wisdom intentionally deceive his own people?" Donald challenged.

"Would he deceive them by giving them a faulty Scripture?"

There it was. Impasse. Donald mumbled his way out of the debate, but Grandfather Abney's eyes followed him the rest of the evening, peering into his heart again and again, probing his brain like it was the two Noah's ark stories, and praying, Donald knew, for his soul. Not with fear or anger, but with love and a bit of pity.

Back at school Donald studied with a vengeance, searing the pages of his assigned books with hungry eyes. His fellow seminarians read casually. They liked their theology hot and shocking, but only to other people; the attraction seemed to depend on who would be offended by it. They loved to talk about the theology of the cross, calling this and that and the other thing a cross, bearing all their crosses with a smug wonder at their good fortune. They disposed of Moses's authorship of the Pentateuch, the miraculous nature of the plagues (all, it turned out, could be explained scientifically), and the parting of the Red Sea as handily as Joshua disposed of the wall around Jericho—except, of course, he didn't. It was a smooth ride from Jericho to Bultmann. The pinched, unemotional New Testament professor declared with authority that Jesus rose in the hearts of his apostles but not bodily in any tomb. Donald suspected there were other broken hearts besides his in the classroom, in which neither Jesus nor anything else rose but despair. Their faces gave away no more than his did, though, so he said nothing to them and they said nothing to him. At night he went home to yet another cousin's house where he lived rent-free. If these matters were hashed out in the dorm at night, Donald never heard it.

Either all of it's true or none of it's true. That's how it worked. His uncles and Grandfather Abney said the first, and Donald couldn't buy it. His professors and fellow students said the other, and Donald couldn't stomach it. Anything in-between was arbitrary, implicitly making Donald the final arbiter of reality.

One day after a discussion of the absolution of sin in systematic theology class, Donald asked Professor Fenstermacher, "If you don't believe any of this is true, how do you get away with telling people their sins are forgiven?"

Fenstermacher laughed at him. Donald was funny; all that Holiness baggage. "It *is* true. People really feel better. They can't believe it coming from themselves, but they'll take it from someone else."

"So it's just psychological?"

"What's *just* psychological about it? Psychology is real."

"But the forgiveness is a big blank. It doesn't actually refer to anything."

"It matters that they believe it. Faith justifies, right? Believe it and it's yours."

"But what *is it* that's yours if you believe it?"

"Forgiveness," laughed Fenstermacher again, squeezing himself away from Donald's further questions.

Jesus didn't rise from the dead, forgiveness was a snake biting its own tail, and Donald thought about becoming a plumber.

Then the second semester began, and a minority opinion surfaced in the form of a professor who *did* think that Jesus rose bodily from the dead, and that the "it" you got from faith was not the psychological rattle on the snake's tail but the risen Jesus himself. The Bible said it, Luther said it, and Dr. Kjaer said it too. As soon as he could, Donald cornered Kjaer and said, "How can you have it both ways? How can you say that Jesus is risen from the dead when Moses didn't write the first five books of the Bible?"

The professor turned slowly from the blackboard and looked at Donald a good while. Then he smiled. "Apples and oranges, Mr. Abney," he said.

"But it's all the Bible," insisted Donald.

"The Bible," said Kjaer, turning back to the chalkboard, "is an earthen vessel. 'Their idols are silver and gold, the work of men's hands. They that make them are like unto them; so is every one that trusteth in them.' Psalm 115," he added.

"I know," said Donald.

"*Do* you?" said Kjaer. He smiled again.

"The Bible is an idol?" Donald pressed.

"In *your* hands," said Kjaer.

Donald went back to his cousin's house and took up his Bible. He stared hard at its cover, willing it to disclose its secrets, then dropped it like a hot potato when he realized the idolatry inherent in the desire. "But this is how I *know* you, Lord," Donald pleaded in prayer.

A notion came to him. He picked up his Bible again, found Mark's Gospel, and paged through to chapter ten. Yes, he'd remembered right. Blind Bartimaeus was sitting on the road out of Jericho, whose walls may or may not have come a-tumblin' down centuries before. "That's me," he said aloud. "That's where I'm at. Sitting in the shadow of Jericho. And I can't see a thing. When will you come knock down these walls and restore my vision?"

An uncomfortable place to live, for sure. But Donald found, and sooner than expected, that he could actually live there. Not comfortably. But honestly.

Such emerging insight, however, did not grip Grandfather Abney the way it did Donald, even though he tried to explain himself over Christmas, and again over a long weekend in February when Donald went home for his mother's birthday. Grandfather Abney would not relinquish the either-or. "If you sacrifice Jericho, you sacrifice the one who was sacrificed for you, and that is a sacrifice you don't want to make," he said, relishing the rhetoric.

"But why?" Donald pressed him. "Jericho was so long before Christ. It's buried in a mass of tradition and superstition and nationalist ideology. It's not like the story of Christ." Donald felt like an eel saying it, implying that the Old Testament wasn't as good as the New. He got the impression some of his classmates felt that way, but in Donald's world there was no preaching of Jesus that wasn't built on a scaffold of Isaiah and the Psalms and Exodus and Joel and much more besides.

"All of it is about God," said Grandfather Abney.

"I *know* it's all about God!" Donald protested. "I believe every bit as much as you do that Jericho tells us of God and his righteousness. I just don't think it happened quite the way the story says it did."

"Donald," said Grandfather Abney suddenly, leaning forward from his rocking chair, "if Jericho didn't happen, what *ground* do you have for saying that a righteous God intervenes on behalf of his chosen people? All you have is an example of something that never actually happened. You can say all you want, 'God is good, God is holy, God is powerful,' but if you don't think the Bible reports to us what God actually *did* to show forth his power, how dare you assert such things about God at all? You are naught but a liar. A pious liar, at that. The worst kind of all."

It was just what Donald had implied about Professor Fenstermacher, coming right back at him.

"Preach me a sermon about Jericho, Donald. Tell me it didn't really happen, yet convince me that God lives and reigns and triumphs over his enemies. You do that, and make me believe it, and you win."

That was the bargain. Donald accepted it, without the slightest conviction he could ever pull it off.

In the end it didn't matter. As it turned out, that February was the last time Donald saw Grandfather Abney awake and alert. Just before Easter he had a first stroke. Donald called off his trip out east with Carmichael to meet her parents—only five months together and they were already at that point—and during his frantic drive to the homestead in southern Indiana, Grandfather Abney had a second stroke. Donald got there in time to hold his immobilized hand, whisper his love, promise to honor him with his preaching.

A few hours later Grandfather Abney slipped away. Donald felt that a mighty bulwark shielding him had crumbled and dissolved into dust.

CHAPTER THREE

September 1988

Some people are apt to regard the portions given
to daughters as so much lost to the family;
but this is selfish,
and is not agreeable to my way of thinking.

Bammy and Bampy were certainly in an expansive mood. Saul and Asher each got a gigantic John Deere tractor toy (identical; the grandparents knew the consequences of brotherly envy by now) and a packet of jellybeans in gem colors that Kitty dubbed, irrespective of flavor, "Sapphire. Amethyst. Topaz. Emerald. *Watermelon tourmaline.*"

To reward that display of cleverness, Bammy bore down on Kitty with a white paper box that was only slightly too large and too square to contain chow mein. Kitty rattled it. "Ooh! Is it what I think it is?" Bammy grinned. Kitty unfolded the flaps and with ceremonial care withdrew the chocolate-coated head of an elephant. "I *love* these!" she squealed. Under the chocolate veneer was yellow cake in the shape of a long trunk and fan ears, and where its brain should've been a lump of marzipan lay hidden.

"I know. For our little treasure," said Bammy, kissing the top of her hair. Saul and Asher ventured a brief jealous glance, but they were still young enough to prefer the lurid colors of jellybeans to the more refined pleasures of zoological pastry.

"Already quite cool up here, isn't it?" said Bampy. He rubbed at his walrus mustache and resettled the golf cap on his head. "Same place as usual, Carmichael?"

Kitty's mother nodded and pointed up the stairs. "Haven't

made the beds yet, but I'll do it before it gets too late," she added.

"Don't worry, I'll take care of it," said Bammy.

"The sumac is the first to turn," Kitty informed her grandparents. "You see it going red already in August."

"Oh, isn't that poisonous?" called Bammy behind her as she followed Bampy up the stairs.

"Only *poison* sumac," said Kitty, barely restraining a punctuation mark of "duh."

"Poison oak's the one you really want to avoid," said Bampy knowingly as he hefted the suitcases into the spare room.

"The sugar maples come next," Kitty assured them.

"Are they the ones that turn red?"

"That's *red* maples. Sugar maples turn lots of colors, like gumball trees. Then there's Norway maples and they go yellow but you can't get syrup out of them. Red maples either. So we're lucky it's mostly sugar maples up here."

"Well, what I want to know is, is it too cold to go out for ice cream?"

Kitty was surprised at the profligate flow of sugar. "No," she said. "Right now? All of us?"

"Right now—but just you. With just the two of us. What do you say?"

"You're not gonna bring Saul and Asher along?"

"Well, we'd like some time alone with our favorite granddaughter."

Kitty rolled her eyes at the old canard. "I'm your *only* granddaughter." Her mother was an only child, which meant Kitty had no cousins on that side of the family. Whereas her dad had both a brother and a sister, they had two and four kids respectively (she was very pleased at knowing the word "respectively"), and Kitty had been exposed to a range of second and even third cousins at more than one family reunion in Indiana.

"All the more reason!" said Bammy brightly.

"Yeah, sure! As long as *you* tell Mommy."

"I'm sure she won't object."

Kitty knew that all objections, valid or not, were rendered irrelevant by the upward chain of parental authority. She grabbed her jacket and buckled on her sandals. Twenty minutes later, sitting at a table outside Tiny's Diner, applied herself to a cone so large it could have fed both her and her brothers without anyone feeling gypped.

"It's dripping down your arms," said Bammy. She dove into her purse and pulled out a little packet of tissues. Without so much as a by-your-leave she mopped the liquefying maple walnut off Kitty's wrists.

"I got it," protested Kitty. She licked herself assiduously in the manner of her nicknamesake.

"Oh, honey, don't do that," counter-protested Bammy. "Act like a lady."

"I'm no lady. I'm a kid." Kitty chomped down on the pinnacle of the blue raspberry wax shell and slurped as loudly as she could.

"Now are such bad manners the way you say thank you to your grandparents for treating you to an ice cream cone?" Bammy looked significantly over at Bampy. "We may not be able to do this again until she has grown up a little."

Kitty took the hint. "Sorry," she rang out in a rote and formalistic tone.

"Funny how it's melting even though it's so chilly out," remarked Bampy. "There was that nice little restaurant in town. We could have gone there and avoided the cold."

"They don't have shell," said Kitty. "Only floats and things like that."

"Next time you come to New York we'll treat you to a proper egg cream."

"Ew."

"It's just called that. There are no eggs in it, actually."

Bammy dabbed at her paper cup of strawberry ice cream and cast Bampy a sidelong glance. He nodded slightly. The pause extended several moments more till Bammy cleared her throat and said, "I suppose you're wondering—"

"—why I've gathered you all here today!" Kitty chortled at her own witticism. "That's what you're supposed to say to a crowd, isn't it?"

Bammy gaped and said, "You're not a crowd," which in turn made Bampy snort.

"Not exactly the most relevant objection, now, is it?"

"Let me start over," said Bammy, waving her white plastic spoon in the air like a conductor her baton. "The reason we brought you here by yourself without your brothers is because we have something very special to tell you."

"You're pregnant," Kitty burst out, doubling over in giggles.

"No, not that either." Bammy paused until Kitty regained herself. Then, regally, "What we want to tell you, Kitty, is that you are a Jew."

Kitty sat bolt upright and knocked her cone so hard on the table that its bottom point broke. She popped the leaky end into her mouth and sucked hard. "No, I'm not," she pronounced.

"Yes, you are," said Bammy. "That's what we wanted to tell you about."

"But I *know* I'm not," insisted Kitty. "I can't be because I know all about Jews and they're not allowed to work on Saturdays but I can. I mean, I *could* if I was old enough to have a job. Mommy works on Saturdays sometimes. And I can eat bacon and shrimp, and I don't *have* to wash my hands before I eat even though I should. Also Jews don't believe in Jesus but I do. So I can't be a Jew."

"But you *are*, honey," said Bammy. "We are Jews, too. You are a Jew because your mom is and so are we."

Kitty looked from one grandparent to the other in astonishment. "But Bampy, you don't wear one of those little caps, and you don't have the curly hair by your forehead or wear the little blue tassels under your shirt. And *you* do work stuff on Saturdays. I've seen you!"

Bampy chuckled. "Observant little thing, aren't you? Fact is, Kitty, there's more than one way to be a Jew."

Kitty ruminated on this while slurping the runoff of her cone. "You're just joking with me," she said at last. "I know for a fact you're not Jews."

"And why is that?" prompted Bammy with an amused smile.

"Because you don't believe in God." Kitty stared intently at her grandmother, who, to her astonishment, blushed.

"It's not a matter of believing in God," Bampy said. "Like I said, there's more than one way to be a Jew. You don't have to believe in God to be a Jew."

"Yeah, you do. You *have* to! God chose the Jews to be his people and he rescued them out of Egypt and then there came Samson, who was a real dope, and King David, who was better, sort of, and later Jesus came along but the Jews didn't like him because they didn't think he really was the son of God, even though he was. But even if Jews don't believe in Jesus they *definitely* believe in God, otherwise they wouldn't be so angry about Jesus saying he *was* God."

Bammy and Bampy pushed back from the table. They exchanged looks.

"You really are kidding me, aren't you?" pressed Kitty.

"No, actually, we're not," said Bammy.

"Did you say Mommy is a Jew, too?"

"Yes, she is."

"But she can't be. She believes in Jesus, too. I asked her and she told me so."

The now-empty paper cup crumpled inside Bammy's manicured hand. "You really have never heard *anything* about this before?"

"About what?"

"About being Jewish."

"I'm not Jewish!" Kitty found herself in tears. She couldn't understand why and wiped them away impatiently.

"I think we'd better go," said Bampy.

∽

As if it weren't bad enough that Kitty came home from ice cream in tears, flung herself despondently into Carmichael's arms, and wouldn't eat dinner, agreeing to sleep only after a long snuggle and a lullaby, Saul got infected with Kitty's distress and spent the better part of the evening in the production of disconsolate sobs expressed as fear of forgetting his lunchbox on the school bus or possibly getting hit in the face with a kickball. *That* in turn led to an even wilder than usual Asher making misdirected attempts at cheering up his big brother, with the result that one of the African violets fell off its stand, its pot shattered, and the mauve blooms got ground underfoot. Amidst the epidemic of hysterics, Asher smuggled leftover butternut squash into the bathroom and frosted it across the tile next to the bathtub, whence it migrated into both boys' hair, but only after the shampoo. Naturally, the second round of shampoo got into Asher's eyes, since he wouldn't sit still and stop thrashing. All in all, a parenting nightmare of the first order.

So it was only well after nine, when Donald had discreetly slipped a gin and tonic into Carmichael's hand and then, as previously arranged, retreated to his office and shut the door, that Carmichael was able to nail her parents with her fury.

"I don't understand this. I absolutely do not understand this. I don't know where it's coming from, I don't know why *now*, I don't know what made you think you had the right to talk to Kitty about this without discussing it with me first or even *warning* me what you were about to do!"

"We had no idea you'd feel this way," said Judith, with a little sniff. "As if you were *ashamed*…"

"*Who* here is ashamed of being a Jew?" Carmichael roared. "When did you *ever* talk to me about it? Isn't this in fact the very first time? Since when do you even care?"

"We've always cared," Frank barked.

"Coulda fooled me," snapped Carmichael. "So what's going on? Are your fancy new friends on the Upper East Side going to bar mitzvahs and you feel left out?"

"I really have no idea why you're so angry about this." Judith rubbed at the lipstick on the rim of a wineglass holding a White Zinfandel she'd brought up from the City.

Carmichael took a deep breath. She studied her parents: mother tucked into the corner of the living room sofa, grubby as it was, as if it were a structural security blanket, at grimy odds with her belted dress, styled hair, and expensive earrings; father meanwhile splayed on the arm of the hand-me-down easy chair, elbows on knees, working over his teeth with his tongue. They are just people, she told herself.

Suddenly she had a memory of herself curled up in Donald's lap during their engagement, when he was preparing her for baptism, reading from the Large Catechism and commenting as he went along, Carmichael doubly in love with him and with God. Donald read the bit where Luther explained the commandment about honoring parents to the effect that however "lowly, poor, feeble, and eccentric they may be," they're still your parents and still from God. Feeble and eccentric! Through her fury Carmichael felt a whisper of laughter rising like smoke from a stick of incense. She paused, regrouped, sat down straddling the ottoman.

"All right," she said. "Let's start over from the beginning. How about you tell me why you suddenly care that we're Jews."

"I don't know why you think we never did before," Judith repeated, stubborn.

"I don't know, maybe because we observed Christmas but not Hanukkah? Never went near a synagogue? Never spoke one word about God?"

"We said a word when you told us you were converting to Christian," said Frank.

"A bit late then, don't you think?"

"You couldn't have *not* known till then."

"Of course I knew sooner, but you gave no sign of caring one way or another. I thought Jewish was like Italian or Polish or Greek. If people asked, most of the time I just said 'Estonian' because *that's* what you actually talked about, about being born there and your parents leaving just in time. But until I met Donald I honestly, truly had no idea you cared at all what religion I was or who I married."

"We *love* Donald," said Judith, meeting Carmichael's eyes. "He is a good man and we know how much he cherishes you and takes care of you and of course he helped give us our wonderful grandchildren."

"But…?"

Judith shook her head. "He's just—or he was, at least—so… religious."

"Hardly surprising under the circumstances."

"Oh, he's much better now."

Carmichael laughed when she realized her mother meant it as a compliment. "Lord, I'm tired," she said. She sucked at the ice cubes and rubbed her eyes. "You have no idea what it's like, raising a boy like Asher. Though he was in rare form tonight, even for him. Look, I have to get to sleep, I have early class tomorrow, but before I go please just tell me why—why *now*."

"I thought Kitty had a right to know about herself," Judith sniffed.

"That's not it. Try again, Mom."

"Well, since you mention the motherland," Frank interjected, straightening up from his perch, "I don't know if you've been following the news, but stuff is happening in Estonia."

"I gave up reading the papers when Asher came along. Better fill me in."

"Well, they're singing together in public. It's a kind of protest. They're sending a sign to Moscow that they've had enough."

Carmichael gave a dubious smile. "Well, good for them," she said. "I hope it turns out well. But how does this…?"

"We might have some family there, you know," said Frank.

"Really?" Another thing her parents had never gotten around to mentioning before.

"It wasn't long between when our folks left and the iron curtain fell. You think *we* don't like to talk about family stuff, but gee, you should've known *my* parents! I guess you don't much remember them, but I could hardly get two words out of them about their life back there."

"I really only vaguely remember them," Carmichael admitted.

"Mine were the same," said Judith.

"Cut from the same cloth. The Bams and the Lazikins arrived here about the same time. Your mom and I always kind of knew each other, before we fell in love, I mean," said Frank.

Carmichael knew that, but she'd never heard her father talk about falling in love with her mother. It was almost as surprising as the talk about being Jewish.

"The way I figure it is, my folks and your mom's got out of there just in time, and losing their homeland like that, becoming refugees, was so terrible that they never wanted to talk about it again. I did try to ask, a bit, when they were old and I could tell the end was near. But they just wouldn't say anything."

"What do *you* remember of it?"

"Well, I was only twelve when we left—"

"I was ten," interjected Judith.

"—so sure, I remember some sights and smells, some food, a little bit about the places we stayed in Sweden and England on our way to this country. But to be honest, I think once we got to America and I realized we were here to stay, I let all that go and put my energy into becoming an American."

"You don't have an accent," said Carmichael. It had never occurred to her before that he should have one, or her mother, either. "I mean, you don't have a foreign accent."

"I suppose we were still young enough, and I was definitely determined not to sound different," said Frank with a smile.

"Anyway, the point is, all connection to our lives there was broken after 1941, and we've never gotten connected again. Till now, we couldn't have, even if we wanted to."

"Wow," said Carmichael, pensive. "But you don't really think anything will change over there, do you?"

"Hard to say," said Frank, standing up and stretching. "But this news has had me thinking about Estonia for the first time since I can remember."

"Well. Wow. It would be amazing if it turned out we had family there and could find them again." She stood up, too. "I just—I still don't quite see what this has to do with being Jewish, instead of just being Estonian."

"It can't be by accident that our parents left in 1941," said Frank drily.

"More to the point," said Judith, "it's time to get back in touch with our roots. You get to a certain age, and family takes on a new importance. Your history and your legacy both." She looked at Carmichael with an odd glint of challenge in her eyes. "You *did* give your two boys Jewish names," she said.

"To me they're Old Testament names," said Carmichael.

"Isn't that the same thing?" said Frank.

Carmichael let out a little huff of exasperation. "That's not something a real Jew would ever say."

She looked from mother to father and back again. Being an only child, Carmichael's sensitivity to their every mood, thought, emotion, and opinion was acute as radar, in no way diminished by the fact that she'd lived as many years out of their home as in it. Something, she registered at a deep level of herself, was still not being said.

But it was late, and she was tired, and they weren't ready—maybe not even able—to divulge. Perhaps they didn't even know the reason themselves.

Feeble and eccentric for sure.

"Good night, Mom," she said, and placed a kiss on her mother's cheek, soft now in the way of aging flesh despite its cosmetic veneer. Her dad reached out and grabbed her hand and squeezed it. "Good night, Dad. Need anything?"

"No, we're all set," he said.

～

The boys of the sixth grade still knew how to play. They also knew, in their bones if not their brains, that opportunities to run riot on the playground out back of the school were rapidly diminishing. In a week or two some dumb cluck would show up without a warm enough jacket or sturdy enough shoes, and then Mr. Van Warts would declare that recess had to be indoors until—oh, March. April, if it was a long winter. So the boys careened down the slide head-first, stood up on the swings, trapped each other on the high end of the seesaw, and, when the overseers dozed or got distracted, chucked handfuls of wood chips at each other.

At any other time Kitty would have looked on with envy. Once or twice she'd tried to insinuate herself into their midst, but they insisted on being tiresome and stupid and holding her off sheerly on account of girlness. But the girls were equally tiresome and stupid by refusing to play at all. Instead they clustered around Megan Moravsky like obedient little soldiers, talking about the boys—who clearly couldn't care less about any of them—and nail polish and The New Kids on the Block. For someone who'd arrived at Shibboleth Elementary only the year before, Megan had all but absolute power over the girls in the class. Kitty despised the other girls for granting her the power almost as much as she despised Megan for seizing it.

Today, though, Kitty had other things to worry about. Like, what if she really was a Jew? If so, was she still allowed to love Jesus? Her dad preached with relentless authority that Jesus loved everybody, even people who turned against him. So, logically, Jesus should keep on loving her even if it turned out that she was a Jew.

But she couldn't shake the weird feeling it gave her. Even

in the safety of her own mind she couldn't go near the fact that Bammy and Bampy and even her mom had known all along but never told her. It was like committing a crime you didn't remember. Or like original sin, something else her dad talked about, which you didn't do but were guilty for anyway.

Or—Kitty thought—it was like you were adopted and they never told you about it. Jenny Ulster was adopted. Kitty found out about it in third grade. For awhile she couldn't even talk to Jenny, because all she could imagine was being a third-grader kidnapped by some strangers who expected her to call them Mom and Dad just because they said so. Jenny must've gone through that kind of weirdness before, though, because a few days later she gave Kitty a friendly whack on the shoulder—Jenny had apparently been born of a giantess because she was the tallest kid in class, round-cheeked and alarmingly robust—and demanded to know why Kitty wasn't talking to her. When Kitty stuttered and reddened, Jenny rolled her eyes and said, "You know my mom gave me away when I was a baby, right? I don't even remember her. It's *cool*." She stalked off, radiating moral superiority. Kitty was so impressed that she went back to liking Jenny again. But the business about being a Jew reminded Kitty of how she felt when Jenny first told her, and how it made her feel sick and icky all over.

Under other circumstances Kitty would try to peel some of the girls away from Megan's thrall and incite them into playing, *like* the boys if not *with* the boys. Jessica usually caved in first because best friends were supposed to do that. Jenny was enough of a loner that she got fed up with Megan second-fastest after Kitty. If Megan had no good gossip, local or celebrity, or was being particularly obnoxious, mousy little Shannon might be pried away, too. With four girls you could do *something*. But preoccupied as she was, Kitty scooched herself into sitting position at the foot of the neglected maypole and enjoyed the rare opportunity for solitude at school.

If she hadn't been so preoccupied, she would've realized

that such outlier behavior was asking for it. She'd have been better off standing at the outer edge of Megan's cabal with a vacant look, keeping her thoughts to herself. But, like an idiot, she set herself up to be targeted.

Slowly, inexorably, Megan shifted her courtiers close enough to the maypole to be overheard. Even if she wasn't good at math or English, Megan was very good at getting a rise out of people. She'd obviously figured out that a direct attack on Kitty wouldn't work. The only really effective bait was presenting herself as a source of unique, authoritative information. Kitty couldn't stand competition in that department.

Megan cycled through a variety of items, none of which elicited any response from the distracted Kitty. Then, by dumb luck, she stumbled into an area of neuralgic passion. Kitty perked up when she heard Megan declaiming, "Alice doesn't even notice Tweedledee and Tweedledum at first because she's trying to catch up with the White Rabbit…"

Kitty emitted a loud and derisive snort.

Megan shifted a hip and stuck her tongue in the lower right quadrant of her mouth, the posture of a female dominance challenge. "Did you say something?"

Kitty found her feet. "You don't know what you're talking about," she announced. "The White Rabbit isn't even in the same story as Tweedledee and Tweedledum."

"Is so," retorted Megan. "I saw it myself. We have a VCR at my house and my mom rents movies for me whenever I want. I've seen *everything* Disney *ever* made."

Kitty dared not let it show that this was a sore point. Despite her fervent pleading, her own parents could not be persuaded to get a VCR. They didn't even have cable. The only way to fend off the shame of technological inadequacy was to seize upon the highbrow route of superior literacy.

"It was a *book* before it was a *movie*," she sneered. "Like, a hundred years before."

"I *have* the book," Megan sneered right back at her, "and it shows Alice chasing the White Rabbit right before she meets them!"

"You probably have some stupid little Golden Book version that's based on the movie. I'm talking about the *real* book. And actually, it's two books."

"Oh, so now *Alice in Wonderland* is *two* books?" Megan cackled. A few craven sycophants in the circle of girls let out short, uncertain laughs of agreement at the absurdity of Kitty's claim.

"Yes," said Kitty with lofty authority. "The first one is called *Alice's Adventures in Wonderland*—" she put a heavy stress on "*Adventures*" to demarcate it from the bowdlerized movie title "—and the second is *Through the Looking-Glass*. The White Rabbit is only in the first, and Tweedledee and Tweedledum are only in the second."

"You don't know what you're talking about," Megan scoffed.

Kitty fumed. Technically, this was a very difficult point to refute. Bringing the books from home to prove her point—or even checking them out of the neutral school library—would not secure victory. It would probably only make her look pathetic. Nobody cared about facts. All they wanted was to enjoy the performance of oneupgirlship.

"I do so," Kitty cried, her tone betraying the weak rejoinder for what it was.

Just then Mrs. Onderdonk strolled over. Adult authority! Kitty smiled and relaxed.

"What are you girls talking about?" inquired the teacher.

"Megan thinks that Tweedledee and Tweedledum show up in *Alice's Adventures in Wonderland*, but they don't," said Kitty. She sidled over next to Mrs. Onderdonk and crossed her arms. Megan looked petrified, teetering on her metaphorical pedestal in the eyes of the sixth grade. Even the boys on the jungle gym had detected the psychosocial turbulence and paused in place to eavesdrop on the teacher's intervention.

Kitty awaited her vindication with quiet calm.

Mrs. Onderdonk gave her a funny little squint. "Don't be ridiculous, Kitty, of course they do," she said. "Haven't you seen the movie? All right now, recess is over in five minutes, so start heading back to the door to line up." She departed without the slightest acknowledgement of the devastation left in her wake.

Megan narrowed her triumphant eyes at Kitty. "Now who's Tweedle-*dumb*?" she hissed.

As if *that* wasn't the oldest insult in the book. Kitty rolled her eyes and held her tongue, as if such jabs were beneath her contempt, but sixth graders by and large did not grasp the power of aloofness. Kitty could tell from their faces they figured Megan had won that round. It made her blood boil.

The walk down the hill after school, past the post office and town square with its tidy gazebo and courthouse, through the lot of the Grand Union, and across the covered bridge to the opposite hillside, took Kitty twice as long as usual. As she idled along she chewed on the recess incident. Megan was bad enough, but Mrs. Onderdonk? Her brainless alliance with Megan confirmed the terrible truth pressing in on Kitty from all sides: adults were not under any circumstances to be trusted. They gave the appearance of knowledge but were just as ignorant as any kid. Except worse, because they acted like they weren't. Adults would cover up their ignorance at any cost. The truth meant nothing to them.

Hours later, or so it felt, Kitty banged through the pantry door. Saul and Asher had actually gotten home ahead of her and were watching Ghostbusters cartoons. *They* got to ride the bus because they were so little, but Kitty had to start walking in fifth grade. Her mother wasn't home from the college yet. Her father craned over a mess of books and papers at the dining room table where he worked during afternoons, the better to keep an eye on the boys. He noticed her vaguely, apparently unaware of her lateness, and said "have a snack" without imposing any restrictions on what that snack ought to be. Kitty quietly helped herself to three oatmeal cookies, making sure her brothers were too engrossed in the TV to notice that she was not partaking of a healthful box of raisins, and snuck upstairs.

In her room, Kitty's eye fell at once on *Alice*, but she couldn't stomach it today. It felt stolen from her. She needed something new. Scanning past *Charlotte's Web* and *Harriet the Spy* and *Bridge to Terabithia* she settled on a pair of glossy seafoam green volumes, a Reader's Digest collection of fairy tales. They had sat on the shelf untouched since last Christmas, gazing at her with mild reproach in the persona of her Arizona grandmother who always asked if she'd read them yet. Evidently Meemaw didn't realize that the asking functioned more as deterrent than incentive.

But the day had put Kitty in the need of both escape and comfort, and nothing fit the bill better than woodcutters and godmothers.

She scanned the table of contents in the first volume and turned to Cinderella. For all Kitty's contempt of the spurious cinematic "Alice in Wonderland," she was a devoted fan of Disney's "Cinderella," what with its singing mice, stepsisters with the hideous names of Drusilla and Priscilla, chilly stepmother, Lucifer the cat. Kitty knew the origin of the name Lucifer, a tidbit she was saving for her classmates when the strategic moment presented itself. As she flipped through the gilt-edged pages she settled into a scholarly thrill gleaned from her mother: she was about to read the *original*. It was a pleasure that rated right up there with a whole bank of post-it notes, green felt-tip pens, and blank notebooks with paisley covers.

The pleasure was short-lived. She read faster and faster. The second she was done, she catapulted down the stairs. Her mother had just gotten home, purse still on one arm and two paper bags precariously balanced in the other. Kitty crashed right into her. One bag hiccuped straight out of her arms and landed on the table, spilling plums, cups of lemon yogurt, and kaiser rolls every which way.

"Mom-*my*!" she shrieked.

"What, what, what?" flailed Carmichael, dropping the other bag and letting her purse slip to the floor. "Are you all right? Are you hurt? What happened? Where are your brothers?"

"No, I'm fine, it's 'Cinderella,'" Kitty shouted, as if this were the obvious source of distress. Carmichael collapsed into the chair behind her and put her hands over her face. Donald collected plums with a fixity of expression that seemed to be suppressing a smile. "It's all a lie, Mommy! The movie! I just read the original. Only one stepsister even gets a name and it's *Charlotte*. There's no cat and the birds don't help her make a dress or anything. And then at the end she's so *nice* to her horrible stepsisters! They ask her to forgive them, and she does, she even finds them husbands, but you don't hear *anything* about that in the movie! They changed everything! How can they do that? Isn't there a law against it?"

"Kitty..." groaned Carmichael.

"Daddy, isn't a *sin* to lie?" Kitty persisted.

"Yes," he replied without further comment.

"Look, honey," said Carmichael, "you already knew they changed things in 'Alice.' Are you really so surprised they did it in 'Cinderella' too?"

"But it's a *classic*, Mommy. You aren't supposed to tamper with the classics. My book says Charles Perrault wrote it. I know about him, he's a French guy who wrote down all the fairy tales. And they just *ruined* it."

"Did they? You've always loved the movie. You can like it just for itself," Carmichael reasoned. Kitty was unmoved. "Anyway, I bet Disney wasn't the first to make changes. You should take a look at the Brothers Grimm version."

"I've heard of them too," said Kitty.

"Germans from, I think, a century or two after Perrault." She pronounced it *pair-OH*. "They collected fairy tales, but also adapted ones that were already well known. Give me a second." Carmichael left behind the scattered yogurt cups to study the bookshelves in the living room. "Found it!" She pulled the book down and handed it to Kitty.

With a barely conscious "Thank you, Mommy," Kitty retreated back upstairs in an entranced daze. This book was not a smarmy sea-green and it wasn't from Reader's Digest, for heaven's sake. Meemaw had a vast collection of abridged novels from them. As far as Kitty was concerned, "abridged" was the Megan Moravsky of books. But this Grimm volume, now, it was over seven hundred pages long, seductively silver, and illustrated with a fine attention to detail that paid no insult to the taste of children.

She lay down on her stomach on top of the rag rug on her floor and found "Cinderella." This version horrified her, too, but for entirely different reasons. The stepsisters chopped off their own toes to fit into the glass slipper. The little birds didn't help Cinderella with her dress but instead tattled on the stepsisters so the prince would notice the blood pouring out of the stumps where their toes used to be. He was a pretty stupid prince, Kitty reflected, if he didn't notice gushing blood inside of glass slippers! And at the end there was no forgiveness for the stepsisters, to say nothing of husbands. Those sweet little birds actually pecked the girls' eyes out.

"I wish Disney had done *this* version," Kitty said aloud. She flipped over onto her back and stared up at the ceiling. There were flaky patches where the paint was peeling off. Her parents conducted a rigid triage in asking for repairs on the parsonage, and this was far down the list. Kitty liked to pick out silhouettes in it, anyway, ceiling-gazing rather than star-gazing.

All at once she jumped up and ran downstairs, out the door, and to her cave at the edge of the meadow to convene the council.

Nutcracker arrived first and she started right in. "It's all connected," she told him. "Like how Tchaikovsky ruined your story, and Grimm ruined—or, at least, really changed—Perrault's." She tried to say it like her mother did. "Then Disney actually did ruin both versions of Cinderella, and Mrs.

Onderdonk didn't know about *Alice*, and..."

Kitty stopped short. She wanted to tell him about her grandparents, not just the agnostic part but now also the Jewish part. This, too, had to be connected somehow, part of the interwoven tissue of adult dishonesty, but saying it aloud—even to so discreet an interlocutor as Nutcracker—felt like a betrayal. But who else could she talk to about it? She hadn't even said anything to her mom about it, not since that night she came home from ice cream crying. "There's more," she mumbled, "but I'll wait till everyone is here."

Nutcracker gave his version of a nod, the apparatus of his jaw opening and shutting again. "Many a night I've grieved over the distortion of my history," he said. "It's very hard on Marie. We have been trying to think of ways to help you escape the fate of adulthood and its lies. Nothing so far, I'm afraid."

Ichabod trotted in and licked Kitty's ear.

"There's another thing I've noticed," she said, leaning in confidentially. Ichabod settled down on his paws. "I think that when girls start to like boys, they lose their imagination. Poof! It's gone." Jo came in during this speech and snorted in agreement. She had nothing but derision for that type of girl. "Megan Moravsky is always going on about boys," Kitty added as proof. "Do you think there's something about falling in love that kills off imagination? If so, I'm never gonna fall in love."

"Me neither," said Jo.

Rhea filled up the entrance in her overbearing way. Kitty tried to remember how exactly the titan got on the council. Kitty was pretty sure she hadn't invited her, but that didn't mean a thing. After all, it was always happening that evil fairies showed up unannounced at baptisms. Not that Rhea was an evil fairy, Kitty hastily corrected herself. She was half-convinced that Rhea could read her mind.

"Well, we're just waiting for Fawn now," Kitty said, to change the subject.

Ichabod exchanged a glance with Nutcracker. Jo stopped

writing mid-sentence. Rhea did not move at all, which was typical. Yet somehow she seemed changed, too.

"What's going on?" Kitty asked.

Nutcracker said, "You don't know, then?"

"Know what?"

"Fawn isn't coming."

"Why not? It's not even hunting season yet. He's still safe."

"He's not coming," stated Rhea.

"What happened to him?" Kitty said. She felt like she was about to throw up.

Ichabod gave the doggy version of a shrug. Jo chewed on her quill. Nutcracker looked to Rhea but at last seemed to resolve to take the responsibility upon himself.

"We don't exactly know," he said in a gentle voice that contrasted so dramatically with his wild painted eyes and teeth. "We just know that he is… not. He is not. Not anymore."

Kitty looked from face to face. They looked back at her with tenderness, sympathy, bewilderment. Nutcracker wasn't holding out on her like a dishonest grown-up. He really didn't know why or how Fawn was—not. But *that* he was not, Nutcracker and the others knew with the knowledge unique to them. They, in any case, would never lie to her.

It didn't matter that they didn't know why, though. Kitty knew exactly why, and she knew exactly when. She felt it in her bones and stomach. It had happened when Megan started talking about the White Rabbit and Tweedledee and Tweedledum. Somehow, in so doing, Megan had managed to poison *Alice* and all its inhabitants from afar. Nixed and annihilated them.

What else could possibly explain it?

"Fawn's never coming back," wailed Kitty. Ichabod gave out a low whine of despair. Kitty threw her arms around him and mashed her face into his floppy golden ears. "Don't you worry," she promised. "Nothing will happen to you. Never ever. I will keep you safe."

CHAPTER FOUR

October 1988

Dreary as this season appears,
yet it has like all others its miracles.

By early October, autumn had already passed through Olutakli County like a fireworks display, every bit as colorful and almost as short-lived. By now the lawns boasted more leaves than the crowns of the trees, and children took their last opportunity to kick and plunge into the piles before wind, compost, and garbage collectors took them all away.

Shibboleth, meanwhile, pursued its never-ending battle between charm and degradation, which took on a special potency during the brief fall blowout. Three-wheelers screeched in the hills, power lines and parking lots popped out to dominate a horizon stripped of all green, college students unleashed their drunk driving and empty bottles on the roads. So many people heated their homes with firewood that the air already bore aloft a smoky scent that wouldn't recede for sure till Memorial Day.

Olutakli County was too cold and the earth too tough for any fruit but blackberries in the summer and apples in the fall, but what apples they were: crisp, juicy, tart, piebald, nothing like the styrofoam-flavored Red Delicious that Grand Union carried ten months of the year. On a clear October day, when the sky was enamel blue and the sun so golden it was almost orange, it felt like God had taken a bite out of a good apple and scrubbed the whole town with its juicy side till everything gleamed with holiness.

Behind the gleam there lurked still the nastiness of mutual use and abuse, no more elevated in dorms than out back of barns, not to mention the domestic brutes, the incorrigibly ignorant, the grifters and drifters, and the snobby transplants whose designs to uplift and improve were colonial at best.

And the pettiness—heavens above, the pettiness; nothing too small to maim over.

But that was reality, apparently: a human race poisoned by one bad apple got shined up with a good one, through the perplexing determination of the divine being, who seemed to find hypocrisy downright endearing in its delusionality.

It was with those exceptional apples of Olutakli County that Carmichael was busy preparing not one, not two, but three apple crisps for the church council to devour after its monthly meeting. Each dish floated a thick raft of streusel that would have done justice to a New York coffeecake. The children were variously occupied with TV and books, so Carmichael's only company in the kitchen was her newly arrived Jewish self.

This Carmichael's hair was just as long but slightly curlier and darker. Though shorter in stature she was towering in personality, for none of the other Carmichaels had shown themselves since her arrival, either as soloists or in chorus. This alternate, it seemed, could clear out a whole orchestra.

The real Carmichael, smoothing the streusel over the top of the third apple crisp, said, "So do you have a wig on today, or is that your own hair?"

"It's our own hair," the Jewish Carmichael replied.

"You had a wig on last time."

"I misjudged. We wouldn't go that far."

"Are you sure? I bet if you'd caught me at the right time I could have gone that way." The only way to cope with these apparitions, Carmichael had concluded, was to bait them with mock seriousness.

"We didn't thirst enough to belong. We would've needed to fall in love with a whole family, or better yet a whole community, and decided that marriage was our only way in. But we've always known ourself and our place in the world."

"Have we now? Known 'ourself'?" The timer went off on the first crisp and she donned oven mitts to trade it out for the second. "Your presence here suggests just the opposite."

"I don't see why you need to alienate me in this hostile fashion. I am you and you are me."

"You are not me. You are an irritating figment of my imagination."

"I am you. We are a Jew."

"I know I'm a Jew."

"Yet you never told our daughter."

Ferocity seized Carmichael without warning. "You keep Kitty out of this," she snarled.

"All I'm saying is, it's not very fair to pin this on our mother without taking responsibility for it ourself."

"She is not *your* mother, and you are not who I have become or ever will become." Carmichael did not notice how she was tapping the wooden spoon on the counter like the stick of a battle drum. "I am baptized. Remember that part?"

"So we are. But that doesn't make this part go away."

"Oh, shut up."

"St. Paul was a baptized Jew."

"What do you want of me?" Carmichael was shaking by now, as much at the content of the conversation as at her inability to stop what was, after all, only in her head.

"To acknowledge me," said the other Carmichael.

They stared at each other.

"I see you," said Carmichael at last. "Now go away."

"Not forever," said the other. Then she was gone.

∽

Whether it was the genetic factor of descending from a line of so many pastors, or the impact of his environment in youth, or the interplay of both, the plain truth was that Donald loved the pastorate.

He loved the olive wood box, given him by his teary mother

on the day of his ordination, made in the Holy Land and carved with niches to hold a little bottle of wine, a stack of wafers in a plastic container to keep them from going soggy or stale, and five solid bronze shot glasses stacked inside each other, for the sake of a holy communion consecrated at a deathbed or a shut-in's side. Donald loved the odor of the church basement, of every church basement, so universal and transdenominational that it ought to rank right up there with "one, holy, catholic, and apostolic" as a mark of the church. He loved the twitch and occasional squawk of outrage from a baby undergoing baptism. "We sure drowned the old Adam out of that one," Donald never failed to quip, in part to mask the glee he still felt at applying the sacrament to one too small to make a verbal confession of faith. He loved the look of surprise on parishioners' faces after struggling through a hard passage of Scripture and arriving at a wisdom they didn't know they had. He loved the warm welcome he could extend to a guilty penitent, slinking back to church after a bender of self-destructive sin and expecting a hot handful of shame from the righteous. He loved parsing Greek, he loved reading Käsemann, he loved the laying-on of hands to welcome confirmands and ordinands into their anointed states. Truth be told, he loved even his desperate and inconclusive mental arguments with his dead grandfather.

But Donald did not love church council meetings.

Lord knows he'd tried. Tried to turn it into a teaching opportunity, a chance to form lay leaders. The result was that Dale Mayer—a dairy farmer put out of business by the regulators in Albany, according to an initiative that Donald couldn't quite wrap his out-of-state mind around—had still not forgiven the pastor for asking him at the outset of his very first council meeting at Mt. Moriah to pray. "Ain't that what we're paying *you* for?" Dale barked. Donald, chastened, replied with an immediate and soothing, "Let us pray." He'd tried to authorize subcommittees to make their own decisions on their own time. He'd tried to pace the meetings with a timer. Finally, a few months back, Donald gave up and appealed to baser instincts. Homemade dessert, prepared by his wife and announced at an agreed-upon hour by his daughter, was the one and only strategy that could rein council meetings in to a reasonable duration.

"Just a quick update on the columbarium and then we can finally bring Mrs. Feuerlein in to talk about her idea," announced Donald.

"I'm not sure we should be so quick about it," said George Pohl, the treasurer.

"*I* got time," added Dale Mayer. Beneath it everyone could hear his rippling resentment at the lack of cows to milk in the evenings. These days he was reduced to driving for Social Services, "carting around juvenile delinquents to privileges they don't deserve," as he put it.

"Let's hear from Sandra first," Donald said.

Eunice Thyssen, staring at Sandra, posed her pencil over her stenographer's pad. Stemming from one of the German families that came to Olutakli County via Brazil, Eunice had in her late teens married a rising Dutch Reformed sofa salesman. After raising their children according to her husband's wishes at Second Reformed Church of Shibboleth (a knot of dissenting Scotsmen got to town first and staked their claim on First Reformed Church of Shibboleth; proposals for Atonement Reformed and Prudence Reformed and Fidelity Reformed got rejected as too Baptist, too Unitarian, and too banker, respectively, so Second Reformed it was), Eunice resigned from the register and repatriated to Mt. Moriah, where she considered taking and transcribing the minutes appropriate penitence for her long sojourn among the tulipers.

Sandra Forrad glanced over at Eunice. "Well, I've heard from the company" was immediately transmuted into the scratchy sound of pencil on paper, a graphite Morse Code. Sandra pressed on, "And yes, the delivery is delayed a bit, but they assure me it'll here by the end of October in good time to dedicate on All Saints'."

"This is the third time now they've delayed," said Dale, a guttural flapping of phlegm at the back of his throat.

"They promise me it'll be the last," Sandra said.

Al Beck always made a point of sounding more reasonable than Dale Mayer, even if he privately agreed with him. "The thing is," Al said in an amicable tone, "we already laid down that concrete foundation six weeks ago. It's just gonna keep on absorbing damp. If we don't get the columbarium on top of it and secured in place before it freezes hard, well then." He stopped, waving a hand toward the window, which suggested the retribution of the unforgiving elements if not, strictly speaking, the divine.

"Not to mention all the work we done for this party," interjected Jackie Holocomb. She was a single mother of three teen boys. Her black bangs marched with hairsprayed rigidity around the perimeter of her forehead. The rest of her mane was streaked with white-blonde and a touch of green. She wore big sparkly earrings, a tight T-shirt with an Iron Maiden logo, and an incongruously delicate gold cross on a gold chain that she'd gotten for her confirmation and, she swore, had worn every day since. This was her first term on council and she still couldn't believe the confidence the church people had placed in her. The All Saints' party was her baby and she was not going to let anything mess it up—concrete, columbarium, or Satan himself.

"I explained all that to them, and they understand, really they do," said Sandra. "They're in the burial business—they know how people feel about All Saints'!"

"Who else cares about it?" challenged Dale. "We never done it when I was a kid."

"Catholics do," said Eunice, sniffing as if in detection of something disagreeable on the bottom of her shoe. "*They* have a huge columbarium, three whole panels front and back and all of them full. Their cemetery is just across the way from Second Reformed, you know," she added, as if the other parishioners at Mt. Moriah might draw the wrong conclusion from her insider knowledge of Catholicism. "I know because they always have so many candles on Halloween and the children thought it was for trick-or-treating but no, they're lit for the dead, to get them out of hell."

"Purgatory," said Donald.

"I care about it," interjected Sandra. "Alan and I have been holding on to his mother's ashes for almost three years now. We've been counting on being able to put her to rest at last this All Saints', and I for one let the company know that."

"So we're doing Catholic stuff now, is that it?" pressed Dale. "Like you in your white robe?" This remark was directed at the pastor, who had defied every single one of his predecessor pastors with his choice of vestments.

"No, we're just remembering our roots," said Donald. "Martin Luther posted his Ninety-Five Theses on the eve of All Saints', which is to say Halloween—'hallowed evening.' We forgot about that for a few generations, but now we're back on track."

"Humph," said Dale. "I liked remembering the dead on New Year's Eve better."

"It doesn't matter one bit if it's trick-or-treat or April Fool's, because the real issue here is that we haven't paid for that columbarium yet," George declared.

"We're halfway there with the special fund," said Sandra.

"Halfway isn't home, as any umpire'll tell you," he retorted. "As it is, we have trouble paying the bills, and you know this roof is going to need replacing soon. We should have done it before winter. I'm up there messing with shingles almost every Sunday."

"You're too old to be climbing up that ladder," piped up Hazel Quinn.

"Costs too much to hire a roofer," George plowed on. "It was a dumb thing to do, buying that columbarium, when we knew full well we couldn't pay for it." He turned the full force of his treasurer's glare on Donald.

"You feel dismayed about the budget shortfall, don't you, George?" said Donald.

"I ain't talkin' about how I *feel*, I'm talkin' about *money* which ain't got no feelings at all," snapped George. The pastor was always saying things like "You must feel very strongly about that" or "This means a lot to you, I can tell." As if they hired him to parrot back their perfectly obvious reactions to things. Paying the bills was surely a more useful skill for a pastor to have than saying things like, "Gee, Bob, you sure must feel sad that your mother got hit by a bus last week."

"Getting buried in God's good earth," declared Dale Mayer, "was good enough for my parents and my grandparents. It's good enough for me, too. I never did like the idea of this thing and I won't be boxed up in it."

"You were happy enough to volunteer to lay the concrete for it," remarked Marilyn Gross in a studiously neutral voice. She was not very fond of Sandra Forrad but she was even less fond of Dale Mayer. As far as she was concerned, he was nothing but a bully.

"I does what needs to get done," said Dale haughtily. He couldn't stand Marilyn's passive-aggressive nips at the ankle.

"What I want to know is," said Hazel in a quavery tone, "are you really sure the Lord will be able to raise us up on the last day if we get all burned up to ashes?"

"You grew up on a farm, Hazel Quinn," said Dale, "and you know as well as anybody that things buried in the ground turn to wormy mush, no more or less like a body than a pile of ashes is."

"Which side are you on?" asked Jackie in genuine bewilderment.

"I don't like the thing, but what I'm saying is, if Jesus can make a new body out of skeletons, and sailors lost at sea, and soldiers blowed up by mines, he can do it just as well out of a handful of ashes in an urn."

"Well said," remarked Donald.

"I just don't know," fretted Hazel. "I just don't think I'll have it done to me."

"You don't have to," said Sandra. She patted Hazel's hand. "Look, nobody *has* to use the thing. It's fine to go on being buried in the cemetery. It's not like we're going to run out of room. But the columbarium is a very nice choice for families that can't afford a big headstone, so it's friendly toward the poor—" Sandra failed to notice the look of universal astonishment on the faces around her; she may have thought some of them counted among the poor, but they certainly didn't think of themselves that way "—and it's also good for the environment."

"I thought burnin' stuff made more acid rain," interrupted Dale. "That's why they tell us now we shouldn't burn our garbage no more."

"Crematoria burn extremely clean," explained Sandra in a patient tone. "Plus, human bodies are absolutely full of toxic chemicals. Returning them to the earth is the same as poisoning the earth. This way, our loved ones are remembered and kept forever, but without damaging Mother Nature."

"Hippie talk," muttered Marilyn under her breath.

"Tell you the truth, I'm not sure I'd wanna be locked up in one of those little squares, neither," said Jackie, gazing at the brochure from the columbarium company. Like a good student, she kept every piece of paper she got at council and brought the whole collection with her to every meeting. She may not have mastered marriage or the pill, but she was going to show them that she was equal to the task of council member. "But if somebody else wants to, it's fine by me. I think it's nice to give people a choice."

"What's done is done," said Donald. "The columbarium will arrive within the next two weeks, we'll install it and consecrate it, we'll raise the money and pay it off. Those who want to be cremated and placed in a niche can do that, and those who want to be buried in the ground can do that. The good Lord will look after us, either way." He smiled on the assembly.

Dale shrugged. George scowled. Sandra returned his smile openly. They let the people say their piece, she thought triumphantly, but in the end the two of us held the line. We'll enlighten these old farmers whether they like it or not.

"Now let's bring in poor Mrs. Feuerlein, who's been waiting for so long," said Donald.

Eunice went to fetch her from the sanctuary upstairs, where she'd been sitting for two hours and praying for everyone she could think of "in German," as she often explained, "because even after all zhese years in America, two zhings I still do in German: I count, and I pray."

"Sorry to keep you waiting, Sabine," said Donald. "We had to take care of old business first. But why don't you share your idea with the council now. I think everyone's going to be really excited about it."

Dale and George exchanged glances. If the pastor liked it, then it was going to happen. It was also going to be expensive.

Mrs. Feuerlein had only just settled herself into the folding chair and propped up her voluminous purse on the table when a sound like bowling pins on an escalator made everyone's head turn. It was Kitty, banging down on each step as hard as she could. When she hit the bottom she turned a magnificent cartwheel, ending in a split, threw her arms in the air, and bellowed, "APPLE CRISSSP!"

The council members applauded.

She stood and made an extravagant bow. "Mommy just took the last one out of the oven and they all smell *amazing*," she said. "Come on!"

"Vell, I am not vun to shtand in the vay of apple crisp," said Mrs. Feuerlein merrily. "I can talk as vell vizh dessert as vizhout."

"Let's go, then," said Donald.

As the council trooped into the parsonage, they heard before they saw Asher and Saul bouncing on the sofa in tandem, shrieking "APPLE CRISP" with a passion equal to their sister's.

The moment Asher laid eyes on Mrs. Feuerlein he landed on the sofa on his bottom instead of his feet, bounced forward, hit the ground running, threw his arms around her in a hug, and whispered, "Did you bring me Lifesavers?"

"Of course," said Mrs. Feuerlein, clawing around in her purse.

"I'll share with my brother. He can have the green ones!" Asher chortled.

"I don't want the green ones! I hate the green ones!" wailed Saul.

"No green in zhis kind," said Mrs. Feuerlein. "*Butter rrrum*," she announced in a tone of high mystery, as if she were a sibylline oracle of confectionery. "And vun for each of you."

At this, Saul also saw fit to grace the old lady with a hug.

Once the living room was fully occupied by the council members swathed in a fragrant fog of apple crisp, Donald attempted to give Mrs. Feuerlein the floor, but she said, "Oh, it's late and I'm tired. You already know vhat I have in mind. You tell zhem for me." She turned to her streusel with zealous attention.

"All right," chuckled Donald.

He proceeded to recall to mind that their very own Sabine Feuerlein was not one of the Brazil families but had escaped the communist secret police of her native East Germany in 1956. She'd been on vacation in Budapest ("Where's that?" whispered Dale. "Romania, I think," replied George with a shrug of disinterest; all commies were the same) and taken advantage of the brief window of liberalization to cross the border before the Soviet troops stepped in. Never married, not much more than a decade away from retirement, she made the abrupt decision to leave everything behind—parents, siblings, friends, native tongue, apartment, clothes—in fact, everything that she hadn't packed for her vacation.

While waiting to receive her final papers guaranteeing asylum in America, she took a job at a German dry cleaner's on Long Island. Once legal, and just shy of sixty, she married Gerhard Feuerlein, owner of the dry cleaner's. They retired to Shibboleth because he'd had enough of the City and the hills reminded her of the Erzgebirge back home. It was a short but sweet marriage. After she buried him (in the cemetery of Mt. Moriah, of course), she decided it was time to reestablish relations with her relations.

It was slow going at first. Every letter was read and censored by the regime, and some never made it through at all. But things were changing. Lately they'd allowed packages, even. She sent blue jeans and perfume to her nieces' and nephews' children and grandchildren. Bit by bit they filled her in on all the news of the townsfolk and extended family. As it turned out, her great-nephew Fritz was a pastor now and had a church in a village not far from where she'd grown up.

"Now this is where it gets interesting," said Donald. The communist government was trying to prove its open-mindedness by allowing a modest number of visas for pastoral exchange between East Germany and the United States. Fritz had written to ask Sabine if she thought her church would be willing to host him for two weeks—to *visit*, not to *stay*, he made very clear in the letter, adding some unnecessary sentences about his admiration for his fatherland. Mrs. Feuerlein knew perfectly well this was for the censors, who might have doubts about his motive in paying a visit to his defector great-aunt in America.

At this point Mrs. Feuerlein took up the thread. "Fritz sounds to me like a very good and honorable man, taking on zhis kind of calling from God in a place vhere no respect is given to it. He has never been out of zhe eastern bloc in his whole life and it vould be zuch a treat for him! I zhink it would be a treat for zhe congregation, too, because you could ask him vhat it really is like behind zhat iron curtain, and here in America, Fritz can speak freely."

"Fritz," said Dale Mayer around a mouthful of apple crisp.

"That's what the Limeys called the Krauts during the war. Never liked it, to tell you the truth. My old man's name was Fritz. You never met a truer American than him, no matter how thick that accent was."

"My ma said they teased her merciless," chimed in Al Beck. "She learned fast to sound American. Wouldn't say a word of German to us when we were kids, even though the family kept it going at home all those generations in Brazil. The war put an end to that for sure. Didn't matter that none of our family was ever in Germany since eighteen-fifty-something. As far as they were concerned, a Kraut was a Kraut."

Mrs. Feuerlein flushed and quivered. "My great-nephew is no Nazi. And today he is courageously shtanding up to an oppressive government."

"Aw, Oma, you know we ain't saying nothing against him," crooned Dale with unexpected tenderness. "Weren't we just sayin' how we hated bein' taken for Krauts just because we're German by blood? I'm sure your Fritz is a good man. Anybody sticking up for God among all them communists must be a good man. Let's have him on over."

George Pohl's mouth hung open, apple crisp balanced precariously on his tongue, at Dale's effortless acquiescence to who-knew-what expense.

"I never met anybody from a foreign country before," said Jackie, eyes shining.

Hazel said, "Bonnie is from Canada."

"I think it's a fine idea," said Sandra, "as long as it doesn't interfere with paying off the columbarium."

"We'll need to see a budget," blustered George, finding his voice at last.

Eunice announced, "I've got plenty of room in my house if he needs a place to stay."

"Ach, he vill stay vizh me," said Mrs. Feuerlein.

"Sure, he can spend the night with you, but he'll want to visit around, see how real Americans live," said Al Beck. "Not to say you aren't," he added quickly. "I bet we can arrange for him to have dinner with a different family every night."

"We can take him to see all the sights!" said Jackie. "The Corning Glass Works, Niagara Falls, the races in Saratoga Springs... but maybe communist pastors don't like to bet."

"He is no communist," insisted Mrs. Feuerlein.

"I think it's a winning plan, Sabine," said Donald.

"Vunderful," she said. "Just like zhis apple crisp. Now it is vay past my bedtime. I am sorry to break up zhe party but somevun should take me home to shleep. I shtill don't know vhy you vouldn't let me drive here myself."

"Because your head don't poke above the dashboard, Oma," said Dale.

~

"It's a crane truck!" shrieked Asher, pointing downhill with a frantically happy finger.

Saul at his left, and likewise standing on the wobbly seat of the swing, shook his head with the superior wisdom of a first-grader over kindergarten ignorance. "It's a *boom* truck."

"Nuh-uh, it's got a crane!" Asher gave Saul a little shove as punctuation to his rebuttal. Saul had to grip the swing's chain not to topple off. The crane, visible at the bottom of the hill from their perch at the top, was of extraordinary length and a bright yellow color, like a giraffe's neck folded forward over the cab.

"That's what you call a truck with a crane on it, dummy, a *boom* truck," repeated Saul.

"It's a disaster is what it is," said George Pohl, standing a few steps away from the boys. His hands were in his pockets and his face was only by the greatest self-restraint not unabashedly smug. Of all the things that Sandra Forrad had told the columbarium company, for all the phone calls and follow-ups, somehow it had slipped her mind to mention the driveway. Narrow, steep, and boasting not just one but two hairpin turns. The fact that it didn't happen also to be icy, this late in October, was proof either that God was merciful or, for mysterious reasons of his own, liked to let fools off the hook.

At the bottom of the driveway, where it intersected with the Shinhopple Turnpike, clustered an impromptu committee of parishioners and passersby. Conversation was noisy and impassioned. The driver, and his associate in the passenger seat who'd come to oversee the installation, had not stopped disputing between themselves since the former, in protest, shut off the engine at the foot of the hill. Dale Mayer offered to drive the boom truck up the driveway, citing his long experience of navigating large machinery all over Olutakli County, but both of them insisted that the insurance forbade any such thing. A neighbor offered his own kitted-out utility vehicle if the columbarium could be transferred over to its bed. But then, without the crane, how would they get the columbarium off again and set into place?

Al Beck figured a pal of his could get them a crane within an hour or two for a good price, or he himself could provide an alternative insurance policy for a different driver. The associate objected that if they didn't oversee every step of the installation, the contract would be null and void, and if the thing got cracked in the process, well, that was on the church and not on the company. So that idea was scrapped.

Sandra, wrapped in an elegant trench coat of shimmery sapphire blue, stood aloof, the constant cracking of her knuckles the only indicator of her nervous tension. Donald and Carmichael stood by to show solidarity but offered no views on the matter.

At last the driver accepted the neighbor's offer to use his phone and called up headquarters, which decided he'd better just try it with the emergency brake on, since whatever damage *that* did was still going to cost less than hiring another truck and driver, or worse yet having to bring the damn thing back and start over again.

So by the time the boom truck actually began its ascent, quite a crowd had gathered, including cars pulled over on the side of the road to watch the proceedings. At the first turn, the driver inched forward and backward at least a dozen times before achieving the necessary angle to advance. At the second turn, the driver seemed to be unnerved rather than empowered by his previous success, taking twice as many back-and-forths and long pauses between each of them. The gawking members of Mt. Moriah kept vigil, staring at the back end of truck and columbarium hovering in space over the steep hillside. At last the driver, satisfied, shot up the final leg of the driveway. Saul and Asher acclaimed his triumph at the top with cheers, but Mr. Pohl only scowled.

The boys jumped off the swing and careened ahead of the truck straight for the cemetery. Saul aimed for the Schickedanzes' grave, their usual destination, but Asher veered to the right and clambered onto the waiting concrete foundation. He lay down, spread-eagled, face up, as if to embrace the columbarium when it settled into its final resting place.

Saul turned to look for his brother and, spotting him, screamed. He tore across the cemetery, clipping a shoulder on one of the tombstones, leapt onto the foundation, and hurtled at Asher. "Get off! Get off! Get off!" He pushed so hard that Asher, unprepared, rolled over onto his stomach and then again onto his back before he could even react.

"Stop it!"

"Get off! You'll get smashed!"

"No I won't! It's still on the truck!"

They wrestled hard, tearing at each other. Asher bit Saul on the fleshy part of his forearm. Saul ignored him and kept pushing and rolling till Asher dropped the foot or so off the far side of the foundation onto the ground, which was hard and bristly with dead grass. Saul climbed over him and then, getting a tight hold of his jacket sleeve, hauled him away.

For once, Asher gave up. "Leggo," he whined. "I won't go up

there anymore." He stood and looked uncertainly at his brother. Saul was panting and heaving and wouldn't look him in the eye. He pressed on his sore shoulder. "I won't go back up there, I promise," said Asher. Saul nodded, rubbed both eyes with the back of his hands, and slunk off toward the house. He sat down on the wooden steps leading up to the pantry door.

Asher squatted in place. He was stranded between two equally compelling summonses: his eternal companion, on the one hand, and the one-time-only apparition of the boom truck, on the other. He surveyed the landscape and intuited that once the truck pulled up to the cemetery, Saul would actually have a pretty good view of the show. Asher burst forward like a pogo stick, checked himself from running over the foundation so as not to upset Saul again, and after a fast dogleg around it ran over to his brother and settled down on the step below him. Normally he'd go on the step above and poke at the back of Saul's head. Something curbed that instinct. Instead he pulled a pair of grubby gummy worms out of his pocket and offered one to Saul, not the yucky green one, either, but the pale yellow pineapple-flavored one he'd secreted away for himself. Saul accepted it with a heavy exhalation of breath, but he seemed to unclench a little.

From that point on, a magnificent display unfurled before the boys' eyes. The driver parked the truck, and in just a few minutes he and the other guy were smearing the foundation with some wonderful gray goo. By the time they finished, the church folks had reached the top of the hill and, still a bit winded, gathered round to watch. The associate hauled a red cooler out from behind his seat—"Maybe he's gonna hand out popsicles!" suggested Asher; "Too cold," rebutted Saul—but what emerged was better than sweets: two blocks of dry ice. With a swirl of seeping mist, like that creepy part of the Ten Commandments movie when the angel of death passes over, the dry ice settled like twin sentinels on the goo-smeared foundation. Before Asher could wonder how the big thing in the back of the truck was gonna balance on two little blocks like that, he and Saul heard the driver explaining that they were there to position the columbarium in place and then lower it to the foundation more gently than even the crane could do. "Cooool," judged Asher. "Too bad Kitty's at Girl Scouts."

Then, the magic of levitation. The crane stretched out its cramped neck. The straps around and above the columbarium pulled taut. The mass rose off the cargo bed, swaying, swinging, twirling a little. Saul was so enraptured that he stood up on his step and gripped the post of the railing to brace himself against the joy. So, so slowly the columbarium traversed its arc up over the edge of the truck and then down toward the concrete, so slowly and yet so compellingly that even the grown-ups could not take their eyes off it, including the skeptical Mr. Pohl.

Once it was within arm's reach, the associate guided the columbarium into position, signaling to the driver at the command post with an eloquent pair of fingers. When it made contact with the dry ice, the whole crowd clapped approval. The associate shook his head to stay the applause; the show wasn't over yet. Crowbar in hand he nudged, shifted, and jimmied until it was just so. A plumb line dropped on each side manifested the result of perfect alignment. Then the driver popped out of the cab and the two men set to slipping off the straps from each corner and peeling away the protective plastic. "Bubble wrap," Asher hissed into his brother's ear. Saul nodded, wide-eyed and open-mouthed: more bubble wrap than he'd seen in his whole life. They could make it last a year.

Then the two columbarium guys stood tall, legs planted, arms crossed, hardhats at a jaunty angle, and with an air of satisfaction invited questions from the audience. By the time the last wisp of dry ice gave out and the columbarium nestled down to sleep, everyone was so taken with the thing that even Hazel Quinn was heard to say, while burnishing one little niche door with her sleeve, "Well, I might just decide to spend eternity here after all."

CHAPTER FIVE

November 1988

*The easiest way of becoming acquainted
with the modes of thinking, the rules of conduct,
and the prevailing manners of any people,
is to examine what sort of education they give their children;
how they treat them at home,
and what they are taught in their places of public worship.*

On Saturday morning Kitty was awoken by Asher climbing under her lilac-colored comforter and snuggling up against her. "Guess what, Kitty," he breathed into her ear.

"Whaaat," she droned, shoving her face under her stuffed wolf, whose name was Virginia.

"I'm polka-dotted," he said. His husky voice was boastful.

"Mommy told you not to draw on yourself with markers."

"No, I'm natural polka-dotted," Asher said. "Look at my tummy." He hauled up his Smurfs pajama top and pushed down the comforter to display his little-boy potbelly. "They're pink!" he announced.

Kitty degrimed her eyes and studied his skin. "Those aren't polka dots, you dope," she said. "They're chicken pox."

"I'm not chicken! I'm brave Asher!" he protested.

"Chicken *pox*. You're *sick*."

"*You're* sick."

"No, I'm not. I already had the chicken pox, when I was little, before you were born."

"Really? What was I like before I was borned?"

"How should I know? There's no way to answer a question like that."

"Please, please, pretty please answer the question."

"I mean I don't *know* the answer. You didn't exist. There's nothing to say about you before you existed."

"I was in Mommy's tummy."

"I'm talking about *before* you were in Mommy's tummy."

"Where was I before Mommy's tummy?"

"I don't know! That's what I keep telling you, there's no answer. You just didn't exist."

"I don't like not existing," said Asher firmly.

"Everyone starts out not existing," declared Kitty. "And everyone ends up not existing. That's what happens when we die." Does that mean Fawn is dead? she thought to herself.

"Do we go back to where we were before Mommy's tummy?"

"No, we go to heaven."

"Wasn't I in heaven before Mommy's tummy?"

"No, you just *weren't*."

Asher shut his eyes very tight, as if trying to relieve his brain of the pressure of new information. Then he popped his eyes open again and said, "I'm polka-dotted."

"Come on, let's tell Mommy," Kitty sighed.

In short order it was discovered that Saul, too, was a mass of pink polka dots that were starting to turn red from all his scratching. While Carmichael rubbed him down with calamine lotion, Asher found a black permanent marker and connected all the dots between his ribcage and his kneecaps.

Kitty, for her part, learned—before she could protest or even speak—that, first, her father would be gone all day at some dumb church meeting in another town, second, that her mother would have to drive the boys over to the hospital in Kuhsota to get a doctor's appointment on a Saturday, and that therefore, third, Kitty herself was to be deported to Mrs. Kipfmueller's house until Girl Scouts at two in the afternoon.

"But I *hate* it over there," Kitty whined. "It smells funny. Her food tastes funny." Every church potluck Mrs. Kipfmueller brought a pot of meatballs seasoned with caraway seeds, which had the texture of fingernail parings. Kitty was especially offended because under any other circumstances meatballs were her most favorite food ever, and Mrs. Kipfmueller had to go and ruin it. Other babysitting occasions had inflicted upon her such horrors as cabbage rolls boiled to rags, tough dry pot roast, and chicken with flabby skin. Why couldn't Mrs. Kipfmueller make a box of macaroni and cheese like a normal babysitter? "Please let me come along! I'll be good and help keep control of Saul and Asher."

"No, Kitty, I just can't handle all three of you today," said Carmichael, flying around in search of keys and purse and checkbook.

"But I'll be good! I'll be helpful!"

"I can't promise to get you back in time for Girl Scouts."

"Then I'll just skip it."

"No. For heaven's sake, Mrs. Kipfmueller isn't that bad. I don't know why you're making such a fuss."

"I *haaate* it over there," whined Kitty even more pathetically than the first time. "You're probably gonna go to Gino's and get strombolis without me."

"I'm not taking the boys anywhere but the hospital."

"Then you'll get drive-through at Wendy's! It's not fair that I don't get fast food just because I'm *healthy*."

"Kitty. Enough." Her mother's voice had that dangerous edge to it.

"Fine," Kitty huffed, but quietly. She slunk off to grab something to read, since Mrs. Kipfmueller didn't have hardly any books and the ones she did were about horses, of all dumb things. Kitty was halfway down the stairs before running back to collect the last of her stash of Halloween candy against the inevitable awfulness of lunch.

Mrs. Kipfmueller lived on the same side of Shibboleth as Mt. Moriah, south of the river, and almost as far up the hillside, but you couldn't get straight there because of the drop-off. Kitty pushed her feet hard against the floorboard of the car to hold off the inevitable as they tipped down the driveway, traversed half a mile along the Shinhopple Turnpike, and strained back up another steep hill, but less than an hour after waking up she was shuffling through the front door of the funny-smelling house. She turned back just in time to see the car pulling away with her mother and brothers.

"Come on, honey, the cold air is getting in," said Mrs. Kipfmueller in an intimate tone, as if being stuck there for five hours was a treat and not a curse. "Set your things down on the chair. Would you like apple juice or orange juice? I know you're a girl who likes to read so I pulled out my favorite from when I was your age—*National Velvet!*" She patted the worn cover, so old it didn't even have a picture on it.

"Thanks, I brought my own," said Kitty listlessly.

"I should have guessed. Well, you just make yourself at home. Or you can go out back and play in the yard if you like."

Kitty almost said, "I don't *play*," but then she thought of Megan Moravsky and her entourage and stopped herself. "OK, I guess I will for awhile," she said with a shrug.

A slow hour passed. Mrs. Kipfmueller wouldn't let her leave the yard, so there was no exploring the forest. The garden was dead. There was a swing set for Mrs. Kipfmueller's annoying grandchildren (once or twice Kitty had had the misfortune of coinciding with their visit) but they'd broken everything except the sliding pole, and Kitty was too tall to get much fun out of that.

She discovered a rudimentary treehouse, with odd ends of lumber nailed in to make a ladder in the trunk of the beech, but halfway up she heard Mrs. Kipfmueller calling from the back door, "Kitty, better not go up there—the floorboards are rotten and I don't want you falling through."

When a misty drizzle began to float sideways through the air, Kitty gave in to her desperation and retreated inside.

She stood in the empty kitchen. "Do you need anything, dear?" Mrs. Kipfmueller called from the living room. She was watching some long-winded news program, so even cartoons were out of the question.

"No," Kitty called back. She opened her tote bag and pulled out *The Little Prince*. She'd seen a few episodes of the show on TV, but once she realized they came from a book she swore off them. She'd had trouble getting into the story, though. Somehow it was sad, even though nothing sad had happened yet.

Suspicious, she flipped to the end for a peek. She came across a picture of a yellow snake rising up threateningly toward the boy. She skimmed the final pages in mounting horror. What kind of book has a little boy die in it? she thought in disgust. She shoved it back in her tote.

Between horses and untimely demise, reading was clearly out of the question.

Kitty looked up. The clock showed it was only thirteen minutes past ten.

"I'll never make it," she groaned.

There was only one possible solution: snooping.

Mrs. Kipfmueller was one of those old ladies who were deaf when you needed something but turned acute as bats the second you got into interesting trouble. Kitty peeled herself off a chair upholstered in plastic and came down as gently as she could on her two stocking feet. So far so good. She took a step and the floorboards screeched like they were being murdered. She froze, then remembered there was nothing criminal about walking around the kitchen. She could always say she was going for a drink of water or to the bathroom.

With a slow shuffle she advanced from the sparkly Formica-topped kitchen table across the room to a wall of built-in cupboards, banked three tall and five across. They revealed the sturdy old age of the house with their thick, precise, carpenter-fitted boards and archaeological layers of paint exposed by chipping. The topmost coat was a color called "desert rose," as Kitty had learned from examining paint samples at the hardware store. It was a dumb name, because it was just a way to not say "pink." Kitty approved of lilac but definitely not of pink.

Now came the moment of truth. Each cupboard had a little metal latch that looked likely to pop free without effort, but would the hinges creak? She thought over her story first. There was still orange juice in her glass, so she could say she wanted a fresh glass for water. Of course she knew perfectly well that the glasses were in the cabinet by the sink, which was the logical place to look anyway, but adults had such a low estimate of kids' intelligence that Mrs. Kipfmueller would probably fall for it. Too bad she didn't have gloves on, like a spy, to keep her incriminating fingerprints off the evidence.

Kitty chose the unit nearest the outside wall and lowest to the floor. Its door swung open in obedient silence. She squatted down on her heels for a better look. She was expecting pyrex pans, maybe the enamel pot that the yucky meatballs always arrived at church in, or a collection of cleaning supplies. It had not occurred to her for a moment to expect something wonderful.

But what wonders she found! More baking tins than you could shake a stick at. Not just round ones for birthday cake and square ones for brownies, but six different Bundt pans positively Gothic-cathedral in their elaborate patterning, tall angel food tins, and squat gugelhupf tins. Large metal sheets punched out in the shape of the castles in a chess game or soaps shaped like seashells (but not like actual seashells). There was some kind of device with a tube, a crank, and two dozen metal plates you could slide on and off to produce differently-shaped squiggles. It reminded Kitty of a Play-Doh set she used to have before Asher wrecked it.

Then she peered into a paper bag with twine handles and gasped aloud. It held shiny wooden rectangles of all sizes. Each was carved with an elaborate Christmas scene, or a single figure in old-fashioned costume, or rows of little pictures like in a game of Memory. She had never seen anything so exquisitely refined. She took out a wooden mold and studied it. At first she thought it might be a decoration for hanging on a wall, but tiny flecks were caught in its crevices. Was that from dough? Did you make cake or cookies with them? By the time she'd handled all the molds, she'd grown careless in her enthusiasm and rummaged into another paper bag, dredging up metal cones with stars snipped out of their tips and a selection of plastic sacks in various bright colors.

She was just screwing a tip onto a blue sack when she was jolted by the sound of Mrs. Kipfmueller's voice: "Snooping, eh?"

Kitty jumped up and blushed as deeply as she ever had, worse even than the time Kenny Creemers had announced to the entire fifth grade that she had a crush on Shane Ferly, which wasn't even true. "Sorry, sorry," she panted.

"Can hardly blame an active young lady like yourself for going stir-crazy in my house," said Mrs. Kipfmueller with what may have been a smirk. "But good manners would have you ask before you go peeking in my cupboards."

"I know, I'm sorry, I'm really sorry." Kitty felt like a skunk.

"I see you found my baking things. I used to be a cake decorator, did you know that? Before the Grand Union came along and put me out of business. Back in the day I did the baptism and confirmation and wedding cakes for just about everybody at Mt. Moriah. Haul that stuff up here on the kitchen table and I'll tell you all about it."

Kitty complied. Mrs. Kipfmueller explained about spritz cookies and springerle cookies, the difference between a genoise and a pound cake and why you might choose one over the other, how to keep an angel's food cake lofty and a devil's food cake dense. She elaborated theories of regional and ethnic differences in gingerbread. This tin for madeleines, this one for financiers, and that one for petits-fours, which were really just mini-cupcakes but square.

Wonderful as it all was, Kitty couldn't keep her hands out

of the bag of piping tips. "Can you make roses with these?" she asked.

"Sure," said Mrs. Kipfmueller. "You'd use this one here. This one is for leaves, this one for a reversed shell border, and this one for stars."

"Do you have to buy the frosting ready-made in the color you want?"

"Well, nowadays they do," Mrs. Kipfmueller scoffed. "But I always mixed up my own. I made a big pot of buttercream for every cake and then parceled it out for each different color I needed. I'd mix it in myself. Always liked that part. Made me feel a bit like a mad scientist, or a witch."

Kitty found that her heart could forgive Mrs. Kipfmueller for the terrible meatballs. Her true passion was cake. Who could fault her for finding meat boring by comparison? The last thing you wanted was colorful meat.

"Would you like to give them a try?"

"*Could* I? You mean, like practice on a plate?"

"You could, but wouldn't you rather decorate a real cake?"

Kitty's eyes flew wide open. "Could I make something to bring to Girl Scouts?" she whispered.

"Well, sure. We'll have to pick something I have the ingredients for. I think I could manage a yellow sheet cake at the very least."

"How about," said Kitty, tripping over her words in eagerness, "how about I make cupcakes but in that tin over there that makes them kind of wide and flat and then I could frost them and put scalloping around the edges and then use the narrow point to write EAT ME in cursive on each of them?"

Mrs. Kipfmueller chuckled. "What else would you do with a cupcake than eat it?"

"It's a reference to *Alice in Wonder*— I mean, *Alice's Adventures in Wonderland*. Little cakes appear that say EAT ME on them. So Alice eats them and then she grows really tall or really small."

"Now that is a kind of cake I never learned how to make," said Mrs. Kipfmueller.

After further negotiation they settled on spice cake with raisins. Since they had to start from scratch, and the cakes needed time to cool before being frosted, the two of them worked with intense focus until, at half past noon, Mrs. Kipfmueller realized it was too late to make anything special for lunch, "so if you don't mind too much, dear, you'll just have to make do with macaroni and cheese from a box."

"It's fine, thank you," said Kitty fervently.

At quarter to two Kitty set the last of her cakes into the wide flat Tupperware containers of which Mrs. Kipfmueller seemed to have a limitless supply. There had not been time for roses or drapery, but each cake smiled up at her with a shiny moon-white face and shouted its message of EAT ME in blue glucose.

During the short drive down the hill and across town to the basement of the Methodist church where the troop held its meetings, Mrs. Kipfmueller reminisced about some of her favorite cakes of yesteryear and said that Kitty was welcome to bake with her any time.

"If only I'd known sooner you were interested," she said. "Before long you'll be able to experiment on your own. How old are you now?"

"I just turned twelve the day before Halloween."

"Well, you're a very bright and well-spoken young lady for your age."

"Actually I was born two weeks early. I was supposed to come on November 11, and Daddy said, if I had, he would have named me Martina instead of Katharina!"

"Is that right?" said Mrs. Kipfmueller vaguely.

"Because of Martin Luther," Kitty explained. This did not in fact explain anything to Mrs. Kipfmueller and, come to think of it, Kitty couldn't quite remember what the connection was, either.

"I think Katharina is a very pretty name," said Mrs.

Kipfmueller. "Anyway, you just let me know the next time you want to work on your decorating skills."

"I will!" Kitty almost gave Mrs. Kipfmueller a hug, thought the better of it, and slithered out. She grabbed the stack three-deep of Tupperware containers.

"Have them cleaned and ready for me tomorrow in time for church," said Mrs. Kipfmueller. "That's good manners."

Kitty nodded and tottered through the side door of the church, down the stairs, and into the basement. It was much bigger than the basement of Mt. Moriah, with a fresh smell of floor cleaner wafting up from the bright linoleum squares. Already the sound of girls jabbering reverberated off the cinderblock walls.

Jessica noticed Kitty first. "Wow! What did you bring? Didn't you know it was Megan's turn to bring snack?" This seized the attention of the other girls, not least of all Megan. They rushed to Kitty and relieved her of her burden, peeling back the lid and exclaiming in delight. Megan turned pale. Kitty looked over at the snack table and, as she'd suspected, it was all bought stuff. Nice stuff, sure, like Pepperidge Farm cookies and Mallomars and a sheet cake from Grand Union with the names of the girls with November birthdays written on it in transparent pink frosting. But there was no doubt that it displayed only money, not skill or care.

Kitty felt her stature shoot up just as if she'd eaten one of Alice's magical cakes. Megan looked at her like the pigeon did at mile-high Alice: *she* saw a serpent, and a poisonous one at that. Kitty had only a moment to wonder whether that made her feel marvelous or repulsive, because Miss Wright came over to admire her handiwork.

"How thoughtful of you, Kitty," she said. "'EAT ME'—like from *Alice*, right? Will these make us grow or shrink?"

"I don't know," said Kitty. "Neither, I guess."

"They look delicious," said Miss Wright. "What a fun idea. Though to tell you the truth, I've always been desperately curious about the dry biscuits the Red Queen gives Alice in *Through the Looking-Glass*. Strange, isn't it?"

She knew the difference! Cleary Miss Wright was the best adult that had ever lived. Though Mrs. Kipfmueller wasn't so far behind anymore. "Do you know what a comfit is?" Kitty asked abruptly. "It's what Alice gives out—"

"—after the Caucus Race, yes," Miss Wright said with a smile. "I was always curious about that, too, so one time I looked it up. It's a kind of licorice candy with a colorful sugar coating on the outside."

"You mean like Good and Plenty?" said Kitty, disappointed.

"Yeah, something like that, I guess."

"I hate licorice. Cake is better."

"Agreed!" said Miss Wright with a big smile. "I hate licorice, too."

Kitty grinned back and looked around proudly, only to realize that all the girls were staring at her. Her specialized discussion with Miss Wright, provoked by the spectacular cupcakes she had brought, made most of them look on with uncomprehending wonder, a few like Jessica and Jenny Ulster shine with pride-by-association, but one girl's face exuded naked resentment. The look in Megan's eyes bored right through Kitty's skin like a pine beetle. It burrowed until it found the part of her that had decided to make something extra-special on what she knew perfectly well to be Megan's day for snack.

"All right, girls, let's get started," said Miss Wright, clapping her hands. Megan wheeled away from Kitty, an angry flush behind her smattering of freckles.

"You drove Fawn away," Kitty muttered under her breath at Megan's back. "You deserve whatever you get."

∽

The Shibboleth Co-op was the only place in town that smelled different. Not in the sense of not smelling of disinfectant, or decaying produce, or motor oil, or dryer sheets. It smelled like the outpost of another world: mostly fenugreek, as if the place were ritually blessed with a strewing of spice, though probably it came from shoppers mismanaging the transfer of curry powder from its bin via child-sized plastic scoops into equally tiny plastic bags. Sometimes the difference was the Zen-like non-smell of tofu blocks floating in water, the Co-op being the only place in Olutakli County that you could buy tofu at all, each cradled in its own green plastic basket. Best of all was the smell of real coffee, so recently roasted it was still fragrant. For woman does not live by bread alone. She must also have coffee.

To Carmichael all of it was a tonic. The Co-op was the one place her alternate selves did not haunt her, for she could lead at least two of her lives in this place, here where she could buy loose dried hibiscus and lavender for home-blended herbal teas, or brewer's yeast by the ounce, or textured vegetable protein by the pound—not that she ever got this last item, but she *could*. Here was sold freesia essential oil, sandalwood incense, tiger balm, and raw honey from an ex-actor's homestead that was rumored to border on Yoko Ono's country estate.

There was even a shelf of books for sale—this in a county without a single bookstore—of a comforting if predictable nature: *The Whole Earth Catalog, Diet for a Small Planet,* a few by Margaret Mead, and, incongruously, *The Late Great Planet Earth*. Carmichael supposed the owners took that last title for an environmental treatise, not a premillennialist one.

There were only three tables, none of them flush with the floor, so they rollicked awkwardly, and the seats were but stools.

No matter. Once a month Carmichael came to the Co-op to be a centered Venn diagram, her selves stacking neatly on top of each another, sealed by the covenant of good coffee.

Sandra pushed open the door and set off a jangle of chimes and beads. Carmichael waved her welcome.

In short order Sandra joined her, cradling a cup of her own—"Lemon verbena infusion, good for digestion and just about everything else," she explained—and a plate bearing two cookies made from honey, oats, sunflower butter, and carob chips.

They settled in with the conventional pleasantries and then Sandra said, "I thought Donald just did a wonderful job with the All Saints' service and consecrating the columbarium."

"It was really nice, wasn't it?" Carmichael enthused. "I didn't expect the candles to be effective in a morning service outside, but it was so dark and foggy they really made a difference."

"What I liked best was getting to sing a capella. I know Marilyn is the original Old Faithful and never misses a Sunday, and I don't suppose anybody else in church even knows how to play the organ, but sometimes—"

"—you'd like to light a fire under her bench and move things along a little faster?"

"I was thinking more like giving her a metronome, but I can't figure out how to do it without her taking offense."

"She is guaranteed to take offense one way or another, so it may as well be at that. Donald has asked her to pick up the pace half a dozen times. It doesn't do any good. I can't tell if it's because she's afraid of making mistakes, or because she thinks it sounds more majestic the slower she goes."

"Well, anyway," said Sandra, "I love that hymn we sang."

"'For All the Saints.' Me too. I saw Alan at the college yesterday and he mentioned how much one of the lines meant to him—'We feebly struggle, they in glory shine.'"

"Oh, I can tell you, he is practically a new man since we finally put his mother to rest. So much lighter at heart. I knew he wanted it done but even *I* didn't appreciate how much it was weighing on him to have her urn sitting on the mantel all this time, like he hadn't performed his filial duty toward her, or something."

"Burial of the dead is pretty primal," Carmichael said philosophically. She rubbed the sunflower grease off her fingertips. "It's meaningful even if you didn't know the people involved. You know, I've never been to the funeral of a loved one, not even family, not that I remember, anyway. My grandparents all died when I was little. I don't have any aunts or uncles, and both my parents are still alive. There have been lots of funerals at church, of course, but I've never been really close to the person who died."

"You haven't missed much!"

"I don't know. Death is there at the other end of life for all of us whether we notice it or not. Seems like I could use the practice. I didn't grow up religious, either, so all this still feels new to me. Which is silly, I guess—Donald and I have been married for thirteen years, so I've been to thirteen All Saints' services by now."

"Well, I've gone to church all my life, but we didn't start doing All Saints' till you and Donald got here, so it's even newer to me. It would be so nice if we could do it out in the cemetery every year from now on, assuming the weather holds, of course. I have to tell you," said Sandra confidentially, dropping her voice, "I hope that the next one to go ends up in the columbarium. It's enough for now that Alan's mother is there, but it does look kind of lonely with just the one panel engraved way up in the far corner."

"I'm sure it won't be long. If there's one certainty of church life, it's funerals," said Carmichael.

"Funerals, yes, but not cremation and not interment in a columbarium. You weren't at any of the council meetings when we talked about it. People are still so uncomfortable with cremation."

"I thought they all seemed pretty excited about the columbarium."

"Oh, that," scoffed Sandra. "A moment's entertainment for these country people who lead such limited lives. They're very primitive in their way. If their parents and grandparents were embalmed and nailed into a coffin and buried underground, they're going to do the same. It's the essentially hidebound nature of these farmers and backwoods types."

"Well," said Carmichael, a little taken aback at Sandra's harsh judgment on their fellow churchgoers. "How did you ever talk them into it in the first place, then?"

"That's exactly what I did—I talked them into it. I've been working at this for over two years now. Donald has been so supportive, of course. But it can be very hard to make people see reason. I've had to work with whoever gets elected to council, and I think we can admit between the two of us that it's not necessarily the most qualified or forward-thinking who get chosen."

"They chose *you*," said Carmichael with a little smile.

"Well, Alan and I have been here for so long now they take us for one of them. I slid in under the radar, you might say. But look, I just want to say again how happy I am that you and Donald are here. I hope you'll stay a long time. Doesn't matter that we're in New York State—this is flyover country for ambitious people. Few are willing to tough it out like Alan and I have. It's thankless work, improving this place, but well worth doing."

"Oh, we're very happy here. It's a great place for the kids, we both have jobs we like, and Donald is really not ambitious at all. He likes to keep his head low, have lots of time to read, and just live life with the parishioners."

Sandra took her wrist and looked into her eyes. "It's not just him, it's you, too," she said earnestly. "You have two jobs—and I'm not even counting mother! Pastor's wife is always a job. I've seen it all my life. You may not get paid, but you count just as much."

Carmichael gently twisted her wrist free of Sandra's reassuring touch. "It just seems like I'm there and part of it, same as anyone else. But then, like I said, I didn't grow up religious, so I've never had anyone for my pastor except Donald, which means I've never observed anyone being a pastor's wife except myself."

"Didn't you ever go to church at all? Not even on Christmas?"

For a moment the whole room hung suspended, silent, still. The plain white walls seemed to refract the light more intensely but the quiet rippled out like a pebble in a pond. Carmichael became acutely aware of the crumbs on the plate, of Sandra's frizzy half-gray hair piled in a messy upsweep and the heavy amber beads around her neck, of the fenugreek, of the presence of the woman behind the counter who had served them. All of it was waiting in tense anticipation. What account was Carmichael going to give of herself, here, in public, even in such a small and peaceable public?

"Never," said Carmichael at last. "Because—well, because we're Jewish."

"Jewish!" repeated Sandra. Her voice sounded very loud to Carmichael.

"We never went to synagogue or anything, either. But that's why we never went to church."

"I knew it!" The voice broke through the quiet and shattered it like a mirror falling off the wall. Carmichael and Sandra both turned to see the clerk—grinning and brimming with vitality—push through the half-height swing door at the counter and stride over to them. "I. *Knew* it," she repeated.

The two women on their stools stared at her wordlessly.

She stuck out a hand covered with plain silver rings of assorted thicknesses. "Rachel," she said.

"Carmichael," said the one, and "Sandra," the other.

"Not you, honey," said Rachel to Sandra, "but you, Carmichael, I had you pegged from the first time you walked in that door. Didn't want to say anything at first, I know you're married to a minister and all, but I just knew."

"How?" breathed Carmichael, unnerved that a stranger could instantly know something about herself that she had taken years to learn and spent many more ignoring.

"Look at you!" Rachel shouted. "How could you *not* be? What's your maiden name, anyway?"

"Bam," murmured Carmichael.

"Bam? For real? All right, I didn't see *that* coming."

"It's Estonian."

"But still Jewish?"

"Yeah. I guess so. I never asked."

"Well, I'm a Leibowitz, so that doesn't leave much margin for error, huh? Not to mention this nose." She turned her face in profile, pointed at her nose, and laughed. Carmichael blushed with shame and perplexity. Since when was it acceptable to talk about Jewish noses? Could you do it if you were a Jew yourself? Sandra stared down at her empty teacup, evidently even more bewildered by the conversation than Carmichael was.

"So, are there many Jews," Carmichael began, and then with an effort corrected herself to say, "are there many of *us* here in Shibboleth?"

"Not so many. Mostly transplants from the City. There are more over in Tryon County because of SUNY Kuhsota."

"Is there, is there," Carmichael floundered, "a rabbi? For services and things?"

"Are you kidding? Isn't that one of the things we came up here to get away from? I stay away from bacon because of the nitrates, not because it isn't kosher," Rachel chortled. "Naw, none of us are religious, at least no one that I know is. But, you know—"

"—there's more than one way to be a Jew," said Carmichael.

"Exactly. Say now, you're married to this minister, so does that mean you..." For the first time Rachel seemed slightly abashed by the course of conversation.

"Got baptized? Yes. I'm a Christian," said Carmichael.

"You're still a Jew."

"I know."

"What kind of Christian? Not that I know much besides Catholic."

"We're Lutheran."

"Wait, like Martin Luther, or like Martin Luther King Jr.?"

"The first one."

"Wasn't he some kind of crazy anti-Semite? Isn't he the one that Hitler got his inspiration from?"

This wasn't the first time Carmichael had heard such things. Back in their days of combined courtship and catechism, she and Donald had talked it over—he'd wanted her to come into not just Christianity but his particular branch of Christianity with open eyes—but all she really remembered of it was the depressing conclusion that the Luther of Lutheranism was typical, not exceptional, when it came to historic Christian attitudes toward Jews. Luther just happened to be more famous, so his nasty ideas got passed right along with his good ones. But she had never had to explain any of this to a real live Jew before. Other than myself, remarked a confused voice inside of her.

"Not really," Carmichael said. "Hitler hated Jews without Martin Luther's help, for racial reasons. What Luther said about the Jewish religion was just convenient propaganda for the Nazis. The truth is that all Christians everywhere have been hard on the Jews." When she said it aloud, it sounded even worse.

"Huh," said Rachel. But she didn't seem upset or surprised. Maybe this was old hat to her. "Well look, we should stick together, whatever you do for religion," she said. "I'm a bit of a Hindu, myself. Don't be a stranger, OK?" Then with a curt nod to Sandra she added, "Nice to meet you, too," and sauntered off back behind the counter.

Sandra and Carmichael looked at each other a moment.

"I suppose I should be going now," said Sandra, awkwardly.

"Me too," said Carmichael. "I'll head out with you."

"Good," said Sandra in a tone that conveyed how she had no problem whatsoever with Carmichael being Jewish and yet never having said a word about it in the three years they'd known each other, and how she sympathized with the uncomfortableness of the moment but would give Carmichael as much time and space as she needed to be ready to talk about it. Carmichael heard all of it and smiled her gratitude.

They pulled on coats and hitched purses over their shoulders. At the door Carmichael looked back to make sure she hadn't forgotten anything.

Sitting on her vacated stool was another self: her Jewish self.

"Told you," she said to Carmichael.

∼

The moment Donald finished his long extemporaneous prayer over the Thanksgiving feast, Asher plunged both hands into the bowl of mashed potatoes and announced, "Mommy's right! They got cold while you were taking so long to get home, Daddy!"

"I've got him," Judith said to Carmichael before the latter could even sigh in dismay, and with a firm grip around his waist she hauled Asher off to the kitchen sink for a clean-up.

"He *did* wash his hands just before we sat down," Carmichael apologized to the table at large.

Frank, always ready with a cliché, remarked, "A little dirt never hurt anybody."

"I'm sorry again about being late," said Donald to his wife. She handed him the oversized fork and knife.

"Make it up to me by carving the bird," she said. "Anyway, how was it?"

Donald studied the joint of the leg. "I never quite know the purpose of these ecumenical services," he said. "Especially on Thanksgiving. My people eschewed them with high-minded suspicion. I think they weren't wrong to see them as a strange exercise in civic religion, with an undercurrent of market competition."

"Really? How so?"

"This is, of course, only the third time I've participated, but the first year I did, it was Quincy the Congregationalist minister who preached, and he talked about how we should be grateful for our rights and freedoms as Americans. Then last year it was Father Pat, and *he* talked about how we should be grateful for our duties and responsibilities as Americans—which even at the time I couldn't help but think was a corrective to Quincy's emphasis on rights and freedoms, despite it coming a whole year after the fact. Then today it was Aaron, the Baptist preacher—"

"Is he at the American Baptist church or the Southern Baptist one?"

"Southern Baptist. He must feel like a real fish out of water here in Olutakli County, way more than I do even. Anyway, he made it clear to all and sundry that it was the providential hand of God that we just got another four years of a Republican in the White House, which guarantees us Americans *both* our right *and* our duty to—can you guess? *Just* the thing I needed to hear," he added with uncharacteristic sarcasm.

Carmichael paused in the act of dividing the cranberry jelly into identical discs and, after a moment's reflection, said, "'Choose this day whom we shall serve?'"

"Hole in one."

"That's a golf term," Frank explained to Saul. Saul nodded around a gigantic mouthful of stuffing.

"So now I can only hope that they choose Scott to preach next year so he'll unleash the most terrifying double predestinarian tirade on the bondage of our individual and collective wills."

"He's the Presbyterian minister?"

"Yes, but I shouldn't get my hopes up, for never was there a less faithful son of Calvin than Scott. Apparently there has been a lot of upset in the congregation because he's tried to install a crucifix in the sanctuary."

Judith returned with a clean-handed Asher. "Now we're going to sit nice in our chair and eat our food like a civilized creature, aren't we, honey?"

Asher nodded solemnly and sat still. Apparently Bammy had applied some choice threats during the hand-washing process that struck their intended target.

"Hey, I meant to ask you, Carmichael," Frank called across the table, "but on the drive up this time, we took a different route, and not too far from here we came around a bend and saw a field all full of sheep and Negroes! Now what's that all about?"

"Oh, Dad, say 'blacks,' not 'Negroes.'"

"'Negro' isn't a term of disrespect."

"I know, but just… People don't say that anymore."

"That was New Aksum you drove by," Donald interjected.

"New what?"

"Aksum. It's an ancient kingdom in Ethiopia that followers of Mohammed settled in."

"Mohammed?" said Frank sharply. "Are they Moslems?"

"Muslims," said Carmichael.

Donald continued, "Yeah, a handful of people in the Bronx converted to Islam and wanted to get their kids out of the City, so they bought a bunch of adjoining properties up here. They're kind of like the Muslim equivalent of the Amish. They use only minimal technology, support themselves by agriculture, and have almost no contact with the outside world. One of my parishioners is a vet and goes out there every so often when there's a problem with their sheep or poultry."

"It was Moslems who firebombed the bus in Jericho last month," Frank remarked, with evident disapproval at the vet.

"These Muslims aren't like that, Dad," said Carmichael.

He shrugged. "Now they're saying they should have their own state, after doing a thing like that, can you believe it? A mother and all three of her children died."

"*Dad.* Come on. Do we have to talk about this over Thanksgiving dinner?"

"There are three of *us* children," said Saul thoughtfully.

"Joshua fought the battle of Jericho, Jericho, Jericho…" Asher sang. Saul joined in. "And the walls came a-tumblin' down!"

"Hey, it's starting to snow," said Kitty.

"It was already starting when I got in," said Donald.

"Look at me," said Saul to Asher. He inserted a whole disc of cranberry jelly into his mouth and bit down so his teeth were magenta.

"Cool!" said Asher, reaching for the dish.

"No," said Bammy, tapping Asher's wrist. He subsided at once. "Saul, that's not proper."

Saul tried to say, "Sorry, Bammy," but in the process all the jelly slurped out of his mouth.

Asher squealed. "Your plate is bleeding!"

Saul smiled and used his spoon to smash the ruined jelly disc into his mashed potatoes. They turned pink.

"Gross," said Kitty. "Mommy, can I run outside and check something quick?"

"No, you can't go outside right now. We're in the middle of Thanksgiving dinner."

"But I want to check before it gets any snowier."

"It's already dark out."

"Please, Mommy, it won't take long."

"What do you need to check on?"

"Just something outside."

"We're in the middle of Thanksgiving dinner. You should have thought of it earlier."

"I was *busy* earlier," Kitty murmured.

Bammy and Bampy had arrived a little before noon with so many presents that they seemed to have confused Thanksgiving with Christmas. They'd brought the very last doll missing from Kitty's Rose Petal Place collection, Orchid—all the other girls in class were obsessed with Lil Miss Makeup, but Kitty had remained steadfastly loyal to her childhood favorite—and along with the dolls came another chocolate elephant head and a charm bracelet. After she'd extracted Orchid from her box, undressed and redressed her, and introduced her to the other dolls, Kitty turned her attention to the charms on the bracelet: funny things like a cheeseburger, the head of Mickey Mouse, a pair of feet, a light bulb, and a hair dryer, but also, she discovered, a star of David.

There was a star of David in one of the two stained glass windows over the altar at church, the one on the left showing Moses and the Ten Commandments, but this one on the charm bracelet made Kitty feel weird all over again. Bammy and Bampy hadn't said anything lately about them or her being Jewish, but this was their little way of telling her that they hadn't forgotten, and they didn't want her to forget, either. Kitty didn't want to think about it. And she was still sad about Fawn. She kept going out to check if maybe he had come back, even though she knew in her heart of hearts he never would.

"The turkey tastes so good," said Judith.

"Thanks," said Carmichael. "I may as well tell you it comes from New Aksum."

Frank looked down at his forkful warily, but Donald quickly interjected, "Last year a parishioner gave us a wild turkey he'd hunted. We thought it was gonna be great, but it was tough and full of shot."

"I just don't understand how people can hunt," said Judith sententiously.

"That doesn't bother me any," said Donald. "We're given a lot of venison. It's quite good. Probably has a better life than the average cow."

"But to take the life of a fellow creature in that way! It seems so bloodthirsty."

"I suppose if a deer has to die anyway, better from a quick bullet than from a coyote running it down and gnawing its back leg off."

Asher grabbed a drumstick from the turkey platter and ripped off a chunk of flesh with his teeth. "I'm a coyote!" he declared.

Judith glared at him. The phone rang.

"Probably your folks," said Carmichael. Donald nodded and rose to answer it.

"When are they getting up here again for a visit?" inquired Frank.

"They're planning to fly up for Christmas," said Carmichael, but she stopped abruptly, turning her ear toward Donald and the phone. The rest of the family noted her alertness and they ate quietly, waiting.

Donald came back looking grim. "That was Dave Fisher," he said. "Terri just went into labor."

"Already?" said Carmichael. "I thought she wasn't due for another couple months."

"She isn't. This is ten weeks early. They're at the hospital in Kuhsota and asked me if I could come, just in case."

"In case what?" said Kitty.

Donald looked at her and the boys a moment before answering. "In case the baby dies as it's being born."

"I don't like you going out in this weather," said Carmichael, rising to her feet.

"I'll drive slow and carefully," he said. "But I have to go."

"I know," she said. "I know. Look, I'll pack up some food for you to take along."

"I'll help," said Judith. "Actually, I was going to bring out some extra treats I brought for dessert."

"Why'd you do that? I made pumpkin pie *and* pecan pie."

Judith was already up the stairs. Donald dashed around the house, stuffing his pastor satchel with his communion kit and palm-sized Bible. "You're in luck, I just ironed your clean clergy shirts," Carmichael said.

"I can never find my collars," he complained.

"I found one in the wash," she said. "Nice and shiny."

Judith reappeared with a big white shopping bag. She lifted out two packages, set them on the table, and unwrapped them ceremoniously. "A chocolate babka," she explained, "and rugelach with prune jam."

"Really, Mom?" said Carmichael. "A little heavy-handed, isn't it?"

Judith responded with wide, innocent, wounded eyes. "They're delicious, from a bakery that makes them from scratch. Normally you love it when I bring specialties from the City."

"I don't remember babka and rugelach being in your repertoire before."

"I need to head out now," said Donald quickly. "You kids, be good for your mother and grandparents." He kissed the little ones on the head. He held Carmichael for a moment. "I don't know when I'll be back."

"I know. Call if you can."

The festive spirit evaporated with Donald's departure. Bit by bit the plates were scraped clean and the dishes transported back to the kitchen. Carmichael and Judith and Kitty put the food away and started in on the stack of dishes while Frank plunked the boys in front of the TV and explained, in great and incomprehensible detail, the rules of football.

But bedtime came and went without the grown-ups issuing the inevitable command. The snow and the premature labor and the uncertainty about where exactly Donald was at any given moment, or when he'd be back, created the rare conditions for the suspension of normal rules. When Kitty suggested a game of Uno at nine-thirty, hardly daring to hope, all three adults acceded with astonishing speed. Not only that, the adults were attentive, exuberant, and funny. Kitty felt mildly suspicious of their good cheer but didn't want to look this particular gift horse in the mouth. Then at eleven Bammy actually said, "You know, I only had one plate of Thanksgiving dinner and, truth is, I'm a bit hungry still. Would anyone object to a second round of dessert?" It was only when they settled back into Uno over their fresh plates of rugelach and pumpkin pie that Asher's unvarying sequence of Draw Four cards elicited accusations of stacking the deck in their absence—but he laughed so hard and so merrily that it was impossible to get angry at him, or teach him a lesson, either. Then all at once he fell sound asleep slumped halfway up the ottoman. Saul wiggled into the space under the coffee table, stuck his thumb in his mouth, and dozed off, too.

Kitty was determined to stay awake as late as she could get away with. She'd only made it past midnight twice in her life and hoped maybe this time she would get to see what one in the morning looked like.

Among other things, it looked like cocktails. Frank brought forth a different-colored one for each of the three grown-ups. He said, "That fire-bombing in Jericho drove it out of my mind earlier, but did you hear the latest from Estonia?"

Carmichael shrugged. "No, I guess not."

"Well, they're independent now."

"What? How does that work?"

"They just told Moscow that they're their own sovereign republic again, and they've been illegally occupied all this time, and they won't have it anymore."

"I can't imagine Moscow takes that view of things."

"Of course not," said Frank cheerfully. "But it seems like a good sign."

"Seems likely to cause an invasion, like what happened to Czechoslovakia back whenever that was, in the sixties, I guess."

"It's been a couple weeks and nothing bad has happened yet. They keep getting together to sing in public."

"But it's still communist, isn't it? What difference will it make as long as it stays communist?"

"It's too late for this kind of thing," murmured Judith. "Let's carry the kids up to bed and call it a night."

"I'm not sleepy," said Kitty much too loudly.

"Shh! Don't wake the boys," said Carmichael. "To tell you the truth, Mom, I feel better staying down here for now. You can go up to bed if you want. You'll be more comfortable there."

"No, no, I'm fine. I'd rather stay down here with you."

They fell silent. After awhile Carmichael put an album of Schubert sonatas on the record player. Kitty thought Marie and

Nutcracker might enjoy dancing to it. It would be a relief not to be stuck with Tchaikovsky all the time.

Kitty only realized that she'd fallen asleep and missed most of the two o'clock hour when, a few minutes before three, the sound of the pantry door opening woke her up. "Daddy!" she cried and raced through the house to hug him.

Carmichael wasn't far behind. "Thank God," she said. She hugged him, too.

"I'm sorry I couldn't call—there was only a pay phone and I didn't have change, and nothing was open to make change with."

"What happened?"

Donald brushed the snow off his shoulders; a thick coating had accumulated on him in the short walk from the driveway to the house. "That was the tiniest baby I've ever seen," he said.

"Oh, no—'was'?"

"*Is.* Sorry! In the NICU now. They asked me to baptize it, I should say *him*, right then and there. So I did. Matthew David Fisher. My first emergency baptism. That was after they put him on a ventilator and got his lungs working. But it looks promising. They think he'll live."

"L'chaim!" said Frank.

"Amen," said Donald.

"Let's go to bed," said Carmichael.

CHAPTER SIX

December 1988

Yet if we attentively view this globe,
will it not appear rather a place of punishment,
than of delight?
And what Misfortune!
that those punishments should fall on the innocent,
and its few Delights be enjoyed by the most unworthy.

The December gathering of the Shibboleth Ecumenical Council was always the worst attended. Donald, along with Father Pat at St. Mary's Roman Catholic and Cathie at St. George Episcopal, added midweek Advent services to the usual rotation of Sundays. The Congregationalists, Methodists, and assorted members of the Reformed family of churches went into good-works overdrive, coordinating presents for underprivileged children in the county as well as at random points around the globe: Ethiopia and El Salvador were particular favorites this year. It was a rare occurrence in any event to see Father Serge from Assumption Ukrainian Orthodox or Jerry from the Assemblies of God: their disdain for the compromised center shot off in opposite directions but converged in a shared aloofness that only occasionally condescended to appear at the meetings, out of a confused blend of pity and proselytism.

"How does a town of four thousand people sustain no fewer than *twelve* churches?" Carmichael had asked Donald a few weeks after they moved to Shibboleth. "I barely even realized there were that many kinds of Christian. In North Dakota there were only Lutherans and Catholics."

Donald pointed out that the number shot up to fifteen if

you counted all the churches within the township, thereby adding to the roster the tiny Adventist outpost on a back road—the last remnant of a Millerite utopian community—which met only once a month nowadays, and on a Saturday, of course; the Nondenominational congregation a couple miles down the Shinhopple Turnpike, "though actually they're an offshoot of one of the Holiness groups that my own kin shot off from," Donald remarked; and the Unprogrammed Quakers, who didn't have their own building but assembled in the basement of High Street Presbyterian to share their news and say "I'll be thinking about you" since it was much too pushy to go so far as to *pray* for someone.

"Fifteen, then," said Carmichael.

"Plus the Jehovah's Witnesses, if you count them."

"Should I?"

"Probably not."

At which point Carmichael looked so bemused (and Asher had just gotten into a cardboard box full of heirloom china) that Donald let her go without an instructive lecture on the Burned-Over District: the local heritage of so many revivals and so many self-proclaimed prophets that every flavor of faith got a toehold but none of them more than that. Despite the number of churches in town, well under half the population was even affiliated, fewer still devout.

Which meant, all in all, that while there may have been mutual doctrinal disapproval among the assorted clergy, they knew they were all in it together, there was to be no sheep stealing among them, and staying afloat from year to year was reason enough to rejoice. Moreover, no recrimination would fall on pastors, priests, and ministers who could barely keep up with the rounds of funerals, weddings, hospital visits, and committees and thus might choose, in December, to drop the ecumenical council meeting.

The stalwarts gathered in the parish hall of Second Reformed, relaxed over bad coffee and good doughnuts, and decided without effort to abandon the agenda. They compared notes on the weather, the flu, and the eternal problem of preaching on Christmas to the faithful and the occasional alike.

Pieter, minister at Second Reformed, said to Donald, "Hey, you lured Eunice back over to the dark side, huh?"

Donald smiled and shrugged. "I had nothing to do with it."

"You can have her," Pieter said with a laugh. "Nothing I did was ever good enough for her. I learned to cringe every time she crept up on me. Her pronouncements always began with 'When I was a girl…'"

"You Protestants," said Father Pat. "I have all these converts who've married cradle Catholics. They spout a never-ending series of critical questions. 'Why do you pray to Mary like she's God?' 'How can you think Jesus is really *in* that little wafer?' 'Why can't I confess my sins direct to God instead of to you?' Always the same, always the same."

Donald said, "If it's any consolation, I also have to explain to my parishioners how I think Jesus can be in that little wafer."

"Well," said Father Pat, with an appreciative glance over a cruller, "at least Protestants care. You may as well invite a cradle Catholic to a root canal as to a Bible study. In and out of mass, that's all they want."

"Don't knock it," said Aaron from the Southern Baptist church. "Small as we are, if I don't offer a men's Bible study, a women's Bible study, a teen's Bible study, *and* Sunday school every week—not to mention preaching at least forty minutes—my folks start grumbling over what they're paying me for."

"See, that's why you should be *American* Baptist," laughed Linda, pastor of the church in question. "The bar is much lower."

"At least you spared us the forty-minute sermon on Thanksgiving!" chortled Father Pat. "Eight minutes strains the patience of my flock."

"I don't mind hearing a forty-minute sermon now and again," said Donald. "I grew up with that kind. Twelve is about the max my people will accept without complaint, though I'm usually pushing up against fifteen and have been known to hit twenty. I notice I don't get compliments on those Sundays."

"I never heard of Lutherans preaching forty minutes," said Aaron.

"Oh, I didn't grow up Lutheran. A variety of Holiness, actually. Pretty small denomination. Firmly believed in a sparsely populated heaven."

"Is that why you left? It's why I left Southern Baptist for American Baptist," said Linda. She cast a sly glance in Aaron's direction, but he stayed focused on Donald.

"Uh, no, not at all," Donald said. He was a little embarrassed to admit to being motivated not so much by the salvation of others as of himself. "It was more about questions of the will—whether a person really can love God above all things. To a lesser extent, about the veracity of certain events in the Bible." All at once Donald felt Grandfather Abney's presence in the room. The question floated from grandfather to grandson: were you dodging the issue by saying "veracity" instead of "inerrancy"?

It didn't matter if he was, though, because Aaron leapt on the comment with the agility of an old-school Abney. "You mean like you stopped believing in the inerrancy of the Bible?"

"Protestants," snorted Father Pat again, in comic exasperation.

"Let's not get off track here," said Pieter, who must have had enough experience of such quarrels to wish to avoid hatching them in his own territory. "All of you can stay here as long as you want, but I've got a funeral in half an hour. There's really only one item of business we were supposed to take care of at this meeting anyway, and that's who's gonna preach at the Thanksgiving service next year."

"That's the real reason no one comes to the December meetings," remarked Linda.

"We can elect someone in abstentia," said Pieter.

"We could give double billing to Serge and Jerry," said Father Pat, and everyone burst out laughing.

"Actually, it's pretty easy," said Linda. "All of us here today have done it now, except for Donald. So you're up."

"Ah," he said. "Well, so be it. I suppose we'll host at Mt. Moriah then?"

"You don't have to," said Pieter, "though I guess it's kind of become tradition. Home field advantage."

Donald felt Grandfather Abney's cautious approval wafting over him. Donald would proclaim the gospel—summon them to faith—ask them to choose this day whom they would serve. Donald interrupted the flow of homiletic instruction with the rejoinder that Aaron had already preached on that verse this year. Grandfather Abney replied: Aaron needs help.

Surprised, Donald glanced over at Aaron, who was staring down at his shoes while the other three discussed who would prepare the Thanksgiving bulletins.

Are you sure? Donald addressed the phantom Grandfather Abney, but there was no further response. He kept up his surreptitious watch on Aaron who, unaware of the fact and uninvolved in the conversation, had allowed his church face to slide off. In its place a sadness settled in. Donald thought he might recognize the sadness for what it was.

The meeting broke up. Pieter headed out to meet the mourners. Father Pat engaged in some banter with Linda over the size of her purse, which she parried with a cheerfully condescending remark about his stereotypical view of women, which he counter-parried by chiding her for neglecting to venerate the Virgin, to which Linda said if she was going to venerate a Mary it would be the Magdalene, thank you very much, and they walked out together chuckling.

Donald approached Aaron. Years of the pastorate had trained him to strike up a conversation with anyone for any reason, but he felt strangely tongue-tied. "Uh, I was really struck by your sermon on Thanksgiving," he said, immediately rueing the doublespeak: it sounded like it could be a compliment, though it certainly was not. But Donald realized now that Aaron's message was not a topic for debate. It was a window into hurt.

Aaron looked around, as if to confirm they were alone, then faced Donald and said, "It was pure bullshit."

Donald raised his eyebrows. "It sure sounded convincing," he fumbled.

"'Convincing' is all they want," said Aaron. He rifled pointlessly through papers in his briefcase, blunting their edges. "As long as you deliver it with conviction, they don't care if it's true. Doesn't matter if you're denouncing godless communists or theorizing about which species of whale swallowed Jonah. Just say it loud and strong and that makes it true."

Donald's curiosity got the better of him. "Is that the kind of thing you usually preach on?"

Aaron straightened up and mounted a bitter smile. "Well, that, or 'Ten Ways to Raise Godly Children.' When I'm not a propagandist, I'm an advice columnist."

"You sound hurt and angry," said Donald.

If George Pohl had been present, he'd have rolled his eyes at Pastor Donald's restating of the obvious. This time, though, the strategy worked. All of a sudden, a demoralized litany spilled out of Aaron every which way. The accumulation of doubts that had pounced and knocked out every last fragment of his faith in a one-two punch. The politicking from the congregational level to the denominational. The obligation to model a godly family, even if your wife was depressed and hated it up here and your kids fought you every night at bedtime and were reported by their teachers to be not paragons of virtue but first-class bullies. And where was it all going and what was the point of any of it?

Donald sat down discreetly during the monologue and the other followed suit. When Aaron ran out of words, Donald murmured sympathy and gave them both a moment to think.

Then he said, "There's a whole lot tangled up in there, but can you tell which of the things is at the core of it? I mean, which is deepest down and makes all the others intolerable?" Aaron looked at him blankly at first, then distrustfully. Donald elaborated, "Because I've been there, you know. It hit me earlier in life, but I went through a long spell of doubt and darkness myself. I know what caused it for me, but I don't want to put words in your mouth."

Aaron nodded. "I guess," he said, "if I tried to get down to the root of it, they always promise you, 'God has a wonderful plan for your life,' and you believe it and act on it, and then… *this*…"

"And you find yourself thinking, is this the best God can do?"

"Yes. *No*," Aaron abruptly corrected himself. "I know a lot of it is shallow, the plan stuff. I'm a lifelong reader of Scripture and can see for myself that things don't always turn out so wonderful for the chosen of God."

"I had a seminary professor who liked to say, 'God has a wonderful plan for your life. It's called the cross.'"

"Yeah," said Aaron. "But the thing is, even the cross is a plan, right? There's another side to it, the resurrection. But what if there's no plan at all? I think I could take the cross if I *knew* it was God's plan. I just… don't know anymore."

Donald sat with the thought a moment.

Aaron said into the silence, "They're just always so sure, you know? So *convinced*. God has a plan, God's in control. I used to really depend on that idea. It helped me, at one time. But it doesn't help anymore. It's like, the more I hear people say it, the less I believe it, or them. I don't hear in it a word from God to me. I just hear people needing to be convinced and saying the same thing over and over until it convinces them."

"I get it," Donald said. He leaned forward. "Look, I can't solve the problem for you. But I think at least part of the problem is putting the plan at the beginning instead of at the end."

"How do you mean?"

"Well, it's not till the last chapter of Genesis, chapter fifty, when Joseph is able to say: you intended it for evil, but God intended it for good. He just didn't know any sooner. So many things went wrong in his life. He'd have every reason to believe that either there was no plan, or that the plan was at his expense."

"But it was still a plan. That's the point."

"I know, but what I'm saying is, a thing can be true in itself but false in the way it's said or used. Try telling Joseph in prison that God has a plan! That would be cruel at best. It's only Joseph who gets to say, and only in retrospect, that God *had* a plan for him. So maybe the problem is that all the plan stuff sounds to you like shouting at someone in prison, 'Cheer up! God has a plan!' when they don't have any right to say so. They don't actually know, so they don't have a right to speak. It doesn't mean there's no plan—it only means that talk about the plan is misplaced."

"I see what you mean," said Aaron. He sat quietly for a moment. "But I have to live life forward, not in retrospect," he said. "How am I supposed to do that? Especially when I feel like I *am* in prison."

Donald wished, momentarily, that Grandfather Abney's assured old voice would tell him what to say next, but the seconds ticked by and it was just Donald and Aaron alone in the parish hall. Donald considered. His own struggle had been long, and he wasn't exactly without doubt still. He'd just learned to live with it, on the outskirts of Jericho like blind Bartimaeus. But if there was one thing his struggles had taught him, it was that you couldn't unleash your own chapter-fifty certainties on someone else. The last thing Donald wanted to do was sound *convincing*. Though he didn't want to leave Aaron without any consolation at all, either.

Aaron interrupted his train of thought with, "'Ten Ways to Get through a Crisis of Faith,'" and a small and bitter laugh.

"I think," said Donald, "and forgive me if I'm overstepping my bounds here, but I think it's possible that you have never really believed in God at all. What you believed in was the plan. I don't think you'll get to God until you drop the plan once and for all."

"But that's what's happened to me already, without even trying!" objected Aaron. "I'm just stumbling around in the dark, trying to figure out how to live another day as a minister without feeling like a complete and total hypocrite. What if I end up having to leave the ministry? What will happen to my family, or me? We won't be able to move home. I'll be branded for life."

"That part I can't say. But I know that pretending to believe something you don't kills you from the inside out."

"Should I just give up trying, then?"

"Maybe. I wonder if God hasn't destroyed your faith in the plan, so you can have faith in him instead," said Donald. "But that's just a guess, and you can't take it as yet another plan to believe in. You have to go into this not knowing how it'll turn out. Otherwise you're still believing in the plan and not in God."

Aaron let out a long breath. "All right then," he said. "You could be right. It's not like I have any other choice."

Donald smiled at the word and saw Aaron out to his car.

∽

The last student exited the classroom and Carmichael breathed a sigh of relief. It was not the sigh of absolute relief that marked the end of the semester—the pile of papers on her desk awaiting grades suggested *that* sigh was at least two weeks away yet. But at least she now had a reprieve from the students' gum chewing, drooping eyelids, and manifest inability to chart out a logical flow of evidence in written format. Carmichael had come to her position at SUNY Shibboleth forswearing the appalling advice of high school teachers nationwide to "tell 'em what you're gonna tell 'em, then tell 'em, then tell 'em what you told 'em." Three years later she realized that it was never intended as a counsel of perfection, but one of despair. Maybe, if you forced a student to write out her point three times, she would figure out what her point in fact was. Though even that was optimistic.

There was a knock on the open door of the classroom. "Got a minute?" said Alan.

"And delay the supreme joy of reading forty persuasive essays on 'Why Education Is Valuable'? Well, all right, but only if you insist."

Alan smirked appreciatively. "Come on down to my office. I've got good coffee."

Carmichael gathered up the essays and a stack of Intro to Lit term papers, slid them into her bag, bade a silent farewell to the faint and frayed whiteboard markers in anticipation of a fresh batch in January, and flicked off the lights. A few moments later she was nestled into an orange suede easy chair in Alan's office, her long fingers wrapped around a hot mug.

"This is what a professor's office should be," she said, nodding toward the shelves with books shoved horizontally on top of the vertical ones, books on the floor, books on the windowsill, books threatening to teeter off the edge of the desk.

"I'll tell you frankly, it's no small matter to stay intellectually alert in this place. These books are my holdout again brain rot. Cream?"

Carmichael waved a polite no with her hand. "You did warn me when I took the job," she said.

"Yes, but I could tell you were idealistic, like all of us are at the beginning, and you didn't believe me. Has hard reality gotten through to you by now?" He ran his fingers through his iron gray hair so it stood up on end.

"I'm pretty sure that at least three of the term papers I got on *The Scarlet Letter* are literal transcriptions of the ones they wrote as sophomores in high school," said Carmichael. "And I'm not quite sure yet because I haven't read it carefully, but it looks like there's a paper on Langston Hughes that never manages to realize that he was black."

Alan shook his head commiseratingly. "Well, look," he said, "it's not glorious work. But Sandra says you and Donald are happy here and planning to stay, and I'm glad to hear it. We might not get the best students here, but it's a real blessing to get good professors, and good colleagues cover a multitude of sins."

"I've obviously led a sheltered existence," said Carmichael. "Most of these kids are from the City, and I'm just appalled at how poorly prepared they are for college, even to get just an A.A. I thought from my own experience they'd be better off."

Alan clucked. "The East 80s are not the same as Long Island, my naïve friend."

"Hey, my parents live there *now*, but I myself grew up in Queens, thank you very much."

"Still. And that's to say nothing of the Vandals and Goths from the countryside. You should look upon yourself as a St. Boniface, taming the wilderness and bring civilization to the savages. Long Island savages as much as Olutakli County savages."

"I'm not sure it's as bad as all that."

"Didn't you tell me last spring about a term paper on Kate Chopin claiming that her goal was to help women graciously accept their roles as wives and mothers?"

Carmichael spread a hand over her face. "All right, you win."

"Good. Now we've got that straight—you won't be surprised to hear this, I hope, but the dean has approved your contract renewal for another three years after this academic year ends."

She smiled. "Not surprised, but glad and grateful all the same."

"And," said Alan, pausing for effect, "I think next fall it'll be time to start you on the tenure process."

"Tenure!" she exclaimed.

"Yes, we do have tenure here in the wasting wilderness."

"I just—wow! I didn't expect it even to be an option so soon. I've only been here three years."

"I know a good thing when I see it. Anyway, I'm tight with the dean, so he pretty much lets me run our lowly humanities department however I want. As you and I know all too well, students come here for ag and tech, so it's not like the stakes are all that high, from the dean's perspective. I'm telling you about it now so you can get a jump start this spring and summer on revising your dissertation for publication."

Carmichael sat perfectly motionless, like a baseball coach trying not to jinx his star pitcher.

Alan dropped his elbows onto the desk. "I'm sure it's not exactly what you always dreamed of—"

"No, no, it's not that at all! It's just, well, tenure is hard to get. I can't believe it's already a prospect. I'm thrilled. I just haven't thought about my dissertation for awhile now. Two small boys tend to drive anything but mere survival from your mind."

"Forgive me for not remembering since I looked at your application, but what was your topic again?"

Carmichael relaxed back into her chair. "Michel Guillaume Jean de Crèvecœur," she said, "better known to his American readers as John Hector St. John."

"Oh, right—something about farming?"

"He wrote a book called *Letters from an American Farmer* that was quite the early colonial hit. Thomas Jefferson loved it!"

"Ah yes. I remember now. As I recall, the fact that it dealt with rural life and there was a New York State connection favorably impressed the committee."

Carmichael smiled. "One always wonders what sways deliberations behind closed doors. Of course, at the time I wrote it, I had no idea I'd end up in rural New York. I chose a Franco-American writer because I'd spent a semester in Montpellier and wanted a topic that would make use of my French. Plus, he was a relatively understudied subject."

"The only really essential quality in a dissertation topic," Alan agreed.

"Another charming coincidence," she said, "is that John Hector St. John was born on December 31, and so was Asher. Donald even suggesting giving him one of the man's many names, but I couldn't see my way to a 'Hector' any more than to a 'Guillaume.'"

"Understandable. I'd never heard the name 'Asher' before. Did you make it up?"

"No, not at all. It's an Old Testament name, Hebrew for 'happy.'"

"Oh, that's nice. I like that."

"It proved to be a very good name for him."

"Yes, he's certainly an exuberant little fellow."

They turned to practical matters of dissertation revision, likely presses to publish it and key journals in which to land reviews; Alan's proposal to let Carmichael design an elective of her choosing for the next fall semester and pulling in an adjunct to teach Intro to Lit in her stead; and finally the downside of tenure in the form of Tobias Gooch Teylow—somehow it was impossible *not* to say all three of his names—a colleague nearing retirement who had long since lost the spark and every semester cranked out the same lectures on Hamlet and Twelfth Night without variance on his part or interest on the students'.

Carmichael stood up and stretched. "I should get going."

"What kind of plans do you have for Christmas? I mean, you're sticking around, obviously, but anything special?"

"My parents are coming up, as usual," she replied, omitting mention of their plea to visit for Hanukkah as well, which Carmichael had firmly rejected, "and so are Donald's, flying up from Arizona a couple days before Christmas. Not quite sure how we're going to manage with so many people in the house, but the kids sure are excited."

"Tom is going to his girlfriend's this year for Christmas—that's a first for us—so we have a spare room, if you need one."

"Gee, that must be strange, to have your own kid going to someone else's for Christmas."

"It is. Sandra's pretty sad about it but trying to keep a brave face. I think it somehow signals to her the death of our family, in its original nuclear configuration, anyway. I keep telling her that's what kids do, they grow up and move on, and after all Cynthia's coming home."

"Oh, it'll be nice to see her again. And thanks about the room. We might just take you up on it."

Alan rose. "If you don't mind, while Cynthia's here we'd like to have a little prayer at the columbarium. She hasn't seen it yet and was really close to her grandmother, so I think it would be nice for her."

"Of course! You don't need to ask my permission. The cemetery is public space for anyone to visit any time."

"I just wanted to let you know since you live there. Anyway, thanks. It was a real load off my mind to take care of that."

There was a knock on the open door. They turned to behold Tobias Gooch Teylow in all his untidy glory. Carmichael saw a fragment of scrambled egg caught in his beard at one corner of his mouth. She dropped her eyes, caught between vicarious shame on his behalf and the primal urge to distance herself from failure in case it might be contagious.

"Yes?" said Alan coldly.

"Good morning," said Tobias pleasantly. Carmichael thought he must get some weird pleasure out of being polite like that. "I just wanted to make sure, before I left for the holidays, that you received my—"

"Yes, I received it. The college's internal postal service works as well as ever."

"Very glad to hear it. I don't suppose you've had a chance to look it over yet?"

Alan only waved a hand over the stacks of student papers on his desk.

"Eloquently expressed," said Tobias. "I'll look forward to

hearing from you in January, then." He gave a brief nod of acknowledgement to Carmichael and shuffled away.

Alan's eyes rolled to the ceiling and rested there until Tobias was out of earshot. "Funding request," he muttered. "As if he deserved it."

"Right," said Carmichael.

"Well, happy grading, let us know if you need the guest room, and it isn't too early to get back to work on John Hector St. John—all right?"

"You bet!" she grinned.

That night, after the kids were tucked into bed—and, glory be to God on high, with less resistance than usual—Donald allowed himself to be persuaded out of his habitual abstention to enjoy part of a bottle of Côtes d'Auvergne with Carmichael.

"I'm so happy I'm kind of in shock," she said.

"I can tell," said Donald warmly.

"You know I wasn't altogether thrilled about moving here," she said. Her eyes followed her finger as she ran it along the grain of the dining room table. "Especially after North Dakota."

"It's no small thing to take a city girl out of her city," Donald conceded.

"I was glad to do it, for the adventure of the thing, at least. I just didn't know how long I could sustain it. But this—this changes everything. I could have a real career here. The teaching isn't the most rewarding, but it's not bad, my colleagues are mostly pretty great, and now with Asher in school I think I really could get back to more serious scholarly work."

"To be honest, it's more than I myself would have dared to hope for. Or even pray for."

"But what about you? I mean, this kind of turns the tables. Before, I was staying for you. Now you'd be staying for me."

Donald reached out for Carmichael's hands across the table. "We're staying for each other." He laughed a bit. "And, at risk of contradicting myself, I dare say it's even God's plan for us."

"How's that a contradiction?" slurped Carmichael through

an overlarge mouthful of wine. He reminded her of his conversation with Aaron. "Oh, right," she said. She dabbed at her chin with a napkin.

"Things couldn't have turned out better." Donald was in earnest now. "The schools are solid, it's great for the kids to grow up here in the country, and for all their quirks I have really come to love the people in this congregation. You know me—I don't aspire to prominence or clerical upward mobility. I actually like the round of baptisms and funerals and hospital visits and potlucks. We should settle in and make this home."

"*Home.* I can actually imagine all the alternate Carmichaels fading into nothingness as you say that," remarked the real Carmichael contentedly.

"How's that?" said Donald, but instead of explaining she crept around to his side of the table, and their conversation gave way to other matters.

∾

"The kids at school talk about Christmas like it's all about Santa Claus," Kitty was complaining to Nutcracker. She was bundled up in long underwear, an oversized sweater, a puffy jacket, purple mittens, a tasseled turquoise cap knitted by Mrs. Feuerlein with a scarf to match, plus heavy boots that took five minutes to get into or out of. It wasn't snowing at the moment but snow lay heavy on the ground, muting the world around like TV with the sound turned off. The sky was a dark gray clamp over the earth, and the edges of Kitty's nostrils furled inward with each breath. But it'd been so long since she'd summoned the council, and she felt bad about neglecting them. It wasn't *their* fault Fawn was gone. It was so unfair that mean old Megan Moravsky could take one of them out like that.

Nutcracker replied with polite disdain, "Do they still *believe* in Santa Claus?" Whatever the nature of Nutcracker's existence, it was evidently not on the same plane of reality as Santa's.

"That's just it," said Kitty. "They *don't*, not anymore. *I* knew ages ago. When I was in kindergarten, back when we lived in North Dakota, I got in a lot of trouble for trying to tell the kids in my class that Santa didn't exist. The teacher even made me sit in the corner for telling lies! That's when I realized for the first time that adults are liars. But by now, *all* the kids have figured out about Santa. They still pretend, though, because they think they'll get more presents that way. It's *corrupt*," declared Kitty with unyielding moral authority.

"Then it would seem that kids are liars, too," commented Rhea from behind her stony face.

"No—" Kitty immediately retorted, but stopped. Rhea had a point. It was clear enough that Megan was a liar and corrupt, but Kitty hadn't expanded the range of kid liars beyond that one infidel. What if it turned out that kids were willing collaborators with lies, too? What if, in fact, kids were no better than adults?

This was exactly what Kitty hated about Rhea. She always spoiled things with a single devastating remark. Kitty sent the titan a furtive glance, but she was like a statue, never affected by anything Kitty said or thought.

"Well, I think *you* are much more important to Christmas than Santa is, Nutcracker," said Kitty. He smiled back at her as much as his rigid mouth would allow.

"Agreed," called Jo from the back. "Sorry I can't talk right now. I'm writing a Christmas story," she added. "Lots of poor children and good works."

"Are you giving *us* Christmas presents?" barked Ichabod. He was curled up on Kitty's feet to keep them warm, but since imaginary creatures weren't affected by the cold, they weren't very good at generating warmth, either.

"Well, of course, but I can't tell you what they are!"

"I like Christmas presents," declared the golden retriever. His tail thumped on the hard floor.

"Me too," said Kitty. "December is great. I already got Hanukkah presents from Bammy and Bampy. They sent a great big package, even though they brought us a ton of stuff at Thanksgiving."

"What's Hanukkah?" asked Nutcracker.

"Oh," said Kitty. She didn't actually know, beyond the fact that it was another way her grandparents were trying to remind her that she was Jewish. She'd overheard an argument on the phone between her mother and grandmother regarding potato pancakes, which had something to do with it. In the end there weren't any potato pancakes, and Kitty had known better than to ask her mother about them. "It's another December holiday, I guess. They gave me a candleholder and some candles to light, but Mommy didn't want me to light it. She said candles were too dangerous with someone like Asher in the house."

"Can't argue with that," said Ichabod, wagging his tail more vigorously still.

"I've gotta get back home for lunch," said Kitty, shivering but also wanting to escape before any more questions about Hanukkah arose. "I'll come back on Christmas Day afternoon, OK? With your presents."

They sent her off with friendly goodbyes. Kitty trooped back across the meadow in the same footprints she'd walked out in. It was so, so cold. A thick layer of snow sat atop the house and the church alike, a perfect simulacrum of icing on a gingerbread house.

It took her nearly ten minutes to get out of her snow gear and by then she was roasting. The downstairs was superheated from the woodstove in the living room. Donald had to keep it going nonstop, day and night, at least five months of the year and sometimes six, the radiators being unenthusiastic warriors against an Olutakli County winter. Kitty gave up her original plan of hot cocoa and poured herself a glass of apple juice instead. She brought it out to the dining room where her parents were talking in low, tense voices.

"What's wrong?" she said.

They looked surprised to see her there and exchanged the

well-known parental glance of deciding whether or not to tell the truth. Kitty waited with interest both for the news and to see whether her parents would prove to be liars in this case or not.

Carmichael said, "She'll hear anyway."

Donald nodded. "Meemaw and Papaw just called and aren't sure they're coming up for Christmas after all."

"Aw! Why not?"

"Well," said Donald with a deep breath, "there's just been a really terrible plane accident, and now they're afraid to fly up here."

"Really? What happened? What kind of accident?"

"No one is really sure yet, but it seems like a bomb went off in a plane, and everybody in the plane died. When it crashed, some people on the ground got killed, too."

"Wow! Did it happen near here?" Kitty wondered what a plane crash looked like and if she'd get to see it.

"No, it was in Scotland."

Kitty made a puzzled face. "That's really far away. It's the opposite direction from Arizona, isn't it? So why wouldn't Meemaw and Papaw want to fly then?"

"It makes them afraid of flying in general. If it was a bomb, that means somebody put it there, but we don't know who—so, maybe, there will be bombs on other planes."

"I can understand their anxiety," said Carmichael, "but don't you think after this the airports will be more careful than ever?"

"Of course, and I think Dad takes that view, but Mom is pretty rattled."

"But what's the point of blowing up a plane?" said Kitty.

Both parents looked at her blankly.

At last Donald said, "I have no idea."

Kitty retreated to her room, more convinced than ever of the madness of adults.

After that it seemed her parents were on the phone nearly

all the time, with one set of grandparents or the other, with the airline, with the airport, and in between they fretted about the cost of long-distance calls. The pattern held through the arrival of Bammy and Bampy by car late in the afternoon, and then on into the night. Only late the next morning could Meemaw be persuaded as to the unlikeliness of a second terrorist attack, especially on commuter flights from Phoenix to Chicago or Chicago to Newark or Newark to Albany, but by then the only option left was to arrive mid-afternoon the next day, which was Christmas Eve. Donald meanwhile had to be gone all afternoon to attend a prayer service at St. Mark's Lutheran in Kuhsota because one of the plane crash dead was a Syracuse University student who'd been a church member there. Carmichael rounded up the children and her parents to join the volunteers across the way in cleaning and decorating the church.

The frenetic activity did everyone a world of good. They changed all the paraments from blue to white and arranged, then rearranged, cascades of potted poinsettias up and down the steps between the pews and the altar rail. The men dragged in an enormous white pine harvested from Dale Mayer's land and spent an hour setting it upright just so. The women spent the same hour cleaning up the snow and dirt that got dragged in with the tree, to say nothing of the boughs and twigs that snapped off of it, and vacuuming up the stubborn pine needles that embedded themselves in the carpet that ran down the center aisle. The three young Abneys were the only children present so they got to do most of the tree decorating. Asher managed to break only three glass globes. Saul insisted on being the one to set the plastic baby Jesus in his little plastic manger at the foot of the tree. Kitty snuck off to examine the bulletins and make sure that all her favorite hymns were listed. There was some intense discussion among the members about running strings of lights along the walls and windows, but consensus was reached that lights on the tree were enough, and special lighting ought otherwise to be provided only by candles. This, however, led to certain recriminations over who had chosen and purchased the Advent candles for the wreath, which were cheaper than those of previous years but burned down faster, such that the purple candle of First Advent wouldn't last through both Christmas Eve and Christmas Day services.

At last the church was shiny and bright, slices of kranzkuchen were passed around and devoured, and the Abneys crossed the driveway for a dinner of meatballs blessedly free of caraway seeds. Donald even made it home in time to eat with them.

On the morning of Christmas Eve, the adults had a long discussion over breakfast about picking up the elder Abneys, who were due in at the airport at two in the afternoon. What with the transfer and the weather and the extra security measures, there was no way to be sure that everything would go as planned. The one certainty was that Donald had to be home for the Christmas Eve service at seven. Frank at last insisted that he would go with Carmichael and could even drive if need be since he was no stranger to snowy conditions. Judith said that she could look after the children just fine without either parent around. So Carmichael and Frank left after an early lunch, Donald stowed himself in his office to finish preparing his two Christmas sermons, and Bammy distracted the children from their excessive fixation on the packages under the tree with a long list of household chores so exhausting that the boys spontaneously took a nap and Kitty became ostentatiously absorbed in her illustrated volume of *The Nutcracker*.

As expected, the Abneys' flight was delayed but the weather never got worse than flurries, so they made it back to Shibboleth by half-past six, giving Meemaw and Papaw just enough time to change into nice clothes. Asher, gleeful, crawled back and forth across their laps throughout the service, and during "Silent Night" he managed to drip wax all over his hands, the hymnals, and the floor. Saul held his candle perfectly upright with a solemnity that befit the occasion. They came home to leftovers with promises of a proper Christmas dinner the next day, and before ten all six adults were sound asleep and not dreaming of so much as a sugarplum.

∼

Sometime after midnight not a creature was stirring, except for Asher. Meemaw and Papaw had been stowed in his and Saul's room for the time being because Bammy and Bampy were already in the guest room, it being too late for them to go to the Forrads', and, after all, it was Christmas. The boys protested at first, then asked to be transferred to Kitty's room. She protested in turn. Finally Carmichael offered to let the boys sleep in their sleeping bags in the living room, nestled between the sofa and the coffee table, and this was so extraordinary, so festive, that they relented at once.

Asher awoke confused as to his whereabouts. His stuffed doggy, so well gnawed and loved that it was shiny and flattened, lay in his arms, but the both of them were in a sleeping bag, not in bed under the covers. The still-lit Christmas tree gave him his bearings. At once he was wide awake. He listened. There was no sound but the embers of the woodstove popping and dying. Gradually Asher realized it was the middle of the night and he was awake to see it, unlike at Thanksgiving when he'd passed out too soon. The sheer novelty was exhilarating. To be the only one awake in a dark house was even more exciting than the pile of presents under the luminous tree, winking back at him in glints of red and blue and green and gold.

Asher peered over to his left to make sure Saul was still sleeping. He was. Mouth open, arms flung wide, a little green race car wedged under one cheek—his single permitted Christmas Eve present. Asher looked down at his own race car, electric blue. He picked it up and ran it along the edge of the sofa but all at once got bored with it. He could play cars any time. Tonight the house was his. He wasn't afraid of the darkness, or the aloneness. He wasn't afraid at all. He was brave Asher.

He padded along in his footed pajamas to the spot where living room, dining room, and staircase intersected. Everyone else was upstairs, sleeping. If he went up there he risked waking them. So some entertainment other than toys had to be found. He passed the staircase and turned into the kitchen. For a long time he stood in front of the refrigerator, considering whether the light inside and the sound of the door opening would wake anyone. For some reason he really, really didn't want Saul to wake up. He decided against the fridge and thought of the pantry. He retraced his steps and turned through the second doorway. The African violets pulsed weirdly under the UV light. His mom must have forgotten to turn it off. He was brave Asher, but there was no way he was going near those little aliens.

Deftly he climbed onto the counter. He pulled at a cupboard door and it opened with a noisy snap. He froze, waiting to see if he'd get caught, but the house slept on. He grabbed a whole wad of fruit leathers sheerly because he could. Afraid of further noise he left the cupboard door open and dropped back to the ground.

On the floor he found himself facing the door to the outside. He squinted through the glass panes set in the door's upper half. The snow was a shimmery blue. A nearly full moon hung pegged into the sky like a pushpin. Asher never got to go outside at night. Even now, when night came on so early, he always got called inside the house once dark fell. The only time he saw night was from the inside of a car or in the rush from building to car and back again. Nobody was awake to stop him now, though. He could go outside and see the night and the blue snow all by himself.

He turned the knob and opened the door. The cold smacked him backward, but Asher hated the fussiness of getting into snow gear. He had footie pajamas on. He wouldn't be long, anyhow. He pulled the door mostly shut behind him and skidded across the thin layer of snow on the little porch, then down the plank steps.

He considered what to do. If he followed his and Saul's route through the meadow, he'd have to wade through deep drifts, and it would be slow going. Not to mention his pajamas would be soaked by the time he got back inside. He crept forward across a thinner layer of crusty snow alongside the house. He came to the corner and turned. Of course! The driveway and parking lot had been cleared by Mr. Mayer with his pickup truck that had a plow in front. There were still some flecks of blue-white on the ground, but the gravel between house and church was mostly clear. Asher could make a circuit around the house and then go back inside. Wait till he told Saul what he did!

Asher trotted as fast as the slipperiness of the ground allowed, past the front of the house to the empty area in front of the church where the cars turned one way or another to park. He walked up to the second building and patted its white clapboard siding like it was a big friendly dog. In excitement he zigzagged back and forth across the passageway between church and home. It warmed him up a little, even though his fingers were getting stiff from the chill. So strange, so wondrous, to be all alone, outside, at night, under the bright white moon.

His last zigzag brought him to the back corner of the church. He was ready now to run the rest of the way around the house and get back inside to warm up, but then he saw it. The ladder. Saul never wanted to climb the ladder, but Asher always did. Saul wouldn't take even one step up it. For months and months it had been leaning against the church. Sometimes Asher and Saul watched Mr. Pohl climb up it and work on the roof, replacing a shingle. Of course Mr. Pohl and their parents and everyone else had said no, they couldn't go up there, it was dangerous, don't be silly, don't even think about it.

But now Asher was alone, with no one to scold him, not even Saul. He could think about it.

==He thought about it.==

He put a foot on the lowest rung. He kept it there a long

time, till his fingers really started to ache with cold. Most of the voices in his head told him to get off the ladder and stay far away from it. But another voice, an insistent one, told him that this was his only chance to do it.

He put his other foot on the second rung.

Holding his breath and willing all the competing wills inside of him to be quiet, he darted up the ladder. He didn't look down or to the sides. He would just go all the way up, and then come right back down again. Then he could tell Saul he'd done it. Asher, who was only five years old! Six in a few days, but still. He would climb all the way up before Saul did, who'd be seven in a few weeks but had never ever climbed all the way up a ladder. He wasn't brave like Asher!

He came to the top. The breeze was a little stronger up here, and colder. The moon looked so close that Asher thought he could grab it, if he wanted to. The roof was covered with a perfectly smooth, unpocked layer of snow, a few inches thick. The backyard snow was all mottled with footprints and cinders from the garbage ring by now. This snow was flawless. Asher thought it would be perfect for a snow angel. Without hesitation he clambered up on his hands and knees.

It was tricky, turning himself around so he didn't mess up the snow before he lay back into it. He dug in his heels to push himself upwards a little more. They slipped and skidded and he lay back hard, against the roof, to brace himself. Well, it would have to be a snow angel right at the edge of the roof, then. The snow was already melting around the collar of his pajamas and behind his ears. He shivered. It would be nice to go inside now and climb back into his sleeping bag, right next to Saul, who always slept hot like he had a fever. Asher swept his arms and legs back and forth quickly to make his angel. There. That was enough. It was time to go home.

But somehow he didn't quite make purchase with the edge of the roof, or with the top rung of the ladder, and all at once Asher's snow angel turned into a slide and he was sailing, he was soaring, out into the night toward the pushpin moon, and it all happened so fast that he had no time to imagine what it would be like in the morning when a lonesome Saul roused the house in a panic, or when all four grandparents squinted into the hallway not yet wrapped in their bathrobes, or when Kitty found snow blown into the pantry through the door still open a crack, or when Carmichael threw herself down on the cold body of her youngest, or when Donald realized that, on the morn of the birth of the Son of God, his own son lay on the hard ground behind the church, dead.

CHAPTER SEVEN

January 1989

View the arctic and antarctic regions,
those huge voids, where nothing lives;
regions of eternal snow:
where winter in all his horrors has established his throne,
and arrested every creative power of nature.

The sacristy was crowded, claustrophobic. The members of the Mt. Moriah church council had packed themselves in, the door on the sanctuary side shut and locked, the stairs to the basement blocked and surveilled, for the sake of a private huddle.

Marilyn the organist was holding court, to Al Beck's great irritation; he, after all, was the congregational president. "So when I spoke to Bishop Cartledge on the phone about the hymns for today," she said, leaning in toward her captive audience, "he told me, in confidence you understand, that under the circumstances we shouldn't expect Pastor Donald to resume his duties until February."

"If it was in confidence, then why are you telling *us*?" snapped Eunice.

"It *wasn't* in confidence, because all of us already know," said Al.

Marilyn straightened up to parry both rejoinders. "What I mean to say is, he inferred strongly that the Abneys are in such a mental state that we shouldn't bother them or expect anything of them for awhile."

"Implied,' not 'inferred,'" said Sandra.

"Well, what else would you expect?" exclaimed Jackie. How

many times had she tormented herself with the prospect of untimely death for her three boys, impetuous and fatherless as they were? And yet they'd all made it into their teens alive. Of course Pastor Donald and his family were beside themselves.

"So this bishop is gonna cover for us on Sundays, then?" snarled Dale. He always snarled when he detected the danger of rising tears, and being far more emotional a man than he ever let anyone know, he snarled a lot.

"Yes," said Al, trying to wrest presidential control of the situation, "he spoke to me on the phone last Sunday evening and said he'd preach and lead the service for us, all this month. Of course, that gives him the chance to check in on the Abneys, too."

"Are they home right now?" whispered Jackie.

The council members as one glanced in the direction of the parsonage, invisible though it was through the walls. But they could imagine their way into that house of grieving well enough. From the outside, the only sign of life within was the smoke coiling out of the chimney like a blurry slinky, indifferently rising above the cares of the earthbound.

"If it were me, I'd want to get away for awhile," said Eunice. "They could go with his parents to Arizona."

Al nodded. "I would too. But it's complicated. What Bishop Cartledge told *me* on the phone—" he cast a meaningful glance in Marilyn's direction "—is that as long as they have to wait for the burial, Carmichael absolutely refuses to leave."

There was a collective nod. The situation was nothing unusual to any of them at Mt. Moriah. Cemeteries down in the valley could manage a winter burial with the use of a propane gun blasting a perfect coffin-shaped rectangle through the hard earth. But even in the unlikely event that the machinery could make it up the church's slippery switchback driveway, the gravestones were too closely and too haphazardly placed, under snowdrifts too deep, to clear a spot for another grave. It was not uncommon for parishioners who departed this earth in wintertime to spend their first few months of death in a rental slot at the mausoleum in Kuhsota. They took up permanent residence in the cemetery only when the snow melted, usually in March, sometimes not till April.

"I'm kinda surprised they want to bury him *here*," remarked Jackie. "Don't they have their own people somewhere they want him to be with?"

Said Dale, "Maybe that means he'll stay pastor here forever. Because they won't want to leave... *him*... behind."

Hazel sniffled and pulled out a lavishly embroidered hanky. "I can't stand the thought of that poor little tyke lying in the mausoleum for months, so far from his mommy and daddy," she croaked. "He was trouble, but what a dear little boy he was. And now for him to be..."

Eunice held out a superfluous tissue. Al patted Hazel on the back. "What a way to start the new year," he sighed, rubbing at the base of his tense neck. He acknowledged to himself that the authority of his presidential office was impeded not only by Marilyn's busybody interference, but also by the fact that he had overindulged at a New Year's Eve party the night before.

"It's just not right that things like this should happen," Dale barked. His eyes were red-rimmed and his face puffed out like a bullfrog's.

The only person who had not spoken all this time was George Pohl. He sat on an overturned bucket in the corner by the staircase and stared at the floor, immobile and unresponsive as if petrified by a divine curse. Dale looked over at him, then caught Al's eye. He gave a tiny jerk of his chin. Al tugged at his sports coat and took a sideways step around Jackie to get closer to George. He laid a hand on his shoulder. George looked up absently, like he was coming out of a deep sleep.

"George," Al said, in a tone that couldn't decide whether it was tender or bracing, "look it, George, nobody blames you."

Sandra pinched her lips but said nothing.

"The ladder was out there for months and months. There

was no reason to think it was a danger to him or anyone else. Like Hazel said, he was a little boy who loved trouble and it was just bad luck that he snuck out in the night. But that doesn't make it your fault, now does it?" Al appealed with his eyes to the council for support. They all chimed their agreement, except for Sandra, but she was at the back and no one detected her silence.

In a low, soulless tone George said, "It was a goddamn stupid thing to do, leaving that ladder out there. I shoulda broke my own neck. It doesn't matter what you say. I've got that boy's blood on my hands and I'll take it with me to my own grave."

All at once everyone was remonstrating with him, some like Dale scolding George sharply for such perverse and pointless thoughts, others like Hazel weeping all over again at the sheer tragedy of the thing. But George only shook his head and resumed his stare at the floor.

The reassurances petered out, a fraught silence replacing them.

"So, um," Jackie said at last, "Bishop Cartledge is coming to cover for Pastor Donald this morning and the rest of the month?"

"He'll be here another four Sundays after today," said Marilyn, "because there are five Sundays total in January this year. I have to keep a close eye on these things since I play every Sunday."

"But what are we supposed to do in the meanwhile—about *them?*" Jackie added in a fearful whisper.

"We need to organize food for them," Sandra announced. "I've been on the phone with Judith, Carmichael's mother. They'll take care of food as long as they're still here, but they and Pastor Donald's parents will be heading back home later this week. I'm going to draw up a sign-up list so people can bring them meals and groceries. Last thing they need right now is to go to Grand Union and have the whole town stare at them while they're just buying baloney. We'll leave care packages of food on the porch and that way they won't even have to talk to anyone."

"But shouldn't somebody say something?" quavered Hazel. "They'll think we blame them if we don't say anything."

"What do you want to do, knock on the door and say, 'Hi there, Pastor Donald, here's some pot roast, and by the way I don't blame you for your little boy's death'? For heaven's sake, give them some space."

"It's terrible and all, but I'm not sure I'd want to be left *completely* alone," said Jackie.

"They won't be completely alone. I'll check in on them daily."

"What about the funeral?" said Eunice. "Has it been scheduled yet? We can talk to them then."

Marilyn seized the chance to project her superior knowledge as organist again. "Yes, it's this Wednesday at two. Bishop Cartledge will come back again and lead it. There'll be a viewing at the church in the morning beforehand."

"A viewing? Is it... I mean, is he... was he..." Jackie stuttered.

"From what I understand," said Al, "there was no real visible damage. A small lesion on the back of the head and a broken neck, but no broken skin."

"A broken neck," sobbed Hazel.

"But the point is, you can't see it. He looks normal enough," said Al, as if this were a consolation.

"But it's only the funeral, not the burial," Marilyn added.

"That'll be sometime in early spring," Al said.

"What an awfully long time to drag this out," said Sandra. "And like you said, Hazel, they have to leave his body in the Kuhsota mausoleum till they can bury him, and Carmichael doesn't want to leave until then. Now what they *could* do instead, right now, is cremate him and put his ashes in the columbarium. They wouldn't have to wait till spring to do that."

"How can you even think of such a thing?" protested Hazel,

bursting into a fresh wave of tears. "To imagine that poor little boy going up in flames!"

"You just said yourself how much you hated the thought of him lying in the mausoleum all this time!"

"Take it easy now," said Al.

"I do hate it," said Hazel, with dignity, "but cremation—it just sounds like, like, the fires of hell, that's what it's like."

Sandra rolled her eyes. "I wouldn't have thought you to be so superstitious, Hazel Quinn. What, do you think God refuses to save cremated people? And anyway, are you suggesting that's what Alan did to his mother—sent her to burn in hell?"

"It just seems different with an old person," said Hazel, cowering in the face of Sandra's intensity.

"Enough now," said Al. "People do what they do and that's that. Now look, the bishop is gonna be here any minute and I gotta be ready to meet him. Sandra, you do that grocery list thing like you said. The rest of you sort out who's gonna stand guard and keep other people from going up to the house."

"It's so cold out," said Eunice.

"I'll go and stand outside," said George at once. He stood up. "It's the least I can do."

Al clapped him on the shoulder again. "You're a good man, George," he said. George shrugged it off and stomped out of the sacristy.

~

Kitty was stationed next to Saul, both of them between their parents, and all four of them behind Bishop Cartledge, voluminous in his white alb, with a white stole draped around his shoulders. They were standing in the narthex. The bishop was so big that Kitty couldn't even see all the people filling up the pews on the other side of him.

She glanced down at her dress, which was black: the first black clothing she'd ever owned or worn, except for a cat costume for Halloween when she was nine. Bammy and Meemaw had driven all the way to Binghamton to buy it. The dress was made of a shiny material called taffeta, with a sheath of lace over top of it. Kitty's toes squirmed inside the black ballet flats on her feet and the black tights on her legs, nowhere near warm enough against the cold seeping in from the church doors right behind her. But she knew enough to keep still, not complain, and look very sad.

It was a weird thing, to feel sad way down deep inside of her, but to feel at the exact same time like her face was not cooperating. She had to make sure she looked right on the outside, or else people would misunderstand about her on the inside. But it was hard to think about anything except the strangeness of wearing black and the uncanny silence they all kept without Ms. Gross's usual organ prelude to cover the settling-in fidgets.

Kitty was startled almost out of her skin when Bishop Cartledge's voice boomed into the narthex, "Blessed be the God and Father of our Lord Jesus Christ, the source of all mercy and the God of all consolation. He comforts us in all our sorrows so that we can comfort others in their sorrows with the consolation we ourselves have received from God." He walked forward. Kitty felt her father's hand pressing lightly at her back and she fell in step. Saul reached out and grabbed her hand and she held it tightly, too tightly, in case he decided to break away.

Everyone's eyes tracked them down the aisle. Familiar parishioners were rendered strange by tissues clutched in front of red eyes and somber mouths. Ms. Bonnie in her oversize glasses, the Fishers with their tiny baby, Dr. Wheeler the veterinarian and his family. Michelle, Lisa, and Tammy crying openly, almost competitively. Daycare-aged kids who didn't know how to behave in church yet, horsing around or scribbling on the bulletin. Kitty fixed her gaze up front where all four of her grandparents waited, along with the aunts and uncles and cousins on her father's side, the first time any of them had ever visited in Shibboleth. Shouldn't they have come while Asher was still alive? Kitty wanted to be mad at them, but for the moment she was just glad to have them as a goal to walk toward, them instead of the coffin. It was closed. Her parents had asked if she wanted to see Asher while it was still open, but she didn't. Somehow it seemed wrong to replace her last image of him lying on the ground with the coffin version of him. They didn't even ask Saul. Meemaw and Bammy kept him occupied all morning so he wouldn't know what was going on at the church next door.

At last they reached the end of the aisle and took their place in the front pew, which lay bare and unprotected before the little coffin. Bishop Cartledge whirled his great bulk around. He invited the congregation to pray, reminding our Father in heaven about how his own Son loved the children and blessed them. The stained-glass window to the right of the altar showed a robed Jesus sitting on a rock with a girl and a boy on each knee and a bunch of other kids, also robed, scattered around him. Jesus was smiling at them and they at him. Bishop Cartledge intoned, "Give us grace, we pray, that we may entrust Asher to your never-failing care and love." Kitty stumbled over the prayer's logic. God had to give *them* something so they could give *him* something, but the thing they had to give God was Asher himself, one of those children that Jesus loved so much. If Jesus really loved him, why did he let Asher slip off the roof and die?

Kitty was so absorbed in puzzling out the prayer that the lessons washed over her unheard until everyone had to stand up for the Gospel. Even then she didn't register a word until Bishop Cartledge was mouthing the words of Lazarus's sister Mary, "Lord, if you had been here, my brother would not have died." Kitty glanced down at Saul, whose eyes were fixed on the bishop, but he betrayed no reaction to this stark accusation against Jesus. She wondered what Saul made of the whole thing. That morning, after he'd wriggled into his own new black clothes, Saul asked Meemaw why Asher didn't get a new black suit, too. Meemaw, horrified, ran out of the room so she could cry without Saul seeing. Actually, Asher *did* have a new suit, but it was grayish-blue, not black, or so she gleaned from the adults' conversation. And a tie, too, which was weird, since he'd never ever worn one that she knew of. She'd gone into his and Saul's room to find his stuffed doggy and asked to make sure it went in the coffin with him. Bishop Cartledge got to the part where Lazarus came out of the tomb. Why is he reading this? Kitty wondered. It's more than four days since Asher died. Whatever miracle Mary and Martha got, it wasn't going to be repeated for the Abney family.

They sat down. Bishop Cartledge preached a heartfelt sermon and said many kindly things toward the family, and the congregation, and Asher's kindergarten teacher Miss Bowden, too, but most of his remarks glanced off Kitty and rolled away into the corners of the church where they soughed out of existence. Then there was a hymn and the creed and a bunch more prayers and communion, which took a long time. After receiving a wafer and a sip from the cup, each and every communicant peeped over at the family in the front pew, directing a bracing or doleful or furtive glance at them. Kitty pointed her eyes downward and kept the sad face on. Mary's disappointed words at Jesus kept playing through her head. Communion ended and Bishop Cartledge wrapped up his final prayer to "the author and giver of life." Kitty figured he ought to say instead "the ender and taker of life." The bishop then spoke over Asher's coffin, "Rest eternal grant him, O Lord," and the congregation read back off their bulletins, "And let light perpetual shine upon him," but Kitty could see well enough that no light was going to get inside that coffin ever again.

They marched back to the narthex. Kitty had to stand by her parents while everyone filed out and shook hands or hugged, cried or reassured. Her grandparents were teary and choked up, but her parents had already cried so much that they were all dried up at the moment. They absorbed the heavy weight of compassion like they were stiff sponges, upright and gracious.

Kitty tried to be like them but envied Saul, released to go play with the other little boys, everyone assuming he was too young to understand. She smoothed out the lace over her black dress again and again and nodded seriously at whatever comments the adults poured on her head. The teenage girls sobbed some more, and so did a lady pastor; the Catholic priest gave her a strange little clap on the cheek, and Mr. Pohl bundled right past them without saying a word. When the church was just about empty but hardly anyone had driven away, lingering in the frigid parking lot and talking in low voices that emitted puffs of vapor all around their faces, Kitty told her mother that she was cold and procured permission to run home and change, though Kitty knew that they both knew she was really asking permission to escape.

In her room she took off her black dress, tights, and shoes, wondering if she'd ever wear them again, but what reason could there be for black again except another death? Kitty shook off the creepy feeling that came with the realization and pulled on fleecy pants over long underwear. She stood still and listened: it was the first time the house had been empty since... well, since almost ever; she didn't often get to be left at home by herself. The parsonage felt extra-full lately, and not just because of the four grandparents, but because everyone was so sad and the sadness itself seemed to take up extra space. She sat at the top of the stairs to pull on two pairs of socks and realized that no one at home meant no one to stop her from going to the council. She hadn't dared go all this time. Her mother was always so anxious about the steep drop-off; now she wouldn't want Kitty even looking in that direction. But Kitty could go quick and come back and claim she'd been up in the meadow. She could even walk up the hill afterwards to leave evidential footprints in the snow.

Five minutes later she was in her boots and on her way. It was slow going. The snow lay thick and deep and soft, and she had to yank each leg out of a sinkhole to take the next step.

She held tight to a limb of the naked lilac tree while she felt for the sheets of slate underneath and kicked the front porch of her little cave clean of snow. It was mostly bare inside, the winds striking it just so to scour out the snow. She backed in and wrapped her arms around her knees. The cold was terrible but she wouldn't stay long, just long enough to say hello and share the news—of course, they would know already—and receive their attentive sympathy in return.

She waited a minute, then two, then ten. She kept calling in her mind: I'm here! Come and let's meet! But only when her toes were so stiff she could hardly feel them did she see Jo and Rhea, together, gliding in from some distant place. That was strange; they never came together. Jo in her Victorian skirts looked out of place on Rhea's chariot. They swooped down and disembarked. But instead of welcoming them, Kitty, feeling the same freeze in her heart as in her toes, asked in a fearful whisper, "Where are Nutcracker and Ichabod?"

Jo didn't say anything. Kitty realized that, in Jo's storybook life, her sister Beth had just died and Jo was too wretched to speak. But Rhea, unflappable as always, stared back into Kitty's eyes. Her unspoken eloquence was too potent to misunderstand.

"Both of them?" Kitty choked.

Rhea maintained her horrible affirmative gaze.

"Forever?" she whispered.

Rhea said, "They are not." She didn't even pretend to offer comfort. She was all hard truth and not an iota more. Jo kept weeping into her handkerchief. Kitty hated them both. She didn't even say goodbye. She scrambled out of the cave and up into the meadow, creating her decoy tracks and feeling the tears freeze into beads on her face as she realized, in a deep and terrible way she hadn't so far, that her brother and Christmas both were gone for good, gone forever, gone.

∼

When the Sunday service was over, Gene Cartledge tugged the

collar out of his purple shirt and unbuttoned it, shrugged his way back into his anorak, and set his face toward the parsonage.

This was his fourth trip to Mt. Moriah in three weeks. First was that terrible Christmas Day, when he'd left three minutes after his own congregation's service ended and drove the two and a half hours to Shibboleth. All the way there, sick at heart, he rehearsed in his mind what to say, what he could possibly say to something so singularly horrible. He felt the weight of his role, his importance, his moral and spiritual authority, but in the end all that came out was, "I'm sorry, I'm sorry, I'm so sorry." It didn't matter. The family's shock had sealed their ears. The only reality was the wails and the tears and a quick trip to the funeral home with Donald to make the arrangements. There had been no Christmas Day service at Mt. Moriah, of course. Gene was frankly relieved when council president Al Beck declined his offer to conduct one later that afternoon. Under the circumstances, nobody wanted to sing "What child is this, who laid to rest..." Gene drove out of Shibboleth long after dark, but only when the elder Mr. Abney had dismissed him with a firm calm that impressed the bishop. "Nothing good can happen now but sleep," he'd said sagely. Gene wondered how they'd manage even that. Despite the long, late drive back home in the dark, he wasn't the slightest bit sleepy, his mind replaying the bitter facts of the day, and his own mute uselessness, over and over without relief.

Gene made the drive again the next Sunday. Instead of knocking at the door, he called the parsonage from the church and reached Carmichael's mother. Judith's voice was shaky but she thanked him for his concern and said they were "doing as well as could be expected"—a worryingly vague communication—but she thought it would probably be for the best to leave them to themselves, if Bishop Cartledge didn't mind, and they'd talk to him on Wednesday at the funeral instead. Naturally he didn't mind. He preached a recycled sermon plucked from his filing cabinet on the naming and circumcision of Jesus that made everyone, himself included, cringe each time the word "baby" or "child" or "boy" was spoken. He ended up abandoning his manuscript halfway through in order to apologize to the congregation for God and his inscrutable ways. It was a remarkable turnout, considering that it was New Year's Day and no small portion of the congregants appeared to be suffering as much from hangover as from grief. They swarmed him after the service and pilloried him with their impossible questions. What could be answered to the demand as to why God would allow such a thing? Gene recalled learning in seminary something about the distinction between the active and the permissive will of God (Augustine, maybe), but philosophical hairsplitting was of no practical use when faced with an outraged mob of the devout.

Then, of course, came the funeral, in which both he and the mourners clad themselves in liturgical armor.

Now on his fourth visit and second Sunday, as he trekked through the thick snow, Gene wondered with no small feeling of shame how quickly he could recruit a replacement for Mt. Moriah. It was not the most attractive of parishes and had taken long enough to fill with Donald, who would no doubt leave the synod and move far away as fast as he could. And who could blame him for that?

Gene knocked on the pantry door. He was dreading the conversation and hated himself for it.

"Come on in," said Donald at the door. He wore half a smile.

Seeing it, Gene was shocked in spite of himself. Maybe these Holiness types could just set their sorrows aside with a disciplined submission. That'll surely backfire, thought Gene, but all he said was, "Thanks."

The living room was tidy, if anything desolate of signs of life. Gene listened but could hear no indication of the two remaining children—he shuddered internally as he noted the turn of phrase—but probably they were just hiding. Gene found that children generally shied away from him. He never knew what to say to them and as a result found himself overly, fakely jovial. To a one they stared back with the contempt of those who will not be condescended to, and children were needle-sensitive to condescension. Just as well. Coping with the adults would be challenge enough.

"Have a seat." Donald indicated the sofa. "It's just me today. Our folks headed home yesterday. I don't expect Carmichael will join us."

"How is she doing?" Gene said in the most serious and sincere of tones, as if this were not an utterly impossible question to answer.

Donald shrugged. The weird half-smile still played around his lips. "She sleeps a lot. Unconsciousness is preferable to the alternative."

"Understandable," said Gene. "Excessive sleep is a sign of depression." He said it like a recitation from a psychology textbook. What an idiot I am, he thought. If she *weren't* depressed I'd be worried. Which is exactly what worries me about Donald. "How about you?"

"Oh, I'm not sleeping at all," said Donald, almost cheerfully. "I mean, at some point I pass out sheerly because I can't stay awake any longer. But I can't lie down and go to sleep deliberately. When I do finally pass out, it's only for a couple of hours. Waking up takes a long time, but it's full of... well. I'm sure you can guess." All this time he looked straight at the bishop, staring out of his bloodshot eyes without blinking.

Gene dropped his gaze to the floor. "I'm sure it's terrible," he murmured.

"I'm getting a lot of reading done," said Donald. He leaned back in the easy chair and took a heavy tome off the side table, displaying it for Gene. "*The Gulag Archipelago.* All three volumes. For perspective, you know."

"Does it help?"

"Only if there's a difference between natural evil and moral evil," said Donald. He stared up at the ceiling and rubbed his chin, the caricature of a dispassionate philosopher. "The thing is, I'm not sure there is, after all."

Gene had no idea what to do with that remark, or Donald's unnerving behavior. He wished for a flood of tears, the kind you saw when strong men had their concrete exteriors hewn apart. That would be honest, clean, and end with a little macho joking to reestablish the compromised masculinity. Donald wasn't that kind, though. Groping for a useful misdirection, Gene said, "How about the kids?"

"Oh, Kitty's all right," said Donald. "She cries a lot and says straight out all the things the rest of us think but can't bring ourselves to say. Good for her. She's doing grief the right way. She'll be fine." Now Donald was the one sounding like a psych text.

"And Saul?"

That seemed to breach Donald's reserve. "Oh, Lord, I don't know about Saul," he said. He sat for a moment in thought. "They were like twins, you know. They never did anything apart. It must be like looking down and discovering the right half of your body is missing. But he acts normal, for the most part. Only sometimes I find him wandering around the house like he's looking for…"

It was the first time either of them had come close to saying Asher's name. Donald bit off the end of his sentence, as if it was too bulky and bitter-tasting to swallow.

"Want a beer?" he said instead.

"Thanks," said Gene uncomfortably. "I have to head back home in a bit, so I'd better not." Wasn't Donald a teetotaler? He couldn't quite remember. Somebody in the synod was, he'd heard the other pastors joke about it, and it had to be either Donald or that weird guy in the Finger Lakes who claimed to speak in tongues.

The silence squatted over them and seeped out in every direction. Donald was unfocused, no doubt from lack of sleep. Gene had to pull himself together, and Donald, too.

"All I can say is how sorry I am," Gene began with an effort. "I just have no words for this unspeakable tragedy. No one deserves to have this happen to them or their family."

"It's not a question of deserving," replied Donald. "I know Job too well for that."

"I know, and of course you know it, too, it's just… I mean, it's hard to believe in God when things like this happen. In some ways it's extra-hard for those of us who make our living off believing in God."

"Well, you needn't trouble yourself about that, if you were inquiring in a professional capacity," said Donald. Now he was being weirdly formal. "Unfortunately, I can't say this has in any respect diminished my belief in God."

Gene was about to offer bland reassurance when he caught the strangeness of the adverb and repeated, "'Unfortunately'?"

"Sure," said Donald. "A sensible person would be knocked right out of the religious delusion by something like this. Or have a good long crisis of faith, which time itself would fix. Or not. Who knows? But it would be nice, I think, to be done with it altogether, if you could. My dad's done with it. He didn't even need a crisis to get there. It was more like somebody pulled the plug out of his drain and the faith went running out and then he was free. I could see that, while he and my mom were here. Mom was just sad, a nice pure clean grief for her littlest grandbaby, but Dad had a kind of stoic calm about him. Life is like that, hard and cruel, sometimes it takes out the littlest and the least, but that's that. Statistics, not fate or providence. I used to despise him for it. Now I envy him. But," he sighed in conclusion, "it's not going to work for me."

The speech washed over Gene with its uncanny speed and clarity. He couldn't quite sort out which thread to follow. Clumsily he settled on, "I'm sure your dad is heartbroken over it."

"Oh, sure," Donald said. "But how nice for him, to have his heartbreak so clean and neat. No God to get messed up in the middle of it. Whereas I have never been surer of God—not even in the good ol' days before I started asking hard questions or learning hard truths or seminary or anything. Put some unbelievers in my path *now* and I will mow them down with my unwavering certainty. I'll be like the hay balers they use around here. Knock down every last objection and tie it up neat, without remainder. No excuses, no objections. God *is*."

"Then it's good you have that to comfort you," Gene whispered. He found himself eyeing Donald like he was a wild animal raised in captivity and only just now discovering his teeth.

"It's no comfort," Donald stated. The hovering smile was at last on full display. "I thought it would be, when I didn't have it. I always craved absolute certainty of God. But now that I'm certain, I realize how brutal it is. God *is*, for sure. But God is not *good*."

If this prophetic deliverance had been spoken with a pitch of rage, Gene thought, he might have needled and provoked it and gotten the hoped-for tears of sorrow. But it was announced with all the passion of a weather forecast or baseball scores: factual, objective, of mild interest only.

"I know you have to argue with me," said Donald, almost pityingly. "Let's just take that part as read. I appreciate the effort, even though it's only your duty. But let's spare both of us the trouble." He stood up. "Thanks for covering for me these Sundays. It's not so much the preaching as the sympathy that I dread. But I'm sure by February I'll be ready to face it again."

Gene mirrored the standing. "The last thing I would do right now," he managed to say, "is argue with you about God."

"You know your job," said Donald. He gave Gene an appreciative pat on the shoulder, as if he were the one to offer comfort instead of the other way around. "Have a safe drive back."

∼

For years, birthday parties had symbolized the essential difference between Carmichael's upbringing and Donald's. She had grown up with them every year without fail, the result not only of being a pampered (this was Donald's adjective, though she couldn't exactly dispute it) only child, but also of the social world in which she was raised. Mothers who would never dream of employment invested their underutilized energies in decorating the house, special-ordering a cake, and having invitations printed on letterpress. "With all that time on her hands, couldn't your mother have written the invitations herself? Or baked the cake?" Donald objected the first time he heard this. Carmichael only laughed at his sheer blind incomprehension. But the tables were turned when she learned that he'd *never* had a birthday party, not because his parents couldn't afford it or opposed it, but because it just wasn't done. Too precious, too silly. The elder Mrs. Abney would of course make Donald his favorite—German chocolate cake, with an extra-thick layer of coconut—and he'd get a couple of presents. But a party with other kids? No. Donald continued to think it ridiculous how much effort Carmichael put into their children's birthday parties, not least of all because she had plenty to keep her busy as it was. However, since all she required of Donald was his presence at the party and a little help with the dishes afterwards, he yielded to the annual indulgence of their children.

It was Saul's fast-approaching birthday in the third week of January that at last roused Carmichael out of her silence.

Since Christmas she had been almost without the power of speech. She did cry, from sobs so violent that they sounded like vomiting to barely-noticed rivulets of tears exploring their way down her inert face. At night, and not infrequently during the day, she clutched at Donald, holding him so tightly that her nails dug into his arms and left crescent-moon marks, but he never loosened them, taking the tiny wounds as the very least of costs compared to the annihilating slash into the heart of their family. She responded to questions like "Will you eat some dinner?" with a "Yes, OK," and afterwards managed a "Thanks" before slipping back into the enveloping fog of speechlessness.

Judith had tried to get her to open up a little while she and Frank were still in the house, but Carmichael only leaned into her mother and cried, cried, cried, wordlessly and hopelessly. Donald wondered if he should push her to talk but couldn't bring himself to do it.

For his part, the sleeplessness seemed to have activated a bizarre loquacity. After both sets of parents left, he fielded all the phone calls, managing with ease the propane tank delivery guy and the woman who called about renewing their newspaper subscription. Even when the caring calls jangled, from his sister and brother checking in every few days, from old friends and former classmates and fellow clergy, Donald found he could talk with them just fine. They said all the right things, then he said all the right things. It had a perfunctory liturgical flow to it, and therein lay the comfort or, if not comfort exactly, then something to help pass the time. January daylight was short but the days stretched long as they all hid inside, blockaded against the brutal world, the children kept home from school and work put on hold for the time being. Each day, Donald thought, takes us further away from his death. *Asher's* death. He made himself articulate the name in his mind. Which is what we need, time and distance. But then, each day also takes us further away from Asher's *life*. There would be no unscrambling that paradox.

What would have been Asher's sixth birthday, on the last day of the year, was even worse than Christmas. Christmas was pure shock, with its protective shelter of denial and rejection and refusal. Blessed are those who have not seen and yet believe, but when Donald was confronted with the almost unblemished body of his dead son, he saw and yet did not believe. Only a week later, when they should have had a ridiculous, unnecessary, too-close-to-Christmas blowout with cake and presents to celebrate Asher's big day, only then it hit them, hit them like a cement roller, like Hurricane Gilbert, like the Soviets dropping the big one. Donald sat at the dining room table for hours, staring at nothing, bleary, gutted. His only company was a mantra in his mind, words spoken by Grandfather Abney so long before: "If the choice is death, is it not because you choose death?" Maybe his wise old grandfather with one eye always on the spiritual world had foreseen this moment and was trying, in his own way, to warn Donald.

When at last he forced himself to get up and check on Carmichael, he found her doubled over in their closet, her tears warping the wrapping paper on a motherlode of presents: the Christmas gifts that Asher never got to open, and all his birthday presents, too, since Carmichael would not let her little one be deprived of a good birthday just because it came so close to Christmas. Donald wedged himself into the closet with her, though his exhausted eyes would not release any more tears. He wrapped his arms around her limp body and peeled her up from its curl around the colorful boxes. Saul found them and climbed in. He cried, chiefly because Carmichael was crying. Soon Kitty found them and climbed in to cry, too. Squashing the unopened presents, in the midst of their tangle of limbs and hair, he felt the vast space between them, the expanding nothingness of the missing Asher. Saul fell asleep on Donald, and Donald's legs fell asleep under Saul's weight until he couldn't feel them at all, but the four of them stayed together half-in and half-out of the closet for some unaccountable time until Kitty said, through a sniffle, "I'm hungry." Then they realized they were smelling something good to eat. The grandparents had left the four of them to their grief but cooked a nice lunch all the same. One by one they crawled out of the closet and found their way downstairs. For the first time they all ate together again, Asher's chair deliberately drawn up to the table, empty but potent. They accepted his present absence during Bammy's chicken soup with rice and Meemaw's tuna noodle casserole.

Three weeks later, the tear-wrinkled gifts were still sitting in the closet, and in the world-upending logic of grief, it was Donald who remembered that Saul's seventh birthday was just a few days off and spoke about it to Carmichael.

Her eyes swung round toward his, paler than usual, as if all the crying had rinsed her irises of their pigment. "You want to throw him a birthday party?" she asked in a dead voice.

"I don't mean we should invite other people over," he said cautiously. "Only that, as much as possible, we should try to normalize things for him."

"Normalize?" She hissed it like an accusation. Donald was simultaneously alarmed and relieved. It was the first emotion she'd shown that was not sheer diluvian sadness. "How could you think—"

He stopped her with a gentle gesture of his hand; the rest of the sentence was too obvious to need saying. "You know I don't mean it like that," he said. "But look, *Saul's* not dead. It's his birthday. It won't help any to take that away from him."

"*Saul's* not dead," she repeated. Her tone was as blank and watery as her eyes.

Donald heard the implied contrast. *Asher is dead* is what I really meant. *Asher is dead. Asher is dead.* It rang over and over in his head like cymbals starting out quiet at the edges and soon drowning out all other sounds.

Carmichael tried to say something but her voice kept catching. She looked at him in mute despair.

"I know," he said, his own voice shaking. "If we have this birthday party for Saul, even with just the four of us, it means we're all admitting that *we* are alive and *we* have to go on..." He wobbled out of speech, but Carmichael's voice came back to her.

"Without Asher," she said. It was a bullet of rage. "We have to keep going. We are going to go on living, one day after another, with no Asher in it. There is going to be life and history, for our very own family, that has no Asher in it. And I hate it! I hate it so much. I want to refuse it and break it. I'd rather die myself than recover and take one single step into a future without him..."

Donald stood helpless before her. His only refutation lay

on the sheer pragmatic grounds that, apart from further accident, murder, or suicide, they would all continue to live. Even as death snatched Asher from them, life would continue to exert itself within them. Carmichael was in the right, life was in the wrong, but life held the power to impose its injustice upon them.

They stared at one another, like gladiators in an amphitheater gearing themselves up for a battle that neither of them had asked for.

Donald held out his hand to his wife. She took it, but with suspicion in her eyes, as if it were a false truce from an adversary. He led her downstairs, out the side door—pulling their coats off the hooks as they went—around the house and toward the back of the church.

Carmichael let go of Donald's hand and stopped walking.

"Please," he said. That was all.

She set one foot out in front of the other, testing the ground as if feeling along the edge of a tooth for the exact spot that would set off an electric shock of pain. Donald went on ahead of her. He stopped. "It was here."

She shook her head. She advanced quickly now, turning her head, orienting herself, a surveyor calculating angles. Satisfied, she squatted down and looked up at the church. "Here. I remember looking up at the roof of the church from here." She let herself topple back and sat right on the icy gravel, picking up a handful and letting it fall through her fingers.

Donald sat down next to her.

"Here's an awful thought," she said. "I wish I could sift through this gravel and find some piece with a little rust-red stain on it, a piece of his blood, because somehow it would make him close again."

"It's not awful. I understand."

She let more gravel clink to the ground.

"You won't find any, though. It's a weird thing, but I keep hearing in my head Ray Jansen saying to me, 'It's a clean wound, very little abrasion,' when we were talking over the funeral arrangements. Like that was some kind of comfort."

"I suppose he's had to deal with some pretty messy corpses."

"He kept on saying it, like he couldn't stop himself. As Gene and I left, he kind of apologized. He said that 'these situations' take it out even of funeral staff."

"Meaning a child's death."

"Yeah."

They sat in the cold and the strangeness of their calm. Inside the house it took every last store of strength to endure from minute to minute. Here, sitting on the very earth that had received their falling son with its hard unwelcoming arms, here the words came back, the hard crisp clarity of thought. At no distance from the site of Asher's death, they were granted the gift of distance on their own pain.

"I remember," said Carmichael, "how I picked him up. And my first thought wasn't whether he was dead or alive, or how I felt about it—which is what you'd think I ought to think—but whether I'd get in trouble with the police for moving a dead body before they'd had a chance to examine it."

Donald gave her a rueful smile. "Brains do funny things in extremity."

"Then I remember, as I was cradling him, that I got worried about his little fingers being so cold and stiff, like maybe he had frostbite. All I could think was how to thaw them out gently so he wouldn't have any pain or damage from the warming-up process. Even though I knew he was dead and that's why he was stiff, all of him, not just his fingers."

"When I took him from you," said Donald, "to lay him in the ambulance, he was all stiff, like you said, and I remember thinking this was my last chance to hug him, but he wouldn't hug me back. He was like that, so squirmy and energetic I was lucky to get more than half a second's hug out of him, and no amount of cajoling would ever make him give in. I got angry, thinking, this is our last chance ever, Asher, hug me back! But he was as unsnuggly as ever. I laid him down in the back of the ambulance feeling angry at him. I still feel awful about that."

Carmichael let out a long sigh and leaned her head on his shoulder. "I get it," she said. "I'm angry at him, too. Except when I'm angry at Saul for not noticing that he snuck out, or my parents and yours for the exhausting day so we all slept through it, or at myself for not knowing he could do something like this, or at God, or George Pohl, or the church, or life, or death, or the devil... I like the anger better. It's better than being sad. But at this very moment I feel nothing, and that's even better than anger. Though I don't know what kind of mother I am that I can be sitting here feeling nothing."

"I think our reservoirs of emotion have been drained dry," said Donald. "Don't worry. They'll fill up again, and sooner than we want."

They remained together in flattened, companionable silence until the cold got the better of them.

Back inside, Carmichael enveloped Saul in her arms and asked him what kind of cake he would like for his birthday. He said "chocolate" as if in surprise that there could be any other answer.

So Carmichael phoned Sandra and asked her to add cocoa powder and extra unsalted butter to the week's groceries, her first phone call since Christmas. It took another day of alternately sad and angry conversation with Donald to decide to give Asher's presents to Saul—"or else they will sit in the closet forever, you know they will, because neither of us will ever have the heart to give them away or even tear the paper off"—and this thought was so terrible that it took both of them out for several hours.

On the morning of Saul's birthday, Carmichael noticed Kitty's existence again and invited her, in a tone so humble that Donald felt sickened on her behalf, to help make the birthday cake. What has Kitty been doing all this time? he wondered. He'd practically forgotten about her. He listened with one ear toward the kitchen to Kitty's steady patter, relating in excruciating detail the plot of all the fairy tales she'd been reading and how they had been bowdlerized by Disney with all the death and gore taken out. He could tell Carmichael was relieved that Kitty's talk required so little of her other than a minimum payment of attention.

Guests were ruled out without any need for discussion, including grandparents—though Judith and Frank had pleaded to come—but Kitty seemed determined to make it festive for Saul all the same. "He doesn't have anyone special anymore," she whispered sidelong to Donald. He knew at once it was not a thought she would express to her mother. Kitty rummaged around the drawers in the pantry until she found seven mismatched, half-burnt birthday candles and bugged Carmichael to get out the fancy cake stand. Saul extracted from his toy trunk a kazoo and party hats leftover from some other kid's birthday and brought them down to the living room. Donald set the presents in a heap in front of the TV but Saul rearranged them, thoughtfully, in a variegated pyramid.

Carmichael carried the cake out to the coffee table. Kitty followed, clutching a spray of four napkins wrapped around four forks in one hand and four rose-patterned china dessert plates in the other. While Carmichael went back for a long knife and the cake server, Kitty arranged the plates, forks, and napkins at the cardinal points of the coffee table. Saul peered over from his pyramid, crawled closer on all fours, and sat up at the far end of the table like a prairie dog poking its head aboveground.

Right as Carmichael returned, he said, "You forgot Asher's plate."

Carmichael, Donald, and Kitty froze in place and stared at him.

Saul giggled. "You're all making the same face," he said.

Donald looked to Carmichael, who looked back at him, the appeal in her eyes obvious. He knelt down by Saul. "Sweetie," he said softly, "you know Asher can't be with us for this."

"Sure he can," replied Saul.

Donald sat all the way down and pulled Saul into his lap. "I know it's really hard, honey," he whispered with a tender hug, "and it's easier to pretend it didn't happen. But Asher is not coming back. He's not coming to your party today."

Saul turned a bewildered face up to Donald. "But Daddy, he's already here."

Donald's eyes flitted up to Carmichael's, but she was petrified in place. "What do you mean, Saul?" he said, hating himself for the caution in his tone.

"Look, he's right there!" Saul pointed to the end of the couch.

Involuntarily Donald looked. So did Kitty and Carmichael.

"There's nobody there," Donald said.

Saul smiled. "Don't be silly, Daddy," he said. "I know Asher pretends he's invisible, but he isn't really." He stuck his hands on his hips, pushing Donald's embracing arms away in the process, and stuck out his tongue. "I see you, Asher! You don't fool me!"

Kitty broke. "There's nobody there, Saul!" she shouted at him. "You're making it up!"

"Nuh-uh!" Saul shouted back. "I see him right there!"

"I don't see him. Mommy doesn't see him. Daddy doesn't see him. And you don't see him either! You're lying! You're making it up!" She was red in the face and screaming now.

"I'm not! I'm not!" Saul screamed back. He burst into tears. "I'm not a liar! Asher is right there!"

"Stop saying that! He's not there! He's dead! You saw him dead yourself!" She lunged toward Saul, and the movement snapped Carmichael out of her stupor. She grabbed Kitty around the waist and yanked her back. Instantly Kitty collapsed and doubled over her mother's interlocking hands, an inhuman moan leaking out of her. Saul kicked and punched to get free of Donald, bellowing over and over, "I do see him! I'm not a liar! I do see him! I'm not a liar!" Donald held him back but nothing he could do, gentle or firm, could break the boy's hysteria. Carmichael angled Kitty around and half-walked, half-dragged her up the stairs and into her room. Donald hefted a still-fighting Saul and carried him, not to his own room with its ubiquitous vestiges of Asher, but into the guest room, and worked Saul and him both under the covers. Mother spent the rest of the afternoon with daughter, father with son, and only late, after a dinner of somebody's gift lasagna half-warmed in the oven, did they eat the cake, without candles and without singing.

After dinner Saul slid off his chair and opened the presents. He carefully detached and folded the wrapping paper from each, saying, "Here you go, Mommy, you can use it again." Then with overstuffed arms he hauled his new presents up toward his bedroom.

At the foot of the stairs, arms full of toys, Saul turned back. "Asher is really excited about the Micro Machines," he told his parents earnestly. "He says thank you, too."

CHAPTER EIGHT

February 1989

*There was besides something extremely moving
to see a man six feet high thus shed tears;
and they did not lessen the good opinion
I had entertained of him.*

It was the first day back for everyone. Saul submitted mildly to school clothes and a packed lunch, remarking that his teacher Mrs. Delve had probably missed him because he was the best at erasing the chalkboard. "But I'm kind of worried about Miss Bowden," he said confidentially to Carmichael. "Because Asher decided he's gonna stay invisible and she won't be able to see him. She'll think he's not there. I keep telling him he should stop being invisible all the time, but he won't listen to me."

Carmichael stared at Saul a moment and then said, "Well, good for you for trying."

Kitty was less willing to return to normalcy, or at least to school. She whined and sniffed and objected, but when she dared to say, "I just don't understand how you can think of going back to normal life without Asher in it," Carmichael gave her such a look that she flushed and fell silent. She said nothing more but was ready to leave the house ahead of schedule and volunteered to scrape the car free of snow and ice.

As soon as she disappeared through the door, Donald said softly, "Weren't you a little harsh with her?"

"I didn't say anything."

"You didn't need to. She's sad, is all."

"Yes, she's sad, but *that* wasn't sad. That was manipulative."

Donald's eyebrows expressed his surprise.

Carmichael nearly smiled, but not quite. She hadn't smiled in a month and a half, and even her husband's absurd ongoing belief in the wholesomeness of women couldn't quite crack her shell. "It won't do Kitty any good to use her grief for any purpose other than grieving," stated Carmichael. "Or me either. That's why we're all going back today, isn't it? Everyone's been generous giving us time. But it's back into the fray sooner or later, and at this point 'later' is only going to make it worse."

"Of course, I don't disagree. I'm just not sure Kitty can see that."

"She does. Her blush told us that."

He shrugged. "You know better than I do. Are *you* ready for today?"

"No," said Carmichael flatly. "But it doesn't matter, does it?"

He enfolded her in his arms and kissed her hair.

She pulled away before the tears could rise. "Have a good meeting with Al this morning. You two can finish up the brownies in the pan on the counter. Don't forget that you're the one picking up the kids from school today." They'd decided that Saul shouldn't go on the bus alone, not yet, so Kitty may as well ride along with him in the car, too.

At school Saul gave Carmichael a big hug before running off to join his friends. Her arms ached, not wanting to let him go, trying to squeeze a hug-by-extension from Asher out of Saul. Kitty barely looked at her and said only a terse "bye" before scooting out of the backseat. Carmichael watched her go, murmuring, "Don't you leave me now, too," but knowing all too well the dangers of any line of thought other than sheer survival, she pulled away and fixed her mind on Principles of Composition.

The students were docile in the extreme, and attentive. Alan and Tobias Gooch Teylow had covered the first several weeks of class for her, obviously telling the students why Dr. Abney was temporarily absent. Once inside the classroom she fell into a lecture as automatic as Tobias's, and as comforting; maybe that's why he did it. Her lifeless recitation didn't alienate or bore the students, but that was probably because they were so uncomfortably alert, watching her for any sign of breakdown, probing her demeanor to learn how you were supposed to deal with this most wretched of tragedies. By the time it was over, she figured, they took her for a cold-hearted witch, or maybe a robot.

She slipped out of the building before any well-meaning colleague could find her—one hurdle jumped was enough for the day—and tucked herself into the car. This semester Tuesdays and Thursdays were her long days, but on Monday mornings there was only the one class, so now, with that out of the way, the hours remaining till she could legitimately go back to sleep stretched out to an endless horizon, threatening in a way that the unoccupied time at home all through January had not. *That* was time out of time, excused, forgiven, without demands or expectations. Now, every minute brandished its second hand at her, admonishing her to the task of getting on with life as a bereaved mother. She was marked like Cain, the mark would never leave her, the mark was going to be set upon her brow always.

Well. Such a line of thought was dangerous and intolerable. Carmichael turned the key and blasted the heat. She could not go home yet. She could not stay in town. She felt sure that, even if not quite everyone in town had known her before, being a pastor's wife and all, they'd surely know her by now. She pointed the car onto the Shinhopple Turnpike and in minutes was beyond the compact node of civilization that was Shibboleth. The hills looked like stubbly cheeks, with the bristle of naked trees over a smooth white skin of snow.

"It sifts from leaden sieves,
It powders all the wood,
It fills with alabaster wool

The wrinkles of the road.
It makes an even face
Of mountain and of plain,—
Unbroken forehead from the east
Unto the east again,"

she quoted aloud.

She drove as slowly as she dared, as if the accident that took Asher's life had been in a car and not from a roof. "Though maybe it's myself I distrust," she said aloud, averting her eyes from the ditch at the side of the road.

For all Olutakli County's sparseness of population, the human presence never really came to an end, not with the abrupt and tidy demarcations she'd found so appealing in France. Americans couldn't make up their minds if they wanted to be in civilization or out of it, so in the countryside they inflicted upon themselves the worst of both worlds. She passed tidy trailer homes and wretched old farmhouses and geometric prefabs set at an unyielding angle to the curvaceous earth, as though a flock of suburban birds had lost a stray. She drove straight through Acernus, which the locals in ignorance or defiance of Latin phonics pronounced "*Ack*-er-niss." A dismal township due west of Shibboleth, its only attraction was the county's first and only Walmart. Just a quarter-mile down the road from the Walmart, and in plain view of it, sat one of the rare prized octagonal barns of upstate New York. It seemed a pity to undermine the integrity of the charming past with the shoddy present, but an octagonal barn did nothing to reanimate Acernus, while the Walmart was rewarded eagerly by the locals. Carmichael, too, on other occasions.

She drove on till she reached New Zutphen, the village at the center of the next township over. Originally little more than a hamlet of Dutch cheesemakers, it had gotten a new lease on life with the construction of the Tammany Canal in the early 1870s, which promised to bring trade and prosperity to the region. Victorian mansions promptly sprouted along Rensselaer Street, but New Zutphen ended up being exactly the last town the canal managed to reach, seventeen miles short of its intended goal at the Nekamisto River in Shibboleth. The town languished for another century until the whole place was reborn as a tourist destination, the only one of its kind in Olutakli County. The two stone arch bridges, a museum built around a farmhouse where a teenaged Millard Fillmore spent a summer, and a spate of boutiques kept the town financially afloat while the canal sank into obscurity.

Carmichael parked and sat in the still-warm car, working up the courage to get out. At last she did. She forced herself into each and every shop. One sold fabric and sewing notions for the unseen army of quilters that inhabited the desolate hills. Another sold fudge and fancy chocolates and colorful if unpalatable candies in glass jars; early in December, Carmichael had dropped in to buy a selection for decorating a gingerbread house on Christmas Day, a project abandoned for reasons so painfully obvious that she had to run out of the store before an untimely sob undid her. There was a shop that sold cards and porcelain figurines and stuffed animals, another that sold pastel polyester clothing for women of a certain age, still another "European" gifts that all looked to have been made in Taiwan. She bypassed both the deli and the Italian restaurant as incapable of pleasing her City standards, leaving only the health food café for lunch, "health food" evidently meaning that all the platters came with avocado and alfalfa sprouts. She tasted her food for the first time since—. The avocado was hard, the sprouts bitter, the overall effect dull. It seemed fitting.

When she got back into the car, the passenger seat was occupied.

"I was wondering when I'd see you again," Carmichael said, as she switched on the ignition.

The woman said nothing but rocked slightly in her seat, hands over her face.

"You must have scared all the others off," Carmichael went on, pulling out into the street. "I haven't heard so much as a whisper from them since—." Evidently sentences containing the word "since" couldn't be finished.

She drove back toward Shibboleth, making the occasional comment to her companion. "I'm always struck by how the same stretch of land looks different in reverse," she said at one point. Later, on the outskirts of Acernus, "I don't know how this hotel stays in business. Who ever comes here?"

They passed the octagonal barn and the Walmart. At the stoplight Carmichael looked to her right. "But are you an alternate *me*?" she asked bluntly. "You don't look quite as much like me as the others. Unless that's the point. Maybe *I* don't look much like me anymore, either."

A faint keening came out from behind the hands covering the woman's face.

The sound triggered a memory that replayed itself as Carmichael drove out of Acernus. Some years ago, back when they still lived in Maurset, North Dakota, the first Sunday after Christmas fell on the twenty-eighth, the Feast of the Holy Innocents. Donald, still in the first flush of escape from the ritual minimalism of his Holiness upbringing, had developed a particular fondness for the "lesser festivals," like the Visitation of Mary and Elizabeth, or the Presentation of the Augsburg Confession. So that particular year, just three days after the annual celebration of birth and motherhood and family and food, Donald had unleashed on his unsuspecting Norwegians a morbid tale of slaughtered babies.

The blowback was immense. The district president even had to come in and talk the congregation down. Donald—something of a holy innocent himself, as Carmichael thought at the time—could only reply in bewilderment, "But I didn't make it up. It's in the Bible." One sweet old lady snarled at him that the Bible was chock full of indecent things but that was no reason to talk about them in church. Donald was saved in the end because there were just enough remnants of Pietism in the congregation that the old lady's bald condemnation of Scripture elicited a counterattack, resolving itself in the firm affirmation of the right of the pastor to preach about anything he found in the good book, however shocking, repellent, or immoral.

As Carmichael had grown up with no holy writings whatsoever, she also had no expectations of what was or wasn't decently to be found therein. But even at the time, she'd noticed the painful contrast between the birth of the savior to his tender parents and the horrifying infanticide exacted upon his young fellows. And all this only to fulfill a prophecy—the horrible ones apparently requiring fulfillment as much as the hopeful ones—from dour old Jeremiah, who could not be pressed to say a kindly word if his life depended on it: "In Rama was there a voice heard, lamentation, and weeping, and great mourning, Rachel weeping for her children, and would not be comforted, because they are not."

"They are not." Such was the stark brutality of holy truth that had made the congregation in Maurset so angry. As if by not saying it, it wouldn't happen! Carmichael tried it out. "Asher is not. Asher is not." She could say it because it was information directed toward the woman on her right, who still did not show her face. Maybe this would provoke her into self-disclosure.

They rolled into Shibboleth. The college sat up high on the hill, the public school halfway down, both opposite Mt. Moriah and the parsonage. Carmichael passed the fire station, the occult shop (college students its principal patrons), a warehouse selling parts for farm equipment and four-wheelers. At a stop sign she glanced over at the Co-op and the penny dropped. She looked again at the woman in the passenger seat.

"Rachel."

A tiny inflection of the head.

"Rachel weeping."

The woman dropped her hands. She was like Carmichael, but not quite like. A transfiguration of grief had altered her.

She was also like the Rachel of the Co-op, but not quite like. Yet looking at her, Carmichael saw for the first time what the real Rachel had seen in herself: a Jewish face, an unmistakably Jewish face. Did it take grief to make one a Jew? Carmichael wondered. Even though it was only as a Christian that she'd come to know of Rachel weeping.

Carmichael was still at the stop sign but no one was behind her. She reached out for the hand that had fallen away from the weeping woman's face. She'd never tried to touch one of her alternate selves before. They were as insubstantial as the mist that spread over Shibboleth on damp summer mornings. But this one was solid, a solid incarnation of sorrow. Carmichael took her hand and comforted her. The other accepted it.

Then Carmichael withdrew her hand and drove the both of them home.

∽

Donald's first Sunday back had been fine. The congregation greeted the family with cautious kindness, Maypo cookies and Nanaimo bars, frozen venison neatly wrapped in white paper and masking tape. They said sincerely how sorry they were about "everything," how happy they were to have him and the family back, and if there was anything they could do, just let them know. Donald got through that Sunday's service with admirable calm, if just a hint of clinical detachment. Parishioners listened to his sermon with the avid attention of detective novel fans for hints and allusions to the recent tragedy, but unless said hints were cloaked in the discussion of how the Transfiguration accompanied Jesus' first revelation to his disciples of his impending demise on the cross, no such word was spoken. Pastor Donald was strong, Pastor Donald was sorrowful but moving on, Pastor Donald was giving them all permission to move on, too. They needn't feel obligated to speak about *it* every time they saw him. Everyone respected this display of spiritual leadership.

But just three days later came Ash Wednesday, and whatever stoic spirituality Pastor Donald was supposed to possess fractured in plain view of them all.

They'd recited and chanted their way through the usual liturgy until the time came to shuffle forward and receive the ashes. Kitty was both eager and sullen. To her great annoyance, Megan Moravsky had turned up at school with the ashes already on her lightly freckled forehead, because Catholics got theirs in the morning, not at night, so, after some stupid remarks from the other kids about the smudge of dirt on her face, Megan bore her religious exceptionalism like a gleaming crown of glory all day. Nobody knew that Kitty would get the exact same ashes at the end of the day, and from her own dad who was a pastor, which meant that *she* was a lot more religious than Megan could ever hope to be.

When it was their pew's turn, Kitty tugged Saul by the hand and marched him up to the altar rail. She and Carmichael formed a protective flank around him. Donald was approaching swiftly, his thumb plunging like a piston into the little silver pot of ash, carefully burned from last year's Palm Sunday branches and mixed with a drop of olive oil (this after learning, his first year as a pastor, that mixing ash with water produces caustic lye—a bit too vivid a reminder of death, even for Ash Wednesday). He recited rotely and unemotionally over each tarnished forehead, "From dust you came, and to dust you shall return." Just as he had always done, year after year, relishing the countercultural denial of the denial of death.

But then he came to Kitty. She looked up at him, eager for her badge and sorry only that Megan wasn't there to see it. As he brushed the ashes over her forehead, his voice faltered in its recitation. Kitty had seen her father cry a lot in the past two months, but never ever in church. The tremor in his words alarmed her.

He took a step to his left. Now he was looming over Saul. Saul looked up at him. He was so small compared to Donald's great height. Donald was dressed in a black cassock, the upbeat white of his alb set aside for the solemn occasion. He looked like the angel of death.

Kitty watched and waited, holding her breath. It was going to be bad, she knew it was going to be bad. The thumb wavered, hesitated. It did not want to draw the cross on the child. Kitty's entire field of vision was taken up by the blackened thumbprint that would not, could not, assign another son to death.

Saul felt none of this, Kitty could tell. He just kept looking up at their dad, patient, expectant.

She looked over at her mother. Carmichael, too, was riveted on the thumb, but she could not break out of the trance any more than Donald could.

Kitty realized it was up to her. "Daddy," she whispered. His eyes flickered back to her and blinked. "Do it," she hissed. Still the thumb hovered. Kitty felt a flush rising up over her skin, felt the whole congregation staring at them in this awkward tableau.

She couldn't take it any more. She reached up and grabbed her father's thumb and pushed it onto Saul's forehead. Donald was startled into action. "From dust you came," he muttered, and then, after only just too long a pause, as if a century's debate occurred within his head in a split second, he completed the line inaudible to any but the four of them, "and to dust you shall return."

Donald straightened up. Kitty exhaled in relief. They'd made it. She'd gotten him through. Once again, a kid to the rescue of unreliable adults. She felt a few motes of the ash on her forehead flake off and tickle her nose.

But then, just as Donald was reaching for Carmichael's forehead, Saul said loudly, "Daddy, you forgot to do Asher."

Kitty heard Ms. Gross the organist gasp. She felt the eyes of the people kneeling on either side of them at the altar rail swivel and stare. Saul pointed to his right, to a tiny space between him and Carmichael. Asher couldn't fit in there, thought Kitty.

Then she realized it was a ridiculous objection because Asher was dead, dead, dead.

"Saul," said Carmichael, in a voice halfway between warning and pleading.

Donald reached again for Carmichael, but Saul insisted, "Daddy, you have to do Asher!"

The dam was breaking now and nothing was to be done about it. Kitty saw Donald's eyes sweep around the sanctuary and take in the fearful expectation. He looked down at Saul and calculated his stubbornness. Quickly he reached into the empty space and swiped a cross. "From dust you came, and to dust you shall return." Saul smiled around at everyone, his duty fulfilled.

But the doing of it broke Donald. When he applied the ashes to Carmichael he was crying, and she was, too. Kitty didn't, if only for the shame of the thing. She scooted Saul back to their pew full of rage and rebuke, but he didn't understand and told her not to shove or Asher would get smushed. Donald wept openly through the last of the applications of ash and then Al Beck, trepidation and sweat leaking in equal measure out of every pore, snuck up behind the altar rail and offered to finish the service, which he did while Donald slumped in his chair off to the side, face in hands, smudging his own cheek with the leftover ash on his thumb.

The moment the service was over, everyone left as fast as they could, and as silently. And when a snowstorm walloped Olutakli County late Saturday night, the parishioners of Mt. Moriah universally regarded it as divine authorization to cancel church the next morning without regret.

~

Dale Mayer was bundled in archaeologically deep layers of long underwear, flannels, and camouflaged hunting gear, a bright orange cap pulled down low over his ears and forehead. Instead of a hunting rifle he clutched two equally orange flags—shockingly bright against the endlessness of white snow, light gray sky, and dark gray trees—with which he waved along the approaching cars up his driveway and into the front yard to park.

It was excessive, not least of all because the cars arrived at intervals of three minutes or more and a simple pointed mitten would have done the trick. But this was Dale's happiest day of the year. His dairy barns stood long, cavernous, and empty, he despised his job and the delinquents he transported even more, he was a bundle of energy and skill that nobody wanted or needed—except on this one day, when half or more of the congregation of Mt. Moriah turned out to help with the sugaring. On this day he was impresario, presider, and high priest. Even lifelong locals never failed to be caught up in the magic of turning sap into syrup.

For all that, a certain pall threatened to disrupt the proceedings. Earlier in the day his wife Arlene had given him a warning while she set up the huge coffee percolator and slid trays of maple-walnut spirals in and out of the oven.

"You better keep an eye on Pastor Donald today," she said. "He's a wreck."

"Of course he's a wreck," said Dale. "Who wouldn't be?"

"You saw how he came apart at the Ash Wednesday service. He was fine, and then he wasn't. He and Carmichael both will be trying hard, but they could snap at any second."

"What am I supposed to do about it?" barked Dale, overwhelmed all at once with an emotional responsibility he felt unequipped to handle.

Arlene gave him a look as if to suggest astonishment that, after all these years and four kids, he still hadn't figured out the obvious. *"You keep them busy."*

"Oh," he said. He was quiet a moment. "I can do that."

Carloads of well-insulated parishioners rolled onto the snowy lawn, with the notable exception of George Pohl and his wife Ruth, who attended Sunday services but otherwise avoided congregational extracurriculars. They set aside encrusted boots and packed into the farmhouse's wide living room to warm up before traipsing into the forest. Arlene circulated with coffee and sweets and low-voiced instructions to keep an eye on the pastor and his family, to keep the conversation light, to keep all four of them busy.

"All *four* of them," remarked Eunice. "Not all *five* of them." Her husband Richard averted his eyes. He still went to Second Reformed and felt a little out of place among all these Mt. Moriah people, though chances were good that at least a few of them were in the market for a new sofa.

"Now that's exactly the sort of thing *not* to say," Arlene scolded her.

"I'm sorry, no, of course not," twittered Eunice.

The Abneys turned up half an hour late, as if giving the parishioners time to work out their game plan. The greetings were jolly to an almost but not quite false degree. Saul in particular came in for praise of his stylish red snowsuit with a picture of Hefty Smurf on the stomach. Unfortunately, to this Saul replied, "It's pretty nice, but I like Asher's better, because it's black and has G. I. Joe on it, and Mommy never lets *me* get G. I. Joe," pointing to the vacant space at his right. There was a loud silence as everyone dreaded a repeat of the Ash Wednesday debacle. Arlene, however, intuited that this was not unusual behavior for Saul, so she interposed with a spiral bun and the room reverted to determinedly cheerful chitchat.

It was no small matter to detach the crowd from their snack and get them all back into snow boots and heavy jackets, but in time it was accomplished and Dale summoned them to follow him up the hill into the forest. They proceeded in single file along the track he had beaten down. Despite the depth of the snow, it was already so well-worn that blades of yellow grass could be seen underfoot. By the time they reached the glade of sugar maples, all of them were managing in their own fashion the winter paradox of being too cold and too hot at the same time.

Dale turned around in front of the doorless entryway to his

sugar shack, its wooden slats inside and out as gray as the trees since it stood open to the elements. Folks drew up around him and waited, their faces obscured by puffs of breath.

"It's real simple," he said. "Fan out in all directions, and wherever you find a bucket check to see if it's more than half full. If so, haul it on back here and pour it into the evaporator." He thumbed behind him to the stainless steel vat, a huge rectangular vessel mounted on concrete blocks. "I already got a good hundred twenty gallons collected from the past few days that I'll dump in to get things started."

"Wow, that's a lot!" shouted someone from the crowd.

"Not so fast," said Dale. He loved this moment. "You know how much syrup you get outta that much sap? *Three gallons.* That's it. So look lively there, folks! Bring along the buckets and we'll pour them in as we go. I'll get the fire started now and, say, Pastor Donald, wanna help me?"

The pastor obliged, and the rest of the company tramped off every which way, eager as children on an Easter egg hunt. Kitty was promptly swallowed up by compassionate ministrations of Lisa, Tammy, and Michelle. Saul set to work on a snowman with a few other boys. Carmichael, abandoned, looked around and arbitrarily chose to seek out a bucket of sap off to her right.

Sandra caught up with her and put a friendly arm around her shoulders. "How're you doing, my dear?" she asked.

Carmichael gave a sideways smile and shrugged. "I'm either thinking about it, or trying so hard *not* to think about it that it's basically the same as thinking about it."

Sandra patted her and gave an understanding smile. "I see some buckets up ahead."

The larger trees had three spiles stuck in at chest height, the smaller ones a single spile. Carmichael and Sandra lifted the blue-gray metal lids off the buckets to peer in. Every bucket they checked was more than halfway full, so they lifted them down, two at a time, and trudged back. It took concentration to keep the buckets balanced without sloshing, and to keep their footing over the snow and uneven terrain beneath. Carmichael found herself appreciative of the sheer physical effort and discovered she could go minutes at a time without gnawing on her grief. She timed her footsteps to bring the buckets into the shack when no one else was around, except Dale and Donald squatting over the fire, which before long worked itself up to a tremendous blaze, the heat shocking compared to the nip of cold outside. By the time she delivered her third pair of buckets, the two men were barely visible through the swaddling cloths of steam. Donald loomed into view like the ghost of sugar shacks past, wielding a huge metal spoon flecked with the scum he'd been instructed to skim off the surface of the boiling liquid. He hummed a few bars of what Carmichael recognized to be a hymn that he loved but the congregation at large (and not just Marilyn the organist) had rejected as too hard to sing. He then chanted aloud the last line, "And all the house was filled with billowing smoke."

"Ezekiel?" she guessed.

"Isaiah," he corrected.

It was the first moment of unguarded—well, *happiness* was too strong a word for it. Maybe contentment. Maybe peace. It lifted Carmichael. She gave him a very small smile and turned to replace the buckets and collect a new pair.

But the moment of peace turned out to be treacherous. For as she trudged back through the snow, it came over her again, with the force of an avalanche, what she'd feared almost from the first moment after she'd found Asher: that someday she would be happy without him. The palest joy, the slightest serenity, a single moment without the torture of grief proclaimed itself a betrayal of her littlest one. That moment of peace was, in fact, collusion with death and evil and tragedy, because it accepted what their family had become. She at the very least, she as his mother, she who had borne him in her own body and birthed him and nursed him—*she* could not allow the slow drift of time and her own need for survival to soothe her grief.

And here it was not even two months later and already she had betrayed him, conceded him to the embrace of death, and taken the first step toward the rest of her life without him.

By the time Sandra caught up with her, Carmichael was standing rigid, her back against the sugar maple on which she'd rehung the buckets, eyes screwed shut. She willed herself not to cry and put the congregation through another scene like on Ash Wednesday. She did not want to move on from her grief, but she did not want to accept their sympathies again and again and again, either. The tortured isolation of misery seemed the only faithful response to her lost child.

"Hey there, are you all right?" Sandra whispered.

Carmichael tried to speak but could only shake her head.

"I know, it's terrible, it's just terrible," Sandra said. Her thickly mittened hand clutched for Carmichael's. "It's OK, you can let it out," but Carmichael shook her head again, clamping her eyes against the tears, willing away the horrible mess of the situation.

"Not here," she breathed. She opened her eyes and brushed away what few tears had slipped out anyway.

"I'm worried about you," Sandra said. She turned to stare at Carmichael's profile. Carmichael kept her eyes fixed on the middle distance, somewhere beyond the edge of the maple glade but not all the way to the opposite hillside. She felt Sandra's eyes on her cheek and it felt like fire. "This is such a heavy burden for you to bear."

"There's nothing to do but bear it," Carmichael said. Her voice came out like a croak, as if the tears denied passage out of her eyes had congregated in her throat instead.

"Of course you need to work through your grief," said Sandra, her words smooth and thick like freshly boiled syrup coating the back of a spoon. "I just think there are ways it could be easier on you."

"I'm not sure I want it any easier."

"You don't need to make it heavier than it is."

"It couldn't be heavier than it is. Anyway, at this point, I'm not sure a therapist would make any difference. It's not like I don't know what the problem is."

"I wasn't thinking of *that*," said Sandra.

There was a pregnancy about Sandra's pause that stirred something deep in Carmichael's gut. Overwhelmed as she was by other emotions, she declined to turn her attention toward it. She said instead, "Did you mean like a support group? There's one at St. Mary's, Donald told me about it, it meets once a month, but I haven't been up for that yet, either."

Sandra stepped around so she was facing Carmichael straight on. Carmichael felt herself push back against the tree ever so slightly and chided herself for it. Was she so proud of her grief that she refused to accept the kindness of a friend, in fact the closest thing she had to a real friend in Shibboleth? Shame piled onto the heap of oppressive emotions. Carmichael made herself look into Sandra's eyes, trying to discipline herself into accepting the kindness.

Sandra said, "I know what's tormenting you."

At once Carmichael's mind was populated with any number of torments. Her hard sleep that night, the unattended ladder, countless failures of parental oversight that had allowed Asher to become reckless, every single harsh word or momentary escape or hired babysitter when she should've known how extremely proscribed was to be her time with her baby boy...

"It's just intolerable that his body is still there in that mausoleum, far from you, waiting for the weather to warm up enough for a burial."

The startled look that flashed in Carmichael's eyes seemed to confirm to Sandra that she was on the right track.

"You aren't getting the closure you need. The funeral wasn't enough; he needs to be laid to rest. *You* need him to be laid to rest. Of course, as his mother, you can't even begin to feel any peace until his remains are also at peace. It's natural and understandable. I hate to see you agonized like this."

Carmichael furnished a faltering smile. "Yes, but the weather doesn't care about my agony."

"That's just the thing," said Sandra, ever more in earnest now. She squeezed hard on Carmichael's mitten, still gripped in her own hand. "There's no need to hold out for spring, not anymore."

Carmichael stared. Her gut prickled again, insistent that she pay attention.

"Now that we have the columbarium, is what I mean. You can have him right there at home with you. He'll be at peace. You'll be at peace, and Pastor Donald and the children. It's OK, Carmichael, it really is," she whispered affectionately.

"I'll think about it," Carmichael temporized. Shock galvanized her back into control of herself. She pulled her hand free and peeled her back off the tree bark. "But look, we're falling behind, there are lots more buckets left to collect," she burbled.

"Of course, yes, let's get back to work," said Sandra. She patted Carmichael on the back like an obedient pupil.

∽

Carmichael waited until the children were in bed before ranting to Donald.

"Can you believe her? Can you *believe* her? I thought she was my friend, but no, it turns out I'm just a conveniently bereaved mother she can use to advance the cause of her goddamn columbarium!"

They were huddled in the pantry, which, being too far from the woodstove or any of the radiators, never warmed up in winter. Carmichael was etching aggressive patterns in the frost on the windowpanes with her fingernail. Donald leaned back against the counter and rested his head on the cupboards behind him.

"I keep trying to come up with some plausible explanation," he said, "to put the best construction on it, but it does seem to be breathtakingly insensitive, at best."

"Oh, it's more than insensitive. It's propaganda. She's using us, our tragedy, to advance her cause."

"Are you sure that's what's going on? She and Alan have always been so good to us—"

Carmichael interrupted him, just shy of a snarl, "How can you think it's anything else? How can you take this so calmly and even try to defend her?"

"Your outrage is sufficient for the both of us," he said, with the mildest of smiles. "I'm not saying I like or approve anything she said. It just seems extremely out of character for her."

"I'm not at all sure I haven't just seen her *true* character."

"I'm just thinking, remember how relieved the two of them were after All Saints', when we interred his mother's ashes? She could just be thinking you'll get the same kind of relief. All I'm saying is, how she dealt with *her* grief could be blinding her to how you deal with *yours*. People are always giving out the advice that helped them but isn't actually useful for someone else in the same situation."

Carmichael left off her patterning in the ice and turned around to face Donald directly. She realized she was shaking all over, the cold and the rage and the grief weaving a braid that bound her. She breathed deeply. "I know that what you're saying sounds reasonable. It *is* reasonable. I know that I am being *un*reasonable, and I know that my sadness makes me kind of crazy."

Donald waited.

"And yet, for all that…" She collected herself. It mattered to get this right. "I don't know how to express it exactly, but I saw something in her, when she was talking to me, that I had seen before but never let myself notice or acknowledge. I don't even know what it was, to be honest. But it unnerved me, Donald. It almost—it almost frightened me. Yes, that's it." It was a relief to identify it. "She frightened me."

"Was it *her* that frightened you, or just the suggestion of—well, of cremating Asher's remains?"

Hearing Donald say the words was its own kind of shock, but Carmichael forced herself to think through his question. She turned to pace up and down the short extent of the pantry. After three laps, she stopped in front of him and said, "Of course I didn't like the thought of cremation. But that isn't what upset me. Really, I don't think that was it."

"All right, then," Donald replied. He reached out and took Carmichael's hand. The same gesture, yet nothing like Sandra's doing the same. "I don't really know what to do, now, other than to keep an eye on, well, on *her*, I guess."

"OK," said Carmichael. She felt flat after her outburst, unmoored without a plan of counterattack.

"But, without agreeing with her, she does indirectly raise a point we haven't talked about yet," Donald said. His tone was careful. It grieved Carmichael that he felt he had to be careful with her, though she could hardly blame him. "The thing is, if we bury Asher here—or anywhere—he's there forever. I know we talked just, just before, about staying here for the long-term, now that you know they're already planning on granting you tenure. But now, well…"

She nodded. "It's an open question," she said. "Whether we want to, or can stand to, stay here. After everything."

"If we bury him here, will we be willing to go somewhere else—without him?"

"I can't even stand to go forward in life *here* without him," breathed Carmichael. As the rage subsided, the sorrow began to rise again, and on its tide more tears.

"I'm not at all saying I want to do this, only that if we cremated him instead, we could bring him with us. If we decide to move on."

Carmichael dropped his hand and paced again. She studied her African violets. Only one was blooming, white with an iridescent sparkle, as if dusted with the tackiest craft-store glitter.

"I can't even figure out why I am so intensely averse to it," she said at last.

"Because Sandra suggested it?"

"No, I'm sure I was averse to it before. I mean, in the sense that I never even considered cremation. It wasn't even on the table. Am I being superstitious, Donald? I remember you said someone on the council was worried that Jesus couldn't raise the cremated on the Last Day, and someone else was like, if Jesus can manage people who drown or get blown up, cremation shouldn't pose any more of a challenge. Right?"

"Yeah. Though I think the early Christians did reject cremation, which was the usual way of doing things in the Roman empire, and buried their dead in the catacombs instead. I guess to give witness to their hope in the resurrection of the body. I suppose it was only later that they were really forced to think through the biology and physics of dead bodies and resurrection."

"I know I should regard their attitude as unscientific, but I get it somehow, in a way I didn't before. I really don't mind other people cremating their dead, and I don't think they'll be denied resurrection, but somehow..." She looked right at him. "I can't do it. I *can't*. I can't send his little body to the fire, awful as it is to have him waiting it out in the mausoleum till spring. Even if it means staying here forever. Oh, God, will my future self hate me for tethering us here forever? But then, I hate my future self already, because she will be even more used to life without Asher than I am..."

Her words ran out. Donald held her, and they wept together again, as they had so many times, a routine expenditure of accumulated grief.

As they wiped their eyes and noses with the palms of their hands, chuckling a little at the strings of snot, Donald said, "I don't want to, either. I want his body laid in the earth here next to us. We don't need to know how long we'll be here. It's enough for now to be next to him."

"It is enough," she echoed.

They stood together, quietly, in recognition of something

great and good unfurling in the unlikely space of a drafty pantry in the aftermath of a hard day. The clear and conscious decision about Asher's body was a decision to go on living, in a way that returning to work and church and school was not. And, at the same time, it was not a betrayal of Asher but a new acceptance of him, accepting the dead and lost Asher into the new life the four of them were forced to live without him, giving him a space and a place within it.

With that was returned to them something else they had lost as a couple, and it came as an unexpected but welcome gift. "Come on," said Carmichael, taking Donald's hand, and she led him upstairs to the bedroom.

∽

Carmichael almost laughed aloud at the sight of her mother descending from the Greyhound. Judith was dressed with the same elegant care as always, hair coiffed, perfectly symmetrical pink pearls wreathed around her neck. She smoothed her twinset before angling her much too narrow high-heeled pumps down the uneven grating of the bus steps. After the hugs and kisses, Carmichael asked, and not for the first time, "Whatever possessed you to do this, Mom?"

Judith exuded an air of quiet dignity as she handed over her luggage ticket to the driver, who unceremoniously dropped a floral suitcase at her pointy beige feet. Carmichael grabbed it and led the way toward the parking lot. "What I don't understand," said Judith, "is why you refuse to believe that I wanted to spend time with my daughter and her family, and keep looking for an ulterior motive."

"Oh, Mom, it's not that," protested Carmichael, "it's the *bus*. I know you don't like to drive this far without Dad, but you won't even take the bus in the City. I remember very distinctly that day when I was thirteen or fourteen, and Dad came home reporting that his business was going so well that he'd finally reached some kind of income threshold he'd been aiming for, and your response was, it's only taxis for me from now on. And as far I as I know, you've never darkened the door of a bus since."

"No, it's the subway I avoid at all costs. I can't stand the smell or the wind. I *do* take the bus," she wavered, "...sometimes."

"All right, all right." Carmichael unlocked the trunk and hefted the suitcase in place, then unlocked the passenger door.

Instead of getting in, Judith turned to face Carmichael directly. "I didn't want to make you pick me up at the airport," she said in a rush.

Carmichael's puzzlement showed on her face. "Why not?"

"Because, you know, it was because of the delays and the late night that..."

"Oh, Mom." Carmichael suddenly melted toward her mother for insisting on a ridiculously uncomfortable bus trip just to avoid the slight association of the airport with the family tragedy. She squashed her mother in a hug, heedless of the twinset. "What a silly, thoughtful thing to do." Judith squeezed back, squeezed hard, holding on to Carmichael as if she, too, might abruptly tumble off a church roof to her death. They released each other slowly, teary but not undone.

Once Carmichael had navigated them out of the lot, she said, "Well, since we're already here in Kuhsota, should we stop somewhere for a bite to eat? You probably didn't get any lunch on the way up."

"I brought a little something along to eat, so I'm fine. Actually, I have lox in my bag that should probably get into a fridge soon. Maybe we could just pick up a cup of coffee."

Carmichael grimaced. "The only to-go coffee in Kuhsota is at Wendy's, and I wouldn't recommend it. There's a pretty cute diner on the edge of town with decent coffee, though. We could could sit down for a cup there and be in and out fast enough."

Judith agreed, though once in place she could not resist the waitress's alluring description of the coconut cream pie. "It's always been my great weakness," she said after placing her order.

"I know," said Carmichael. She ordered a gigantic cinnamon bun, her own personal weakness.

They chatted of mild and unimportant things through their coffee and dessert, Judith apologizing again that Frank couldn't get away just at the moment to visit, but he sent his love and hoped to see them soon. After abandoning an attempt to capture the last crumbs with the tines of her fork, Judith settled herself and took a deep breath. Carmichael instantly recognized the sign that her mother was about to unload something heavy. Oh, God, no more surprises, she thought despairingly.

"I found a book," Judith began.

This was so surprising, set against Judith's gravity and Carmichael's dread, that the latter let loose an eruption of laughter.

"What?" challenged Judith.

"Nothing. A book is a great thing to find. My favorite thing to find, actually."

Judith squared her shoulders and started again. "It was in the, well, in the Judaica section."

Carmichael's guard rose again.

"I was just passing through, honestly, because it was between the foreign language section and the magazines."

"You don't need to apologize to me for looking at books in the Judaica section."

"Well, I thought I might," said Judith, with the subtlest of rebukes. Carmichael could not deny that she deserved it. "Anyway, it was on Jewish mourning practices. It caught my eye and I picked it up. Because of. You know."

"I know." Carmichael pointed her face down to her almost-empty cup of not-terrible diner coffee and tasted the remnants of sweet sticky cinnamon on her lips.

"I didn't pick it up right away, I promise you that."

"Really, Mom, it's OK."

Judith shook her head. "It's just that, until that moment, I never really made the connection. About Asher, I mean. Silly, isn't it? After everything—after last fall, and you being so upset about Kitty. I was thinking about myself that way, and your dad, and you and Kitty, but somehow the boys—I suppose it's because they were too young to talk to about it. But I looked at that book and suddenly a phrase jumped into my head: 'Another dead Jew.' That's what Asher is, now. It just, it just hit me all over again, in a way I hadn't felt it before."

Carmichael exhaled the air she hadn't even realized she'd been holding in her lungs. "That's really heavy."

"I mean, he *is*, or *was*, I mean he *is* a Jew, isn't he? Because I am and you are and he is your child. Even though he never got…" Judith's voice dropped low, and she looked furtively around her.

"What?" said Carmichael, bewildered.

Judith whispered, "*Circumcised.*"

"Oh," murmured Carmichael. "No. No, he didn't."

Judith rubbed her napkin over a smudge on the formica tabletop. "Well, it's a bit irregular, is all. But that doesn't make him any less a Jew."

"I guess not."

"It doesn't, because it goes through the mother's line. Anyway. I don't know how long I stood there staring at the spine of that book," Judith ventured afresh, "but at last I took it off the shelf to look through it. I want you to know that I have never, *ever* read or even picked up a book on a Jewish topic before."

Carmichael hid a smile as a scene flashed into her mind. Asher as he might have been ten years on, caught with a copy of Playboy stashed under his pillow, swearing up and down he had never, ever looked at pornography before. This particular lost future didn't pain Carmichael, but it did give her a wry buoyancy. She assured herself that she'd no doubt have that very exchange with Saul at some future date. And in the meanwhile, it was pretty funny that her mother was acting just the same.

"Well, what I found out, just paging through it, you understand—"

"You didn't buy it?"

"No," said Judith, an expression of genuine shock on her face. Apparently there was a dramatic difference between perusing a book on Jewish matters and actually purchasing it. "But I did read this little bit about a thing called shiva. It's what you do after someone close in the family dies."

"I know. Do you remember my high school friend Annie? Her father died our freshman year, and her family sat shiva for a week. She showed me her black ribbon after."

"Yes, exactly. Well, I guess you're supposed to do it immediately after the… after it happens, you know, it helps the family grieve and cope in the immediate aftermath, and friends bring food and things like that."

"Makes sense."

"But it also assumes that the person gets buried right away. It's the week following the burial. So my point is, Asher still hasn't been buried yet."

"Hopefully next month, but maybe not till April," Carmichael said. The pain momentarily held at arm's length was migrating inward again. She tried to push it back.

"So that's another irregular thing, but I was thinking…" Judith trailed off. She rubbed at her dark nail polish with the same vigor as the smudge on the tabletop. Then she looked up. "I don't know if your dad is going to do it, I did mention it to him, but *I'm* going to do it. After Asher is buried, I'm going to sit shiva for him for seven days."

"That's beautiful, Mom," mumbled Carmichael. Her mind was torn in so many different directions at once she didn't know which trail to follow. For the moment, all she could safely do was register the sincerity of Judith's desire to grieve well for her grandson.

"And apparently," said Judith, "the ideal way to do it is in the house of the deceased. So I'm running this by you now, well in advance, because of course we'll both be up for the burial, but I was hoping it would be all right with you if I stayed the full week after, so I could do this. Your dad might leave sooner to get back to work," she added, as if this were a tremendous concession.

"Yes, of course, Mom, you can stay as long as you like, and I'm sure we'll all need your support anyway," Carmichael tipped out in a steady stream, all the while trying to get a grip on her own reaction.

One part was aggravated and offended that, yet again, her mother was injecting this abrupt new interest in being Jewish into her own life, and over such a painful matter, too. Was it like Sandra pushing cremation? she asked herself. She thought about it. No, it wasn't, not at all. Judith was trying to grieve well for herself, not extort something out of Carmichael's grief to advance her own agenda.

All at once, the prospect of her mother sitting shiva gave Carmichael a tremendous feeling of comfort. She tried to imagine herself doing the same, like Annie in high school. That didn't work, not even in her mind's eye. It fit badly. However unlikely a candidate for Jewish piety her mother seemed to be, she wore it better than Carmichael did. It was in some way the real thing.

"Thank you," Judith breathed, taking Carmichael's hand for a moment. Then, as if enormously relieved to have gotten through that hurdle, she ran headlong into the next topic. "Speaking of which, your dad has located a whole pile of letters and documents and things from his parents and mine, way in the back of the attic, boxes we'd never looked through before."

"Oh, really? What have you found?"

"It's hard to say, because they're mostly handwritten and it's not so easy to figure out the cursive they used, and also they're all in Estonian, which neither your dad nor I have spoken or even thought in for decades, really. So we're working on it, but it's slow going."

"Is it coming back to you? The Estonian, I mean?"

"Bit by bit. The brain really is a funny thing. Your dad will read a sentence out loud to me, and my first reaction will be, 'I understood that!' before I even register *what* I've understood. There are all these words I never could have called up, but when I hear them, I know them. Not all of them, of course. Actually, the reason I went to the bookstore that day when I saw the book I told you about, it was because I was looking for an Estonian-English dictionary. They didn't have one, so I ordered one. That should help."

"So no leads yet on why exactly they left, or whether we have any family there?"

"Well, no, nothing concrete. But we can read between the lines, can't we? Not many Jews have family in that part of the world anymore. I'm sure that's why my parents, and your dad's, never talked about it. Even if they didn't know for sure, they could make an educated guess. It must have been too painful to even think about."

"I imagine so." Carmichael allowed her thoughts to flit, for a few seconds, to this also never-mentioned-at-home Jewish topic. The Holocaust was something she'd learned about in high school history classes. It was horrible, shocking, evil. But not something that touched her in any way.

But now it might. Another dead Jew, she thought, and then shook the thought away.

"Time to head home," she said and stepped up to the cash register to pay the bill.

CHAPTER NINE

March 1989

*We know, properly speaking, no strangers;
this is every person's country.*

At four in the morning, long before the March sunrise, Jackie, Al, and Sandra pulled into the Mt. Moriah parking lot but stayed put inside their cars, motors running, staving off the moment of facing the cold. The snowdrifts, shoved up against church and parsonage and dusted with the latest flurry, stood luminous and sparkling in the headlights. Even more snow lay banked against the near end of the cemetery. Winter conspired to keep the poor little pastor's boy in the mausoleum as long as possible.

The snorting roar of another vehicle clambering its way uphill broke through the lulling putt-putt of idling engines. It was Richard Thyssen, skillfully navigating his sofa delivery van around the icy turns. Behind him crept Eunice in their sedan. Even before they came to a stop, Pastor Donald shuffled out of the house, feeling his way forward one sliding foot at a time, his pastor satchel slapping at his hip from its long thick strap. Al remembered Dale dismissing it as a "man purse" but Al, for his part, thought it made the pastor look both classy and scholarly, traits that he himself could never hope to possess.

What Al did have, however, was an insurance business. That was how the delegation could travel in Mr. Thyssen's van with Al himself and Pastor Donald taking turns at the wheel, a well-crafted policy being the only way that stingy Dutchman who wasn't even a Lutheran could be talked into it. Somehow nobody even suggested that any of the women take a hand at driving; that would've been a dealbreaker for sure. Al found this funny, since nobody knew better than an actuarial expert how much more dangerous men were behind the wheel than women. But the goal had been to persuade this Thyssen fellow, not to reason with him.

In the glare of the headlights, Al wrapped up the paperwork with Richard, who exchanged keys with Eunice and drove off in the sedan. Al took the driver's seat and the rest of them piled in, popping the fold-down seats into upright position. Jackie could barely contain her excitement. She'd arranged to have the day off two months in advance. Sandra and Al had flexible schedules and Eunice didn't work anyway, so the four of them plus the pastor formed the welcoming party traveling to JFK airport to collect Fritz Hartmann, pastor from East Germany and great-nephew of Sabine Feuerlein.

Fritz was due in at eleven, which gave them more than enough time to anticipate ill-favored weather and traffic jams, not to mention regular pit stops for toilets, coffee, and breakfast. They reached the parking lot at five minutes to eleven but had to loiter outside of passport control and customs for a full hour and a half—ready to despair that Fritz had never boarded the plane at all, no doubt kidnapped by the Stasi and deported to some Siberian gulag—until there emerged a solitary figure of middling height, thick dark hair, rather more than a five o'clock shadow, and chunky black eyeglasses that took the Americans back a decade and a half. He carried two huge suitcases, each fastened with the equivalent of a pair of belt buckles. On his back hung a rucksack made of canvas pitched on an aluminum frame. It could not be other than their guest, though Jackie murmured to Sandra, "I thought he'd be blond."

Fritz had no trouble recognizing them—the poster board with his name hand-blocked across it probably helped—and bounded forward with a huge grin. "Your government trusts me not!" was his first declaration. He looked positively gleeful. "They have questioned me more than thirty minutes! They have searched all my bags. And you see, that is no small job! But when they asked what I am to do in America, I said, 'I am come to declare the gospel of the Lord Jesus!' Ha! Your government hears this with so much gladness as our government." He dropped his bags and leapt toward Donald, whose role was obvious on account of the clerical collar. "My brother pastor!" he shouted, yanking the much taller Donald into a bear hug. "And who are your friends?" he asked, swiveling toward the others, as if he were the host and not the guest.

Each in turn passed through an equally exuberant introduction to Fritz, each captivated by his charm, Jackie positively besotted despite being fifteen years his senior and noting, instantly, the plain band on the ring finger of his right hand. She inquired as soon as it seemed not indecent as to this untraditional choice of hand and learned, to her unsurprised disappointment, since men were always a disappointment anyway, that Germans generally wore their wedding bands on the right, and Lenchen would not like it if he switched, even at risk of confusing Americans. "Lenchen, from Magdalena, like Martin Luther's daughter, yes?" he put in a loud aside to Donald.

"Very good," agreed Donald. "My daughter is Katharina, after his wife, though we call her Kitty."

"I will call her Käthe!" declared Fritz. Everything he said was in the manner of a declaration. On the way back to the van, this included declarations about the size of the airport and the wonder of seeing both bananas *and* oranges for sale, inexpensively, at the several newspaper and tobacco kiosks they passed. "Only on Christmas in the DDR," he declared.

"Day-day-air?" Eunice whispered to Al.

"I think it's what they call East Germany, *in* East Germany," Al whispered back.

Jackie, pausing at a kiosk for a pack of cigarettes, added six oranges to her order and passed them around.

"Thank you, my new American friend!" Fritz bellowed. "You have given me an early Christmas!"

Jackie beamed and thought maybe communists weren't so bad after all.

Fritz's wonder only got louder as they fought through the everlasting snarl of Queens traffic. Despite the cold and, eventually, the speed, they could not dissuade him from rolling down his window to point a clunky Praktica camera at the Whitestone Bridge. Nor could they persuade him that it was *not* the Brooklyn Bridge. "This is the Bronx, dear," said Eunice fondly.

Oranges notwithstanding, by the time they made it to Route 17 ("This is New Jersey?" gasped an astonished Fritz, unable to believe his good luck at adding a second U.S. state to his lifetime tally so soon) everyone was starving. Pastor Donald pulled into the lot of a Lucky Panda. Fritz narrated them through the all-you-can-eat buffet, his plate piled high more from curiosity than gluttony. He bit into a cream cheese wonton, eyed its creamy white contents suspiciously, and muttered, "Quark?" All five Americans burst into laughter, Jackie explaining that he sounded like a duck. Fritz shrugged and applied himself to the moo shu pork. Sandra offered him chopsticks, but he shrugged at them, too. "Of course, I have seen films about the Chinese farmers, because they gladly show us the life of brother socialists. But I have never tried them. This is the first time that I eat Chinese food." Of all the staggering things Fritz had said so far, this was surely the most staggering.

The enormous meal knocked out the jet-lagged Fritz, so within minutes of their resuming the northward journey he was slumped against a window, his chin migrating away from his mouth and snapping shut again with a smacking noise. The others disciplined themselves to whispered conversation until the mountains rose claustrophobically around them, blocking the sun from sight, and Fritz woke up again. He rubbed his eyes and gaped theatrically at the stark winter forests all around. "So, you have stolen me!" he declared. "Where are your great American roads and tall towers? Are we now in Canada?"

"Not even close. This is still New York," said Al.

"This is *New York?* This is not the New York they show us on the news."

"A lot more of New York looks like this than like the City," said Sandra.

"Is it so?" He sat back, hands folded in his lap, at last subdued by America into pensive silence.

"Pastor Fritz, how did you even *get* here?" interposed Eunice. She was in the row behind him, next to Jackie, and had to lean forward to see his face.

"In the airplane," he replied in astonishment.

"No, what I mean is," she dropped to a whisper, "you can't fly right out of a communist country to America, can you?"

"Oh, that is what you ask." He laughed. "No, there are no direct flights between communism and capitalism! I had to pass from East Berlin to West Berlin and then take a bus to Frankfurt, what a long way it is, but the roads are so good and so smooth that it went for me very fast. But that is only the last part of my trip. I will tell you what I did to win approval for my trip. First, I have spent one year writing to the superintendent of my Landeskirche and also to an office in the Bezirk of Karl-Marx-Stadt, and I have asked for a Dienstvisum to come to America to help the work at a church."

For being such a short speech, the number of details in it threw the auditors into confusion. It took some time to sort through the German vocabulary, the fact that you could pass from East to West Berlin at all, the further fact that the reference to Karl Marx meant a city, formerly known as Chemnitz, and *not* the father of all lies and communists, and finally the startling fact that Fritz could admit openly to wanting to visit America for religious reasons.

"I thought religion was illegal in East Germany," said Al.

"No, no, not at all," said Fritz cheerfully. "You think probably of Soviet Russia. They are much worse there. Also in Czechoslovakia. My church is in a village near Ehrenfriedersdorf, close to the border, so that we hear news about them. It is quite bad for the believers there. But actually our government is very eager to prove that it persecutes no believers. If I did not help the government's image, I was not here, believe me, my friends! They want the world to think that they are very tolerant."

The dismay on the faces all around him was plain. "You're not persecuted at all?" said Eunice, a little sadly.

"'Persecuted' is not the right word," said Fritz. "They are interested only in people who they can—how to say this? People who are not in clearness over what they think. On one day this, on the next day that. If they are not inside sure what they believe, then the government notices and tries to make them…"

"Compromise," supplied Pastor Donald.

"Yes! Compromise. But if you are clear in your head, if you say what you think, they leave you in peace."

"So wait, you mean, the more open you are about your religion, the *less* they bother you?" Al was baffled.

"No, also that is not quite right." Fritz stretched his arms and clasped them behind his head. He was obviously enjoying the audience. "For example, they did not let me go to the Gymnasium because I did confirmation in the church."

"You can't exercise because you got confirmed?"

"No, no! The Gymnasium is what we call secondary school."

"High school?" said Al.

"Yes, high school, that is what we call Gymnasium."

"German is weird," said Jackie fervently.

"It's just different," corrected Sandra.

"So you couldn't go to high school at all? How'd you get to be a pastor then?" said Al.

"There are three high schools of the church, this is allowed," said Fritz. "I went to the school in Leipzig because it was closest to my home. You know Leipzig, yes?"

"Bach's city," said Pastor Donald.

"Genau. And then I could go from there direct to study theology at the university."

Over the ongoing surprise that you could go to a church school and even study theology in a godless nation, more questions pressed, demanding answers. Fritz tackled the next one with the astonishing claim, "I learned English from television!"

"You have TV in East Germany?" breathed Jackie.

"Yes, but only black-white," he reassured her. "I think here you have color?"

Jackie nodded. Forget the Corning Glass Works. She was going to make sure Pastor Fritz watched color TV before he left America.

"Some nice socialists from England came to us to make a program named 'English for You.' I loved this show very much. I learned every episode by heart! Since you are so interested in Karl Marx, please listen." He clasped his hands together and declaimed, "'Thousands of workers look after the grave of Karl Marx. They put flowers on it on March the fourteenth, the day he died in 1883.'" He grinned at his rapt audience. "Good English, yes?"

"They have Spanish on Sesame Street, I used to watch it with my kids, but I can't speak Spanish like you speak English!" exclaimed a dejected Jackie.

"I studied in school also. And the novels of your cowboy writer Mr. L'Amour are very beloved. Most people read the translations from West Germany, but I have also found them in English. I have compared them when I did not know a word. 'He rolled the cigarette in his lips, liking the taste of the tobacco, squinting his eyes against the sun glare.' Now this 'squinting,' it is not in the textbook. But from my German book I have learned that it is English for schielen."

As the desolate miles unfolded through forest and hill and past the occasional other car, Pastor Fritz relayed still more unexpected and perplexing facts about his life. How he did not consume a steady diet of Soviet propaganda, because West German TV and radio could not be blocked from reaching the eastern side, not even by an iron curtain. Yet he also spoke

Russian, because it was the required foreign language in primary school. How he had learned to play the organ when he realized that the regime would try to press on the musicians if the pastors would not collaborate, so he might need to play for his own congregation. As it turned out, he often did play, but mainly because his church shared an organist with another village. Pastor-plus-organist was as unlikely a chimera, in the minds of the Mt. Moriah parishioners, as a mermaid or a centaur. Then Fritz told them how, since it was a cornerstone of DDR ideology that the voting rate was one hundred percent and always unanimous, the citizens negotiated with their politicians not by voting, but by refusing to vote at all, until the desired concessions were granted.

"We should try that here," joked Al.

The catalog of wonders continued until the Americans were even more astonished than their foreign visitor. It was a relief of the mind and not only of the Sitzfleisch, as Fritz so amusingly called it, to pull into a dark and sleepy Shibboleth at last.

"We'll take you straight to your Aunt Sabine," Pastor Donald explained. "You can have tomorrow to catch up with each other, and also to catch up on your sleep, before we put you to work on Sunday!"

"This is very good. You are so kind to me, my friends."

"When did you last see Sabine?" Eunice asked.

"Never! We have never met. I was born in 1960 and she has left Germany in 1956. But I can say that my father was her favorite nephew and she was his favorite aunt, therefore I have always heard many good things about her. I was so happy when my father showed me the first letter from her, six years ago! Always 'Tante Sabine, she was so good to me,' that was what my father said. Now I will learn to know her myself."

The van pulled into Mrs. Feuerlein's driveway. Instantly the front door swung open and there stood the tiny old lady, undeterred by the cold or the icy front porch. Suitcases and rucksack transferred indoors, the group bashfully declined the invitation to come inside, hearts full and overawed at this reunion, which wasn't even, technically speaking, a reunion. Yet all of them were struck by the peculiar feeling that the long day of driving had somehow been midwife to a miracle.

∼

It was a good thing that Fritz had an apparently inexhaustible supply of enthusiasm, because Donald lived off it for the next two weeks as if it were his air, food, and water all in one.

Fritz preached on Sunday from I Corinthians about the foolishness and weakness of God, then proceeded to take not only seconds but thirds, too, from the lavish potluck the congregation laid out to welcome him after the service, attendance at a record high despite not being Christmas or Easter. He handled the many and repetitive queries about communists during the Q and A with wit and aplomb. The festivities concluded with his presentation to the church of an elegant map printed in 1983 for the five hundredth anniversary of Martin Luther's birth, displaying the cities in the present-day DDR in which the reformer had been active, and, as a bonus, all the cities where peasant revolts had broken out, "because of course the DDR had to make our Luther a prophet of the proletariat revolution," Fritz explained with boisterous good humor.

A couple nights later Fritz gave the first of two organ concerts at St. George Episcopal, which had the best organ in all of Shibboleth, to a standing-room only crowd that came as much out of curiosity to see the "communist pastor" as to hear him play J. S. Bach's Orgelbüchlein—Bach's fame compensating for his unfortunate Christianity in the eyes of the DDR government that had approved Fritz's volunteer service visa. The next night's midweek Lenten service, too, was unusually well attended, even though regular old Pastor Donald preached. But the soup supper afterwards afforded plenty of opportunity to satisfy the ravenous curiosity of small-town Americans. Fritz responded to promptings to say something in Russian with tongue-twisters of propaganda, thrilling every last person with how he sounded exactly like General Orlov in "Octopussy."

Another day the monthly ecumenical council meeting elected to drive over to Kuhsota so Fritz could try Mexican food. Great was the hilarity when the confused German attempted to cut his crispy-shelled tacos with knife and fork. The prospect of both Fritz and burritos had lured out even Jerry from the Assemblies of God and Father Serge from Assumption Ukrainian Orthodox, the two of whom once again found common ground in their intense hatred of the evil empire, if for rather different reasons—Jerry opining that it was preventing the seizure of Jerusalem and consequent rebuilding of the temple to trigger the Lord's return in glory, Father Serge that it was infiltrating the mother church with both communists *and* Russians, and who could say which was worse?

Aaron from the Southern Baptist church only listened, a sad and vacant look on his face. Donald asked how he was doing, but he just shook his head and shrugged. "'Where there is no vision, the people perish,'" he quoted. Donald couldn't tell if that meant his congregation without cheerleader preaching, or Aaron himself.

"Sure you don't want to stay, now that you're here?" Father Pat asked, licking hot sauce off his fingers.

"America, she is a beautiful bride, but I like my own wife better," said Fritz. He remained unwilling to pick up his tacos by hand, but balancing fragments of shell on a fork proved to be slow business. "I am in my heart a true Saxon. Also, in the DDR, I know how to hold the gospel. The enemy is very clear. Here, in America, I am not sure who the enemy is."

"The Soviets," said Jerry and Father Serge in unison.

"OK, yes, they are enemies. But they are far away. Who are your enemies right here?"

"Radical individualism," said Father Serge.

"Secularists and liberals. Also Dungeons and Dragons," said Jerry.

"Fundamentalists," said Linda loudly. "The so-called Moral Majority."

"Washington," said Cathie.

"Shopping malls and television," said Pieter.

"You make my point for me!" laughed Fritz. "You are all pastors of the gospel, you all live and work in the same town, but you are not united about who your enemy is. I think you must always look in every direction. It makes me tired when I think on it. That is the nice thing in the DDR—we need to look in only one direction to find our enemy."

Each afternoon Donald and Fritz paid a visit together. To Mrs. Kipfmueller at home, Jackie at work (who showed off the tiny color TV in her manager's office), Eunice at her husband's store, the high school for an assembly, and healthy baby Matthew whose parents recounted his whole dramatic birth story, complete with emergency baptism, on Thanksgiving.

Fritz's second Sunday did not warrant a potluck but it did earn him and the Abneys an invitation to Sandra and Alan's for lunch before the second organ concert. Carmichael had angled discreetly and then pleaded overtly to get out of the lunch. Ever since the conversation during the sugaring at Dale's, she'd been steering clear of Sandra. "You have to talk to her about it," said Donald. "Both as your friend and as a parishioner. You can't avoid her forever."

Carmichael shook her head, buttoned her lip, and agreed to the lunch after all.

It went fine, mostly. Alan talked Fritz through their collections of first editions, original paintings, and eclectic antiques from Danish modern to Art Deco. Sandra was a skilled cook and, having seen Fritz's wonderment at Chinese and heard of it at Mexican, decided to treat him to a Middle Eastern feast, speciality ingredients supplied by the Co-op. She made her own pita and a bowl of hummus—as new to Donald as to Fritz— and baked eggplant stuffed with lamb and cucumber tzatziki, halva with unseasonal fresh figs for dessert. The Forrads were less overtly voyeuristic in their questions about life in the DDR. Donald could tell that Carmichael was gradually thawing in their presence.

That is, until Sandra asked Fritz, while handing him a tiny cup of syrupy coffee flavored with cardamom, "Tell me, Pastor, do you only bury people in your country, or is there also cremation?"

"What is this 'cremation'?" said Fritz, looking in puzzlement into his black coffee.

"Not like 'cream,'" she said. "It means burning a body after death and preserving the ashes."

"Ah yes, Einäscherung," said Fritz.

"Asher?" Saul perked up.

"No, honey, this is something different," Carmichael said softly. She twisted around and helped Saul pick the pistachios out of his halva.

"Yes, we have both possibilities," said Fritz.

"Is there a preference for one or the other? By the church or the state?"

"No, I think not. It is adiaphoron, like we say in the church. It makes no difference."

Donald willed Sandra to drop the issue, but she pressed on, "So you're saying that members of your church are OK with cremation? They have nothing against it?"

"No, I don't think so." Fritz looked rather puzzled. "Why should they?"

Sandra dove into an impassioned description of the recent addition to the Mt. Moriah cemetery, concluding with the fact that "some people" were still hostile to the idea of returning their beloved dead to ashes, which was unfortunate and backwards, considering that it was a cost-effective option for the poor, better for the environment, and permitted the mobility of the dead.

"Americans move around very much," Fritz observed. "But in Saxony, we stay there where we are born. Even the people who move to a big city, they are never far from their home village." Then he asked if someone could please explain to him this very confusing game of American football.

Donald didn't know if Fritz detected the subtext of Sandra's queries about cremation and changed the topic on purpose, but he was grateful all the same.

The meal concluded without further incident and they escaped politely, needing to get Fritz over to St. George Episcopal to warm up his fingers before the concert.

On the drive over, Kitty said, "Mrs. Forrad sure loves to talk about her columbarium."

"It's not hers, it's the church's," Donald said automatically.

"She talks like it's hers," said Kitty.

∼

It was mid-afternoon on a Thursday, and Fritz's last day. He sat with Donald in the sacristy, relaxing over a plate of cookies sent along by Mrs. Feuerlein and idly filling in some forms that he'd have to hand in to his superiors in both church and state upon return.

Donald bit into a lebkuchen, stretched out his legs, and said, "You know, I thought I was doing you a favor by bringing you over here, but the truth is, you've really done me the favor. I can't even tell you how much good the past two weeks have done me."

"Ah, that is wonderful, my friend," said Fritz. He scrawled something in his elegant hooked German cursive and tossed the pen aside. "It is good when capitalist and communist pastors trust each other, is it not?"

"I'm not sure I'm much of a capitalist," said Donald with a smile. "Or I'd get myself a more lucrative call and offer my family a better life."

"You know that I make a joke. I am also no good communist. Some type of socialism is OK, I think, so the people have what they need. But I see in America that sometimes it is also good not to have what you need. I have not expected to discover this in America."

Donald opened his mouth to pursue this intriguing line of political theory, but Fritz stopped him.

"We have only a few hours' time, my friend. We will not solve the conflict between our countries. I want instead to put a question to you. It is a question about your soul. I hope you will not be offended that I ask this question."

It had been so long since Donald had heard a Lutheran pastor inquire after the state of anybody's soul, much less his own, that sheer curiosity overrode any objections. "By all means, ask away."

Fritz balanced his elbows on the armrests of his squeaking swivel chair and laid his fingertips together over his lap. After a moment's silence he said, "It is hard, in a foreign language, to ask polite. But I try."

Donald nodded encouragement.

"You see," said Fritz, "I have lived in the DDR all my life. Until now, I have never been in a country where there is no Stasi and even your neighbor hears everything that you say. In such a country you learn already as a small child that in public nobody says the truth. It is not *all* lies. I do not say that. I say only that you learn fast that what is said at home, and what is said in the public, is not the same. So you learn to listen different. One ear for what is said—" Fritz pointed to his right ear "—and one ear for what is meant." He pointed to his left.

"That makes sense," said Donald.

"So, even if English is not my language, I can maybe hear things that even the born English speakers cannot. Yes? It is possible. Public and private language are not dependent on German and English."

Donald reached for another lebkuchen. He took a bite and realized that his own left ear was cocked at attention, trying to discern what, exactly, Fritz was driving at.

"Yes. So, my friend, two times I have heard you preach.

Yesterday evening you led the Bible study before I preached. Also on our visits to people's homes, yes, there also you read from the Bible and you give no sermon but you explain it to the people. So I have had the chance to hear what you say, and also to hear what you mean."

Donald felt he was ready to do some of the talking. "I know what you hear," he supplied. "I grew up kind of fundamentalist, you know what that is, right?" Fritz barely had a chance to nod before Donald barreled on. "I've done my best to overcome it. I got a really good education at seminary with some excellent teachers, who helped me get over my initial shock at discovering that Moses didn't write the first five books of the Bible and there were no nephilim but lots of dinosaurs, and the documentary hypothesis and Q and the quest for the historical Jesus and all that. I get that Jonah is a folktale, not literal history. But the fundamentalism still haunts me, like a ghost almost. The ghost of my grandfather, who was a real old-school preacher." He laughed a little; it was the first time he heard himself calling his grandfather a ghost. Grandfather Abney had believed in demonic possession but definitely *not* in ghosts. He would be offended at the comparison and no doubt haunt Donald's mind in vengeance. "I have never really been able to find an easy place between the extremes—between 'all of it's true' and 'none of it's true.' Anywhere in between makes *me* into the final judge of the truth of Scripture, and I can't quite make myself easy with that, either. So probably what you hear is me wrestling with all of that. I try to keep it to myself and not bother the congregation with it, since most of them don't know or care, but it still leaks out, sometimes. That's the private stuff I avoid saying in public. I don't know if you have those kind of issues in East Germany."

Fritz nodded through Donald's speech. "We have some of this fundamentalist type," he said. "But not so many. I think this is more an American problem. We have maybe the opposite problem. Some of my professors in the theology faculty were believers, but some of them believed more in Marxism than in God. The state favors them to take positions in theology, to cut the church down from the inside. It is more effective than persecution, because persecution makes martyrs, and the people like martyrs. So at the theological faculty I heard very much that the Bible is a fairy tale for small children. They said that everything is like Jonah. Jesus also is like Jonah, they said. Jesus was a good teacher, who loved the poor and hated the rich, therefore he was at heart a communist! But, he was also a bit crazy and thought he could force God to overthrow the Romans. But God has not saved him, and the Romans have killed him instead. Ha! You can guess the message they wanted us believers to learn: God will not save us if we try to overthrow the state! But I have always been a boy who loves to read. I found the book of Albert Schweitzer where he says this about Jesus. It is old news, not new scientific study of the Bible. I found my ways to argue with them."

"I got some of that too, actually," said Donald. "Weird, isn't it, that some seminary professors in America would take as much delight in crushing the faith of believers as in East Germany? But I wasn't as good at arguing back at them. What did you say?"

Fritz leaned back in his chair with a big smile. "I have one very happy memory," he said, fingering a chocolate chip cookie. The sheer gracious revelation that was a chocolate chip cookie—unknown in the godless East—had been a constant refrain of Fritz's visit. "It was about this Jonah you mention. My Tante Sabine, she was one of seven children, yes? My grandfather was her brother Gottlieb. There were two more boys in the family, Gottfried and Gotthilf. You see what good Christians my great-grandparents were, who have named all their boys after God, yes? Now, this Gotthilf, he was the youngest in the family. When there are seven children, the parents cannot watch so close. They pray to God and hope for the best.

"So," continued Fritz, "this story I tell you, it happened

when my great-grandfather worked for the railroad. This was just before the First War. At the time there was a good relationship between Germany and Russia. It was still the imperial Russia before the Revolution. My great-grandfather had the possibility to do an exchange with a railroad man near St. Petersburg. The railroad paid for the family's travel to Russia for one month, and the Russian railroad man and his family came to our town in Germany. It was the spirit of international cooperation, as the Soviet Union always talks about today. But back then it was better!" Fritz crowed.

Donald pressed another chocolate-chip cookie on him and begged him to continue, though he could not imagine what a rail station outside of St. Petersburg could possibly have to do with skeptical seminary professors.

As the story had passed down to Fritz, his great-grandparents Hartmann and his Tante Sabine and all the other children, including his two-and-a-half-year-old grandfather Gottlieb and year-and-a-half-old great-uncle Gotthilf, loved their month living in the stationmaster's house in a small Russian town just north of St. Petersburg. They loved the black bread and the fresh fish and the pretty wooden houses.

The local people were very friendly and tried speaking to them in French, as was the fashion at court. A wealthier family in town was descended from the Volga Germans and claimed a distant connection to Catherine the Great. Since they could speak together in German, they became friendly.

At the end of the month's visit, this family invited the Hartmann family to their dacha, even farther north, for a few days. By then it was late October and cold and snowy already, but the chance was much too exciting to pass by, for great-grandfather Hartmann could never hope to give his family such a holiday again.

It started out fine. The little cottage they were told about was in fact quite a fine house, deep in the woods and far from neighbors. The Volga German family was very kind and gave them good food and played musical instruments and led them on walks in the surrounding hills and forests.

But on the last afternoon, the weak autumn sun already hurtling toward the horizon, as they were turning back home, the host family realized it was a bit late to be out still. The Hartmanns followed along, but they did not understand why their hosts were becoming nervous. And they did not worry about the children, who were enjoying the romp through the snow. So the great-grandparents Hartmann were not prepared when, all at once, a gigantic wolf swooped down upon them.

"It was a wolf such as you never see in Germany," Fritz declared to Donald. "Most of our wolves are gone."

"Here, too," said Donald.

"But they live still in the far north. And they are *big*. Big like you cannot imagine. If it stands on its feet, it is taller than you."

"I can't believe it."

"Genau!" pounced Fritz. "That is my point. A wolf of such size is unbelievable. And yet, it exists. And this big wolf was alone. Somehow it was thrown out of its, its…"

"Pack."

"Yes. So it was lonely and hungry. And it found this group of very delicious persons who walked through the woods. But even a hungry wolf is smart. It seeks the most small and the most weak. And that was my great-uncle Gotthilf, only one and one half years old. The wolf jumped on Gotthilf and swallowed him."

Donald stared. "You're telling me 'Little Red Riding Hood.'"

"'Riding hood'?"

Donald gestured over his head. "A fairy tale, about a little girl who wears a red—"

"Ah yes! Rotkäppchen. We have this story, too. You Americans think it is a magic tale, but it is quite realistic, if you live so far in the north that the wolves are as big as in Russia. No wolf could swallow a girl who is nine or ten years old, this is true. But a baby? Yes.

"Now, this Volga German man, he was rich, like I said, and he was also a smart man who knew about the woods. He had with him a pistol and a knife. Before five seconds passed, when they all noticed what happened to little Gotthilf, he pulled out his pistol and shot the wolf through the head. It fell dead to the ground. Then he ran over, took the knife, and cut the wolf open."

Donald chuckled. "You're making this up."

"No, this is the truth. Everyone in my family knows this story. Ask Sabine, she will tell you also. She was there when it happened, twelve or thirteen years old. So, the man cuts the wolf open, and inside they find Gotthilf. He still lives! Yes, he is crying, there is some blood, but the hungry wolf has swallowed the boy whole. No bite. My great-grandmother pulled him out of the wolf's stomach and held him and comforted him. And he was fine.

"Do you know that 'Gotthilf' means 'God helps'? After that, they all said this child, my great-uncle, he was the living proof that God helps.

"The reason I tell you this, my friend, is that, I have told it also to my professor at the theological faculty. This professor always said to us that Jesus is a fairy tale like Jonah. We should not believe that it is history. But I told this professor about my great-uncle Gotthilf. And the professor said, even if this fairy tale you tell about your family is true, why do you give honor to God, when it is the pistol and the knife that saved your great-uncle? I said that I did not want to argue with him about that. I only wanted to say that the world is full of strange things."

"'There are more things in heaven and earth, Horatio...'" Donald quoted. Fritz nodded, though Donald doubted he got the reference.

"I told the professor, maybe it happened once, just once, a very long time ago, that a man fell out of a boat and somehow he came inside of a whale. And then somehow he came out of the whale. And then he told people, and they told people, and *they* told people. Such wonders that people experience, these are the best stories, and these stories spread very fast. 'And you believe this one man swallowed by a whale was Jonah?' said the professor to me. He was very sarcastic. I said no, probably not. Probably the story of the man who lived inside a whale has survived, and such a story was too good to die. And the Hebrew people heard it and they mixed it with their prophet story and that is how we have Jonah. It is true and not true, you see."

Donald stretched his arms and smiled. "OK, why not," he mused.

"You do not understand my point," Fritz pressed on. "Our Jonah story, true and not true, is one type of story. It is not very important. But it needed to happen only one time, this one man in this one whale. It is enough, satis est, like we say in the Bekenntnisschriften, yes? I have said the same to my professor, because he wanted to make a science of the resurrection. He wanted to make experiments with temperature and atomic tests to learn how it works and then make it happen again in a laboratory. But I said to him, it happened only once. The whole Scripture tells us it happened only once. With Jonah, it makes no difference if it happened to this man Jonah or not—the whale, I mean. But everybody agrees that if the resurrection happened only once, it happened to only one man, and that man was Jesus.

"And then—this was my best moment! Then I asked my professor, where is the tomb of Jesus? There is no tradition of Jesus' tomb until many, many centuries later. So many people loved Jesus, but they did not come to pray at his tomb. They had not forgotten his tomb, if he died and stayed dead like any other famous man. But he did not. So they did not."

"What did your professor say to that?"

"Nothing. But he gave me a bad mark on my final exam."

Donald laughed.

"What I say to you, my friend, is that each case is its own case. Jonah is one case, Jesus is another case. I judge the case for myself," said Fritz, "but I do not judge it alone. I judge it with the others who also judge. That is where you make your mistake."

Donald leaned in. He liked this train of thought. It didn't solve everything but suggested a way forward that he had not yet explored. "So you're saying—"

Fritz cut him off. "I am sorry! My friend, you are very clever, and I am too glad to hear myself talk. Because actually it is not what I wanted to speak with you about. Ha! Yes, you put me to solve one big problem for you, but I have wanted to speak about another."

Donald sat up straight again and pressed his back against the folding chair. "All right, and what problem is that?"

"You hate God very much, because he took your little boy away from you."

A sharp intake of breath, as if Fritz had punched Donald in the gut. In a sense, he had.

The topic of Asher had not once arisen during the whole course of Fritz's visit, except obliquely when Sandra asked about DDR burial practices. Surely, Donald acknowledged to himself, that was one reason the visit did him so much good. It had been an escape from the constant accusations of failed fatherhood, an excuse to submerge himself in work and not think or feel. It gave him the platform to act the part of a good pastor. A pastor who actually *liked* God and could give other people reasons to like God, too.

"I knew about it before I came. Tante Sabine's letters come now quick to me and she has told me the terrible story. I am so, so sorry, my friend Donald. It is not as it should be."

"Not as it should be," Donald echoed. He thought of Aaron and his murdered faith in the plan. Every possible answer surrounding Asher and the plan was evil. It *was* God's plan—so God killed my son. It *wasn't* God's plan—so some power greater than God killed my son. There *is* no plan—so God's as much in the dark grip of chaos as the rest of us.

"Please believe me, I do not speak to you so with a light heart. You know my Lenchen and I are married since three years, but we have no children. But we had one child, one boy. He died in the seventh month, inside Lenchen. She gave birth to him already dead."

"I'm sorry," murmured Donald.

"I do not say it is the same as with a child of five years," said Fritz.

"Almost six, actually."

"Yes. It is not the same. You had these years with him. You knew him and what he liked and you played with him and held him. It is harder, the more time you have together. But even the small ones, before the birth, they are your children. Do you know, Lenchen and I chose a name. If the child was a boy, do you know what we would name him?"

Donald shook his head.

"Gotthilf. 'God helps.' After my wonderful great-uncle. A very unpopular name now, even in West Germany! The first Gotthilf came alive out of the wolf. But the second Gotthilf came dead out of his mother. Sometimes God is very hard."

Donald thought he'd never heard a truer word. How had Grandfather Abney dealt with it? Did he ever experience God as hard? Or did his immense confidence in the Bible and the Spirit wipe out all doubts and pains?

No, no, not at all.

Donald heard Grandfather Abney speak but could not attend to him just now.

"So you're saying that my hatred of God comes through in my preaching, is that it?" Donald turned an empty face toward Fritz.

"I hear it with *this* ear," said Fritz, pointing to his left. "In the other ear, I hear you preach with great love for God. And I can see the people, they hear you and they start to believe and love God, too."

"Huh," said Donald.

"But with the left ear, this ear says to me that you preach the love of God because you do *not* love him. You preach to make yourself believe again."

"I *do* believe," said Donald, "unfortunately."

"Yes, you are right. I said it false. You believe in God. But you do not believe in the *good* God."

"No. I don't. I even told my bishop that. The strange thing is, I've never experienced so little doubt in all my life. I had no idea that confidence in God's existence would be so bitter."

"Like the demons who believe and tremble, yes?" Fritz smiled kindly. "It is OK for now. You have pain because you loved your little one so much. But there is a danger here."

"I know—it's no good for a pastor not to love God. It's dishonest. If I stay this way, I'll have to leave the ministry."

"That is not what I think. If a pastor left the ministry every time he lost his love for God, there had been no pastors! No, no. Rather, the danger is that your people will come to believe because of you and your strong preaching."

"Isn't that how it's supposed to work? 'Faith cometh by hearing.' How will they believe without someone to preach to them?"

"Yes and no. You cannot answer a hard question so simple. If you preach too strong, their faith will come out of you instead of out of God. That is the danger of the good preacher, yes? You are *too* good in this moment. It is a gift of the Holy Spirit that helps you through the sad time. But you must not try to keep this gift after its time. Then it will be a temptation for you, and it will hurt your people. They must believe in God for God's sake, not for your sake."

Donald sat in thought. At last he said, "What am I supposed to *do*, then? Preach less passionately? Or convince myself that God isn't so bad after all?"

"No. You also must come to love God again for God's sake, not for your sake. You must not even love God because you need to love him, but only because God *makes* you love him."

"He'll have a rough job of that now," muttered Donald.

"He is not much of a God, if he cannot handle the rough jobs," said Fritz. "You can continue to preach as you do now. Only you must not preach so when it no longer comes pure out of the sadness. Do not imitate yourself, when it is at an end."

Donald ate the last lebkuchen. "If God sent you to help me," he said, "then maybe God isn't all bad."

"Not *all* bad," Fritz agreed. He took the last chocolate-chip cookie.

∼

The exit committee was not quite as large as the welcome committee—only Donald, Al, and Sandra saw Fritz back to JFK, and this time in Al's car, since the four of them could fit. Fritz's luggage was stuffed to overflowing with gifts from the Mt. Moriah parishioners: T-shirts with logos from Thyssen Sofa Superstore and Shibboleth High School, a tiny plastic jug of maple syrup, blue jeans from J. C. Penney's in an array of sizes, bags upon bags of Reese's Cups and Baby Ruths and other American candies that could practically function as a secondary currency in the DDR. Acute as ever to unspoken tensions, Fritz wore on his head both a Yankees cap *and* a Mets cap, switching the stacking order at every pit stop during the drive.

As the mountains slunk by and gradually shrank down to nothing, Fritz described to the other passengers the Friedensdekade, ten days of public prayer for peace sponsored by DDR churches every November.

"I still can't get over how you can do that without getting in trouble," said Al at the wheel.

"You are very blessed in your pastor," said Fritz. "In him I have found a friend for life. So I invite him to take part in the Friedensdekade this year. I have so many benefits from visiting America. I think he will have many benefits from visiting Germany. He can see how we live there as the church."

Donald nodded but kept quiet. Fritz had put the idea to him

the night before. He wanted to go, for sure, but getting both time off and financing from the church was another matter.

"You sure they'll let him come back?" Al joked.

"Yes," said Fritz. "To hold an American pastor, that will hurt the image of the DDR. He will be quite safe."

"You like this idea?" Al asked Donald.

"I like it," he admitted, "but only if it's all right by the congregation."

"That is why I ask you first," said Fritz, "since you are the president of the council."

"I'm a council member, too," interjected Sandra.

"Yes, very good," said Fritz.

"Do you need us to pay your way?" Al asked bluntly. Insurance men did not need to be squeamish about money, as he'd told Donald more than once.

"Well, yes. I mean, I'm happy to contribute. But if my costs are anything like Fritz's, it would be hard for us to manage all on our own. Plus I'd need you all to help Carmichael while I'm gone."

"Of course we'd do that," Sandra said impatiently. "It's just that, we're still paying off the columbarium, and like you said, Fritz's trip wasn't cheap. There might be some resistance among the other council members."

"I won't go if it causes dissension," said Donald. "Only if it's agreed that this visit is a good thing for the whole church and not just for me."

"I promise you, much good will come to my congregation in Germany from my visit in America," said Fritz.

"Praying for peace in a communist country sure sounds like a good idea to me," said Al. Then abruptly they were sucked into the tangle of City traffic.

Once they got to the airport, Al and Sandra dropped the pastors on the curb with the luggage and proposed to circle a few times before coming back for Donald. He in turn wrangled a trolley for Fritz and saw him to passport control.

Fritz paused to dig out his dark blue Reisepass.

"What's the insignia?" Donald asked.

"A compass on top of a hammer," explained Fritz. "With rye all around, no wheat. We have very good rye bread. I will say this about America—she has terrible bread! I am astonished that you are healthy people with such bread. When you visit me in November, I will prove to you that our bread is better."

"Sounds good. I hope it works out. Al seemed open to it."

"Yes, my friend." Fritz paused and a serious look came over his face. "Before I go, I want to say one more thing to you."

Donald smiled warmly. "Yes, I will look after my soul. Thank you for alerting me to its danger. Whenever people talked to me about my soul before, I only got anxious or resistant. But when you said it, I took it to heart."

"Ah yes, this is also good. But this is not what I mean."

"What then? Are you going to retell the story of Goldilocks and the Three Bears and use it to prove that Elijah really did set that bear on the boys who mocked his baldness?"

Fritz didn't take the bait. If anything, he scanned the crowd as if expecting Stasi agents on his tail, then leaned in close to speak. "This Sandra..."

"Sandra? Who came with us in the car?"

"Yes, this woman." Fritz paused to make sure he had Donald's full attention.

"What about her?"

"Watch out," said Fritz. "That is all. Watch out." He leaned down and seized his suitcases off the trolley.

"Wait, wait, you can't just say 'watch out' and leave it at that!"

Fritz shook his head. "I cannot say more to you, because I do not know more. But I hear something with my left ear when she speaks. I do not understand what she says. But I do not like it. She is like the snake in the garden. You must watch out."

"She's one of my wife's best friends at the church," Donald protested, even as he recalled Carmichael's outrage over their conversation during the sugaring and Sandra's tactical mention of cremation at the lunch with Fritz.

"Then you must really watch out," said Fritz. "There is no person who is more dangerous. But now, enough!" He put his bags down again and gripped Donald in a bear hug, the perfect bookend to his greeting two weeks earlier. He spoke once more his profuse thanks for the visit and promised to treat Donald with equal kindness when he came to Saxony in November. "Until then!" he cried, reclaimed his bags, and marched off to passport control with a lively step.

Donald waved to Fritz and kept on waving till he vanished from sight. Then Donald pivoted and dodged between travelers to wait on the curb for the reappearance of Al and Sandra.

"'Watch out!'" he repeated under his breath. Then he let out a long exhale and a chuckle. Nobody bats a thousand, he thought. Just because Fritz is right about one thing doesn't mean he's right about everything. No doubt living in communist East Germany makes you paranoid, on the lookout for traitors at every turn. Not here, though. That doesn't happen here.

When the car pulled up and Donald climbed into the backseat, Sandra rummaged around in her knit bag full of healthy snacks and pulled out a shiny green apple. "Hungry?" she said with a smile. "It's good for you. Makes you smart."

In spite of himself, Donald shuddered a little.

He declined the apple.

∼

A week later, the church was hushed and dark, stripped bare for the Good Friday service. Carmichael had grabbed a generic church outfit from her closet and was therefore surprised when Kitty appeared in her black dress. Before Carmichael could say a word, Kitty offered her retort. "It's Jesus' funeral today."

"Good choice, then," Carmichael answered in a mild tone to conceal the clenching she felt inside.

Donald, she could see, was master of himself again, here at

the far end of Lent. Fritz's visit had a lot to do with it, but it didn't hurt that the service was all singing and speaking, no communion or ashes requiring a personal touch that might unglue him.

It wasn't quite dark yet; sunset by now held off till after seven. Carmichael was grateful that the worst of the winter darkness was over, though the snow still refused to recede. And with such an early Easter, there was no hope for daffodils and tulips or even snowdrops and crocuses springing up underfoot, pagan nature's respectful acknowledgement that a greater power than itself had triumphed over a greater foe than winter. A white Christmas was one thing, a white Easter another thing entirely. Donald read from the pulpit of Jesus' scourging and mocking. Carmichael scolded herself for getting stuck on something as insignificant as the weather.

She stood with the congregation to sing "Ah, Holy Jesus." They stayed standing for the final reading from the Passion. Saul leaned against her, pressing his right side hard against her thigh. Asher always used to stand on his right, she thought. He's trying to fill in the missing piece of himself.

Donald spoke, "And at the ninth hour Jesus cried with a loud voice, 'Eloi, eloi, lama sabachthani,' which means, 'My God, my God, why have you forsaken me?'"

Wait, where did *that* come from? Isn't he supposed to forgive his enemies and commend his spirit to God?

Saul reached his arms to her, yearning to be picked up. She managed, awkwardly. Hefting a seven-year-old was not the same as with a toddler.

Did God really forsake him?

Saul nuzzled her neck. She felt him missing Asher, longing for him. He wouldn't say it. He never said it. He still spoke to and of an invisible Asher hanging around the house. Maybe here in church, on this day of all days, the terrible reality was pressing in even on Saul, and he couldn't hold it off anymore.

Another dead Jew. Carmichael recalled her mother saying

it. That's all Jesus was, in the end. Not the first, not the last. Maybe just the deadest of all dead Jews.

She felt tiny tears leak out of Saul's eyes. He made no sound, no shudder or sob, just anointed her neck with two drops of the undeniable and irrefutable truth.

Nobody forsook him, because nobody was there to do the forsaking. It was a scream at an empty universe.

Donald, speaking as the centurion: "'Truly this man was the Son of God!'"

The son of nothing. No son, no God, no lord, no nothing.

Just another dead Jew.

CHAPTER TEN

April 1989

*How easily do men pass from loving
to hating and cursing one another!*

At last the snow melted.
Saul wasn't sorry to see it go. Dutifully had he built snowmen and thrown snowballs and steered the toboggan from the state forest down through the meadow straight toward the house, peeling off at the last second before it crashed against the wall, but none of it was much fun with invisible Asher, who happened also to be weightless Asher. No added momentum to the sled, no delicious terror of not being able to bail out before the bust-up. In previous years Saul and Asher had ended each and every day of sledding with a busted lip or jolted wrist, but this year Saul didn't manage so much as a bruise. Kitty came out to sled with him once or twice, but she wasn't much fun. She complained about the cold and lacked Asher's daredevil impulses. Saul was cautious enough as it was. He didn't need Kitty to warn him against disaster.

Usually the end of snow meant a boring in-between stretch of cold mud until green things, plants and bugs alike, reasserted themselves. But this year the end of the snow meant an uptick in activity at home. There were meetings and phone calls and whispers. One afternoon when Saul got home from school, Mr. Mayer was in the house. Halfway up the stairs Saul paused to listen to him and his mom and dad talking at the dining room table. After awhile Carmichael noticed. She came over and sat on the step next to Saul and talked to him in a soft voice. She only ever talked to him in a soft voice now, even when he was naughty. Saul didn't exactly miss getting yelled at, and anyway Asher was the one who used to get yelled at most of the time since he caused all the trouble. But something about his mom's soft voice made him worry about her, like she was one of the fancy teacups with roses on them that she kept on the top shelf of the pantry where nobody could reach them.

"Do you know what we're talking about, Saul?" she asked him.

"Yes. You're going to make a grave in the cemetery for Asher."

Her eyes got wider, like she was surprised he understood.

"Can I help you pick where it goes?"

She glanced over at Donald and Mr. Mayer, who had paused to engage in a little eavesdropping of their own.

==Because I know where he wants to be. He *told* me,==" said Saul.

"Well," Carmichael faltered, "we already picked a spot. Mr. Mayer helped us figure it out. I'll show you."

"We'll come, too," said Donald, nodding an invitation to their guest.

They made a solemn cohort, slipping into coats and treading single file across the crunchy pale grass. Saul thought of the choir processing down the aisle in church. Mr. Mayer stepped over the low chain enclosing the perimeter (the altar rail, thought Saul) and planted himself to one side of a rectangle marked out with yellow spray paint and tiny flags at the four corners.

Carmichael squatted next to Saul. "See, this is the closest we can make it to the house," she said. "That way Asher is right next to us."

Saul shook his head vigorously. "He doesn't want to be buried there."

"Honey," Carmichael began, but Saul swung his head back and forth like a frantic pendulum.

"This isn't his spot. He doesn't like it here. He will be sad and mad if you put him here. I'll show you where you're supposed to put him."

Saul stomped right across the marked-off rectangle in a way that made all three adults suck in their breath. He took himself to the far side of the cemetery where stood the one lavish monument, a little taller than Saul himself, under which lay the mortal remains of Mr. and Mrs. Schickedanz, founders of Mt. Moriah Lutheran. Saul grazed his fingers across the engraved surname. "Asher liked it here because it was the first time he found his A," Saul informed them. "And then I showed him his S, his H, and his E," pointing out each letter in turn. "He was sad that there wasn't his R here, but I showed him a littler R right here," pointing to "FRIEDA" lower down. "So we have to put him right here." Saul hopped onto a bare patch on the east side of the grave. "Then he will be happy."

Donald opened his mouth to speak but Mr. Mayer said, "It's a bit narrow in here, between the Schickedanzes and old Mr. Feuerlein, but after all it's not gonna to be a very big grave, is it now?" Saul nodded in agreement, though he noticed that his mom and dad only stared at Mr. Mayer as if he'd said something mean. But it wasn't mean, it was just true. Asher was a *lot* littler than Saul. "I think we can manage all right. Would you like that, son?"

Saul realized Mr. Mayer was asking him for permission. It made him feel important. At least *somebody* understood that Saul knew best of all what Asher wanted. "Yes, I would like that," he said clearly and firmly, feeling much older than his seven years. "Asher would like that, too."

"What do you say?" Only now was Mr. Mayer asking Donald and Carmichael what they thought of the arrangement.

"It's really not that much farther away," said Donald in an uncertain tone.

Carmichael looked down at Saul. He couldn't tell what her face meant. "How do you know he wants to be here, Saul?" she said at last.

"He's sitting up on top of this one," Saul replied, patting the Schickedanz gravestone. "And he keeps pointing down at this spot." Saul waved up at where Asher was. "He knows it's naughty to climb on the stones in the cemetery. But I think if you give him his own stone he'll only sit there. Then he can look at his letters all day long and he won't have to look for them somewhere else."

There was a long silence among the adults. Saul wasn't used to Mr. Mayer keeping quiet and watched him curiously. But Mr. Mayer was watching his dad and mom, who seemed to be having a conversation with their eyes only. Then his mom said, "Do you think this is a good idea?" with a tiny shrug of her shoulder in Saul's direction.

After a pause, his dad said, "It's no worse than any other idea."

All the air seemed to go out of his mom like from a balloon, but she turned toward Mr. Mayer and said, "All right, I guess this is it, then." His dad put his arm around her shoulders and held her tight.

Mr. Mayer reached into the deep pockets of his baggy jacket and pulled out a can of spray paint and a measuring tape. "I'll get this all marked out," he said.

"Can I help?" asked Saul. Mr. Mayer's eyes flickered up to Donald, who nodded and turned to guide Carmichael back toward the house.

"Sure thing, little buddy," said Mr. Mayer. "How about you go get those four flags over there for me?"

Saul skipped over to the other end of the cemetery and pulled them free, then ran back to Mr. Mayer. He got to hold the measuring tape while Mr. Mayer figured out just how big of a hole was necessary to fit Asher inside of his coffin. "It's too bad Asher can't help," Saul told Mr. Mayer. "He would think this is really fun."

"Is that right," said Mr. Mayer.

"He's afraid it's going to be boring in there, but I keep telling him it's just like taking a nap. Nobody *likes* to go to sleep, but once you're asleep you don't even know it, and it's not boring, because you don't notice. So I keep telling him not to worry. But he still gets worried, because it seems like a really long nap to have to take."

Mr. Mayer bit his lower lip and fiddled around with the can of spray paint.

"Also he's kind of jealous, because when you take a nap you don't get to play or have snacks. I told him I'll bring him some of my snacks to share. I'm not sure about playing, though," he said in a quieter voice.

"I guess you know how to take care of your little brother," said Mr. Mayer.

"I'm not very good at it," said Saul. He sat down inside the brand-new spray-painted rectangle and patted the earth. "I slept too hard and didn't wake up when Asher woke up. If I woke up, I could've stopped Asher from going outside. But I didn't. I just slept through it. I shouldn't've stayed asleep but he was too quiet and fooled me." Saul had never talked to his mom and dad about this, but somehow it felt OK to tell Mr. Mayer. "So I just keep saying to Asher, you should sleep real hard, like I did on Christmas. Just go to sleep and sleep through everything. If I did it, you can do it, too."

Mr. Mayer said, "Is that what Asher's gonna do, then?"

"I don't know. He hasn't made up his mind yet."

"Well," said Mr. Mayer. Even though it was cold out, he pulled off his orange cap and stuffed it into a capacious pocket, scratching hard at his thin hair. "Well, let's you and me make him a nice little bed here to take a nice long nap in, all right? Then maybe he'll be able to sleep good and hard."

"I hope so," said Saul.

∼

Even though the snow was gone, the earth remained frozen hard beneath the tepid grass, so the day before the funeral Dale

Mayer showed up again leading another driver in another pickup carting a scary-looking machine. After a lot of time and fuss, the two of them got it around back of the cemetery and settled it in place to blast a concentrated stream of fire along the spray-painted rectangle marking out Asher's grave.

A little while after that, George Pohl appeared in a third pickup, this one towing an excavator machine. George and Dale had quarreled at length because George wanted to dig the grave with his own sweat labor, insisting that he owed that much to the little guy who lost his life on account of George's carelessness with the ladder. Dale said that was plain stupid and wouldn't bring the boy back or set things right, it would just give George a heart attack because the ground was too hard to dig this time of year, and did he really want the Abneys to have *another* death to cope with? In the end the quarrel was resolved by George paying for the excavator out of his own pocket and overseeing the dig, which he proceeded to do wearing a scowl that even the not especially perceptive Dale could tell was clamped over a bottomless well of guilt. "But I'm gonna use a shovel to cover the grave when it's over," George informed Dale defiantly, "and set the sod in place myself." Dale didn't argue, since that at least wouldn't cause a heart attack, and trotted off to wave into position the fourth pickup of the day, this one carrying the tombstone.

Kitty looked over the tombstone with Saul the next morning. He was tracing out with his finger the letters that read "ASHER MARTIN ABNEY," remarking how happy it would make their little brother. He studied what was engraved below the name and cried ecstatically, "Look! It even says his birthday!"

"And his *death*day," Kitty added.

"Wow! You're right!" said Saul. "They're both in December. Isn't that cool? But wait, it says he died *before* he was born. See? He died on December twenty-five but got born on December thirty-one. That doesn't make any sense."

Kitty's aggravated instruction about the difference in years trumping the difference in days was lost to the scrunching sound of tires over gravel. The car came to a standstill and the bulky bear shape of Bishop Cartledge emerged. He noticed the two of them in the cemetery, pretended not to—Kitty was pretty sure of that by his shifty eyes—and leaned back into the car for his briefcase. He shut the car door, eyes on the ground, and trudged around the side of the parsonage until he realized he couldn't pretend anymore not to see them. He straightened up and waved. "Hello, children!" he called in the false voice he reserved for youth.

"Hi," said Kitty flatly. She wasn't going to help him out.

"This is my brother's," Saul shouted, pointing at the gravestone.

Bishop Cartledge gave a small weird nod and said, "I'm going inside to say hello to your parents."

Kitty watched him disappear through the pantry door as Donald beckoned him in. She thought of him eating the nice doughnuts her mom had bought, which Kitty wasn't allowed to touch until he'd had his choice. You'll probably eat all of them, you big fat bishop, she thought at him. Then, remembering what he'd read out at the funeral: "If you had been here, my brother would not have died!" She shook herself. She didn't like the bishop, but even she had to admit it wasn't exactly his fault that Asher fell off the roof.

"So where's Asher right now?" she asked Saul.

"He's a little shy because he knows lots of people are coming," said Saul. "He's gonna stay up inside the tree line. It's kind of cold there because of the shadows, but the cold doesn't bother him so much anymore."

"He got used to the cold while he was lying in the parking lot after he fell, huh?" As soon as she said it, Kitty was appalled at her own nastiness.

"No, it's just part of being invisible and also not weighing anything. You have to weigh something to be hot."

"What, are you a science teacher now?"

"Uh-uh. Asher just explains this stuff to me."

Kitty had the feeling that if she stayed with Saul a moment longer she'd end up decking him, and he'd fall in the grave and break his neck, and then she'd have *two* dead little brothers...

The thought was so intolerably shocking that she reached over and suffocated Saul in a huge hard hug. He accepted it for a few moments, then shoved her off, laughing at her funny behavior.

Eventually the two of them got summoned inside to sit at the dining table and keep quiet while Bishop Cartledge walked their parents through the bulletin. He spoke in a bland voice like a newscaster, even while saying things like "Since almighty God has called our brother Asher from this life to himself, we commit his body to the earth from which it was made." He's *my* brother, not *your* brother, Kitty thought, concealing a glower. At last she was allowed to take a jelly doughnut. When its lurid purple jam popped out the other side, she imagined that she'd bitten into the bishop himself and his guts spilled out. She swallowed a giggle.

As soon as she could get away with it, Kitty excused herself to change into her black dress. On her way to the bathroom to brush her hair, she saw that the door to the guest room was open. Bammy and Bampy were inside and evidently had as little wish to talk to the bishop as Kitty did, since they hadn't come downstairs all this time, forgoing any claim on the doughnuts. They were the only extra family to come for the burial. Everyone on Donald's side of the family had come to the funeral and it was just too far and too expensive to make the trip again. Kitty thought it was rotten of all of them, but it warmed her heart toward the grandparents who did take the trouble to show up.

"What's that on your arm, Bammy?" Kitty asked from the doorway.

Judith was dressed head-to-toe in black, from her tights and fancy high-heeled shoes (they'll sink in the dirt, Kitty thought) to her skirt suit and blouse and even a kind of rounded hat that clamped around her hair. Kitty imagined her with black lipstick, too, which was almost as funny as the bishop's exploding guts.

"It's a ribbon," said Judith by way of explanation. She extended her arm so Kitty could get a better look. "It's something Jews wear when they are grieving for a lost one."

Not again! Kitty froze in the doorway, electrified by a surge of anger so stark and sudden she hardly knew what to do.

"I have one for you, too, if you'd like, honey," said Judith softly. She was so nice, so solicitous. "For the whole family—your mom and dad and Saul, too. Bampy's already wearing his." He obligingly turned his arm to show it off.

"*No!*" Kitty screamed. "I don't want it! I won't wear it!" She tore back to her room and slammed the door. That didn't seem protection enough, so she crammed herself into the closet on top of piles of stuffed animals and stuck her face in the corner. She knew she'd get in trouble, yelling at her grandparents like that; her mom would not go easy on that kind of crime. And Bammy didn't mean any harm. Kitty didn't know why she was so angry about the ribbon. Or about Bishop Cartledge, who was dumb and fat and awkward but not a mean person. Mrs. Onderdonk had been so nice to Kitty since she went back to school, but Kitty hated her, too. Also Jessica, her self-appointed best friend, who had spent Kitty's first week back at school sheltering her and fending off both kindly sympathy and cruel mockery from their classmates. Instead of being grateful, Kitty criticized, then ignored, and ultimately dissed Jessica. Even now Kitty could conjure up Jessica's hurt shocked face. But she took Kitty seriously and withdrew. Now Jessica mostly hung out with stupid little Shannon. Jenny Ulster still talked to Kitty sometimes, but that was it. Kitty didn't mind. She hated all of them.

The hatred was growing into a thick, lush, buoyant, beautiful thing. Kitty cast around and realized with delicious certainty that she hated all the people at church, too. Everyone was always so nice and thoughtful. They were trying to make dead Asher into an OK thing instead of the kind of thing that should make the whole world stop, just stop, right in its tracks. Sympathy was evil because it tried to calm you down and trick you into thinking that bad things were good things.

What else was there to hate? Kitty recalled that she'd seen the tiniest little buds starting on the lilac bush. She hated lilacs. She hated spring. She hated crocus shoots, the yellow ones and the purple ones with equal withering passion, because they didn't care that Asher was dead. They insulted his memory by springing back to life, which was the one thing that Asher would never, ever do. Or if he did, it would be in heaven, and it would happen at the same time as Kitty and Saul and their parents and everyone else who'd ever lived, so what good was that to them right now? As long as Kitty and Saul and their mom and dad were on this earth, they would be alive without Asher, and Asher would be dead without them. It was a rotten deal. Kitty felt shooting through her limbs a lightning bolt of perfect, universal, unrestrained hatred of absolutely everything.

Some unreckonable amount of time later, her mother came along and extracted Kitty from the closet. She didn't scold Kitty for shouting at her grandmother. If anything, she seemed to understand how Kitty was feeling. More sympathy. Kitty hated that, too. She permitted herself to be led downstairs. She buckled on her shoes and followed Saul and the adults to stand outside the church where, it seemed, pretty much the whole congregation was gathered. Wasn't the funeral enough for them? Kitty thought. Why do they have to come and gawk at the coffin?

The hearse was already waiting in the parking lot. When Bishop Cartledge gave the magic signal with his hand, the funeral home men, somber and stiff in their suits, swung open the back door and pulled out the little coffin. Kitty had seen it at the funeral but somehow it seemed even smaller now, out in the open air instead of framed by the altar inside the church. At other church funerals she'd seen six grown men carrying the coffin, but you couldn't fit more than four around this little thing.

Crunch-crunch-crunch went the pallbearers' footsteps across the gravel. They got to the edge of the cemetery and walked around it, their fancy leather shoes sinking into the softening top layer of the earth, making a squelching noise each time they pulled free. Kitty imagined one of them tripping, the other three thrown off balance, the coffin flying off the rods and tipping over, Asher's body rolling out. How rotted is he by now? Kitty wondered. Is he already a skeleton? Are worms crawling in his guts and out of his eye sockets? She remembered someone talking about embalming to preserve the body. Maybe he was a mummy inside, all wrapped up in long bands of cloth, like swaddling clothes, like baby Jesus. It was weird to be so close to Asher and not know what he looked like. If it even *was* Asher. Was it? How could a dead thing be the same as her little brother who never sat still?

By now everyone had found a place in the cemetery or in the little bit of meadow just beyond Asher's grave. Mr. Pohl stood farthest back, behind the big pile of dirt, guarding the shovel lying at the foot of the mini-mountain with a ferocious grimace. Ms. Jackie wasn't in one of the rock band T-shirts she wore to church every Sunday, but a long pretty dress with flowers and a big lace collar. Kitty was surprised how nice she looked, even with her bits of green hair.

Way far back were a few of the other local pastors, as alike in their black collars and white tabs as they were different in shape, height, and convictions: Pastor Linda with her gigantic purse, Reverend Cathie whose collar went all the way around her neck underneath a Nancy Reagan haircut, Father Pat who was round like Bishop Cartledge but not nearly so tall and somehow his fatness didn't make you hate him, Pastor Aaron who didn't look sad like the other three but just plain angry. Kitty liked him the better for that.

She dropped her eyes to the people close by her. Bammy's pointy heels had sunk right into the ground, as Kitty expected. Saul picked at a loose thread on the sleeve of his little black jacket. Mrs. Forrad was wiggling her way closer to the family. She was dressed all in black, too. In fact, she was the only one dressed all in black besides the Bams and the Abneys. Who does she think she is? Kitty thought angrily. She's not part of the family. She doesn't miss Asher like we miss Asher.

Bishop Cartledge droned on and on. The prayers sounded like all the other prayers Kitty had ever heard, a lot of "through Jesus Christ our Lord" and "May the Lord God" and "Grant to us." There was a part that involved chucking dirt on Asher's coffin. Kitty found it horrible, Saul went at it with indecent glee. At last Bishop Cartledge said, "Let us go in peace," as if such a thing were possible, and the whole assembly exhaled in relief that it was over.

With the sole exception of Mr. Pohl, who stayed back and set at the mound of dirt with his shovel, the congregation withdrew silently from the cemetery and filed back toward the church for the potluck lunch. Kitty could already smell the ziti and the sauerbraten and the meatballs (probably with caraway seeds) floating up through the basement vents. Father Pat came over and grabbed Donald's hand in a warm clasp. "'The Lord giveth and the Lord taketh away, blessed be the name of the Lord,'" he said. Donald displayed a pallid smile. "How are you holding up?"

"You know," with a shrug. "Thanks for coming."

"Glad to do it," Father Pat said. "I can't stay for the lunch, unfortunately. I've got to get over to Kuhsota to see one of my parishioners just taken into custody."

Kitty noticed that the news startled her sad father out of himself for a moment. Custody? What exactly did that mean? Kitty focused her ears, though not her eyes, on Father Pat.

"Is it bad?" Donald said.

"Yes, though not like you'd think," replied Father Pat. "It's not for a violent crime, thank God. Insider trading, as it turns out. That's one I haven't seen before in all my years as a priest! He was involved in what led up to the crash of '87, but they've only just caught up with him now. He left the finance business and moved his family up here right around that time, I guess in hopes of getting a fresh start, but the feds came for him last night. His wife called me. She's a wreck. They've got two girls, too—one right about Kitty's age, I'd guess, and the other in first grade."

"That's awful," said Donald.

"Yeah. He goes before the judge on Monday. I suppose he'll get out on recognizance before the trial, but if he's convicted he could be looking at a few years at the FCI in Otisville. Not a pretty situation for the family."

"Well, good luck with that, and God bless," said Donald. Father Pat moved off.

Kitty stood rooted to the spot. It was—it had to be—Megan Moravsky's dad. Megan had a sister in first grade. Megan started school in Shibboleth just a year and a half ago. Megan always bragged that her dad was a banker and they were rich. And Kitty knew for a fact that Megan was Catholic. Who else could it be?

No wonder she's such a rotten person, Kitty thought with profound satisfaction. She tramped across the frozen earth with a lighter heart.

~

The church basement hummed. Arlene Mayer, Hilda Kipfmueller, and Lynn Beck lined up on the kitchen side of the counter to dole out cheesy broccoli casserole and cornflake baked chicken, Watergate salad and butterkuchen. People talked loudly and piled their plates high, relieved that finally, finally, the little one was laid to rest, the terrible thing was over, and they could talk about other things, like how down in the valley you could see the first daffodils blooming.

Carmichael felt their relief. It was hard not to share it, in some small way. Of course, would that none of this had ever happened; that Asher had not died; that they had gone on as a normal family should. But it did happen. It was done. Asher was dead and now, also, buried. What choice was there but to live the life that remained to them? Sure, it was the insult of an uncaring, nonexistent heaven, insult added to injury. So be it.

Parishioners and visitors and colleagues passed by. They extended their hands and expressed their condolences again. They said it was a lovely service and hoped it had been some comfort to her. Just a few church members were bold enough to express their confidence that Asher was at rest with God. She accepted their words, kept her doubts to herself, and let them move on to the food.

At last the stream out of the cemetery ended. The lunch line shortened. Carmichael came out of her cloud of gracious politeness and noticed her parents at the counter. They stood out startlingly in their black attire with the ribbons on their arms. Frank had decided to take the week off and sit shiva with Judith in the parsonage. Carmichael felt softer toward them than she had in a long time. They'd never endured the grief of losing a child to death, but they had suffered through other griefs she'd imposed on them: such an eagerness to start her own life that she barely wrote or called the whole time she was in college, her time in France with even less communication than that, her conversion to Christianity, her self-absorption during her doctoral program, the neglect borne of sheer exhaustion when the children came along, especially having Saul and Asher within the same year. And she'd had no siblings to sop up the excesses of their parental attention, though she knew vaguely that they'd tried and hoped and even visited doctors for help. Probably, in the fifties, fertility treatments weren't very advanced. Their kindness and strength since Asher died changed things between the three of them, and for the better. It seemed treacherous to allow even one good thing to come out of Asher's death, as if in some superstitious way it retroactively caused his death. Carmichael waved the thought away as foolishness. She couldn't afford to reject any good thing, however tiny and compromised, that trickled into her decimated life.

As she looked on, Sandra, likewise all in black, approached Judith and Frank and gestured toward the center table where a few empty seats were left. She grabbed and held aloft two cups of coffee and led the way. Judith and Frank followed and took their seats and their coffee. Sandra sat down across from them. Carmichael scanned the room and found Donald at a table against the far wall, Kitty in conclave with the teenage girls, Saul horsing around with the other boys. At her shoulder Arlene appeared. "Aren't you eating?" she asked, and Carmichael allowed herself to be led to the remnants of the worked-over feast. She had no appetite to speak of, but as the pastor's wife she knew better than to play favorites. She took a dab of everything and still had an overstuffed plate by the end of it. The only seat left was the one next to Sandra. Carmichael was less than eager but there was no alternative, and anyway her parents might need defending from Sandra's—whatever.

"All this food is delicious," said Judith. "What a treat."

"Pretty standard fare for a church potluck," Carmichael replied.

"You never told us it was this good!"

"How often do you have these things?" asked Frank.

Sandra said, "As a matter of fact, quite often. When there are midweek services in Advent and Lent we have supper after, and there's a potluck whenever we have a congregational meeting or special occasion, and once a quarter for all the birthdays. It's such an important aspect of community-building. We're like one big family here."

"Well, that's a pretty good deal. No wonder you turned Christian," Frank joked to Carmichael.

"So then is this your very first time at a church potluck?" Sandra inquired.

"It is," said Judith.

"Well, you should come up for a visit every time we have one," said Sandra warmly.

"Thank you," said Judith, with equal warmth.

Don't fall for her friendliness, Carmichael thought. Every word Sandra said nauseated her.

Eunice Thyssen was sitting on the other side of Frank. She leaned in and said, "Well, I for one am glad that we had to hold out till spring for the cemetery service. It's such a lovely day. I'm sure God was smiling on us all, and on little Asher especially, with such beautiful weather."

Marilyn Gross opposite her chimed in, "I agree. Some things are worth waiting for."

Eunice and Marilyn had spoken just as one of those unpredictable lulls in the conversation fell over the basement. All at once it seemed like everyone in the room was in on the discussion. Over on Judith's side, Al Beck contributed his agreement with the sentiment, and Hazel Quinn on the far side of them both said maybe it was even an advantage to have time to come to terms with terrible news, instead of being rushed right through a funeral and burial, like she'd had to do when her own father died quite suddenly of an aneurysm a few years back. A general rumble of approval followed this speech.

"Come on, now," said Sandra reprovingly to Hazel, though the rebuke was unmistakably broadcast to all who had spoken and agreed. "What a thing to say. This whole delay has been a real shame, dragging things out the way it did. I'm sure it was a terrible burden on the family." She gave a possessive pat to Carmichael's hand.

Carmichael involuntarily jerked her hand away. It was a sharp gesture and everyone at the table saw it.

Sandra threw her a sidelong glance. Even she could not fail to grasp the meaning signaled by Carmichael's instinct.

Something shot through her own face. She said, "It *was* a burden. I've seen how you've suffered."

"I've suffered," said Carmichael in a low voice, but the quiet that continued to reign over the room meant that she was perfectly audible to one and all, "because my son died."

"I know that, I'm just saying, you've had no closure till now. Four months is a long time to go without closure. If you could've laid him to rest sooner, I think it would've been a little easier to deal with."

"The ground was frozen, so there was nothing we could do." Carmichael forced her fork into a meatball and tried to lift it her mouth. Why wouldn't Sandra let it go?

"There *was* something you could have done," Sandra said. Her words came out soft and gentle, but they veiled a smoldering pile of resentment, of accusation, of disappointment that Carmichael had let Sandra down.

Carmichael's heart thudded. How dare she. How *dare* she? Who had the right to be hurt here?

She turned to face Sandra full on, feeling her parents' eyes on her.

"You mean to say we should have cremated him and put his ashes in the columbarium," Carmichael said.

"It was always an option," said Sandra. She was retracting now under the weight of Carmichael's stare. She fiddled with her empty, stained paper plate and smoothed out the napkin on her lap.

"It was *never* an option," retorted Carmichael. She knew she should stop. She knew nothing good would come of it. The whole basement remained still and silent, including the bishop one table over. Every last person was listening. But a righteous anger possessed her and directed her with a power she could not gainsay. "Do you know *why* it was never an option?"

Sandra gave an uncomfortable titter, an awkward shrug. It was clear she regretted her words. But only being caught saying them, Carmichael thought. She hasn't said anything she doesn't think. She just doesn't like looking bad. Well, let her badness be exposed for what it is.

"I'll tell you why," said Carmichael in a cold hard tone.

"Honey," Judith whispered from across the table. "You don't have to do this."

Carmichael turned and looked at both parents fully, openly, unreservedly. "The reason why," she said, "is because we are Jews. *And we do not burn our dead.*"

Sandra shrank back as though she'd been slapped.

Carmichael felt Sandra's weakness and pounced on it. "There have been enough Jews already put into ovens, don't you think, Sandra?" she asked. "Don't you think so?"

Sandra dropped her face toward her lap. "I'm sorry, of course, I wasn't thinking," she murmured. But Carmichael could see her expression. She was not sorry. She was furious.

Let her be furious, thought Carmichael. Let her taste just a little of the fury I feel.

All at once the sound of renewed conversation built a hasty shelter over the four of them, a willing conspiracy of the crowd to bury with alacrity the supreme discomfort to which they'd been made unwilling witness. It was loud, too loud, artificially loud and cheerful to boot, trying to erase with the noise the rupturing that had just taken place.

As soon as she decently could, Sandra excused herself, whisking away her plate and napkin and plasticware. Surreptitious glances followed her as she deposited her trash in the big can, collected her blue pottery bowl of hummus, the least emptied of all the potluck dishes, unknown and uncolorful item that it was. She seemed to regard it as a deliberate insult. She scanned the room and found Alan already on his way to meet her. Yanking her coat and purse from the rack, Sandra swirled up the stairs and out of the church in a whirl of hurt pride, Alan sucked along in her wake.

Carmichael watched them go. Frank and Judith kept their heads low over their plates, eating with careful attention. At last Judith dared a quick peek over her shoulder to verify that Sandra was gone. She swallowed. Carmichael noticed that all her lipstick had rubbed off. Her lips looked wrinkled and vulnerable.

Judith said, "Honey, I appreciate what you said just now. I appreciate your accepting and claiming what we are."

Carmichael nodded.

"Still," Judith dropped her voice and looked to either side, but the parishioners were talking animatedly to prove that no, of course they had not seen or heard that terrible exchange or even noticed that Sandra and Alan were gone and anyway there was nothing remotely surprising or disturbing about finding out that the pastor's wife was a Jew because obviously she was a churchgoer and my, aren't the buttered spaetzle delicious? Judith leaned in closer all the same. So did Frank. "But don't you think you were a little hard on her? I'm sure she wasn't thinking of, of, you know, *that* aspect of it."

"No, Mom, she was *not* thinking, that's exactly the problem. She has not thought *once* about us or Asher at all. She has only thought about how to advance the cause of her columbarium so that her mother-in-law wouldn't have to be all alone in it anymore, and so no one in the congregation would hold it against her that the thing cost so damn much since she's the one who talked them into it. The fact is, she has done nothing but exploit Asher's death for her own purposes under the cover of sharing in our grief. And to do it again, now, on the day we finally got to bury him? I'm sorry, but I'm just not playing along and being polite anymore."

"All right," said Judith placatingly.

Frank added, "OK, all right, but to bring in the—the burning?" he finished in a whisper.

"Dad," said Carmichael, "have you not been telling me that you're looking into our family tree precisely to find out what happened to the ones who got left behind in Estonia? Isn't that why your own parents fled? For God's sake, it could've been *you.* This is our reality. This is part of who we are. It's part of who Asher was. We're not going to pretend like it's of no consequence."

Her parents exchanged a look. Frank murmured, "Ah. Well. I guess I didn't ever realize that *that* was actually your reason for not wanting to cremate him."

"Well," Carmichael said, faltering, "it wasn't, exactly. Not originally. It's part of the reason now. But even before I thought about that aspect of it, I just couldn't bear the thought of cremation. I know it won't make a difference to God what state our dead bodies are in on resurrection day. But I just couldn't have him burned." Carmichael listened to herself with puzzlement. I don't believe in God anymore, she thought, but I won't have my dead son burned because I want God to raise him on the last day. How does that add up? It doesn't. Oh, well.

"Jews believe in the resurrection of the dead, too," said Judith reassuringly. Then, looking guilty, she added, "I've done a little more reading."

"It's OK, Mom," said Carmichael.

As if by common consent, the guests stood and cleared their places and moved out. A team of women got to work cleaning the kitchen while the men folded the phalanx of putty gray chairs, then the tables, hanging them on their respective racks. People nodded and shook hands with the Abneys one last time before exiting. So did the bishop. Carmichael sent Kitty and Saul back to the house with her parents. When the basement was clean and empty enough for the pastor respectably to withdraw, Donald caught up with Carmichael on the way out the door and across the gravel.

"What happened there?" he asked in a low urgent voice.

"She wouldn't stop," Carmichael hissed. From his tone she couldn't tell if he was on her side. "Why couldn't she leave it be? Why did she have to bring it up again, today of all days? And why in God's name did she think it was all right to dress up like a chief mourner?"

"I don't know. I don't understand what motivated it. But you shamed her in front of everybody."

"She deserved it!"

"Maybe. But," and here Donald paused for so long and got such a strange look that Carmichael had the unsettling feeling that he had fallen into a prophetic fit, "we are the ones who are going to pay for it."

"Why should *we* pay for *her* propagandistic cruelty?" snarled Carmichael.

"No good reason. It's just how these things happen. Strangely enough, Fritz warned me."

"He did?"

"Somehow he saw it coming."

"Oh, God." Carmichael shook all over, equal parts rage and sorrow, her clean sadness over Asher tainted and tarnished with human ugliness. They stepped through the pantry door. Donald clasped her to himself. "Oh, God," she sobbed. "Why did I let her bait me like that? I shouldn't have said it. I know I shouldn't have said it. But I couldn't not say it."

"I know. It was an impossible situation."

"So what do we do now?"

Donald exhaled long and slow. "We wait."

CHAPTER ELEVEN

May 1989

*So prevailing is the disposition of man to quarrel,
and shed blood;
so prone is he to divisions and parties.*

Marilyn the organist was the first to fall. At choir rehearsal she shared sniffily that Pastor Donald had vetoed yet another hymn she'd wanted to introduce, "I, the Lord of Sea and Sky," on the obviously spurious grounds that it "reminded him of sock puppets." Instead of eliciting sympathy this fact only elicited giggles, and the choir went on to belt out "Lift High the Cross" with gusto.

But afterwards, as the baritones and sopranos departed one by one into the apple-blossom evening, Sandra lingered long enough to express her solidarity with Marilyn. It *was* a little high-handed of the pastor to run every hymn and anthem through some kind of a litmus test. Shouldn't the music director be trusted to make her own judgments?

"And I am here *every* Sunday," Marilyn added, as if this were further proof of her good taste.

"I don't know what we'd do without you," said Sandra.

"We have so few men in the choir, it's really a shame that Pastor Donald won't join us," said Marilyn. "It's not like his voice is bad. He sings the liturgy every Sunday and sounds just fine."

"It could be that he just doesn't like choir music all that much," suggested Sandra.

"You might be on to something there," Marilyn agreed. "I'm sure Carmichael doesn't. She always says she won't join the choir because she has a lousy singing voice, but I'm not sure about that."

"Well," said Sandra, "it's not the strongest of voices. I've sat near her in church so I know. But in a whole choir, no one would notice. Maybe she feels uncomfortable doing anything that makes her look less than outstanding."

"Now there's a thought," mused Marilyn. "Huh. But what's a church for but to accept people as they are? It's like she doesn't trust us."

"Even after almost four years," Sandra sighed. "You'd think that would be er   ne."

"If she doesn   s now, she never will."

"I don't reall   ow a congregation can flourish if there isn't fundament   etween the people and the pastor."

"Oh, I agree completely." Marilyn finished stacking the sheet music in her cubby in the basement.

"Well, I doubt they'll stay here much longer anyway," said Sandra. "It will be too painful to be reminded of the tragedy every single day."

"I never thought of that!" exclaimed Marilyn. "But I'm sure you're right. It only makes sense. They'll be gone before too much longer."

Sandra nodded gravely.

∽

A few days later Marilyn ran into Hazel Quinn at the deli counter of the Grand Union. They greeted one another frostily; they had never been the best of friends. But while Hazel was waiting for her pound of pimento loaf, Marilyn said, "You were on the search committee last time, weren't you? I wonder how soon we'll have to go through all that again."

"What are you talking about?" said Hazel in abject puzzlement.

"Getting a new pastor," said Marilyn.

"Is Pastor Donald leaving?"

"Well, not yet. Not officially. But how *could* he stay after what happened? To be reminded of it day after day. It's just too painful. I think we'd better be prepared to act fast. After all, it took so long to get Pastor Donald in the first place. Maybe we should start looking for a new pastor right away."

"What I can't understand," said Hazel, "is why they buried the poor little thing if they were going to leave again so soon, instead of being able to take his ashes with them."

Marilyn squinted at her. "I remember you being so upset about the idea of cremating him."

"Yes, personally, but what I mean is, if they were planning on leaving anyway, why leave him behind in the cemetery? I sure couldn't do that to Jean or Debbie. Though maybe to Len," she added darkly in reference to her ex-husband. "A pound of Munster, please, sliced thick," she directed at the clerk.

"I think Carmichael just took a disliking to the columbarium from the start. I mean, you heard what she said to Sandra at the lunch after the burial."

Hazel shook her head. "I'll tell you frankly, I was shocked."

"Me too. What a thing to say to poor Sandra, who was only trying to help!"

"Oh, that. I guess. *I* was shocked to find out she was Jewish. Are you allowed to be Jewish and Christian at the same time?"

Marilyn waved away the irrelevancy of the topic. "It just means her parents are. Carmichael takes communion and says the prayers like the rest of us. I think that's actually what makes it so offensive, what she said to Sandra. I mean, it's not like she *knew*. None of us knew."

"Actually, ever since the columbarium was installed, I've been thinking about reserving one of those little niches for myself. That way if Jean or Debbie ever move far away they can take me with them. I don't expect Len to lay flowers at my grave," she snorted.

"I think it would mean the world to Sandra if you did that," said Marilyn. "She's really hurting. It would give her a boost."

"Are you *sure* the Abneys are planning on leaving? With little Asher buried here?"

"I can't say anything for sure," Marilyn averred in a tone tinged with just enough confidentiality to ensnare Hazel's trust, "but let's just say, odds are more likely that it *will* happen than that it *won't*."

"Well, that's too bad," said Hazel. "I always like his sermons. I think some of the new families have come because of his preaching. They'll probably leave again once he's gone." She sighed and asked the clerk for a pint of coleslaw.

∾

Later that night, Hazel called up Dale to ask him how to go about reserving a niche for herself in the columbarium.

"You gotta pay for it," Dale shouted down the line. "We're still in debt for that thing. We can't just give the niches away."

"That's fine with me," said Hazel with dignity. "I wasn't looking for a handout. I'd have to pay for a tombstone anyway but I'm sure this will be less."

"Probably," said Dale. "Why are you bringing this up now, anyway? Didn't just get diagnosed with something deadly, didja?"

"Don't be ridiculous," snapped Hazel. "There's nothing wrong with looking ahead. Besides, I thought it might be encouraging for Sandra. I know she's sad that only Alan's mother is in there and no one else has shown any interest in it. Not even the Abneys, who you'd think would support her."

"I remember you getting all upset at the thought of burning the little guy."

"Yes," said Hazel, exasperated. "I *did*. But now I'm thinking, why didn't they just cremate him so they could take him along with them when they leave? It must've been to stick it in Sandra's eye."

"Wait a minute, did you say they're leaving?"

"Would *you* want to go on living right next door to the

church your little boy fell off of? Would *you* want to be reminded of that every single day of your life?"

Dale emitted a reel of creative profanity. "But they haven't even been here that long. You mean we gotta go through the call process all over again?"

"Looks like it. I mean, it's more likely that they *will* leave than that they *won't*."

Dale shook his head vigorously at the receiver. "Do you know what," he said to her in a low growl. "Do you know that Pastor just talked to me and Al the other day about financing his trip to Germany this November? For some prayer thing Fritz was talking about when he was here. He's asking the church to pay for part of his way, even though we're still in debt for the columbarium *and* for part of Fritz's plane ticket. Does he think we're some kind of rich city church that can just go on financing one fancy project after another?"

"He's going in November, you say?"

"Yeah, that's when that peace prayer thing is, I guess."

"You know," said Hazel, unconsciously echoing Marilyn's confidential tone, "think about it. He wants to go in November to this thing in Germany. But in December—that'll be the first anniversary of the, you know, the tragedy. On Christmas. Do you think they'll stick around for that?"

"Not after what happened on Ash Wednesday," said Dale.

"I bet," said Hazel, "that Pastor Donald will stay on at Mt. Moriah just long enough for us to pay his way to Germany. Then he'll come home and hand in his resignation. And we won't have a pastor on Christmas."

"But we *will* have a big ol' pile of debt," concluded Dale. "I wouldn'ta thought it of him."

"It's not just him," said Hazel. "It's Carmichael, too. I mean, you heard how she treated Sandra at the lunch after the burial."

"Naw, I wasn't there when it happened, I was checking on George while he was covering up the grave. Arlene mentioned something to me about it."

"Well, I was there, and so was Marilyn and Al. You just ask Al about it."

"I will," said Dale.

∽

On Friday Dale sat Al down over a beer at the VFW, which was haunted by the odor of chili dinners past, and asked what he knew about the pastor leaving soon.

"I don't know anything about it," said Al. "Who told you that?"

"Hazel Quinn."

"Oh, well. You can't trust everything she says."

"She made it sound like a sure thing. And who can blame them, with the tragedy happening just next door? But listen to this." He explained all about Pastor Donald's plot to get an all-expense-paid trip to Germany and then ditch the congregation upon his return.

"That doesn't sound like him," said Al. "And anyway, he didn't ask for all the expenses, just part of them."

"Not being concerned enough about money sure sounds like him," retorted Dale.

"Well," said Al weakly.

"Hazel and Arlene both told me something about Carmichael taking down Sandra during the burial lunch. I wasn't there but you were, weren'tcha? What exactly happened?"

"I'm not sure I'd call it taking her down," said Al. "Though I guess it was kind of tense." Emotions were not Al's forte, but he had to do better than Dale. "She just said they didn't want to cremate the little guy because they were Jews and enough Jews had already been burned in the ovens. Which I guess is true."

"You see," said Dale.

"What?"

"That explains it. That explains Pastor Donald thinking he can skim off the church for his own projects. Jews are known for being stingy, aren't they? Well, she got to him. Carmichael."

"*Dale*," said Al, shocked. "How can you say such a thing? You told me you liberated one of those camps. You saw what happened to them."

"It has nothing to do with that. I don't agree with the Nazis, of course not, didn't I fight against them? You never saw it 'cause you served in Korea but I saw, it was the most disgusting thing I ever seen in my life, what had become of the ones who were still alive, like walking skeletons. And I'm a farm boy, so I'd seen my share of disgusting things. I'm glad I helped kick those Nazi bastards' asses. What I'm saying is totally different, just that Jews have a reputation for being a certain way about money, and maybe it's rubbed off on Pastor."

"That can't be right," said Al mulishly.

"Well then, how do you explain Carmichael being so hard on Sandra? I talked it over with Arlene and she agrees with me it don't add up somehow. The two of them always seemed pretty tight. Sandra was the one who organized the groceries for them back in January. Heck, Alan is Carmichael's boss. They've done nothing but good for the Abneys. You know what it is? I'll tell you what it is. People always bite the hand that feeds."

"That's true," said Al. He'd certainly seen that phenomenon more than once. Nobody hates an insurance man more than when it turns out he was right about needing a policy for some disaster. No gratitude at all.

"I mean, I'm not saying it isn't rough on them. You can't expect people to lose a little kid and not go kinda crazy. I'm sure that's why they want to leave."

"Maybe it's better this way anyhow," sighed Al.

"Yeah, remember what happened on Ash Wednesday? What are the chances he'll make it through a Christmas service ever again?"

"It's a shame to take it out on Sandra, though."

"Yeah, and her just trying to help."

Al said, "Well, don't go talking to anyone else in the congregation about this just yet. We don't want people to panic or stop coming. We should discuss it only among the council members for now."

∼

After Al had ascertained, to his annoyance, that not only Dale and Hazel but also Sandra and Marilyn knew about the Abneys' plans to move on after Donald's partially-paid-for trip to Germany, it fell to him to inform the other council members who remained unaware of the plotting afoot.

Telling Eunice turned out to be easy enough. Al made a run to the nursery on Saturday morning to pick up tomato, eggplant, and pepper seedlings for Lynn to plant in the backyard. There he ran into Eunice clutching seed packets splayed like a hand of poker. After hellos and garden inquiries, Al told Eunice that, while she wasn't to mention it to anyone else, she should know that the Abneys would probably be leaving before the year was out.

"Well, I should think so," replied Eunice.

"Really?"

She leaned in. "*I* wouldn't show my face again after that sort of shocking treatment of a friend."

"You mean—"

"You were right there! You saw it. I could hardly believe my ears."

"Well now—"

"I have been in touch with Sandra," Eunice announced importantly. "She is *very* hurt. And after all she's done for the Abneys. Alan, too. It's disgraceful treatment. I don't care how upset Carmichael was over the, I mean, you know, it being the day of the burial and all. There's no excuse for that kind of talk, and in front of so many people."

"I guess it didn't strike me as being quite so bad as all that."

"Oh no?" retorted Eunice. "It's all part of a *pattern*, is what it is." Al suddenly had the feeling that Eunice was not so much speaking as quoting. "Pastor and Carmichael both. A pattern of passive-aggressive behavior. Nothing overt or obvious, but a subtle pattern."

"I'm not sure that what Carmichael said was all that subtle."

"Take *my* case, then," insisted Eunice. She tapped her seed packets together like she was getting ready to deal a hand. "I returned to Mt. Moriah after years of going to Second Reformed because that's what Richard wanted for the children, but then I came back home again. But has Pastor Donald done *anything* special to welcome me back? No. Just that one Sunday when he had me join with those other people, the Fishers, who were brand new, not returning after years away like I was or from an old church family. I am, after all, the last of the Krauss line at Mt. Moriah."

Al couldn't think of anything to say except that Eunice was too full of her family line for her own good, but that seemed impolitic.

"And then there's the fact that he's made all these *changes*," she continued. "When I was a girl, the pastor wore black, reminding us to repent, not white, like everything is always so cheerful and sunny. It's *not*," she concluded with a bite.

"Well, I gotta get running so Arlene can plant these before she goes antiquing this afternoon, but it looks like just us on the council are going to meet tomorrow morning early before the service, around eight, at Tiny's, since they do breakfast on the weekends. Do you think you can make it?"

"Certainly," said Eunice. "It's my duty as a council member."

"Fine," said Al, and he peeled away past begonias and fuchsias toward the checkout.

~

Al couldn't get through to Jackie all day. He tried one last time the next morning at seven-thirty before heading to Tiny's. She picked up, sounding a little bleary.

"Sorry to call so early," he apologized, "but you weren't picking up yesterday. I guess you had to work a late shift."

"No, actually, I was up at the casino on the reservation with my mom and didn't get back till late."

"Win anything?"

All that came across the line was a derisive snort. He invited her to the council breakfast if she could make it. "Why're we doing that?" she asked.

"Oh, I'll explain it all once you get there. It's too complicated to say over the phone just now. You'll see."

But, as it turned out, Jackie didn't see. Clad in a Mötley Crüe T-shirt, the fringes of her hair now blue instead of green, and not touching anything but black coffee—McDonald's had ruined her for breakfast, she said—she listened to Al, Sandra, Marilyn, Hazel, Dale, and Eunice each say their piece on the Abney situation as her face turned stonier and stonier. At last the others' words ran out.

"So now you're up to speed," said Al.

Jackie shook her head. "I do *not* know," she said, "how all of you can sit there digging away at your pancakes while you're basically just *firing* our pastor."

"Whoa now," said Dale, and Eunice chimed in, "Who said anything about firing?"

"Maybe it hasn't happened to any of you," said Jackie. She leaned in with an aggrieved air and the rest of them leaned back. "Because, you know, you got the kind of jobs where you're secure and protected." Dale huffed but didn't interrupt. "But I've worked a ton of jobs where you are at the mercy of your manager, and when I say 'mercy' I don't mean it like we mean it in church. I mean like if he wants to pinch your ass or make you work Memorial Day last minute even though you already had plans, you do it or you're out of a job."

"I really don't see," said Marilyn, but Jackie was finding her preacher voice for the first time and cut her off.

"And I know what it's like when somebody decides they want you out and they start planting the little seeds, you know, like poison, in the mind of your manager and the other employees, and they squeeze you out. And they *always* find cause, the employment laws don't do shit to protect you if they're determined to get rid of you, not at the level I work at, anyway. People like you are probably safe from that kind of thing." Jackie pointed a martyred cigarette at Sandra.

"I think it's outrageous that working-class people are treated that way," Sandra protested.

"Sure. I bet thinking that helps you sleep at night," scoffed Jackie.

"Now look," Al attempted to interpose.

"It's not about *us* pushing *him* out, it's about *him* leaving after taking *our* money," insisted Dale.

"Where's your proof of that?" demanded Jackie. "That's what I want to know. Where's your *proof*?"

"It's a pattern," said Eunice.

"Oh, no, oh, no, I'm just not sure anymore," sniffed Hazel into a tissue.

Just then George slunk in through the door and dragged an extra chair over to the table. He looked like he hadn't slept. He always looked like he never slept anymore, a hangdog shadow trailing after him at all times. As he shoveled the dirt over Asher's coffin, Dale had tried again to persuade him that it wasn't his fault. But George was determined to cling and cleave to his guilt, like *it* was his wedded wife and not Ruth.

"So what're we talking about?" he mumbled, beckoning to the waitress.

After an awkward pause so the waitress wouldn't overhear their top-secret discussion, Al once again unrolled the whole sordid series of facts, punctuated by Dale's hot outrage and Eunice's haughty disappointment in Donald and Carmichael alike.

When he finished, Jackie leaned over to George and said, "And what I'm saying is, where's the *proof*? Sounds to me like they're judge and jury both, trying to squeeze Pastor out without any proof at all."

A dim but unmistakeable light flared in George's eyes for the first time since Christmas. "Who's behind all this?" he uttered in a low, dangerous tone.

The rest of the council looked around at each other with shrugs of bewilderment. "What do you mean, George?" said Al.

"I mean, where did it start? Who said what first?"

"Well—I guess Dale called me up and said the Abneys were going to leave."

Dale said, "Hazel told me when she asked about getting a niche in the columbarium."

Hazel said, "Marilyn told me at the deli counter."

But Marilyn got so flustered at the tracing of the rumor back to herself that all she could think of was self-defense, not passing the buck. She protested, "Listen to all of you! Like this is some nasty game of telephone, and turning on each other like that. We are all in this together. Pastors come and pastors go, but *we* are the church and we have to look out for ourselves, no matter who's in the parsonage and pulpit."

"I agree," said Eunice. "No pastor has stayed with us more than five years, not since Pastor Weber when I was a little girl."

"*You* didn't exactly stay with the church, either, Eunice," snapped George.

"I just question whether Pastor Donald really has our best interests at heart," said Marilyn.

"If one of my boys just died, I wouldn't have *your* best interests at heart, either!" Jackie snarled.

"Settle down, please," begged Al.

"Don't you pin this on me, Al Beck," said Jackie. "I'm not the one trying to drive the pastor out."

"If anyone's trying to drive anyone out, it's Carmichael trying to drive Sandra out," declared Eunice. "Say what you like, Jackie, but never in my life have I heard such a thing said in public by a pastor's wife to a parishioner."

All eyes turned toward Sandra. She was dressed in a cream-colored pantsuit with an apricot blouse. The understated professionalism was offset by a necklace of chunky agates and curly hair upswept with a tortoiseshell comb. She looked unimpeachably correct in every way. "It was very painful," she said, in a quiet, sad, respectful tone.

"Bullshit," countered Jackie. "I heard you hounding her about cremating little Asher. Why couldn't you just leave her alone?"

Everyone jumped on Jackie at once, except George, who crossed his arms and glared at Sandra. The rest of them defended Sandra's good intentions, criticized Carmichael's disproportionate harshness, skirted the matter of Jews and ovens, speculated on the timing of the Abney departure vis-à-vis the visit to East Germany, and arrived at no conclusion whatsoever.

"So now what?" George shot into the silence that settled over the group. The smells of maple syrup and sausage grease on the plates intermingled with old coffee and cigarette smoke.

"I have to go and warm up before the service," said Marilyn, fiddling around with her purse.

"But where does that leave things?" pressed George.

"We don't know *anything* for sure," said Jackie.

"I think we should give them a chance to tell us their plans," said Al.

"How long should we give them? Till the end of November, I suppose?" said Eunice.

"Not that long," said Al, "but a little while more. We'll see how things unfold about the trip to Germany. And meanwhile, let's not say anything to anyone, OK? It'll just discourage the rest of the congregation and they'll stop coming. We want to give Pastor Donald the chance to tell us himself, not because word leaked out."

Jackie shook her head and shoved off. "You're driving out a good pastor. Hell, I actually *remember* his sermons the next day. Never remembered a damn thing Pastor Whitney ever said."

Eunice slithered into her lightweight cardigan and said,

"He just makes it up as he goes along. I have never once seen a manuscript in the pulpit."

"But they're still good sermons," said Hazel as she followed Eunice out the door.

George stayed put in front of his undrunk coffee. The rest of the council members filtered out.

When he finally got through with his mug, George stomped up to the cash register to pay. The cook stood there, none other than Tiny himself, a man of gigantic girth and stature. George barely looked at him as he handed over a couple of dollar bills.

As Tiny dropped the change into George's hand he said, "So your pastor's leaving, huh? Tough luck."

∼

Kitty spent several weeks watching and waiting for hints from two quarters, namely, her father and Megan Moravsky. Her father disappointed. If he'd heard anything more from Father Pat about the ex-financier now in jail, he didn't say a word of it within earshot of Kitty. She knew better than to ask. Inevitably, living in the parsonage, she gleaned this, that, or the other salacious detail about people she barely knew, but asking outright was verboten. Sometimes, if she calculated her questions with precise vagueness and a tone of innocent incomprehension, Carmichael might let a little fact slip out. But even that was rare.

Lacking help at home, Kitty took to studying Megan. Kitty had to go right back to school after the burial—no long break like after the funeral—but Megan wasn't at school on the Monday or Tuesday after. Wednesday she turned up looking unusually pale, her freckles standing out like polka dots. Instead of playing kickball at recess, she complained of a stomachache and got sent to the nurse's office. The next two days she went to the library at recess. She hardly spoke up in class. None of the rest of their classmates seemed to notice anything was wrong with her at all. Kitty realized that Megan didn't have friends so much as followers. The followers took Megan's power for granted but never noticed her as a person, even when she was sad. Kitty, having achieved a state of friendlessness by choice, took grim joy in the realization.

The next week Megan's behavior went from withdrawn to childish. She returned to recess—and it was finally warm enough, and no longer too muddy, to go outside—but this time she didn't organize a dance routine like she'd seen on MTV or give a lecture about Molly Ringwald, whom Kitty was pretty sure Megan liked only because they both had red hair. No, instead, Megan wanted to *play*. Like the boys still did. She suggested acting out *A Wrinkle in Time*. A few of the other girls had read it, though Kitty was sure none of them had read it as many times as *she* had. But Megan had trained them to forget how to play, so they were at a loss when she tried to reinstate it. After forty minutes of abortive effort, an exasperated Megan suggested that everyone bring in their Barbies the next day. That suggestion took effect. Even if imagination was dead when left to its own devices, the hair and clothes of plastic perfection could partially reanimate it. Kitty was disgusted. She did not have, never ever had Barbies, and if at one stage in her girlhood she'd resented her mother for refusing to indulge—even forcing Bammy to take back one such gift unopened—by now Kitty wore her Barbielessness as a badge of pride.

Barbies lasted the rest of the week but lost their luster by Friday afternoon. The next Monday, Megan announced a new plan. They were going to try again to act something out, something less challenging than *A Wrinkle in Time*, a story better suited to a gaggle of girls. Kitty expected something dopey like the Baby-Sitters Club. "And of course you'll want to be Kristy," Kitty sneered under her breath.

But Megan said, "We'll play *Little Women* by Louisa May Alcott. I read it over the weekend. It's really good."

The by-now familiar jolt of rage shot through Kitty. She leapt off her swing and bore down on Megan, who was loitering by the jungle gym. "There is *no way* you read that whole book over the weekend!"

"Did so," retorted Megan, though she looked more startled than offended. It had been months since the two of them exchanged words directly.

"You must have read the abridged version, then," Kitty sneered.

"No, I read the real version."

"That book is like five hundred pages long! If you read it, you couldn't have done anything else all weekend."

"I didn't. I read all weekend. It's a good book and I liked it."

"I don't believe you."

"I don't care if you believe me or not. I read the whole thing."

"You didn't even go to church?"

"No, I didn't even go to church, what do you care?"

Kitty was sorely tempted to say something about Father Pat. She bit her tongue and said instead, "I bet you want to be Jo, then, don't you?"

"What? No," said Megan. "She gets married to that old professor. Yuck. I want to be Amy. She's the one who gets to marry Laurie."

Kitty fumed. The one and only thing she hated about *Little Women*—well, besides the fact that Beth died, though Beth was a bit annoying, to be honest—was that Jo refused Laurie, and he went off with Amy instead, who didn't deserve him. How like Megan to side with Amy instead of Jo!

And in that moment Kitty knew, without even having to go home and check, that Jo would never again visit the cave by the lilac tree at the edge of the drop-off. Megan had managed to destroy yet *another* member of her council.

Megan pressed on, "I suppose *you* want to be Jo, then? Sure, go ahead. You can have the stinky old professor." She tittered and all the girls joined in, despite the fact that they obviously had no idea what she was talking about.

All of a sudden Kitty felt herself the object of everyone's gaze. Since she'd gone back to school in February she'd been cold and, where necessary, offensive, to make everyone stop looking at her—stop looking at her as the girl whose little brother died, who was marked with death, who was somehow implicated in it, who might infect them with death, too, if they didn't watch out, so they had to watch *her*, closely, carefully. Kitty's elaborate indifference to anything and everything, set off by the occasional show of claws and bristles, succeeded in averting their attention altogether. But now they were seeing her again. Curious again. About Kitty, not Megan! Stupid idiots.

She took a deep breath. The sweet smell of mown grass acted like an intoxicant on her brain.

Kitty said, "What part of *Little Women* did you like best?"

Megan was clearly caught off guard. It sounded like a fair and honest question. "Well," she wavered, "I don't know, I guess the part..."

"The part where Mr. March comes home after being away for such a long time?" Kitty said pointedly.

Megan stared at her.

"He was away more than a year," said Kitty. She crept closer and looked straight into Megan's face. Her freckles popped out like punctuation against the sickly plaster of her skin. "I bet the girls really, really missed their dad. Don't you think so?"

"Yes," said Megan faintly.

Kitty felt the other girl's weakness. It was like a tonic. She gulped it down and kept going. "Imagine being a *whole year* without your father. Or even longer. Imagine wondering if he'll ever come back again." But even dads in prison come home again, thought Kitty. Dead little brothers don't. Ever.

Megan said nothing but tears pooled in her eyes. She was close to breaking.

"I don't think I could stand it," whispered Kitty. "I think I'd be crying my eyes out every day. I mean, if I *really* loved my dad."

All the other girls gawked at the standoff. Megan's damp eyes flitted to the audience and back to Kitty's inexorable stare.

"*Do* you love your dad, Megan?" she breathed. "Are you going to miss him when he goes away?"

All at once Megan broke. She bawled and ran off toward the door leading back into the school.

"What was that all about?" asked Jenny Ulster loudly.

"Nothing much," said Kitty, turning away and kicking at the wood chips underfoot. Then, casually, she tossed over her shoulder, "Except that Megan's dad is in jail."

With that she resumed her place on the swing and swung higher than she'd ever dared go before.

∾

It took four months in the company of Rachel weeping before Carmichael worked up the courage to approach again the real live Rachel who worked at the Shibboleth Co-op. There was a lot of weirdness to process first: the sheer ongoing fact that these apparitions haunted Carmichael's consciousness at all, that the former phantom iterations of herself had all merged and morphed into this one not-quite-herself icon of maternal sorrow who went by another name, and finally that the living bearer of the same name was a real live Jew, a Jew who knew it and admitted to it, a Jew who was not also a Christian like Carmichael was, in fact a Jew more like her parents were becoming—a-whole-nother level of weirdness right there— and maybe, in some way, what they hoped Carmichael herself would turn into.

But it was late May now, and the weather was irrepressibly gorgeous after so much snow and cold and then rain and clouds. It was a day to make you forgive upstate New York; the fraternal twin of the perfect October day, a different palate of colors but the same shameless exuberance. Carmichael had to do something festive, had to rejoice in the glory of the sunshine. Rachel weeping was always at her side, but by now so fixed in place that she no longer required constant attention. Some part of Carmichael grieved the tiny retraction of her grief. And yet, it was a relief to want to be alive and enjoy it, just for one bright day.

So then. A cup of the excellent coffee at the Co-op. Some kind of bakery treat. And an attempt to befriend Rachel. After all, Carmichael had declared to the world—or at least to the church basement—that she was a Jew. Rachel at the Co-op had figured it out long before. Why should they not be friends?

The odor of fenugreek enveloped her the moment she walked through the door. Some kind of essential oil trailed faintly behind; freesia, maybe. The café was blessedly devoid of people. The copy of *The Late Great Planet Earth* was still on the shelf, bookended by *The Moosewood Cookbook* and *Silent Spring*. The tofu glistened in its water bath and the sundried tomatoes in their tiny jars of oil. All of it breathed "home, home, welcome home" at Carmichael. She inhaled gratefully.

Rachel-for-real banged out of the back room at the sound of the tinkling chimes. "Hey there!" she called merrily. "Haven't seen you around here in awhile." Then a cloud crossed her face as the immediate recognition of Carmichael was overtaken by the reason for her long absence. "Understandably, of course," she added quickly.

"Don't worry about it," said Carmichael, surprised to realize she meant it. "It's hard to know what to say. I wouldn't have known before, either."

"Yeah, sure, of course," said Rachel. She became a portrait of solemn sympathy. Then, "Actually, what *do* you say? If you don't mind telling me. I don't want to say the wrong thing."

"'I'm sorry' is fine."

"I really *am* sorry."

"I'll tell you what the worst is," and suddenly Carmichael found herself unspooling a preposterously long discourse on helpful versus devastating responses to tragedy, the latter category considerably longer than the former, with "Here's how you could have prevented it" and "Everything happens for a reason" topping the list.

"Oh, man, do people really *say* that?"

"Not the people closest to us. But some people do. I think it's a form of protection. They're not really telling *me*, they're telling *themselves*, because if they can learn the lesson, then it won't happen to them."

How easy it was to tell Rachel this. Strange, since they barely knew each other. Carmichael was tempted to relate Sandra's cremation campaign and her own public rebuttal thereof. But maybe Rachel wouldn't feel the same way. Or might be offended. In Rachel's presence, Carmichael wasn't sure anymore that she had the right to her reasons.

She grew self-conscious and gabbled on, "Are you roasting today? I don't smell the beans."

"No, but I did a couple days ago and it's still perfectly fresh. Give me a couple minutes and I'll brew you a cup."

"Perfect. Can I have one of those black-and-white cookies too? They remind me of home."

They chatted lightly of favorite places in the City, what they missed most, and why it was worth it to both of them to live in Olutakli County anyway.

"I just couldn't take the crime anymore," said Rachel. She set down the cup and saucer on the table and accepted a seat in response to Carmichael's friendly gesture. "I only got mugged once, and it wasn't that big of a deal in the end, I guess, he just snatched my purse and ran, but afterwards I couldn't ever *not* think about it. The crime was worst in the most interesting places, and I couldn't afford to live in the safe places. Up here you can get a house for a *song!*"

"Do you live right here in Shibboleth?"

"Yeah, up on Iroquois Street." She described the Victorian extravaganza that she and her "total goy of a partner" had bought and renovated.

Carmichael recognized it at once. "Wow, that one?"

"You wouldn't believe the hardwood floors. They could be a museum exhibit all on their own. Where do you live?"

"In the parsonage. It's the house right next to Mt. Moriah, you know, the church way up on the hillside. It's pretty common, or at least used to be, for the church to give the pastor a house to live in. Pastors' salaries aren't usually enough to make them homeowners, even in an area like this."

"Oh, right. Is it nice?"

"Not bad," said Carmichael. "A little rough around the edges. But they take care of the main stuff and keep us well-supplied with firewood for the winter. In fact, it's kind of cute, every spring the men of the church get together and chop down trees on one member's property and leave them to dry out over the summer. Then in the fall they get together again and split them into firewood and haul the logs over to the parsonage. The church ladies always make a big lunch. It's kind of a festive day, actually."

"Huh," said Rachel. "That's real old-school. Well, I'm sure you'll miss that part of it."

Carmichael paused mid-sip. "What do you mean?"

"After you've left. After you've moved on to wherever it is you're going next."

"Oh." Carmichael resumed her sip and then set the cup down. "I suppose. But it's so far off, I hadn't really thought about it."

"Is it? I thought you guys were leaving before the year was out."

"No!" exclaimed Carmichael. All at once her heart was pounding. "We're not leaving. We haven't even considered leaving. Where did you get that idea?"

"Oh," Rachel faltered. She shifted around on her stool. "I thought it was common knowledge. You know, in a small town word gets around and you hear things. Where *did* I hear it? It was a few weeks back already. I guess people were saying you'd leave because…"

"Because who would want to stay and be reminded of it every day?"

Rachel nodded.

"It would be worse *not* to be reminded of it every day," said Carmichael and again was surprised to realize it was true. "But is that all? Is it just people inferring we'd want to leave because of—because of Asher? My son," she added.

Rachel pushed back her seat. She looked like she wanted to make a run for it. "I mean, that's the *reason* I've heard people give. But it seemed like they were saying it was a sure thing you were moving away."

"We're *not*," Carmichael retorted, more forcefully than she meant to. It wasn't Rachel's fault. She didn't want to alienate her.

The tinkling of the door chimes drew both pairs of eyes away from the half-eaten cookie on the table.

Sandra stood there, momentarily framed in the doorway as she took in the sight of Carmichael.

Her. It's *her*.

Sandra squared her shoulders and gave Carmichael a curt nod. Rachel popped up and retreated to the counter. Sandra explained all too elaborately that she hadn't come in for a coffee, she didn't have time to stay just now, she'd only take a muffin and be on her way, thanks. Rachel narrated her own actions loudly and cheerily. Sandra accepted her wax paper-wrapped treat, counted out exact change, and whooshed through the door again.

Carmichael was making a pattern out of her cookie crumbs when Rachel sidled up to her. She seemed unsure of her reception. "Um, isn't that, wasn't that, isn't she a friend of yours? I thought I remembered seeing you in here together once."

"You did. She *was*," said Carmichael bitterly in spite of herself.

"Ah. OK. Well, it was her."

"Who told you we were moving?"

"She didn't tell *me*, but I overheard her talking to someone else about it. I only just remembered now. Some other woman who'd never been in here before. I didn't know her and I'm not sure I'd recognize her again if I saw her. But they were definitely talking about it. Sorry, it must have been a quiet day, and I can't help but overhear sometimes," she apologized.

"That's all right. It was probably someone else at the church. We can quell the rumor fast enough. I'm glad it hasn't spread wider."

"The thing is," said Rachel, hovering over her vacated stool until Carmichael gestured her back onto it, "it was her I heard it from first, but I definitely heard about it again from someone else. Let me think a minute." She clamped her eyes shut. "Wait… almost… got it. It was the wholesaler. He makes deliveries and is really chatty. Nice guy. He came here after Tiny's, I guess. Heard it from him. That guy is a real chatterbox, too."

"Why on earth would Tiny and a delivery guy be talking about *us* leaving Shibboleth?" demanded Carmichael.

"Beats me." Rachel shrugged. "But what I'm saying is, if those two guys are talking about it, then everyone knows by now. I'm really sorry. You should just assume that everyone in town knows for a fact that you're moving away."

"I can't believe this."

"That's the downside of small-town life," conceded Rachel. "I've had a taste of it myself. Word got out that Todd and I smoke weed sometimes. So now at least once a week someone comes in asking if they can buy some off of me. They think a co-op is the same as a head shop!"

"I need to go. I need to tell Donald about this." Carmichael gathered up her things.

"You bet. Look, I'm really sorry. About everything."

"Thanks. Better to have found out about the rumors, though. Thanks for telling me."

"I didn't even know I was telling you anything." Rachel cleared away the empty plate and mug.

Carmichael stopped. This was not how she wanted the conversation to end. She wanted to ask Rachel about something, something that would connect them, something about the huge stuff—life and death and whether there was a God and being Jewish and what was and wasn't friendship.

No. Not now.

Ever? Maybe.

If they stayed in Shibboleth.

This is all my fault, thought Carmichael.

∼

As Carmichael banged through the door into the pantry, Donald replaced the phone on the hook. "I just had the weirdest conversation with Al," he told her.

"Oh, no. Oh, God. What did he say?"

Donald looked at her in surprise. "You seem flustered," he observed.

"Just tell me, tell me what he said!"

"Well, I was looking over the agenda he dropped off for the council meeting next week, and I noticed that he'd forgotten to add the item about my proposed trip to Germany in November. Because we have to talk about the budget, since it wasn't in the original year's plan. I figured he just forgot, so I called him up to ask him to put it back on. But he was just kind of silent, at first, after I mentioned it, so I said, 'Al?' and he answered, 'You really want to go through with this?' and I said, 'Well, if the council agrees to it,' and he said, 'You sure?' I figured he was worried about my safety over there, so I said, 'I think we can trust Fritz that I'll be all right,' but then Al said, 'I'm not worried about *that*' and clammed up again. So I said, 'What *are* you worried about, then?' but all he said was, 'All right, if that's what you want, I'll put it back on the agenda.' He said 'back on the agenda,' which means he must have taken it off on purpose, but I never got an explanation out of him as to why."

"They think we're leaving!" shouted Carmichael.

"What do you mean? And keep your voice down," he added, glancing out toward the dining room where Kitty was working on long division, Saul on penmanship.

In a low frantic tone Carmichael conveyed all she'd learned from Rachel.

"Tiny?" Donald said in disbelief.

"Yeah. But why? How? I racked my brains on the drive home and I can't think of anything. Who do you think Sandra was talking to at the Co-op?"

Donald reflected a moment. "Now that you mention it, I noticed that Eunice sat in the same pew as Sandra and Alan last Sunday. They were behind you, so you might not have seen them."

"Oh, it *would* be Eunice," said Carmichael viciously.

Donald could not bring himself to argue.

"It's been weird the past few Sundays, but everything is so weird since—since all the way back in December. One weirdness doesn't necessarily distinguish itself from another. But do you think, after what I said," and Carmichael's voice switched from hostility to anguish, "do you think I broke something? In the congregation. That I turned them against us?"

"Not all of them," said Donald. He stared at the ceiling. There was a stain like an inkblot test where rain seeped through a small chink in the shingles over many years, not serious enough to fix but sufficient to fascinate. It looked like a Holstein. "But it does explain some things. George was a little warmer to me this past Sunday. He muttered something I couldn't quite catch, but his tone was apologetic and supportive. And then Jackie, too—"

"Oh, yeah!" Carmichael interrupted. "Sorry, I didn't think of it at the time, but as she was walking to her car she saw me and said something like, 'You're a good woman and a good mother and don't let anyone tell you otherwise.' Which I took to be her way of trying to comfort me after, you know, after letting one of my children die." She let out a harsh little bark of laughter. "And I did find it strangely comforting. But now, I wonder, was she saying it because—"

"Because a faction is turning against us," Donald finished her sentence.

"Because of what I said to Sandra."

"Well, that might be part of it. But something else is going on here. Why was Al being so weird about my trip to Germany? And what about *Tiny*, for heaven's sake?"

The phone rang. Donald and Carmichael both stared at it like it was a feral dog gathering itself up for the attack.

Donald took a deep breath before answering. "Oh! Mrs. Onderdonk," he said after a pause and leaned out of the pantry to look at Kitty, who perked up and returned his gaze upon hearing her teacher's name.

"What?" Carmichael hissed at him.

He waved her to silence. An alternating series of "oh" and "I see," and then, "I'm so sorry, of course, I'll have a talk with her." He hung up. "Saul," said Donald, "why don't you take a break from your homework and go upstairs and play for awhile."

Saul opened his mouth to argue, then looked from his father to his mother and over to her sister, who had turned as red as Spiderman. He slid off his seat and trotted upstairs.

"Come on in here with us," Donald said to Kitty. He could tell Carmichael was barely holding in her anxiety at what was coming, but it was obvious enough that Kitty knew.

She slunk into the doorway and fidgeted with her charm bracelet.

"How did you find out about Megan's dad going to jail?"

"I overheard Father Pat telling you about it."

Donald was horrified at his carelessness. Though how he could have been otherwise, right after the burial, and Father Pat telling him openly about it—"But he didn't name any names!"

"I know, but I figured it out. He said it was a girl my age and all the other stuff added up. I am a detective," she said defensively. "I *deduced* it."

"Even if you deduced it, that was no excuse for using your knowledge against her."

"What did she do?" Carmichael demanded.

"She made Megan break down in tears and told the whole class that her father was in jail."

"I only told the girls!"

"First of all, he's not in jail right now. Father Pat let me know. He's been released pending trial. But he could get taken away from his family for a very long time."

"Then she could've argued back and told me I was wrong. But she didn't. That's *her* problem, not mine."

"Kitty," said Donald, sounding severe, a severity so rare that when it did manifest it turned his children's bones to water, "we are a pastor's family. We are entrusted with private information about people's lives. I know you can't help overhearing things, but this rule extends to you, too. If you betray trust, it reflects on your mother and me. It reflects on God. You damage the reputation of all of us."

Kitty stared down at the floor, her hands dug deep into her pant pockets.

"I know you've had a hard time with Megan," added Carmichael, "and I know she isn't your favorite person. But think about it, Kitty. Her dad was arrested and might end up in jail for a long time, and you just exposed her secret to the whole class. How do you think you made her feel?"

"I don't know, maybe like *you* made Mrs. Forrad feel!" Kitty screamed at her mother.

Carmichael staggered back like she'd been walloped.

"Kitty!" Donald rebuked her.

"I didn't do anything Mommy didn't do! I heard her! Everybody heard her! How come Mommy can do that and I can't?" She whirled and ran off, sobbing furiously. They heard her bedroom door slam shut.

"She's right," said Carmichael softly. "She learned it from me."

"It's not the same," said Donald. "What you said wasn't, well, it wasn't the wisest thing to say, but you weren't exposing any secrets, and Sandra had been using you, in her own way."

"No, there was no secret, but the fact is I had a choice about how to deal with Sandra and I made a bad one. And I'm an adult, Donald. Let's not excuse me more than I deserve. Yes, my son died and she used it against me. But I didn't have to say what I said. Kitty's a child, and I know better than you do what a tense relationship girls can have with each other. Kitty and Megan certainly have that. But I'm the one who taught my daughter to smack down her enemy in public."

"I still don't think—"

"Oh, let me have my sin, Donald. I don't mind. Maybe that will make me believe in God again."

He raised his eyebrows. "Don't you now?"

Carmichael looked at him straight on, a slight smile pulling at one side of her mouth. "No. Not really. Sorry. I really am an awful pastor's wife in every possible way."

"I envy you," he replied.

She snorted. "Really? How?"

"Well, I always knew it would come, sooner or later. I mean that unbelief would catch up with you. It's been so *easy* for you. The whole time I've known you. I used to envy how easy your faith was. I guess it was compensation for a childhood and adolescence without it. You know how I've struggled after growing up right in the heart of the church. But since Asher died—" this time there was no faltering before he said it "—oddly enough, all doubt has vanished. I've never been so certain of God. And it's terrible. I miss my doubts, to be honest. They could give me some buffer against the God who let my son die."

"I can't believe in a God who let my son die."

"That's probably more tolerable than believing in a God who *did* let our son die."

"Aren't we the iconic pastor's family," Carmichael choked. She leaned her head against Donald's shoulder. He stroked her hair. "All right," she said. "I'll go talk to Kitty. And then—oof. Then I'll have to apologize to Sandra."

Donald said nothing but squeezed her a little.

"Thanks for not asking me to do it sooner," she said. "I know it's the right thing to do, and not doing it sooner has hurt us, but I couldn't, till now."

"I understand," he murmured and kissed the top of her head. "I'm sure she'll understand. She means well. She'll forgive you and we'll sort out what went wrong."

Carmichael straightened up and patted his chest. "You've lost your gift of prophecy, dear," she said. "What you said just now, that was wishful thinking plain and simple. I'll apologize because it's the right thing to do, and because I have to, for Kitty's sake. But I am not at all sure it will set things right again."

Carmichael headed off to Kitty's room. Donald thought again of Fritz at the airport, of Sandra holding out an apple in the car.

Please let this be over, he prayed. Please let this apology be the end of it.

But heaven responded only with its habitual resounding silence.

CHAPTER TWELVE

June 1989

Oh, virtue!
Is this all the reward thou hast to confer on thy votaries?

Rachel weeping did not want Carmichael to apologize. She didn't say as much. She never spoke at all. It was rare even to see her face, covered as it usually was by her hands. Sometimes, in the middle of the night, Carmichael snuck out of bed if she was sure Donald was sound asleep. She slipped on a coat and out the door and sat down on the gravel behind the church. She looked up at the roof and then, leaning against Rachel weeping, let loose her own weeping. Rachel made for good company at such times. She let Carmichael experience her grief and, at the same time, study it from a certain remove. She let Carmichael do strange and unsettling things, like hold her arms up to the roof to catch Asher as he hurtled toward the ground, or imagine him as a flicker diving down with a precision that was both mathematical and artistic, swooping upward at the very last moment with a laugh at having fooled her, his white bottom bobbing off into the distance just like a real flicker's. Carmichael would laugh at Asher's trick. He fooled her, all right. Then Rachel would take her hand and lead her gently back into the terrible truth, and Carmichael would cry again, just because she missed him. Grief in Rachel's presence was pure. It didn't have the nihilism of daytime thoughts about a nonexistent God, a meaningless universe, the delusional lie of faith that had given such richness and joy to her life over the past fourteen years. The nighttime tears under Rachel's tutelage were always and only for Asher alone. But then the sun would rise, and Carmichael would have to face all the other losses and all the other griefs that crowded out the grins and jokes and little hands of Asher.

On the Sunday morning that Carmichael determined she would stage her apology to Sandra—personal and private, yet within plain view of the congregation, a public fact to stand on, just in case—Rachel weeping was not happy with her. Not at all. Cold and distant and disapproving as she had never been before.

"I have to do it," Carmichael tried again to explain. She was having a go at making croissants from scratch, fiddly and precise to absorb her nervous energy.

Rachel turned away from her, staring out the kitchen window.

"It's the right thing to do. There's too much at stake not to. For Kitty, if no one else." She thought there was a faint softening along Rachel's jawline. Appealing to maternal duty worked on her. "But also for the church. This is our life. I can't let this go on unchecked."

Rachel stiffened up again.

"I *know* she doesn't deserve it," agreed Carmichael. Her shoulders tautened as she pressed down and rolled out the cold butter inside its envelope of dough. "I *know* that. But isn't that the whole point? Aren't we supposed to forgive regardless?"

Now she felt that Rachel was not just disapproving but outright angry.

"Yes, I know that evildoers should repent, but it's not like it's Sandra's fault that Asher died," Carmichael insisted. She was getting angry in turn. "She's not the one who took him away. It's not like in your case. I don't blame you for not forgiving Herod. My situation is different. Can't you see that?"

Rachel turned and unveiled one of her rare direct gazes. There was something unfathomable in those eyes that knew grief with a level of expertise that even Carmichael could not reach. Carmichael had lost her boy to gravity, to chance, to bad luck, to relaxed vigilance, to the sheer random coldness of the indifferent cosmos. Rachel lost hers to malice: deliberate, pointed, sneaky, snaky, shameless, proud.

Which was worse? Maybe Rachel couldn't help but see malice everywhere. Her world was *too* meaningful in its battle between good and evil. She was importing meaning where it didn't belong.

Unless—what was it Donald said that time? He'd been reading Solzhenitsyn. That maybe there was no real difference between natural evil and moral evil after all. Herod's infanticides were an act of nature, while Asher's fall was the outworking of a moral evil woven into the very fabric of the reality.

Carmichael folded the dough in overlapping thirds. She rolled it out and folded it again, checking that the corners stayed sharp and square.

"Look," she said to Rachel, "this really doesn't mean that much. I'm making a small sacrifice for the sake of my family. Surely you get that. It's not the linchpin of the universe or giving way to evil. Apologies and forgiveness are what set things right again."

Rachel weeping walked out on her.

∽

During church Kitty couldn't help but notice how out of sorts her mother was. She kept singing the wrong line of the hymns, one verse too early or one verse too late. During the Apostles' Creed she inserted lines from the Nicene Creed by accident. When she got the communion wafer, she actually said "Thank you" instead of "Amen"! Not to mention fidgeting with her rings, Saul's earlobe, Kitty's braid, the frayed ribbons trailing out of the hymnal... Clearly, something big was about to happen.

So after the concluding "Go in peace, serve the Lord"—"Thanks be to God," Kitty let Carmichael shoot out of their pew, down the aisle, and out the main doors to loiter in the parking lot. Kitty slunk out the other way, through the door on the parsonage side of the church, and circled around. The fluffy hydrangea bushes afforded some camouflage. She pressed herself into the clouds of blue pom-poms at the corner of the church building and waited.

People exited, chatted, lingered before heading either toward their cars or back into church for Sunday School and Bible study. Carmichael shifted her weight from one foot to another, nodded hello, deterred with her very posture any attempts at conversation.

Until Mr. and Mrs. Forrad came out. Kitty saw her mother's body change, tense, turn. She saw a deep breath drawn. She heard, "Excuse me, Alan. Do you mind if I have a word with Sandra?"

Mr. Forrad nodded, curtly, and continued on to his car parked on the other side of the driveway.

Sandra was dressed in a periwinkle suit. She looked important and almost beautiful. Carmichael was in a paisley-patterned dress with a collar that reminded Kitty of a bib. She felt ashamed. Her mother shouldn't be lower than Mrs. Forrad, not in how she dressed or how she acted. Kitty *liked* it when she told off Mrs. Forrad in front of the congregation. Mrs. Forrad deserved it. Why was her mother acting all lowly and nervous now? It wasn't right.

"Sandra," Carmichael began, "I owe you an apology."

The other woman didn't say anything. She just held Carmichael in place with those cold eyes, the same color as her suit.

"What I said to you, after Asher's burial—it was unfair of me."

Still nothing.

Kitty watched her mother drop her face to the ground, take a breath, and try again. "It was a hard day. I was very upset. I overreacted." She looked up again. "But it wasn't right of me to take it out on you, not in that way. I'm sorry."

The crunch of gravel underfoot caught Kitty's attention. She peered around the corner of the church and saw other people filtering out—the organist, Ms. Bonnie, Mrs. Kipfmueller, and Mrs. Feuerlein. They saw the two women in conclave and gave them a wide berth, and yet, Kitty could tell, they didn't move so far off as to be out of earshot. They were listening.

Mrs. Forrad apparently decided she was ready to reply. Because she has an audience? Kitty wondered.

"What you said," came out the words loud, clear, and clipped, "was extremely hurtful."

"I know." Kitty felt her mother's shame and hated it.

"What you suggested—that was the very furthest thing from my mind."

Carmichael nodded humbly. She was taking the scolding from Mrs. Forrad like a puppy caught chewing on the furniture. Kitty had a sudden vision of herself kicking Mrs. Forrad to death.

"I have only ever wanted the best for you. Since you first arrived here, I've been looking out for you. Alan, too."

"I know." Just a whisper now.

"I just—I just don't know what to do with it. With what you said. How you could have… *turned* on me like that." She swept a hand across her forehead and let it trail off expressively.

More people were coming out of the church now, slowing down, pretending not to watch and listen. Mr. and Mrs. Beck, Mr. and Mrs. Mayer, Mr. and Mrs. Pohl. Ms. Jackie and (miraculous indeed) two of her three sons. Tammy, Michelle, and Lisa trailing admiringly after them. Mrs. Thyssen, who didn't even pretend to ignore the scene but seemed eager for an excuse to jump right into it.

Mrs. Forrad's eyes were like laser beams now, pinning Carmichael in place. "I need to know," she said, "that you understand that I have always had good intentions toward you and your family."

Carmichael did something funny with her head, like she

was trying to nod but her head decided to shake instead and the collision of the two actions was the result.

"I need to know that you understand that I'm on your side and was only trying to do the right thing."

Donald came out the door, still in his white alb and green stole, talking to a couple Kitty hadn't seen before—visitors, maybe tourists, who knew. And the Fishers. And Dr. Wheeler and his family. Kitty watched as all of them gradually noticed the attention of the others in the parking lot and followed their gaze to behold the subtle dressing-down being visited upon the pastor's wife.

Carmichael looked up, not at Sandra's face, it seemed, but over Sandra's shoulder, as if making eye contact with someone who wasn't there. "I have told you that I am sorry for what I said."

Pow! thought Kitty with glee.

"I'm glad to hear it. It hurt me very deeply. I'm completely willing to forgive you and put this behind us."

A line came zipping into Kitty's mind: But only if you bow down and worship me.

"I just need to hear that you understand what my intentions have been all along," Sandra pressed. "I need to know that you understand me."

A long pause.

It was silent across the parking lot, except for the sound of a chainsaw buzzing through a tree trunk somewhere deep in the state forest.

At last Carmichael said, "I understand you all right."

Puzzlement and offense wrestled for dominance across Sandra's face. "You know what kind of a person I am," she said.

Carmichael: "I do now."

The charade broke. Not like the shattering of a mirror or one of those gigantic icicles dropping off the church roof and impaling the snowdrift below. But everyone felt it. The congregants on the way to their cars snapped out of their freeze-frames and hustled along, reaching for handles too soon. They broke into noisy chatter. Donald asked the visitors for their phone number so he could arrange a visit. Sandra peeled away from Carmichael and practically ran to Alan waiting in their Volvo.

Kitty pressed back against the wall and let herself slide down to her heels. The hydrangeas kept her covered. A moment later Carmichael came into view, heading for the parsonage. She seemed to blaze, her face flushed and her very body sending off ripples of heat and energy. I could roast marshmallows over her, thought Kitty. She tore out from behind the bushes and caught up to her mother just as she turned the corner of the house, out of sight of the parking lot. She flung herself at Carmichael and hugged her with a fierceness she hadn't since fourth grade.

Carmichael was startled. "What's this?" she said, but she accepted the hug.

"I saw the whole thing," said Kitty.

"Oh, no," said Carmichael, pulling away. "That—you should know, Kitty, that didn't go at all the way I planned."

"I know! But it's not your fault, Mommy. I know girls like that. Don't feel bad. You did the right thing and said sorry, but she didn't want your apology. She wanted you to curl up at her feet and die."

"This doesn't mean you can treat Megan—"

"Yeah, I know, I know, I know," interrupted Kitty. She tugged Carmichael up the steps toward the pantry door. "Can I help you finish the croissants? I want to try rolling up the triangles."

Just then Donald appeared. He was still in his alb and stole and looked as comical wearing it here in the backyard as he looked stately wearing it in church. He saw Kitty and his open mouth snapped shut.

"She heard the whole thing," said Carmichael.

"What just happened?" His tone was not as friendly toward her mother as usual. Kitty felt it like an electric shock.

"Mommy apologized! She really did. It was a nice apology. But Mrs. Forrad wouldn't accept it. It wasn't enough for her. She wanted Mommy to say in front of everyone that she had always been a nice and wonderful person and never did anything wrong, but that's not true, and Mommy wouldn't lie about that, because you can't fix things with apologies if you lie to do it, can you, Daddy? *Mommy's* no liar!"

Carmichael directed an awkward shrug toward Donald. "She's summed it up pretty well, honestly."

Donald stared off at the forest and said nothing.

"Don't you believe us, Daddy?" Kitty demanded.

Donald turned back toward them and trod the path to the foot of the steps. He looked up at Carmichael.

"I know, I know," she said. "My attempt to make things better just made them worse. But I *did* apologize, as sincerely as I knew how." All the blaze had winked out of her. She looked like cold ashes in the trash ring.

"I can't pretend I understand any of this," Donald said at last. "I don't know why a simple apology couldn't work."

Carmichael said nothing. Kitty felt the tiny rupture between her parents. She had never felt any such thing before. It made her feel supremely icky, way worse than finding out she was Jewish.

"Don't worry about it, Daddy, maybe Mommy scared them off and they'll just leave Mt. Moriah and never come back!" Kitty gabbled, trying to fill in the rupture with cheerful words.

"We should be so lucky," Carmichael muttered.

"The thing is, they won't," said Donald.

"Why not? Too proud to admit defeat?"

"I was actually thinking of Alan's mother. She's in the columbarium."

"They can always take her and go somewhere else."

"And leave behind an empty columbarium and the church in debt? And Alan's position at the college? No, Carmichael, they are not leaving."

"But we aren't leaving either!" shouted Kitty. "They can take Mr. Forrad's mom and go away, but Asher is in the ground and he has to stay right here and so do we."

The three of them turned to look toward the cemetery and all at once realized someone was at Asher's grave. Donald reacted first as if it were grave robbers; he hitched up his alb and ran for it. Kitty tumbled down the steps after him and Carmichael followed.

A few seconds later they realized it was Saul. He was stretched out the full length of Asher's grave, the seams from the digging still visible in the grass. His palms were pressed against the gravestone, his toes pointed straight like a ballet dancer's.

"Honey, are you OK?" Carmichael panted when she reached him.

He rolled over to face her. "Yeah, I'm OK," he said.

"What are you *doing* here?" Kitty shouted.

Saul sat up, drew his knees forward and balanced his elbows on them, then dropped his chin into his hands. "Asher won't come out anymore," he said. He pouted as if Asher were hogging all the Legos. "He won't play with me or talk to me. All he wants to do is nap. He's so *boring*," Saul whined.

"Oh, sweetie," said Carmichael. She plopped down next to him and pulled him in close.

Donald squatted to keep his alb from trailing in the dirt. "I think it's time for Asher to sleep now," he said gently. "I think his playing days are over. Maybe it's better just to leave him to his nap. You should spend your time playing with your sister instead, or with some of the kids at school."

"I don't like any of the kids at school."

"Me neither," added Kitty fervently.

"You know what, Kitty had a great idea," said Carmichael. "She offered to help me finish making the croissants. We have to roll them up and bake them. Would you like to help us?"

"Asher likes croissants, too," Saul said. "Can I bring some

out to him when they're done? Maybe the good smell will wake him up!"

Kitty let out a strangled sound and stormed off.

"We'll see about that," said Carmichael.

～

The school year ended the next Friday. On the Sunday following, Alan, Sandra, and Eunice were conspicuously absent from church.

"See, I *told* you they'd just leave!" Kitty crowed when she overheard her parents talking about it after the service.

"Maybe," said Carmichael. "Are you done packing?"

"I think so. How many books can I bring? Meemaw has lousy books."

"Only what you can manage on your back."

Kitty vanished and reappeared with her knapsack. It bent her double with the weight.

"Take a few out."

"You said whatever I could manage!"

"That's not managing, that's becoming a hunchback."

"Fine," huffed Kitty. "You'd better check Saul's bag too, then."

Carmichael's eyes appealed to Donald.

He went upstairs. "What've you got in your bag there, sweetie?"

Saul proudly opened it to show.

Donald said, "Wait, aren't those Asher's clothes?"

"Mommy forgot to pack them for him."

"But... I thought he was staying in his, you know, in his napping place."

"Well, yeah," agreed Saul. "But if he stays behind, then *I* can wear his clothes."

"Aren't they too small for you?"

"No, look!" Saul peeled off his green Ninja Turtles T-shirt and plucked a long-sleeved black He-Man shirt out of the bag.

He tried to wriggle into it. His head didn't want to go through the collar and his arms got stuck in the sleeves.

"Saul…"

"Wait! Just wait! I'll get it!"

"Even if you get in, how will we ever get you out again?"

"I can do it!" came muffled through the cloth.

"Anyway, it's going to be too hot in Arizona to wear long sleeves."

Saul quit trying and shimmied out of the shirt again. He shoved it back into the bag. "It's OK, the rest of them have short sleeves."

The next morning George Pohl picked them at half-past five in the morning.

"I can't believe the sun's up already," remarked Carmichael as the men loaded the suitcases in the back of the van.

"Summer solstice in a few days," said George in the tone of astonishment he reserved for City people who failed to notice the pattern of something as fundamental to existence as the sun.

Before climbing in, Saul turned toward the cemetery. "Byebye, Asher!" he called with a wave of his hand.

The other three Abneys followed suit, not quite as loudly or enthusiastically. "Are you all right?" Donald whispered to Carmichael.

She gave him a rumpled smile. "He'll still be here when we get back," she said.

It was not yet the longest day of the year, but it may as well have been. After the drive to Albany there was a short commuter flight to Newark—besides the Abneys, only businessmen in uncomfortable suits. Carmichael distributed sugarless gum to the children to chew through the ear-torturing descent. Then a mad dash through Terminal B to make the flight to Chicago. Saul and Kitty ate with wild enthusiasm the cold bland inflight pastries that Carmichael passed over in horrified silence. In Chicago they had to wait a few hours before their departure for Phoenix, passing the time with a lunch of greasy deep-dish pizza and a bag of fancy candied nuts. Saul passed out the moment he was belted in to his seat. Kitty kept her nose pressed against the window and pestered Donald to tell her which state was which. Kansas was the most exciting for cultural reasons, since that was the home of Dorothy from *The Wonderful Wizard of Oz* (the book title, not the movie title, Kitty informed her father), but New Mexico was more exciting to look at. In the late afternoon they unfurled their cramped legs and stumbled down the jetway to find Papaw and Meemaw waiting for them. Meemaw enveloped Kitty and Saul in a tight weepy hug. Donald was surprised when his father did the same to him, and then both parents did to Carmichael. Kitty and Saul shot off and ran up and down the hallways to baggage claim.

"Get that energy out now," said Papaw. "We got a long way to go yet! Your mother and I drove down yesterday and spent the night in a motel," he confided to Carmichael and Donald. "With traffic slowing us down on the way out of Phoenix, we'll be lucky to make it in under five hours."

"You couldn't have chosen a more obscure corner of the country to retire to, could you, Dad?" joked Donald. "Well, I'm glad we're seeing it at last."

"I'm only sorry little Asher never got to see it." Dot wrapped herself around Donald's left arm and leaned her head on his shoulder.

"Me too, Mom, me too," he whispered.

Luggage in hand, they made their way to the parking lot and clambered into the station wagon. Meemaw presented the visitors with a huge bag of chimichangas. "Wow, these aren't like any tacos *I've* ever had before," Kitty marveled. Saul burst into tears after drinking down a little plastic container of red fluid that he thought was tomato sauce but turned out to be chiltepin salsa.

They drove on till dusk. The second and third generation of Abneys struggled to comprehend a landscape of such breadth, not the least bit green, and mountains on the horizon that never got closer no matter how steadily you drove toward them. Kitty tried rolling down the window once and choked on the blast of hot air. "Not while the air conditioning is on, honey," chided Meemaw.

At a rest stop they dashed through the blistering heat to use the bathrooms and Papaw handed the keys to Donald to drive them the rest of way to Hardyville. "Sure you're awake enough? You got up earlier, and three time zones behind, besides."

"I couldn't fall asleep in a car this cold anyway," replied Donald.

"We told you this was the worst time of year to visit," said Dot as she snuggled in the back seat with Saul who, shivering, tried again to wriggle into Asher's He-Man shirt.

Everyone slept late the next day. Kitty and Saul didn't rouse themselves from their stations on the two sofas in the living room until the smell of pancakes got to them. "Where's the maple syrup?" inquired a puzzled Saul.

"In Arizona you get prickly pear jam," said Meemaw proudly. Kitty was game but Saul stared at the purple ooze distrustfully and would have nothing but gobs of margarine on his pancakes. As soon as breakfast was done Kitty dashed for the TV because Meemaw and Papaw had cable. "I *love* this show!" she shrieked, settling herself three feet from "Down to Earth."

Donald and Carmichael declined the offer to head straight out sightseeing—they wanted a day just to recover from the trip—but there was plenty to see from the subdivision of modest split-levels stacked on the hillside: the electric blue of the Colorado River, the jawbone of the Black Mountains, and the tremendous quantity of tall neon signs advertising casinos.

"Hardyville isn't *that* big of a town, is it?" asked Donald. "How does it support all this gambling?"

"We draw the locals," said Dot. "We're not that far from Las Vegas, but lots of people would rather come here instead."

"How far from Vegas?" asked Carmichael from over a cup

of Earl Grey. She loved her in-laws, but their idea of coffee was not to be borne.

"Oh, just thirty miles up the road," said Jimmy.

"Then..." Carmichael furrowed her brow. "Couldn't we have flown in there instead?"

"And give our business to the Sin City?" Dot was shocked.

Carmichael gazed through the window at the lurid strip along the riverside and held her tongue. Later she whispered to Donald, "I never thought of your mother as all that religious."

He shrugged. "You can take the girl out of the Holiness church... Besides, I think the only reason she doesn't go anymore is because my dad doesn't approve, and she never disagrees with Dad about anything."

Despite the astonishing heat—some days breaching 120 degrees, so that even with all the air conditioners running at full blast it was a cool 80 indoors, leaving everyone in a gilamonster state of lethargy—the next week was the most restful Donald and Carmichael experienced since Asher's death. His absence was nevertheless potent, not least of all because of Saul's daily struggle to fit into clothes too small for him. But also because they knew, even though they didn't say it aloud, that they were adding to their fund of family history something that Asher had not been and never would be a part of. This further act of living on without him was equal parts relief and treachery.

They visited the Hoover Dam, the closest to Las Vegas that Dot would agree to. No amount of wheedling on Kitty's part could persuade the adults to make the trek out to the Grand Canyon. "A few minutes of looking in this heat isn't enough to justify seven hours of driving," explained Papaw. Meemaw made it up to her with a trip to the mall for a new bathing suit, real moccasins, and a dozen piggy cookies. Saul ducked outside for five minutes at a time to study the saguaro cacti in the backyard, artfully arranged by Papaw amidst pink and red rocks. Carmichael, who had never seen a live cactus in her life that wasn't planted in a pot, decided to try to make something of the nopales paddles for sale in the supermarket; the effort was fun, though the result was something less than delicious. She had better luck with a salad made of tepary beans, corn, tomatoes, and another novelty, a leafy herb beloved of the local Mexican population called cilantro.

"They put it in everything here," Dot informed her.

Saul spit it out. "It tastes like soap," he complained.

Sunday morning Donald did the unthinkable: he skipped church. "God won't strike you down for it. I mean, he hasn't gotten me yet, has he?" said Jimmy. It was almost six in the morning, the sun winking pink and gold over the eastern horizon as they pulled into a golf course with grass as unnaturally green as one of the casino signs. Donald was startled by the lingering chill of the desert night. "Don't you worry," said Jimmy. "By the time we've done our eighteen holes, you'll be begging the sun for mercy."

Jimmy was an excellent golfer, Donald rusty at best. The concentration required to reanimate his muscle memory during the first six holes relaxed Donald enough to start talking to his father. First and foremost of Asher. How the four of them were managing, what made it worse and what made it tolerable, the burden of opting into life day after day after day. Jimmy talked mostly about Dot's grief, which manifested as a smothering blanket of depression that would swallow her up for days at a time. Then she'd spring up as if launched from a trampoline and devote herself frenetically to some project, crocheting or pickling peppers or playing euchre with her new friends in the neighborhood. Jimmy said less of himself, only what kind of a world was it that things like this happened, and Donald knew it wasn't the world that Jimmy objected to but God.

At the thirteenth hole Jimmy got around to speaking plainly. "What I don't get is why God treats his fans so terrible."

"It wasn't God who did this to us," said Donald automatically, though he wasn't sure he believed what he was saying.

Rationally he didn't buy that line of thought at all; he'd left behind tit-for-tat religious logic long ago. But the deep, scared, furious part of his soul couldn't assign any other meaning to a pastor's boy dying on Christmas. How could *that* be nothing more than a rotten coincidence?

It was precisely the awful co-incidence, the happening at the same time, that had rolled away all of Donald's doubts about God and left in their place a gigantic boulder of immovable certainty.

"It's not just you," said Jimmy, as he watched his ball sail away in an elegant arc against the shimmering sky. As predicted, the heat was decorating his forehead with a tiara of sweat. "He did the same damn thing to my dad, your grandfather."

Donald stopped mid-swing and looked up. "How do you mean?"

"I don't suppose anyone ever thought to tell you," said Jimmy. He was peeling off his gloves, his fingers pink and swollen like little sausages. "My folks got married in 1911 but your Uncle Mort didn't come along till 1920, then your Aunt Helen, then Aunt Vera, then last of all me. Back then, nine years was a long time to go without a baby, and of course it wasn't on account of birth control."

The prospect of Grandfather Abney even contemplating birth control was so startling that Donald said nothing and leaned on his club.

"Don't lean on your club like that," said Jimmy. "Well anyways, the reason why is that my poor ma had one miscarriage after another. I figure it's 'cause they were so poor she couldn't eat right to sustain a baby. I know your church doesn't pay you what you deserve, but you're raking it in hand over fist compared to my pa way back when. Mort has had health problems all his life, he was born so scrawny. Ma and Pa were doing better by the time the rest of us came along."

"Miscarriages are really hard on a couple," said Donald in a detached pastoral tone.

"Yeah, that was bad enough, but what really did it was baby Benjamin. He was the first of us to be born."

"Your—your brother?" stuttered Donald.

"Yep, the brother I never knew. He came along in 1918, just as the war was ending. My dad didn't fight, you know, he was already a preacher then and whoever it was decided about the draft said they needed him to preach more than to fight. He was kind of a pacifist so I guess it suited him fine. Anyway, he and Ma took it as a sign of hope—a baby finally lived to birth, the war was over, life was winning out over death."

"What happened?" Donald whispered. He felt a tidal wave of worry and grief and loss for this uncle he'd never even known he had, all his sorrow for Asher abruptly redirected to the phantom baby.

"He choked to death," said Jimmy. It came out harsh. "You should probably take your swing so we can move on. It's not gonna get any cooler." Donald started to protest but Jimmy said, "Swing and I'll tell you the rest as we go on."

Donald swung. It was his best all morning. They alighted the cart and proceeded to the green.

"It happened at home, one of them little tiny houses they built around the turn of the century. I know it only from one or two pictures that survive, you know, those square black-and-white ones with crinkle-cut edges? Anyway, I guess little Benny was crawling by then and he found something and shoved it in his mouth and it got stuck in his throat. Ma tried to pull it out with her finger but it just went farther down. Pa wasn't home, I don't know where he was, a prayer service probably, and they didn't have a car and weren't near any hospital, so she carried him into town in her arms, watching that poor little guy turn blue. By the time she got to a doctor it was too late. Pa only got to see his little dead body. He didn't know when he left home that morning he'd never see his boy alive again."

Donald was beyond words. The sunlight, growing stronger by the minute, dazed him and pinned him in place.

"Nowadays I guess a couple would wait awhile to recover before trying again, but that wasn't an option for them, so Mort came along soon after, then the rest of us. Our ma sure did love us, though sometimes it was a bit much. I guess losing Benny did that to her."

"What did it do to your dad?" Donald asked.

They got out of the cart and Jimmy handily putted his ball into the hole. "I don't know," he said. "Actually, I never heard the story direct from either of them, only from my Aunt Minnie when I got older. Of course I didn't know my parents before it happened, so I couldn't compare. But it must have done something."

"Must have," said Donald. He tapped his own ball into the hole.

"First time under par!" said Jimmy. He beamed, then took a deep breath and continued. "I know you don't approve of me not going to church, son," he said. "It's not because I don't believe in God. I surely do. It's just that I hope if I don't show up in God's house, he won't notice me and will just leave me be."

"Dad…"

"I know you gotta argue. I respect your faith, Don, and I respect your courage. But from where I'm standing, God struck down the child of my father and now he's done it again, striking down the child of my son. He's got a thing for killing off sons, doesn't he? It's all over the Bible. That's always had me worried about *you*, to tell you the truth. So can you blame me for not wanting anything more to do with God than I can help?"

The sun was so strong now that Donald thought he was going to faint. He could barely see through the glare, even with his visor pulled down low and sunglasses slipping on his sweaty nose. "No," he said at last. "I don't blame you one bit."

"All right then," said Jimmy. "Let's finish up quick and head home before we get heatstroke."

∽

A few days later the weather forecast said it wasn't to exceed a mild 95 degrees in the afternoon, so Donald decided to take an excursion of his own to Spirit Mountain on the other side of the Nevada border. He invited his parents and children and Carmichael along, but even the comparatively gentle 90s could not offset the prospect of a steep uphill climb with no shade. Donald didn't mind, and as he drove off before dawn, he admitted to himself that he'd chosen an outing that wouldn't appeal to anyone else, precisely to be alone for awhile.

The analogous loss of sons between him and Grandfather Abney had haunted his every waking minute since Jimmy told him about it. "The analogy of faith?" he asked himself with a grim little laugh. "Not quite what Barth had in mind." He turned onto Christmas Tree Pass Road and offered God ironic thanks for the reminder of Asher's death in this most un-Christmasy of places. No other cars were parked at the trailhead lot. Donald felt genuine gratitude at that. He stepped out of the car into a slender stream of cool air flowing down and around the granite litter scattered across the slopes before him.

He set out, following the mute instructions of cairns that reminded him of flying saucers. He wondered for a moment what would happen if aliens were tiny. Shaking his head at the strangeness of his thoughts, he turned his face toward the peak. The terrain was pebbly and dusty underfoot, continually drawing his eyes away from the goal. The plants were uniformly strange to him. The only one he could identify was the barrel cactus, shaped like its namesake. Other cacti stuck out twisted limbs at awkward angles, like a TV antenna or a crucified arm. Still others were clumps bound at the root, huddled together as if for protection against the sun. Surely no other predator could be interested in anything so thickly covered with spines. In fact, Donald realized, there was hardly a plant to be seen without an armory of needles or thorns. He tapped a black-hued bush gingerly. That was enough to draw blood. He stuck his finger in his mouth and sucked on it. "'They shall look on him whom they pierced,'" he quoted aloud to a pair of hawks coasting on the air currents far overhead.

Soon sheer physical effort drove all thoughts from Donald's mind. He panted, sweated, conserved the quart of water in an old apple juice bottle that Dot had found for him to carry in the string bag on his back. Every so often he stopped to catch his breath in the inadequate shadow of a granite projection like a faceless statue. But it was only going to get hotter. He pressed on.

Three hours into it, a few awkward scrambles on his gangly untrained limbs gained him the summit. Grandfather Abney was waiting there for him.

The white-haired man gestured to an outcropping that offered a sliver of protection from the sun. Donald picked his way over and hunched down on his heels. Grandfather Abney lowered himself to Donald's right with surprising grace. They looked together out over the plains, at first glance dusty and brown, but as they gazed complex patterns of light and dark emerged.

Donald said, "I'm sorry about Benjamin."

"As am I about Asher," Grandfather Abney replied. He set a large bony hand over Donald's. Even now Donald felt dwarfed by the man.

"Is that why..." Donald stopped. Grandfather Abney nodded his approval of any question. This was not a place to dissemble. "Is that why you always needed to be so certain? Because of the sorrow."

"It started there," the other acknowledged. "Your father doesn't know the whole story."

"Will you tell me?"

"Yes." Grandfather Abney settled his back against the rough wall of rock behind him. "No false modesty, Donald, but I was a gifted preacher. I remember hearing once that some father of the early church was called the Golden Tongue—"

"John Chrysostom," Donald supplied.

"Could be. That was me, for as long as I could remember. I did love the Lord, and I knew he'd blessed me with the gift. I wanted to use it for his good. I got recognized for it early on. Back then, it didn't mean money or fame—not like the preachers you see on the television nowadays. Back then we liked our preachers poor, to keep them honest. I see the point and don't argue. I was glad to do it all for God. Only it was hard on your grandmother, and the more so as we lost all those babies, and finally Benjamin, the 'son of my right hand.'"

A hawk swooped low and seemed to regard quizzically the two of them (can it see us both? Donald wondered) in anticipation of a meal.

Grandfather Abney continued, "You don't know the gospel till you know pain. And in the pain of all those lost little lives, my preaching caught fire like never before. All my anger and sadness at the Lord was lead that he turned into gold. When Mort finally lived, and then Helen came along, the elders decided I needed a better post to support the family, but also to put my gifts into greater prominence. My successes reflected well on them, too. Finally things were looking good for us."

Donald kept silent. He recalled his conversation with Carmichael early the previous December: her prospect of tenure, his contentment at Mt. Moriah, the favorable environment for raising their children. Why didn't he perceive it then? The false sense of security that precedes the tumble into the abyss.

"And then... well, you'll laugh at this. I'm sure you won't understand it for a moment. You have a life insurance policy, don't you?"

Donald was startled into speech. "Well—yes. Of course. As soon as Kitty was on the way, I set one up to look after her and Carmichael in case something happened to me, and one for Carmichael, too. And one for each of the kids, to cover funeral costs." He felt a shudder run through him as he recalled that he'd actually had to cash in one of those child policies. "There's a church agency that takes care of it."

"A church agency," said Grandfather Abney with a chuckle, but he was shaking his head. "You didn't even have to think twice about it. But when I was a young man, the very notion of life insurance was still a pretty new thing. We had huge debates about it. It struck a lot of us as blasphemous. Calculating the lifespan of a man like he was just another entry in a bookkeeper's ledger. Placing a price on his head. Charging more for this or that health condition. It looked to a lot of us like trading and gambling on a man's body, and above all defying the creator and giver of life. Would he not in his infinite wisdom provide both the lifespan of the man and the livelihood of his family?"

"But…"

"You needn't rehearse all your objections. Believe me, I've heard them all. Seems the world and the church alike have come down in favor of it. Maybe that's all right after all; I don't know. What I'm telling you is, there was a time when it was a fight. A big fight. These matters of life and death will rend a church like nothing else."

Again Donald fell silent, but this time what he saw in his mind's eye was the columbarium.

"So there I was in a big congregation of our church, I was preaching like I had never preached before, our numbers were growing, and this dispute erupted. We had a bunch of prominent businessmen in the congregation by then, a lawyer and a judge, too, I remember, and other notables of the town. Some had left their home churches to come to ours. They were buying life insurance policies and saw it their Christian duty to get others to do the same. I opposed them."

A movement across the toe of his sneaker attracted Donald's attention. He squinted over the top of his sunglasses and saw a beetle marching on some kind of mission. It had an off-blue patina, like rusted copper.

"I wouldn't blame you for thinking I was crazy to make such a stink about life insurance. But who knew better than I and your grandmother that you can't make any hedge against death? They talked a good game, 'providing for your loved ones' and 'in case the worst happens.' The worst had happened to us so many times already, and these men were saying that money would shield you from it. They said it was to look after the womenfolk and their children. You know how back then it was hard for women to work in any case, all the more so when they were young mothers. But something about it just sat wrong with me. Big companies turning a profit looking after these women, instead of their kin and their church looking after them. I guess sometimes kin and church fail people in need. But I thought I could see where it was all going. Before long, nobody would need kin or church because the company and its policies would cover you. Kin and church wouldn't even try anymore. Does that make for a better and godlier world?"

Donald sorted through objections as the beetle climbed off one sneaker and headed straight for the other. "You know," he said, "I feel like I ought to argue, but the truth is, I don't really know."

"Well, it's your world now, and yours to figure out, not mine. The point is, I took a stand, and it was not popular. And it clove that congregation right in two. I wouldn't back down—and I couldn't let down the folks who'd sided with me—and the other team wouldn't back down, either. Before long the elders of the denominational board got sucked in, too, and they couldn't reach any kind of agreement. We ended up splitting off and forming our own new denomination. I couldn't see any other way. I lost some good friends. Fellow believers." He exhaled and stared off at the endless expanse.

"I'm sorry," said Donald.

"The thing is, by the time it was all over and we'd set up our new church, even my allies came to the conclusion that a great preacher is not the same thing as a good pastor. I may have done the right thing, but at the cost of fracturing our church's biggest congregation. Let's just say they didn't exactly trust me not to do it again. For that matter, I didn't trust myself."

"I had no idea about any of this."

"It wasn't something I was proud to talk about. Time passed and people forgot. Your own dad and uncle and aunts were too little to know anything about it anyway. And to tell you the truth, life only got better for us after that. Our new denomination recommitted itself to the old-school model of itinerancy. I spent the next four decades preaching everywhere you can imagine, not just in congregations but at tent revivals in farmers' fields and high school stadiums. We were mostly a rural church but sometimes I went into bigger cities and we rented out a warehouse or abandoned restaurant in the poorer neighborhoods and I preached there. That got less effective as the years went on, but I was always in high demand in our congregations in the countryside, so I didn't worry about it too much."

"But you never served full-time as a congregational pastor again?"

"Never." Grandfather Abney's eyes followed the hungry hawks still circling overhead.

"Did you miss it?"

"Hard to say. I never stopped being a preacher, and a good one. They loved what I had to give them. I think I did some good. Would I have done better if I'd gone back into the parish? I might have done more harm. But then I wonder, would I have *become* better if I'd gone back into it? Maybe hopping around all the time deprived me of something I needed. And yet, I saw too many of my fellow preachers chewed up and spit out by their congregations. That doesn't make a holy man out of you, either. Some of them ended up bitter and mean-spirited. There were times when I thought, this yoke is too heavy for mortal men, Lord. There's no way to do this job right."

The beetle had traversed the second sneaker and was advancing steadily to the edge of the rock shelf. "Is that why you've come to me now?"

Grandfather Abney reached out his huge hand, which had laid so many blessings on so many souls, and clapped it to Donald's shoulder. "Donald, you were always dear to me, because I saw the same yoke laid upon you, already when you were a boy. I know my son saw it, too, and that he didn't like it because he knew, without knowing exactly why, what it had done to m[...] [*is he a ghost?*] [...]at I never knew how [...] could accept. You [...] w much it would extr[...]

Donald leaned into the phantom bulk on his right. It was almost like a hug.

Grandfather Abney said, tenderly, "You know you don't have to preach any sermon for me. You don't have to talk me into anything. Not anymore."

"I'm always trying to write it in my head, but I don't even convince myself."

"Let it go, grandson. I don't pretend to understand some of the decisions you've made, or how you manage to believe one thing and not another. But I see your faithful heart, and I trust it."

"That's where you make your mistake. You shouldn't trust me, because I don't trust *him*. I believe in God all right, but I don't trust him one bit. Not after what he did to us. All of us. You, too."

Grandfather Abney reached up and ruffled the lank sweaty hair at the back of Donald's neck. "Oh, it's worse than that," he said. "You *do* trust him. You can't help it. You just don't like him any. He doesn't need you to, though. He'll keep on pushing you forward to do his work no matter what."

"It's a rotten deal."

"Sure is. But we don't have a choice in the matter."

Donald dared a smile. "Are you saying that we *don't* actually choose this day whom we shall serve?"

Grandfather Abney smiled back. "I suppose I am. I suppose I am."

∽

George Pohl picked up the four of them at the Albany airport. He inquired distractedly about their trip and seemed bemused at best when Saul proudly offered him a lollipop with a scorpion entombed within. He declined. Carmichael pressed on him a box of candied nuts from the Chicago airport in thanks for shuttling them to and fro.

It was only once they'd gone a dozen miles along a virtually empty I-88 that George cleared his throat expressively and said, "Things been happening since you've been gone."

Kitty and Saul kept fiddling with their pins of the Arizona state flag, but Donald and Carmichael both snapped to attention. "Is that right?" said Donald in a voice so unnaturally calm that it betrayed how agitated he felt.

"People been talkin'," George continued cryptically.

"You mean, at church?" Carmichael prompted.

"Yes, indeed."

"What are they saying?"

"To be honest, not very nice things about you." George stopped short. "Carmichael" was too long and strange to say, "Mrs. Abney" too formal, "Ma'am" too southern, so he never called her anything at all.

"About Carmichael?" Donald supplied, in a sharp tone.

"It's that Sandra Forrad," croaked George. "She's spreading word that you're not fit to be a pastor's wife, saying harsh things about people and all."

"I never said a harsh word *about* anyone, I said a harsh word *to* her. And not to anyone else!" Carmichael exclaimed.

"You don't need to defend yourself to me, and anyway I think she had it coming. But there are some who are weak-minded and fall under the spell of a smooth talker like her. She always was a smooth talker. Talked us into that columbarium nobody wanted."

"This is all very unfortunate," said Donald, "but I'm sure

it can be smoothed out. I'll have a word with her and whoever else has taken her side of things. We'll work it out."

"I wouldn't count on that," said George. "She's been hard at it since you left. She got Eunice and Marilyn entirely on her side, and Dale mostly, if you can believe it, and I think she's got Al, too, though I woulda thought him a more sensible man than that. They're saying you're weak because you don't hold your wife in check…"

Carmichael snorted.

"…but also that you're planning to scam the church, asking for this trip to Germany but planning to quit soon as you get back."

"You're quitting the church?" shouted Kitty.

"This is insane. This is preposterous," sputtered Donald. "I mean, I gathered that a rumor about us leaving was going around, but there's no truth to it. No truth at all. No, I am *not* leaving the church!" he said to Kitty.

"Truth don't mean a thing to them as are determined to think otherwise," declared George aphoristically. "It's a shame you had to be gone just now. Two weeks do a lotta damage when people go spreading poison about you."

"There's poison in scorpions!" cried Saul, waving around the lollipop George rejected.

"There's poison in all kinds," said George.

CHAPTER THIRTEEN

July 1989

It is strange that misery, when viewed in others, should become to us a sort of real good.

"The fireworks are due to start at nine," said Carmichael to her parents, "so let's get ourselves set up now." Her arms were full of mismatched old blankets.

"We have an *amazing* view from up here," Kitty announced. Of her mother she asked, "Can I bring out the lemonade?"

"You know I don't like you having sugary stuff right before bedtime."

"Mommy, it's the Fourth of July! We're supposed to celebrate!"

"How about some popcorn instead?" suggested Judith.

"Popcorn! Popcorn!" shouted Saul.

With time to spare, the family was spread out across a patchwork field of blankets close to the cemetery, ideal for viewing the fireworks to be shot up from the college on the opposite hillside. They were well supplied not only with lemonade *and* popcorn but also a fantastically oversized cheesecake imported from the City. Frank became engrossed in a serious conversation with Saul about the mechanics of fireworks, assuring him that plenty of fire engines and ambulances would be standing at the ready, just in case.

"We're lucky it's not raining," Carmichael remarked to her mother. "We ended up having to cancel this party last year on account of rain."

"'Party'?" said Judith with a laugh. "Is this a party?"

"Oh," said Carmichael. "Yeah, that sounded funny, didn't

it? Up till now it's always been a congregational event. Since the church is so well situated, years ago they got in the habit of having a Fourth of July picnic supper and staying on for the fireworks."

"But not this year?"

Carmichael licked butter and salt off her fingertips. "It's like I've been telling you, Mom. Things aren't going so well right now. Calling it off was the best choice, under the circumstances."

"I guess I still don't really understand why things have gotten so bad. Nothing seemed abnormal at the service this morning."

"Look! Fireflies!" screeched Kitty. She and Saul bounded off to catch them.

Carmichael took advantage of their absence to lean in and say, "They put on a good show on Sundays. To tell you the truth, I don't really understand how so many other people have gotten sucked into it, either. What I do know is that Sandra is at the center of it."

"But she was always such a nice friend to you."

"Yeah, I thought so, too. I didn't really grasp what she thought our friendship was all about, though. More like a patron than a friend, with corresponding rights over me, or something like that. It's partly my fault. I should've seen it coming, and I shouldn't have said what I did at Asher's burial."

"Oh," said Judith. "Are you getting enough popcorn, Frank?"

"I'm fine, I'm fine, I don't need the empty calories anyway," he replied loudly, taking a swig of his Genesee.

"But I stand by it," said Carmichael, almost as loudly as Frank, trying to regain her mother's attention. "Look, Mom, Dad, I want to say something to you both. I know I didn't react so kindly last fall when you told Kitty about us being Jewish, and I haven't been very open to it. But I want you to know that things have really changed for me. Inside of me."

She reached out for Donald's hand and held it. He squeezed

it. She had talked this all out with him ahead of time, discussing what to say to her parents, wanting his insight and ideas and, not least of all, consent to opening a window in their lives to Carmichael's Jewish heritage. But she'd also involved him, she had to admit to herself, to try and regain his trust and high opinion of her. She could tell he was still unhappy about how she'd handled Sandra but was holding it in. That itself made her sad and a little scared.

"I was really moved," she continued, "by the two of you spending the week with us sitting shiva for Asher. I can see the good things that reclaiming our Jewishness has done for you. I'm not sure it will ever be the same for me, but I'm glad you've found it, and I want you to know that I support you. And I'll try to be a part of it, in whatever way I can, and share it with the children, too."

"I second that," Donald added.

"Well, thank you, honey," Judith said. She patted Carmichael's knee and emitted one of the chuckles she always used to fill in conversational silence.

"I think I'll help myself to another beer," said Frank. He heaved himself to his feet and pattered toward the pantry door.

Carmichael glanced sidelong at Donald. He shrugged.

"Mom," she said cautiously.

"Should I have your dad get you a beer, too?"

"Mom," she repeated. "I just said something big here. Why are you acting like I didn't say anything at all?"

"I said thank you."

"I can't keep up!" Carmichael said in exasperation. "This was such a big deal last fall, and now you're acting like it's nothing. What's going on?"

Just then the first starburst crackled across the sky, a predictable trio of red, white, and blue. Kitty and Saul came careening back and settled down between parents and grandparents to watch, their hands cupped tight over fireflies. The noise precluded any conversation beyond appreciative oohs and aahs.

When the rumble of the finale died away and all that was left in the sky was tatters of smoke, Carmichael shooed the children inside to get ready for bed. Judith reached to fold their just-evacuated blanket but Carmichael stopped her. "Mom," she said. "Dad. What is going on?"

"I'll make sure the kids brush their teeth," said Donald, rising.

"You may as well hear it, too," said Frank. Donald dropped down again.

"Now, Frank," said Judith.

"She already can tell something's up. There's no point in keeping it a secret any longer."

"*What?*" Carmichael demanded.

"It's nothing bad *now*, this is old news," Frank said reassuringly. "You know how your mother and I have been working through our parents' old letters and papers and things?"

"In Estonian," Judith added.

"Right," said Carmichael.

Frank continued, "Well, the thing is, we just assumed, and because of that, we led you to believe that our families fled in 1941 because of, you know."

"Hitler? The Holocaust?"

"Right. It hadn't started in Estonia by then, but Europe just wasn't a good place to be a Jew then. So we always just assumed. We had no reason to think otherwise."

"Well, naturally," said Carmichael. "But wait—what did you find out? Are we *not* Jewish after all?" A clenching panic overtook her. She hadn't guessed till then that it had become so important to her.

"Oh, no, we are," said Judith. "It's just not exactly why our families left."

"I can't even fathom what you're leading up to. Just tell me already!"

Frank said, "Well again, our Estonian is pretty primitive, even with the help of a dictionary…"

"*What is it?*" Carmichael could barely keep herself from shouting.

Judith said all at once, "Our parents were Soviet collaborators."

"You're kidding" erupted out of Donald.

"No," Frank answered for her. "No doubt about it. We've found paperwork from the USSR with 'Abraham Lazikin' on it."

"My father's name," said Judith by way of unnecessary explanation.

"And others that say 'Saalomon Bam.' We've got letters between our dads, and more between them and some officials in the Estonian government who were friendly to the Soviets. And even some our moms wrote. They were all communists, true-blue communists. Real believers in it. It's right there in my own dad's handwriting—all this stuff about the 'proletariat' and the 'revolution' and how this was the only real solution to world peace against the forces of warmongering capitalism."

Carmichael, hardly able to process what she was hearing, said, "You found the word 'warmongering' in Estonian?"

"Well, along those lines. Also 'dialectical materialism' and 'opiate of the masses.' I still don't know what the hell 'dialectical materialism' is supposed to be."

"The first Estonian dictionary I got wasn't anywhere near adequate, let me tell you," Judith interjected.

"As much as I can fit the pieces together," Frank went on, "it looks like both our sets of parents got caught up in the communist cause early in life, which is how they met each other and fell in love and got married and decided to give their lives to bringing it to Estonia. I'm not sure they were spies, exactly, but somehow they got into government and were in close communication with the Soviets. Our mothers supported them."

"Wait, I don't understand something here," said Donald. "Estonia *did* get taken over by the Soviet Union. So why did your parents have to leave?"

"Well, actually, I didn't realize this till just recently, but Estonia changed hands a couple of times. The Soviets annexed Estonia and their neighbors in June of 1940. Looks like our dads got nice government positions in exchange for the role they played in welcoming the Russians. Can't imagine it made them popular with the neighbors."

"Well, maybe they were already unpopular on account of being Jews," said Carmichael. She felt she was slipping down some slippery yet jagged precipice, trying to clutch at anything to break her fall.

"Could be, could be," said Frank. "But then the next year, Hitler turned around and broke his treaty with the Soviets and invaded Russia. By the summer of '41 Estonia was under Nazi control."

"That's when your parents decided to flee, then," said Carmichael. "They saw the writing on the wall for themselves as Jews in Hitler's Reich."

"Nope," said Frank. "They saw the writing on the wall for themselves as Soviet collaborators. The letters we read don't leave any doubt about that. There's hardly a mention of us being Jews anywhere in all the stuff we've gone through, but being a communist is all over the place. They say straight out that's what made them run for their lives."

"And did they leave any family behind? What happened to them?"

"We still don't know. You get the impression there wasn't any love lost between them. Communism was their new family *and* their new religion. The thing is, when it was time to run, they went west into Sweden, not east into Russia. Hitler was invading Russia, but they had no way of knowing that he wouldn't succeed. I guess some English communists brought them over from Sweden and tried to get them legal status, but communism wasn't exactly popular there, either. So in the end they got hooked up with some agency that brought Jews over to the States."

"So they came back around to their Judaism in the end," Carmichael suggested.

"Sure doesn't look that way. Soon as they got settled and legal in New York, they cut all ties with the people who brought them over. I guess the agency wasn't so keen on our folks by then, either. I remember how my mom always put up a Christmas tree in December—just for decoration, she always said. One letter I found mentions how the agency was trying to push a menorah on them instead and she just refused."

"I can't make any sense of it," said Carmichael. She looked up at the sky. Half the stars were blotted out by the haze from the fireworks.

"From what I've been reading, not just in our letters but in some other books, a lot of Jews gave up on their religion and believed in communism instead."

"'There's more than one way to be a Jew,'" she quoted back to him.

"Even more than I thought," he agreed. "I'm just guessing here, because they stopped writing letters and keeping journals soon after we got to the States, but just going by my childhood recollections, they must have realized it wasn't a good way to make a new life in America, being communists. So they kept it quiet, and who knows, maybe after awhile they stopped believing in communism."

"And you had no idea about any of this?"

Frank and Judith exchanged a look, the same one Carmichael had seen them exchange at the lunch after Asher's burial. "Well," said Frank.

"Dad, I need to know."

"I guess somewhere in the back of my mind I always knew. Or suspected. I wasn't *that* young when we left. I had to have heard things."

"Honey," continued Judith, "you can't imagine this now, but in the fifties you just did *not* admit to having anything to do with communists."

Carmichael said, "And is this also why you never talked about us being Jewish?"

"*They* never talked about us being Jewish. We didn't start that," said Frank. "Now this really is total conjecture, but I think the fact that they didn't leave because of the Holocaust or have any connection to it was sort of a dirty secret. Everyone else we knew who was Jewish had some kind of terrible story to tell, at least of extended family if not personally. But us? Not a thing. And even if we did, we had no way of knowing, since our folks long since broke contact. I guess it was just better not to say anything about being a Jew at all. We didn't fit in with the others."

"Holocaust envy," Carmichael murmured.

"I wouldn't go so far as to say *that*," protested Judith.

"So—so I'm going to ask again what I asked you last fall when you told Kitty. Why now?"

"I told you," said Frank, "it's because of what was in the news. There were all those protests in Estonia. It got me interested again."

"OK," said Carmichael. She reflected a moment. "All right then, let me ask you this. Did you *really* not know, when we talked about this last fall, that your parents left because of being communists when Hitler invaded? I mean, did you really not know that it had nothing to do with being Jews who would be sent off to death camps?"

"I really didn't know. I didn't know how deep my dad was in the communist thing. I always just assumed he took us and ran because it was 1941 and that's what Jews did if they could."

"Well then, at least my ignorance is still left to me."

"How's that?"

"God, Dad, don't you realize what I've done? What I said to Sandra, when she kept berating me about cremating Asher, and I made it sound like we had some part in the Holocaust personally. Like it really affected us and that's why we couldn't cremate Asher. And now—now I've had my boy taken from me, and my God, and it looks like our church before long, and on top of everything else my moral high ground, because however awful she was, I don't even have a right to what I said to her. It never had anything to do with us at all."

"Oh, honey," said Judith. She leaned over awkwardly on her knees and plucked Carmichael away from Donald to give her a hug. Frank rubbed at the label on his beer bottle, radiantly uncomfortable in his silence.

After a very long pause, Donald said, "So, are you still thinking of trying to make contact with whatever relatives you might still have there?"

Frank shrugged. "I don't see the point, to be honest. Even if there are any left alive, after all they've been through, would they want to hear from the children of the communists who escaped to America and had a good life? And that's if we could even find them. Or do anything about it, if we did. Nothing's ever gonna change over there."

"I don't know, you remember how that East German pastor was allowed to visit us back in March."

"That's Germany. Estonia's part of the Soviet Union."

"But the protests are continuing. I read something again in the paper about their public gatherings to sing."

"Yeah, but look at what happened in Tiananmen Square last month. That's where all this is headed. Those communists will never give up power. They'll shoot or send off to Siberia anyone they have to."

"Gee, Dad," snuffled Carmichael, "don't be such a Pollyanna."

There was a scuffling at the pantry door.

Kitty banged through the screen and shouted, "Saul just rinsed his toothbrush with water so you'd think he brushed his teeth but he didn't really!"

"Yes I did! I did so brush my teeth!" Saul shouted from right behind her.

"Party's over," said Frank.

∼

Halfway through the week of Girl Scout camp, on Wednesday afternoon during free time, Miss Wright plopped down next to Kitty, who had stationed herself in the shade of a sugar maple overlooking the lake.

"What're you reading there, Kitty?" she asked.

Kitty stowed her bookmark in place and closed the book to display the cover. "*Below the Root*," she said. "It's about this amazing planet with gigantic trees that people live in and can glide from one branch to the next with their shubas because the gravity is extra-light. I like sitting under this tree to read it because it turns the light green and the name of the planet is Green-Sky."

Miss Wright nodded. "It's wonderful weather this afternoon. Don't you want to go swimming?"

Kitty shrugged. "The water's too cold."

"With the sun so bright, it's not too bad. If you were swimming around and playing with the other girls, you'd keep warm enough."

"I'd get sunburned."

"All the counselors have sunscreen you could use."

"It's OK. I'd rather read anyway." Kitty flipped her book back open again, hoping Miss Wright would take the hint.

Miss Wright just sat there, though. She looked out over the lake, squinting against the shards of light reflecting off the caps of the little waves that fluttered to and fro in the mild breeze. She had tightly permed hair, which Kitty thought looked stupid, and ridiculously white sneakers that she tried too hard to keep clean. But there was a kind of softness about Miss Wright that was genuine without being weak, and she was smart, so Kitty could forgive her fashion choices.

When Miss Wright spoke again she said, "I notice you haven't been hanging out with the other girls very much."

"No, not so much. Do I have to?"

"I'm just surprised. I thought you'd be excited to hang out with your friends during summer vacation."

"I see them every day at school the rest of the year."

"Most girls like to see their friends every day."

"Yeah, well, I'm not like most girls." Kitty recited it like a creed. "Anyway, I've been hanging out plenty with the littler girls and helping the counselors with them."

"But it's not the same, is it now?"

Another well-meaning, interfering adult. And here Kitty thought Miss Wright stood out from the pack. But she was just going to badger Kitty into pretending that she liked people she didn't and wanted to do things she didn't, like pretty much every other annoying adult. When all Kitty wanted was to be left alone to read her book.

"Why aren't you married yet, Miss Wright?" she said.

Miss Wright's eyes flew open and darted over at Kitty in surprise. "Well, I, I just haven't met the right man yet, I guess," she stammered.

"A Girl Scout camp is a lousy place to meet men."

"Olutakli County is a lousy place to meet men," said Miss Wright.

"So why don't you move away?"

This time Miss Wright turned toward Kitty for a better look. Kitty felt suddenly and uncomfortably seen. "All right, then, Kitty, I'll leave you alone," she said at last. "But it's not a good policy to push away your friends." She sprang up on her white sneakers—Kitty could see little specks of dirt marring their pristine appearance—and jogged off.

Kitty stared for awhile at the delicate pale blue dragonflies that darted over the weedy part of the lake before returning to her book.

At craft time Kitty avoided the girls in her own age group again and sat down amidst the six-year-olds. Some of them had been in Asher's class. As she'd hoped, one of the gaggle of girls, Allison, clambered over her neighbors and cuddled up to Kitty, showing off a white, green, and red God's-eye she'd been working on. "Nice choice of colors," Kitty said.

"I'm gonna give it to my mommy for Christmas!" Allison lisped through the gap in her teeth. The other girls held up their own God's-eyes for Kitty to admire, but she reserved her most lavish praise for Allison. Kitty accepted their collective plea to sit with them at dinner—a noxious mixture of ground beef, canned tomatoes, and macaroni called "goulash," although it was nothing like the dish of the same name that Kitty was accustomed to eating at her mother's table—and afterwards joined them at story time, and then at the campfire to make s'mores. Another counselor tried to extract Kitty and reinsert her among the girls her own age, but Kitty's indifferent response and the eager cries of the little ones to keep her with them defeated the counselor in the end.

Once it got dark and the inevitable could be forestalled no longer, Kitty trudged to her cobwebby cabin. The moment she came through the door the other girls fell silent. "Hi," said Kitty flatly, grabbing her pajamas to change in the outhouse.

"Hi," said Jenny Ulster back, in an automatic though not unfriendly tone. Jessica Hodyl echoed with another faint "Hi." Kitty looked away. The sight of her former best friend made her squirm. Only Megan Moravsky didn't say anything, but that was to be expected. They had reverted to their usual poisonous silence after Kitty's revelation about Megan's dad.

What Kitty couldn't understand—she reviewed the matter again in her mind as she halfheartedly splashed cold water on her face and pushed back her greasy hair; she refused to take a shower in the very unprivate conditions of camp—was how Megan still managed to be popular. It was like having her dad go to jail for just a few days gave Megan an additional mystique instead of taking away from it. Maybe it was because his crime (which Kitty still didn't fully understand) wasn't violent or seedy but had something to do with money. People worship money, thought Kitty savagely. They worship Megan because she has money, and it doesn't matter what a horrible person she is. Kitty stomped all the way back to the cabin, clambered up to her bunk, and turned her face to the wall so she wouldn't have to pretend to talk to her hateful bunkmates.

Thursday unfolded much as the three preceding days, Kitty eschewing the company of her own and planting herself among the six-year-olds, who loved her with greater passion as each hour ticked by. Same on Friday, as the approaching end of camp kicked up the level of devotion to frantic. Kitty gave the girls piggyback rides and showed them how to stick maple helicopters on their noses.

After one last repellent supper of fish sticks and tater tots, the whole camp gathered around the bonfire for a final dose of inspirational speeches, trust falls, and heartfelt songs about friendship. This time Kitty was stuck. The counselors had seated them by their age groups and forced them to talk to each other, answering dorky questions about their favorite color and pop singer and personal goal for the school year ahead. Kitty answered flatly, "Purple," because it was true; "Danny Wood," because she knew that choosing the ugly guy of the New Kids on the Block would offend the other girls; and "getting all As," also for the express purpose of alienation. The strategy worked well.

As the others chattered in expansive detail, Kitty leaned back and glanced around. The six-year-olds weren't so far away and pretty distractible. Kitty waited till Allison looked around in her direction, then waved. Allison waved back. Kitty beckoned to her and mouthed, "Come over here." Allison sat frozen a moment, her desires for obedience and for Kitty's approval working at cross purposes. One more gesture of encouragement was all it took. Allison found her feet and dashed off, landing seconds later on Kitty's lap. "I'm being naughty!" she cried gleefully.

"Allison!" Megan hissed. "Get back to your own group!"

"No!" Allison shouted. "I'm gonna stay here with Kitty."

"You're gonna get in trouble! You're gonna get us all in trouble! Go back to your group!"

"I don't *want* to."

"Let her stay if she wants to stay," Kitty said to Megan with a satisfied smile. She stroked Allison's long red hair.

Megan turned evil eyes on Kitty. "Fine," she barked. "But Allison, you should come and sit with *me*."

"I wanna stay with Kitty," Allison said.

"Come over here to me!"

"No!" pouted Allison.

Megan was panting with rage by now. The bonfire picked out the tears at the edges of her eyes like tiny diamonds. "But you're *my* sister!"

"I think she likes me better," said Kitty.

"I *love* Kitty," said Allison, wrapping her arms around Kitty and giving her an adoring hug.

"I hate you," Megan snarled at Kitty. "I hate you, I hate you, I hate you!" In a moment she was on her feet and screaming. The others girls were shocked into paralysis but not Miss Wright, who heard the kerfuffle and came running. Megan was full-on bawling by the time Miss Wright got there and still screaming abuse at Kitty, who sat in perfect ease, an expression of mild puzzlement carefully pasted over the smug joy she felt inside.

"Megan, that's no way to talk to your friend," said Miss Wright.

"She's not my friend!" Megan shrieked. "I hate her!" She gulped and hiccuped. Miss Wright led her away, but not without a curious glance at Kitty before she left.

"I'm more fun than Megan, aren't I?" said Kitty.

"Yes," said Allison. She snuggled up and closed her eyes and pretended to go to sleep.

The other girls stared. Kitty smiled back beatifically upon them all.

~

Just as Jackie was reaching out for a lamp with a bulbous glass body full of seashells and capped with a turquoise lampshade, another woman reached for it, too. They pulled back at the same time.

When they made eye contact Jackie said, "Wait, don't I know you from somewhere?"

The woman gave an embarrassed smile. "Probably not," she said. "I just moved here a couple months ago."

"Well, a yard sale is a great place to find what you need. I go early bird every Saturday in July and August. My house is totally *stuffed* with things I bought at yard sales. I got *this* at a yard sale," displaying the Iggy Pop T-shirt she was wearing.

The other woman took in its peeling decals and said, "Oh wait, I think I know where you might have seen me. Do you go to church?"

"Mt. Moriah in Shibboleth," replied Jackie proudly.

"Right," said the other woman. "I'm Carol. My husband Larry is over there looking at the fishing tackle, as if he doesn't have enough already. Anyway, I remember you because you were wearing a Van Halen T-shirt and I was surprised but thought it was cool that it was OK to wear that to church."

Jackie waved an expansive hand toward the broad blue sky, which was dotted with clouds like lumps of biscuit dough. "Pastor Donald doesn't care about stuff like that," she proclaimed. "You should come again sometime."

"Oh," said Carol. She blushed.

"I mean, no pressure," Jackie added in haste.

"Well, it's just that, the first time we went, I thought his sermon was really good, but the second time..."

It was Jackie's turn to blush. "Yeah, he's been going through a rough patch lately, but normally he's a really good preacher, not like the ones on TV, because he has a *message*, you know, and he never asks for money from the pulpit."

"I'm sure," said Carol, but Jackie could tell she was trying to pull out of the conversation.

"It's been a tough year for him," Jackie pressed on, adopting a confidential tone. "Their little boy died on Christmas."

"Oh, my God," said Carol. "What happened?"

"Well," said Jackie, suddenly dubious of her strategy. "He fell."

"Where from?"

"…the roof of the church."

"Oh, my God," said Carol again, all the color draining from her face. She took two steps backward, as if in self-defense.

"So you can't really blame him if sometimes his sermons aren't quite up to par. Hey, did you want this lamp? You can have it. I don't really need it."

"No, no, you can have it," protested Carol, as if the lamp, Jackie, the church, and everything associated therewith were tainted and contagious. "I was more in the market for a sofa, to be honest. Nice to meet you," she mumbled and scuttled off.

"One of our members is married to a sofa salesman!" Jackie called after her.

Carol was already collecting her husband and tugging him toward their car.

"Shit," said Jackie.

∼

A few days later the skies reverted to a gumptionless drizzle, which was some consolation to George, stuck inside Blackwell Memorial Hospital in Kuhsota, screening one patient after another for telltale lumps in this or that body part. Mid-afternoon he saw a face he recognized—not altogether uncommon—but it happened to be someone he knew from church.

"Harold Clark," he said, after a quick glance at the chart to be sure of the name.

"That's me," said Harold, and then, doing a double-take, said, "Aren't you—?"

"George Pohl, from Mt. Moriah."

"Oh, right." Harold's eyes fell to the floor.

"Haven't seen you there in awhile," said George amiably.

"Yeah, I been meaning to come more often, it's just that Sunday's my only day off, the County has me working on Saturdays most weeks..."

"That's fine, you come when you can," said George. "Have a seat while I set things up."

George was, in truth, setting things up, but the silence of his concentration agitated Harold enough to unspool further justifications. "The thing of it is, Pastor Donald's a really nice guy, I like him a lot, so does my wife and our kids, it's just that, you know, it's hard to know what to say, after what happened."

George blanched. Harold took it as a rebuke.

"I mean, I'm sorry for him and all, and I guess if I was a better Christian I'd reach out more or something, but I mean, what do you *say*?" As George held his tongue, Harold babbled on. "And also, it's not like I'm blaming him or anything, but the last time or two I came, his sermons weren't like before."

Glad for a change of topic, even if not the exact reason for it, George said, a little more harshly than intended, "He's a good preacher."

"He *was*," said Harold, rattled. "But the last time we went, he just sort of... stopped."

George let out an ambiguous noise. He stared hard at Harold's chart and finally said, "Blood pressure's 140 over 90. A bit high. Better get a prescription for that."

"All right," said Harold meekly.

∽

Donald stared at the typewriter on his desk in dismay.

He was not a manuscript preacher. "Or a typescript preacher, either," he said aloud to the machine. It leered back at him, the wide grin of the ribbon reminding him of the manic antagonist in a horror movie.

He pecked at a few keys with his index fingers. It took actual effort to force them down. Just in the heading "The Ninth

Sunday after Pentecost" he made three mistakes. He flopped over backward in his chair and groaned.

Hate it he might, but there was no other option. He could not afford to choke in the pulpit as he had the last four Sundays in a row. He could not again lose his train of thought, stare into space, leave the faithful squirming in humiliated agonies on his behalf and unable to hear a single word of the Lord because all they heard was their pastor's struggle to emit any word at all. It was a malady without precedent in Donald's ministry.

He let his mind wander back to his hike up Spirit Mountain, to his visitation from Grandfather Abney—who, not at all coincidentally, Donald was sure, had failed to manifest himself even in the shunned corners of Donald's mind ever since. On the mountain Grandfather Abney entrusted Donald with his griefs, his hard-won wisdom, his harder-won questions. They met as colleagues, in a sense, a finer blessing than any other Grandfather Abney ever bestowed, which was saying something, because he'd always been generous to Donald with his blessings. In that shared space, Grandfather Abney released Donald from his dying charge to preach a Jericho sermon that convinced him.

And so, despite the bitter revelation of another dead son, Donald came back from Arizona feeling lighter, ennobled and uplifted. Isn't that why one went to the desert? To face the demons, but also to wrest the blessing out of God's clenched hands? In the desert one beheld an earth scoured of all pretense, the starkness of rocky truth that underlay the fertility of grace.

But then, his first Sunday back, Donald ascended the pulpit, opened his mouth to speak, and everything he'd intended to say dissolved like salt into the sea and vanished. He was tongue-tied as he'd never been before.

Where did the words go?

Donald stood up and took two steps to the picture window that overlooked the east edge of the meadow. The lilacs were long since past their blooming, only a few crunchy brown skeletons of their former white and purple selves left, but farther up the hillside the rose-of-Sharon bloomed, and so did a line of gaudy gladiolas in tropical colors. His eyes stretched over the drop-off and the treetops rising out of the wooded saddle between the hills down below. In the winter, his office was almost unbearably cold with all this exposed window. Now he felt like a specimen in a glass box. Even the breeze blowing in through the screen did little to relieve it. "Still, nothing like the peak of Spirit Mountain," he said aloud.

He turned again to that mountaintop meeting. Grandfather Chrysostom, he thought, golden-tongued preacher. He recalled Fritz's admiration for Donald's preaching but also his warning not to imitate himself when it passed. In the first blaze of grief, Donald's preaching was on fire. He knew it, he felt it, he took it for the consolation it was. But why not anymore? Why did that mountaintop revelation—for so it seemed to be—deprive him of his gift instead of empowering it further, or moving it on to the next stage? Surely no one benefited from the preacher losing his words. His own humiliation was one thing, but the enforced famine on the congregation was something else, and unconscionable.

"I know how to compose a sermon," Donald told himself. He turned back and settled into his chair in front of the typewriter again. "It doesn't have to be inspired. It doesn't have to be great or original. It just has to explain the Scripture to them. That's the minimum, and I can do that. Anyone who can read the Bible can do that. You don't even have to believe to do that."

Painful as it was, Donald kept himself at the typewriter, one pecked key at a time, until he had a sermon of sorts.

Sunday morning. Invocation, singing, prayer, lessons. Then the sermon. "Grace to you and peace," he said, quoting St. Paul as he did at the outset of every sermon, "from God our Father and the Lord Jesus Christ."

He took a moment to survey the congregation. There was no

mistaking the fact that the numbers were down. He told himself it was July, of course the numbers were down, they'd stay down through August, then bump back up again in September. But the numbers were low even for July. And the new people who'd visited through the first half of the year, whom he'd called and visited—not a one of them had been back. Surely they weren't *all* on vacation at the same time. And even the infrequents were more infrequent than usual. Only the core of the church was there, the core of the apple, the bad apple… Donald's eyes flickered over Sandra and Alan. They had been in attendance every Sunday since the Abneys returned from Arizona. Present and bristling with hostility, presumably over Carmichael's harsh words and botched apology. Eunice always sat with them now. In fact…

Donald swept the room with his eyes a second time. He saw it then. His congregation had split itself into two factions, one on the pulpit side and one on the lectern side. Team Abney consisted of, naturally, the Abneys, Jackie, George, Mrs. Feuerlein, and Mrs. Kipfmueller. Team Anti-Abney featured Sandra and Alan and Eunice at the center, the others arranged around them as if a protective phalanx: the Mayers and the Becks and the Wheelers and Bonnie and… He stopped the tally in despair. Marilyn was stuck at the organ, but her very posture conveyed her Anti-Abney allegiance. At the back of the church, as if they didn't realize they were supposed to pick sides and just picked empty pews instead, were the Fishers and a hovering Hazel, who kept finding reasons to pop up and shuffle the bulletins.

Donald realized he'd been staring without speaking. He cleared his throat and dropped his eyes to the typescript, covered with white-out and hand-scrawled corrections. He started reading. But it was only that, reading. It was not preaching. And not just because it was a typescript. His mind was disengaged, his heart was dulled, it was only words and not *the* word. He spoke the typed words aloud and they died in his mouth. They tripped and stumbled over the rim of his lips and tumbled to the pulpit and bounced off it and skittered across the floor, lifeless things, fractures and fragments that refused to link arms with one another. Each wanted to go its own way, none wanted to take its place as part of the one body of the sermon. The result was noise disguised as intelligible speech but in reality only sound and fury signifying nothing, "which makes me the idiot," thought Donald, and then wondered if he might have said it aloud, because Carmichael looked stricken and Sandra triumphant.

He read the next six pages like he was a seventh-grader giving his first book report. It was hard to say who in that church was most relieved when it was over.

∼

"I can't effing believe we're doing this again," said Jackie. She slammed her pack of cigarettes and lighter on the table, causing several glasses of soda to slosh.

"Language," sang out Eunice reprovingly.

"George and me wouldn't have come at all, except we know how you're all plotting against Pastor and no one else will stick up for him."

Al halted the reuben sandwich clasped in two fists midway to his mouth and said, "Now Jackie, let's try to have a civil conversation."

"I'd like to know what's civil about sneaking behind the pastor's back," said George.

"Your guilt feelings are coloring your view of things," said Marilyn.

"Guilty about *what*?" he snarled.

"You know," she said, but in a chastened tone.

"No, I don't know, Marilyn, why don't you tell us?" Jackie snapped. "Are you saying that George feels guilty about leaving out the ladder so little Asher died, and you think that's clouding his judgment on your plot to take out the pastor and his family?"

"Whoa, whoa, whoa," said Al, wiping the Russian dressing off his sticky fingers, as everyone else erupted. The recriminations mounted in volume till Al caught sight of furtive glances from the other diners and he barked "*Enough*" like he was back in Korea. That had the desired effect. "Now look," he said, "the reason we're here is to talk things out like adults before we speak to Pastor Donald at council tonight. I know we're in disagreement here, but we're not gonna act like this in front of him, OK? Some of us might be unhappy with him and his wife, and think it would be better if they moved on, but he *has* had a rough year and we're gonna be polite about it. All right?"

There were nods of agreement, some glowering, some supercilious.

"Now last time we left it unresolved whether we were going to help pay for his trip to Germany."

"I will withhold my tithe if we do," announced Eunice.

"Then I'll double mine," said Jackie.

"Oh, really? Do you think that will make up the difference?" said Eunice with artificial sweetness.

"At least I *earn* the money I give," hissed Jackie.

Eunice gathered herself up for a hurricane of outrage but Dale said, "Shut up, Eunice," before she managed to say anything. She pinned her lips.

Al continued, "So in our last discussion, I think what we came to is that we're going to decline to pay for the trip, but if he wants the time off we'll let him have up to one extra week beyond his allotted vacation time."

"What discussion are you talking about?" said George. "I never heard anything about this before now."

"Well," said Al.

Jackie cut him off. "Oh, I get it. This isn't the *only* secret council meeting they've had. Except you and I weren't invited to the other ones, George."

"There was nothing official about the other times," said Dale in self-defense.

"Oh, God, I knew it." Jackie stabbed at her pork chop savagely.

"But how are we going to pay for a guest preacher on his extra Sunday off?" pressed Marilyn. "That costs money, too, money we haven't budgeted."

Al said, "I think there's enough in the discretionary fund to cover the difference."

"I'll donate the difference out of my pathetic McDonald's manager salary," said Jackie. "If I'm still a member of this church by then."

"I'm staying as long as Pastor Donald stays," said George.

"None of us is going anywhere," said Al. "But that does bring me to the other question, which is, how much longer is Pastor Donald staying, and when is he going to tell us? The call process takes such a long time, so the sooner we get on top of that, the better."

Jackie said, "And I say you still don't know anything about any plans to leave."

"Sandra?" prompted Al. "You seem to know the most about the Abneys."

Sandra pushed back her chicken caesar salad with a sigh. "Well, of course, Carmichael doesn't confide in me anymore," she said. "So I wish I could tell you, but I can't. Alan doesn't know anything, either."

"Oh yeah, she works for Alan, doesn't she?" said Dale. "Wouldn't he know if she was planning to leave?"

"You'd think she'd be forthright with him," agreed Sandra, "since it would really leave the college in the lurch if she quit midway through the year. But I'm afraid he doesn't know either. It's been very strained. I can't break through her hostility. You expect a grieving mother to be a little unbalanced, of course. But rejecting offers of friendship..." She sighed again. "We've all seen it, haven't we? People who could use a helping hand but can't bring themselves to accept it, they're in it so deep. I see it all the time in my work with Hope for Olutakli."

All the others murmured agreement over this mysterious flaw in the human character, except for Jackie and George, who murmured under their respective breaths something to the effect that a helping hand from Sandra was more likely to push you farther down than pull you up.

"I don't think we've quite gotten to the heart of the issue," said Eunice. She straightened her blouse and glasses, waiting for full attention to land on her. When she had it, she said, "Maybe Pastor Donald's planning on leaving. And maybe he's not. The question, as far as I'm concerned, is, even if *he* wants to stay—do *we* want him to stay?"

"Well, of course we do," said Hazel.

"I'm not so sure about that," Eunice said. "Let's face up squarely to a few facts. First, I'm sure everyone has noticed that attendance has been down lately."

"It's summertime," Al pointed out.

"But still lower than usual. Which I bet we can prove by the giving lately. How about it, George? Is the offering up to the usual level?"

George stewed in protracted silence before allowing a reluctant "No" to slip sideways out of his mouth.

Eunice continued, "Also, have you noticed that even though a lot of new people have visited in the past half year or so, none of them have been coming regularly or joined? When was the last time new members joined?"

After an extended pause Al said, "Well, I guess last year sometime. I don't remember exactly."

"That's my point," said Eunice. "I think people are *spooked* by the pastor, when they find out what happened to his little boy." At this even Al and Dale bucked, but Eunice hastily explained, "I'm not saying it's fair, I'm just saying that if *you* found out that the pastor's little boy fell off the church roof and died, wouldn't you feel odd about joining?"

Jackie became intensely interested in a chip in the lime green nail polish on her right pinky finger.

Marilyn cleared her throat. "I'd like to add something to what Eunice has been saying. I'm sure I don't need to repeat what I've said before about Pastor Donald's controlling attitude toward the hymns and the choir—"

"You just did," muttered George.

"—but I think it's fair to say that whatever other issues we may have had with him, we all enjoyed his preaching, didn't we?"

"We *did*," said Eunice, meaningfully.

"Exactly. He *used* to be a great preacher, even though I've always thought it kind of strange that he just makes up his sermons on the spot without a manuscript or anything. It worked fine for a time, but it doesn't anymore. Something happened and now he doesn't preach like he used to."

"I think we all know exactly what happened!" said Jackie.

"But he preached just fine all through the first half of the year after *it* happened," retorted Marilyn. "He's only gotten bad in the past two months, so you can't blame it on *that*."

"Six weeks," said George, "at most. And I noticed he's started bringing a sermon with him into the pulpit. A typed one."

"But that didn't fix the problem either, did it?"

Against this even Jackie and George could mount no defense.

"Maybe we've all gotten a bit spoiled by his good preaching," said Al. "Maybe it's normal for preachers to go through a bad spell. Heck, Pastor Whitney went through a bad spell the whole four years he was here." Nobody else laughed at the joke. "I think we should give him some time."

"That's your answer to everything, give him more time," said Eunice. "But how much time is too much? Are we just going to sit by and watch attendance drop, visitors get turned off, lose money, listen to lousy sermons—that is, if he manages to say anything at all—and then just have him leave us anyway? And make us wait so long for the next pastor? Is that fair to *us*?"

A longer silence this time. Last bits of dinner were scraped off plates, last chunks of ice slurped out of soda glasses, napkins crumpled and set aside.

Sandra said, "It might seem a little harsh, but I really think it will be best for them to move on. How can they carry on with their lives staying in that parsonage, always seeing the place where their son died, walking past his grave every day? They'll just get stuck in a never-ending loop of grief. But I'm afraid they won't have the courage to walk away from it. It could be that the friendliest thing we can do for them is give them that little nudge to move on to the next stage in life. It's like pushing the fledgling out of the nest, or pulling a sore tooth—painful in the moment, but ultimately for the good."

Eunice and Marilyn nodded in shared admiration of Sandra's wisdom about grief and ethics and personal growth. Hazel saw their admiration and tentatively added her own. Jackie and George scowled. Dale and Al exchanged glances that expressed confusion more than anything else.

"Council starts in fifteen minutes and we probably shouldn't all pull in at exactly the same time," observed Al. "I say, we just tell Pastor Donald that we aren't gonna pay for his Germany trip and leave out the rest."

"That's what we decided last time," said Eunice, "and things have only gotten worse since then. We need to get this out in the open."

"*That* at least I agree with," said Jackie. "I am absolutely *done* with these secret meetings."

"I think it's for the best," said Sandra.

Al looked around at the others. Eyes averted, tongues held.

"Oh, all right," he said.

CHAPTER FOURTEEN

August 1989

*Thus impiously I roam,
I fly from one erratic thought to another,
and my mind, irritated by the acrimonious reflections,
is ready sometimes to lead me
to dangerous extremes of violence.*

"I wish you didn't have to go," said Carmichael. She straightened out Donald's tab collar and his black sports coat. "I know you don't exactly love synod assemblies even at the best of times."

He shrugged.

"Hey, Daddy!" Kitty said. "I just realized something. You know that hymn we sing on Good Friday, the one that goes *some-thing hath sin-ned,* and 'sinned' is two syllables instead of one like usual?"

Donald considered a moment. "Oh, right. That's in 'Ah, Holy Jesus.'"

"Well, I just realized that when you pronounce it that way, it's *exactly* the same as 'synod'! 'Sin-ned,' 'synod'! What do you think of that?"

Donald gave her a wan smile. "I think you have perceived the heart of the matter with rare insight."

Kitty beamed.

A few minutes later Donald clambered into the passenger seat next to Al. Sandra and Marilyn were in the back already. The two women had been elected as representatives during the annual congregational meeting way back in March; Al, as council president, was coming along, too. Every year the trip to synod was made in one car to save on gas, even if it was a bit cramped with everyone's overnight bag. This year was to be no different, maintaining the polite fiction that the worst council meeting in living memory wasn't just a week behind them.

The awkwardness of the two-hour drive to a motel on the outskirts of Schenectady was managed by Marilyn's ostentatious nap, Sandra's quiet study of wads of documents pertaining to Hope for Olutakli's latest grant proposal—"I think I actually do more work as a volunteer on the Board of Directors than the full-time staff do," she sighed—and Al's nonstop commentary on the underwhelming sights of I-88. Donald focused on his breathing and presenting a non-anxious presence. He failed at the latter, and when he noticed the former it was only because he'd held his breath for so long that he had to gasp for air.

They checked into their separate rooms, then headed back in the direction they'd come for half an hour on winding county routes till they reached St. Paul's Lutheran in the hamlet of Berne. It had been chosen not so much for its aptness as a meeting place or even as a house of Christian worship—its red brick façade capped by a white bell tower suggested "federal building" more than "church"—as for its historic significance as the site of the first Anti-Rent War convention of 1845. The synod staff had determined that this stellar example of non-quietism on the part of apolitical, lackluster Lutherans had to be flaunted, flogged, and altogether drummed into the heads of the clergy and laity, lest their market share in the crusade for a more enlightened republic slip away entirely.

Donald heard barely a word of the plenary harangue, running over and over in his mind the council meeting that had not ended in something sweet, only a tense cessation of hostilities until the battle could be resumed. He felt sick and sweaty as he replayed Dale's accusation that he wanted to extort the congregation of money for his "vacation" in East Germany, Marilyn going so far as to suggest that the supply preacher should be paid for out of Donald's own pocket. He heard Eunice ticking off point by point his recent failures, both homiletic and evangelistic, all but stating outright that he was single-handedly driving the church to extinction. Then Al prompted him, politely but firmly, to tender his resignation sooner rather than later so as to give them time to find a replacement. Donald heard his own baffled bluster that he had already told them more than once that he had no intention either to extort or depart. Then Hazel was flapping her plump hands around and wailing, "This is terrible, this is just terrible, I don't know what to believe anymore," and Sandra said, "I think we all know that this would be for the best." Then George and Jackie simultaneously exploded and flung around their own accusations until Donald realized that the council had been meeting behind his back for months already, a fact he could barely register amidst the slander that his elect band of Christian lay leaders hurled at each other, which came to an end only when Donald came to his senses and declared, loudly but spiritlessly, "I am not leaving. I have no plans to leave. I'll pay for my ticket myself. I'll take only my two remaining vacation Sundays this year." The hubbub subsided and the rest of the meeting's business was conducted in grunts, for the first time ever finishing an hour ahead of schedule. When it was over everyone made excuses to shoot home. The Abneys were left with a gigantic bowl of summer pudding and no one to eat it but themselves.

During the late afternoon, the synod assembly dispersed to workshops on how to navigate the clergy's new health insurance system, or how to use the adult education resources generated by the national headquarters on the heartfelt assumption that local clergy were incompetent to generate their own. Donald sat in the back row of a workshop on "Preaching Tough Passages in the Bible." It proved to be an exhortation not to preach on them at all, delivered by a fiftyish pastor dressed in a neon pink sari that did nothing to flatter her buttermilk skin, and who, amidst tears of distress, explained how she'd made it a policy to tell people what they actually needed to hear and not what some exclusionary legalist like Ezra or St. Paul claimed to be the will of God. Donald was surprised she knew enough about Ezra to hate him. He passed the hour monitoring the headache spreading its tight tentacles across his skull until he could escape in search of an aspirin.

Following a dinner of brats and sauerkraut on a bun, the whole assembly stuffed into the sanctuary for a communion service that compensated for its lack of theological heft with an abundance of liturgical flourishes, including a long-handled silver spoon that the presider swished around in the chalice for no reason that Donald could discern. When the last hymn drew to its show-tune-derivative emotional crescendo, Al and Sandra and Marilyn found him and together they shuffled off in search of Bishop Cartledge to inquire whether he'd found a time to meet with them before they left the next day. He vacantly proposed right after lunch and bolted. On the drive back to the motel in Schenectady they didn't even try to talk to each other.

The next morning was dedicated to voting on matters that no one cared about except those who proposed them and that would carry no weight except with those who enforced them. There was another communion service showcasing a new liturgy that eschewed such pedestrian concerns as singability, then a sandwich buffet for lunch. Donald sat with a handful of other pastors in the synod he'd gotten to know a bit. Over ham and cheese they complained in turn of each and every aspect of the church from the local to the global and back again. Donald surmised that the steadiness of complaint was, as much as anything, a way to avoid the topic of Asher, judging by the sidelong glances they cast him whenever there was a lull in the conversation. He wondered what would happen if he said, "My son died on Christmas. Got any words of comfort for me?" The temptation to interrupt their blather almost got the better of him, but in the nick of time he spied the purple shirt and excused himself to follow Bishop Cartledge and the three parishioners into a Sunday School room. The door clicked behind them like in a jail cell.

"Albert Beck, Mt. Moriah council president," as he introduced himself, unfolded a reasonably neutral account of the conflict, though he omitted to mention the secret meetings. Marilyn and Sandra contributed the occasional nod or "that's right" to the tale. When Al ran out of things to say, Bishop Cartledge asked Donald if there was any truth to his plan to leave soon. Donald flatly denied it. Bishop Cartledge's relief was obviously more about not having to oversee another call process than anything else. "And you've come to an agreement about the proposed trip to Germany?" Al said they had and detailed it. "I take it you've got your visa and whatever travel insurance you need? I don't know that I have the clout to spring a political prisoner," Bishop Cartledge joked. The rest of them remained stony-faced as Donald said yes, the visa was in process, and as soon as he got it he'd buy the ticket with his own money. "Well then," said Bishop Cartledge, "I don't really see what more you need from me." The parishioners stared at him, uncomprehending. He rose and gestured to the door. "Let me just have a word with your pastor," he said, and they left.

Donald could barely contain his frustration. "That's all you have to say to this situation?"

"Look, Don," said the bishop. Donald cringed at the nickname that no one but his own father ever used. "I gotta level with you. I'm putting out fires right and left here. Just two days ago I got word that a pastor up by Saratoga Springs has been having an affair with the organist, and they're both married. No danger you'll be having an affair with your organist, at least, am I right?" He grinned with a nod toward the door after Marilyn. Donald said nothing. Bishop Cartledge cleared his throat and continued. "I *have* to deal with pastors who get themselves tangled up in scandals. But there's nothing I can do if your congregation just turns on you like that. I've seen it happen, but what can I do? I can't *make* them like you again. I know it's unfair.

God knows this has been a terrible year for you. But honestly, Don, why do you even *want* to stay?"

"This is my life," said Donald. "I like the area. Carmichael has a great job. It's a good place for the kids."

"But you're reminded of—*it*, every day. Is that what you really want?"

In a flash, all the anxiety and sorrow and uncertainty transmuted into tonic towering anger. "Why are you, why is everyone, so afraid of me remembering every day that my son has died?" Donald demanded. "Do you think if I left I'd *stop* remembering, and stop loving, and stop grieving, my lost child? We're pastors, Gene! Aren't we supposed to be courageous in the face of death, we above all others? Or do you expect me to run away from it, too?"

Bishop Cartledge put up his hands and took a step back. "No, no, no, of course not, of course not," he said in the soothing tone reserved for the very sick and the very young. "I'm just saying, the ministry's hard enough as it is. Why keep pushing when they just don't want you anymore?"

"But it's not right," Donald insisted.

The bishop shrugged. "That doesn't have anything to do with it."

"It should."

"But it doesn't. Look, you can fight it out if you want to. You have the right to do that. But there really isn't anything I can do to help you. Besides, there's always two sides to every story."

"What's *that* supposed to mean?"

Bishop Cartledge waved his hands mollifyingly again. "I don't mean anything particular. It's just that in my line of work, you learn that there's more going on than meets the eye. I heard what your wife said to that Sandra. I was there. It was pretty harsh. I'm sure there's some kind of history behind it, but I can't help with that. I don't pick sides."

It was on the tip of Donald's tongue to retaliate, to tell him exactly how much was going on behind the scenes that Al had not related, to remind him that a bishop was not a legal mediator but a shepherd of the shepherds, for God's sake...

And then his tower of rage collapsed. This was not the place to seek or find justice. Or even grace. Just lukewarm comfort covering an unspoken plea to take his troubles elsewhere.

"Well," said Donald, "next time I need your help, I'll be sure to have an affair first."

Then he pivoted and stalked off.

∼

The faculty meeting was winding to its unhasty close. Carmichael had entered with a measure of caution. She'd seen little of Alan over the summer break except when he and Sandra appeared at church, a strident air hovering about them. Awkward as that was, there'd been no occasion for it to spill over into their professional relationship. Carmichael presumed that emotions were one thing but work was another, and, despite a marked decline in interpersonal warmth, matters would continue much as they had before.

The enormous number of items pertaining to the ag and tech departments dragging on endlessly, she gave herself over to doodles in her notebook, interspersed with florilegia of corrections to her syllabus for Nineteenth-Century American Literature. It wasn't quite final, because when she had been able to bring herself to work over the summer at all, it was to dive back into her dissertation on John Hector St. John. No matter. Even if she had a thing for undervalued eighteenth-century lit, she could teach an introduction to the nineteenth-century without effort—or at least no more than was required to disabuse her students of all the nonsense stuffed into them by high school English teachers. So that meant Emily Dickinson for sure, *Moby Dick* tragically not, *Uncle Tom's Cabin* and *The Turn of the Screw* (of course, students were always disappointed when they realized what the book *wasn't* about), something of Edgar Allen Poe other than the predictable "Tell-Tale Heart," extracts from *Knickerbocker's History of New York*, and maybe one of Louisa May Alcott's saucy potboilers to shake things up. And of course nonfiction: Douglass, Thoreau, Emerson...

She came out of a reverie sketching a bumblebee, as copies of the course catalogue for the next school year were sent around the table. She took hers, passed the stack, and flipped over "Golf and Sports Turf 101" and "Advanced Dairy Cattle 350" to the slim selection from the humanities department.

"Um," she said aloud. The monosyllable skimmed across the sound of shuffling papers. Several people looked up.

"Yes, Carmichael?" said Dean Stanhope.

"Sorry, this isn't probably the right place to bring it up, but I just noticed that my elective has been left out of the catalogue. Could we make sure it gets back in before students register? Otherwise it'll be undersubscribed and canceled."

The dean turned all shifty and squirmed in his seat. "Oh, I thought you knew already. Alan?"

Alan nodded curtly. "I'm sorry, I should have told you sooner, but I guess the busywork of running the department made it slip my mind. The adjunct we'd slated to cover for you dropped out last minute, and as you well know, we just don't have the faculty to cover all the basic sections of Comp and Lit, so you'll have to take your usual load again. Chances were pretty small you'd get any takers for that particular elective anyway. Sorry."

Carmichael stared at him gap-mouthed until she was brought back to her senses by the downcast eyes and abrupt paralysis that spread like contagion from the dean to all the other professors. They knew a takedown when they saw one. It hardly mattered what had caused it, only to keep quiet and avoid getting tarred with the same brush.

"I see," said Carmichael at last. "Well, I can't say I'm not disappointed, and I wish I'd been informed sooner."

"It's a terrible oversight, I feel so bad about this," said the dean. He continued to burble apologetically until someone had the courage to change the subject.

Carmichael looked down at her syllabus, the printed words dissolving into a matrix of meaningless gray dots, her handwritten corrections as lucid as hieroglyphs. This is not right, this is not right, she chanted in her head, and everyone will think it's because of something I did and never know what's behind it and what if it hurts my tenure process...

At which, on cue, the dean took the floor again and announced proudly the enrollment of a professor of hotel and restaurant management and another of horticulture in the tenure process for the year ahead, and how proud SUNY Shibboleth was to retain such talent for its faculty and wished them both the best of luck and a long and prosperous career.

This time Carmichael knew better than to say anything. Her eyes flicked over to Alan, who was waiting for her. He stared back in stony impassivity, but the message was clear enough.

She began to shake deep within, whether of fear or rage she couldn't quite tell. It threatened to dislodge the carefully managed grief for Asher that she had learned to box up with care for times like these when she had to be public and official. How dare he, how dare he, how dare he, the chorus sang in her brain, and then she wondered how hard it would be to get a hold of arsenic and whether she could poison his coffee without getting caught.

The meeting broke up, the dean and Alan shot out the door at the other end of the room, the rest of the faculty skirted her as if she might be contagious, and it was only the sound of a throat clearing that told her she had not been left completely alone.

"I saw what just happened," said Tobias Gooch Teylow in his nasal, slightly-too-high-pitched voice. He was in his early sixties and wearing a bow tie that drooped to one side. Carmichael couldn't imagine the point of wearing a bow tie if you weren't going to be dapper about it. He nodded solemnly and dislodged a sprinkling of dandruff that settled on his shoulders like in a snow globe. The unflattering small details made him, for the first time, snap into focus as a person. His extension of mercy to her filled Carmichael with shame.

"What *did* happen?" she asked. "I wasn't imagining it?"

"Oh, no," Tobias replied. "At my age you've seen every little thing faculty use to destroy one another. I'd surmise that Alan is hell-bent on taking you out."

"That's a little…" Carmichael began, still feeling obligated to deny reality as a matter of principle.

"It's not. I know the man. Believe me, I've been here a lot longer than you have. He didn't make department head on sheer merit. He elbowed me out."

Carmichael's raised eyebrows were question enough.

"I'm sure, if you've heard anything, it's that I'm an incompetent old fart better consigned to the dusty basement of Kinderhook Hall than any position of real responsibility. I don't pretend that I'm any kind of superior scholar, but the fact is, my only crime was naïveté. I didn't see him coming for me and had no preparation when he pulled his stunt. I'm not going to tell you the whole sordid tale," he interrupted her unspoken query. "Mostly because I refuse to donate any more of my life's energies to that man's machinations. I don't know what it is he has against you, but watch out. He's going to try and take you down."

"I know why," said Carmichael. She stood up to face Tobias like the equal he had suddenly become. "It has nothing to do with my work or the college or anything."

"Well, don't tell me. I don't want to know."

"Did you know that he'd talked about putting me up for tenure this fall?"

"My dear, he waved it around all last spring like he was Santa Claus bringing a bag of goodies to some poor child in the ghetto."

Carmichael glanced around the empty room wrathfully. "And *nobody* stuck up for me—"

"Come now. You've been the departmental darling ever

since you got here, and everyone took you for Alan's pet. He made no bones about playing you up as his favorite and starting you on tenure ahead of schedule. If he's turned on you now, what is that to the rest of us?"

"But I had no idea," Carmichael stammered.

Tobias shrugged. "Live and learn," he said. "I sure did."

"Isn't there some court of appeal?"

"Appeal what? It was out of order to start you early anyway, and it never got any further than a promise. If Alan decides not to proceed, he's only reverting to what he should have done in the first place."

Carmichael leaned back against the cinder block wall and exhaled. "So what am I supposed to do now?" she said.

"Work on your résumé," Tobias suggested.

"Like I'd get a good recommendation out of him," Carmichael scoffed. "But wait—what are you implying? Not getting tenure is one thing, but you don't think I'll be fired, do you? My contract has been renewed for the next three years. I have a signed copy. That at least can't be undone."

"He can't fire you without cause. But he can certainly make you want to resign."

"Oh, God. Oh, my God." Carmichael felt the deep wracking hiccups that forecasted a crying spell.

"Or you could fight back," Tobias said.

Carmichael took a very deep breath. She forced herself to look at Tobias straight on. "How on earth would I do that?"

"Don't know," he said lightly. "I never did figure it out myself. Wish I did, now."

"Well, if you figure something out, you'll let me know, won't you?"

"If I do, I'll not only tell you, I'll join you." He smiled for the first time.

Carmichael stuck out her hand. He took it. "Tobias, I've done you wrong. I haven't taken you seriously."

"I know. I'm used to it."

"That's not the kind of thing a person should get used to."

He shrugged. "And yet." He dropped her hand and adjusted the strap of his carrier bag. "Good luck."

~

Five minutes into the Sunday service, just as Donald was pronouncing the absolution, a commotion at the back of the church announced the late arrival of little less than a crowd. As all heads turned to ascertain the identity of the noisy latecomers, Donald conceded the necessity of a pause and squinted for a better look.

Lord-a-mercy, he heard himself say in his mother's voice. It's the Schickedanzes. *All* of them.

Frieda and Hermann Schickedanz had been the founding members of the congregation in 1910, repeating their ancestors' initial emigration from Germany to Brazil by emigrating from Brazil to Olutakli County. A forty-year sojourn in Latin America had not put so much as a dent in the family's language habits, and they arrived in Shibboleth speaking the exact same dialect as when they'd left Franconia. The second requirement they made of their new home, after the primary requirement of dairy pasture, was a Lutheran church that held services in German. Thus was Mt. Moriah born, though the congregation discreetly abandoned German somewhere around 1917. The Schickedanzes and the other families that joined them kept up German at home until the early forties, at which point all ties to the Vaterland but culinary ones were severed once and for all.

Several generations on, however, being descended from the founding members was taken as a matter of entitlement, not devotion, a matter about which Dick Schickedanz did not mince words the first time he met Donald. This was at the new pastor's installation. The entire clan turned out in force—Frieda and Hermann's sons Ralph and Clarence, along with their wives, Clarence's sons Dick, Steve, and Curtis, along with *their* wives and children, and a few odd cousins through Ralph's line that Donald never did manage to sort out. They filled in the back three pews on the lefthand side—to the disgruntlement of the regulars—and ate abundantly of the celebratory potluck without talking to anyone but themselves. At one point during the luncheon Dick took Donald aside, introduced himself, explained his exalted status in the lineage of Mt. Moriah, assured Donald of his general goodwill and approval that the church was once again in the care of a competent pastor, and promised never to trouble him again with attendance at worship, because after all someone of his family line didn't need to bother with continual renewal of the covenant, as it went without saying anyway.

Since that time, not a single one of the Schickedanzes had graced the church with their presence, except for about a year ago when Steve's youngest daughter Cheryl came back from college in Philadelphia with a baby but not a husband, and Steve ordered Donald to "baptize the bastard" as if that were the only suitable act of revenge. Donald endured six miserable sessions of catechism with Cheryl, who sat passive and resentful throughout, and approximately fifteen seconds after the water dried on little Justin's forehead, Cheryl shot out of Olutakli County with the baby, and for all Donald knew never returned. He didn't exactly blame her.

And now, without any justifying occasion for it, Ralph and Clarence, not to mention Dick, Steve, and Curtis, spouses and progeny in tow, were fussing and chatting their way into church. The back pews already being fully occupied, they spilled down the aisle and, with a great deal of discussion and changing places, took possession up front.

On their way up Donald distinctly saw Dick turn and nod at Sandra, who nodded back. It was as ominous a sign as the sun black as sackcloth and the moon as blood.

After the blessing and dismissal, Donald had little choice during the announcements but to acknowledge the rare pleasure of the Schickedanzes' presence and bid them welcome.

Dick took this as an invitation to speak. He popped up, was next to Donald in three strides, and after looking around fruitlessly for a microphone launched into a well-rehearsed speech. After a good deal of faff and jokes that failed to land, he got to the heart of the matter.

"Now I know we don't come around much, but you all know how much we love this church, and how proud we are that Oma and Opa started it all those years ago, and right after we're done here we're gonna head over to the cemetery to pay our respects. Anyway, the point is that even though we're not here much, we love this church, coming up on its eightieth anniversary soon, and we want it to go on another eighty years at least, but we all know that there's no bigger burden on a church, or I might add on a federal government, than debt. It's come to our attention that our beloved Mt. Moriah is suffering under a big ol' debt on account of that gorgeous new mausoleum you got out there—"

"Columbarium," Donald could not help but interject.

"Right. Columbarium, a real fine piece of craftsmanship, I have to say, and a great addition to the Mt. Moriah complex. I'm sure if Oma and Opa were around now, they'd have chosen it instead of their graves. Anyway, what I'm saying is, we've had a family consultation, and none of us want to see Mt. Moriah suffering under a crushing load of debt just because you took the risk of faith to add on this mauso—uh, columbarium, and so, since business has been really great, thank God for that, we've decided to pay off the whole debt. That's right, all of us Schickedanzes are pitching in, so you just get your treasurer to show us what remains to be paid, and I'll write you a check and see to it that Dad and Uncle Ralph and my no-good brothers reimburse me for my share. I won't make you good folks try to squeeze blood out of those two turnips." He grinned.

The congregation burst into applause. Sandra, Alan, and Eunice stood up as they hammered their hands together, and in moments the whole congregation was on its feet for an extended ovation. Dick bowed like an opera diva. Donald half expected him to blow kisses. When the applause died away, Donald managed to choke out thanks and say perhaps the Schickedanzes would be moved to come again soon and enjoy the fruits of their labor. Donald could not resist the dig, but Dick and company seemed to be so dazzled by the crowd's adoration that it sailed right over their heads.

Then Donald tried to shift Dick back to his seat but after another failed grab for a nonexistent microphone he carried on, "And look it, we're not gonna bail you out every time you do something expensive, but the thing is none of us even knew about this debt—" here Donald had to bite his lip to keep from pointing out that the current debt load was published in every single monthly newsletter "—until Sandra over there picked up the phone and told us all about it, and once she explained the situation, well, like I said, we weren't going to let our beloved church go under just on account of something like that. So how about some applause for her, too, since she's the one who reached out to us?"

There was another round of clapping, though Donald noticed that Jackie sat on her hands and George balled up his fists and stuffed them into his armpits. Sandra rose, gave a graceful nod to both sides of the aisle, and sat down again.

Donald repeated his official thanks, persuading Dick with gentle cues to relinquish the stage. Then there was nothing for it but to work his way through the whole body Schickedanz, one after another, expressing his insincere pleasure at seeing them and especially on the occasion of doing the church such a kindly turn. Before he knew it he was surrounded by a hive of Schickedanzes and carted off bodily to the cemetery to say a prayer over Frieda and Hermann. The underchurched younger Schickedanzes, having apparently absorbed their catechism from the movies, wondered with trepidation whether their great-grandparents were not perhaps "still suffering." Donald managed to wrangle the petitions away from intercession for the lost toward thanksgiving for the saints. The excessively boisterous "Amen!" of the opportunistically pious capped it off. One by one the Schickedanzes pumped Donald's hand with an overtone of appreciation and an undertone of possession.

Just as he was turning to go, Dick glanced around and said loudly, "Hey look! There's a new grave right here by ours."

Every Schickedanz head spun around as Dick squatted and read aloud, "Asher Martin... Abney. Oh. Oh, right."

It was very nearly comical. The entire family stood petrified in place, all the bravado draining from their posture.

Donald said quietly, "My older son Saul said that Asher liked to identify the letters of his own name in Frieda and Hermann's names. He insisted that Asher would have wanted to be buried right next to them, so we granted him his final wish."

Dick gaped like a largemouth bass, nodded, and zipped off, the whole swarm trailing in his wake.

~

"Are you home?" Carmichael called out as the pantry door slapped shut behind her.

"Over here," Donald called from his office. He emerged and added, "The kids are still with Hilda Kipfmueller. She decided to take them over to the county fair, so prepare for them to come back all hopped up from funnel cakes and scary rides. But I figured you'd want a little quiet to recover from your first day back. How was it?"

"Not bad," said Carmichael, sloughing off her blazer and scarf. "I mean, considering I'm teaching the same course for the seventh semester straight, and not the one I was hoping to teach."

Donald gave her a little sympathetic twist of the lips. "And the students?"

"No worse, though no better than usual. I used to think they were bored. Now I think they're terrified and trying to cover it up. Maybe because I know better now what it is to cover up emotions."

Donald crossed the rest of the way through the dining room to hold her. They were still in each other's arms when the doorbell rang.

"That's weird," said Carmichael. "Who ever uses the front door?" The well-meant intention to preserve the privacy of the pastor's family meant that the front door faced the drop-off on the opposite side of the parsonage from the driveway and the church. None of the parishioners ever used it, and guests were always directed to the pantry door, too.

Carmichael heard the surprise in Donald's voice as he opened the door and said, "Lynn! Hello. This is a surprise. What brings you here?"

Lynn? Carmichael wondered. She reviewed the Lynns they knew and still couldn't figure why any of them would come to the front door.

This particular Lynn's voice came through clipped and defensive. "Good afternoon, Pastor Abney. May I come in for a moment?"

"Of course, yes, of course," but the way he said it told Carmichael that something was wrong.

The woman stepped into the living room. She was in a dark suit that fit her badly, low pumps, and an excess of makeup. Even across the room Carmichael could see the smudged eyeliner. She gave off a conflicting aura of being both kindly and tough, sympathetic and brutal. Carmichael couldn't make the picture add up.

The bewildering woman said, "I'm Lynn Truscott, from Child Protective Services. May I speak with you both a moment?"

Donald gestured to the sofa. "Of course. Please have a seat."

Carmichael watched in horror as the woman tiptoed over a spill of Lincoln Logs and seated herself gingerly on the grubby old sofa. All at once the house took on a different aspect: every speck of dirt, every stray toy, a crumpled-up piece of paper that hadn't quite made it into the trash, all of it screamed out the

Abneys' parental incompetence, testified that they were filthy and cruel and neglectful and unfit to be parents and that their children should become wards of the state...

"Carmichael," said Donald softly, "why don't you join us?"

She was across the room and seated rigidly upright on the ottoman before she knew it. "Why are you here?" she whispered, and then hated herself for the whisper, as if it were an admission of guilt.

Lynn was all professionalism. "Child Protective Services received a call expressing concern about the condition of your household for your children." Here she paused to consult papers on a clipboard she pulled out of her vast purse. "Katharina Emily Abney and Saul Wilkinson Abney."

"We call her Kitty," Carmichael said, still in a whisper.

Lynn gave a clipped nod. "The caller expressed concern about neglect and reckless endangerment of the children."

"Who called? *Who*?"

Donald answered before Lynn could, "All calls to Child Protective Services are anonymous." Carmichael looked her question and Donald explained, "Lynn here has made presentations to the Shibboleth Ecumenical Council so we would know what to do if we encountered situations of child abuse in our pastoral work. Though I have to say, I never did expect to be on the receiving end of one of these visits."

Carmichael could hardly sort out which question to ask next. "You mean you have *no* idea? It could have been just anyone?"

Lynn replied neutrally, "All calls to Child Protective Services are anonymous."

"But then someone could use the anonymity to persecute someone they didn't like!"

"Ma'am," said Lynn sternly, "we take seriously every call we receive. Not every call proves to be grounded and not infrequently the charges are dropped. But we always have to operate on the assumption that there was substance to the complaint."

"Guilty until proven innocent, in other words!" Carmichael's fear shed off her like a skin as she knew, knew for sure, that this was Sandra's doing, or someone Sandra put up to it, a low-down dirty betrayal to make all the rest of what she'd done to the Abney family pale in comparison...

"No, it's not like that at all," said Lynn, and Donald said at the same time, "She's just doing her job."

"What is the *basis* for the complaint against us?" Carmichael demanded.

At this Lynn had the decency to look uncomfortable. "Well, the complainant mentioned that the home site was insufficiently safe for children, leading to a high probability of accidents, and a further look revealed to us that last December..."

Carmichael was on her feet and could not control the furious wobble in her voice. "Do you think we haven't put the goddamn ladder *away*? Do you think it doesn't take every ounce of willpower I have not to surveil my children every second because I'm so scared they'll get even a splinter? And at the exact same time scared that I'll end up making them incompetent to deal with the world by being overprotective? Do you think I don't wish every single day that I could undo the very force of gravity so I could get my little boy back?" And then she lost control and was sobbing and Donald had to ask Lynn if it would be all right if Carmichael sat out the rest of the conversation and Lynn looked down as she said that would be fine.

When Donald returned from settling Carmichael in their room he didn't know where to begin. Only the fact of Carmichael's uncontrolled anger kept his from exploding as well.

"Look, Lynn," he said, accenting her first name and their hitherto collegial relationship, "you know as well as I do that Asher's death was ruled accidental and no one pressed any charges against anyone for it. So why is this complaint coming against us *now*?"

Lynn steadfastly maintained that the caller gave no indication one way or another, just asked CPS to look into the safety conditions at the Abney home, no more, no less.

"And are you satisfied?"

Lynn bit her lip and said, "I had a look around outside before I rang the bell, and to be frank it looks to me like a baseless claim. But according to the law, the case has to stay open for sixty days. If no further evidence beyond the call itself comes to light, we'll dismiss the case." She stood up. Donald walked her back to the front door. As she stepped outside she turned around and said, in a hushed and confidential tone, "It's hardly uncommon to get revenge calls. I'm really sorry, but I have to investigate them all, regardless. I didn't think there'd be anything to it, but you never know."

"A pastor knows that as well as a social worker," said Donald.

"My advice would be, watch your back. Someone has it out for you." Her heels made a clicking noise as she scurried down the steps.

"Oh, God, I'm so ashamed of myself," moaned Carmichael when Donald came up to her in their bedroom.

"Don't be," he said. "You were right all along. I'm the one who's sorry. I've been holding it against you that you screwed up your apology to Sandra. But I get it now. We are not dealing with someone who deals fairly. This is the lowest of lows."

"So you think it's Sandra, too?"

"We'll never know for sure. Calling CPS is a diabolically clever way to hide. But I can't imagine why anyone else would."

"She's going to drive us out no matter what." Carmichael wiped the tears and snot off her face with a corner of the sheet. "Her and Alan both. This is the final proof. They win. No one at church is going to hold the cost of the columbarium against them now, not after that brilliant stunt with the Schickedanzes, and what's to stop them from making a child abuse complaint against us every month until we just can't take it anymore? Sooner or later it will get out. Everyone already thinks we're tainted because of Asher. We won't have any friends, our kids won't have any friends, and if Alan can't bring cause against me in the next three years he'll certainly see to it that my contract isn't renewed, and then I'll be out of a job..."

"...and meanwhile the church will split right down the middle."

"That too."

"It's an impossible situation," said Donald. He flung himself down the length of the bed next to her and screwed the heels of his hands into his eyes. "If I stay on much longer, the congregation is going to fracture. They're not *all* on the Forrads' side, you know. People will applaud money no matter what. But there are definitely two factions. At *least* two. Who knows how many more before it's all over."

Carmichael propped herself up on an elbow and stared earnestly at him. "But it's a trap! If you resign now, you'll end up confirming the rumors about us and *make* them true, even though they weren't true in the first place. Sandra will claim she was right about you leaving, and about everything else, too."

"You're right. I hadn't even thought of that. I'll become the person they think I am." Donald peeled his hands away from his face and stared at the ceiling. "Should I care so much about my reputation? I mean, if I really was a good and holy person, wouldn't I sacrifice my reputation for the good of the church?"

"But is it good for the church if people end up believing untrue things about you? You know that's why I couldn't give Sandra the apology she wanted. She didn't want my apology. She wanted me to say something about her that I didn't believe, for everyone else to hear."

"No. It wouldn't do the church any good. If only because it would set up the next pastor for a fall."

Carmichael put her head down on his chest. "It doesn't matter what's the right thing to do. All that matters is what we *have* to do. And what we have to do is leave. They'll make us leave if we don't go voluntarily, and then they'll win even more than they've already won. They have us every which way. Even if we hang on three more years, after that I'll be out of a job. Olutakli County isn't expensive, but even so, we can't get by on your salary alone."

"I'm sure my parents would help us out. They have enough to spare."

"So do mine, for that matter. But is that want you want? To take handouts from our parents to stay in a couple of miserable jobs?"

Donald exhaled long. "No. No. Not at all." Then, "What about Asher?"

"We'll take him with us," Carmichael said. "We'll exhume him—that's not the right word, is it? You say that for murder investigations. At least we haven't gotten to that yet, but who knows what CPS is going to require of us before this is all over. We'll bury him with my grandparents in Queens. Or yours in Indiana."

"And settle there?"

"I don't know. I hate the thought of not being near him. But we have no way of knowing where we'll be in ten years, or fifty, or when we die. Oh, God, we should have cremated him after all, shouldn't we, so we could take him with us… She's going to win on that one, too…"

They wept as they hadn't in months. Every effort to carry on, to opt back into life, taunted them all over again as a betrayal of their son. Good parents don't get over it. Good parents don't move on. Good parents remain permanently locked in grief beyond all consolation. The whole unfolding debacle of suspicion and recrimination was the rebuke of an impersonal yet judgmental universe, condemning them for trying to find reasons to live and in so doing abandoning their dead son to his grave like that was where he belonged. How dare they call themselves parents at all. How dare they presume any right to the two children who yet lived. It was their fault Asher died, their fault, their own most grievous fault, because good parents could have foreseen and averted every danger, there are no accidents but only executions of the nonexistent divine will upon the wicked, and who but wicked parents would allow their little boy to die, to die, to die...

The phone rang.

"Let it ring," begged Carmichael.

"Might be a church emergency," said Donald heavily. He rolled off the bed. Carmichael made herself stand up and pad down the stairs after him, her heart pounding so hard she could feel it in her throat.

"Hello," said Donald. A long silence. "Yes, yes, I'll come right away, thanks for calling me."

"What, what?" she said, frantic.

"Not one of ours," he said promptly. "It's Aaron, you know, the Southern Baptist preacher I'm friends with?"

"Oh, no. What?"

"That was the hospital in Kuhsota. Aaron's there now. He tried to kill himself."

CHAPTER FIFTEEN

September 1989

*Good and evil I see is to be found in all societies,
and it is in vain to seek for any spot
where those ingredients are not mixed.*

Through the open car window Donald smelled the Labor Day barbecues already underway as he drove over to Kuhsota for a second visit with Aaron.

On the first visit, Aaron had still been groggy and disoriented from the overdose of valium he'd taken. Donald had spent most of that visit with Missy, Aaron's wife, distraught and incoherent and furious all in one, blaming herself for being such a failure that she needed the valium prescription in the first place, blaming Aaron for failing to get them the out of Olutakli County, for failing to be stronger than she was, for failing full stop. Her makeup ran and her hair wilted and she didn't even notice her two sons, sitting immobile on the waiting room bench, taut and seething children who weren't allowed to be angry. Donald saw there was nothing he could do but absorb her words till they ran their course. He promised to come again soon.

When he checked in at the nurse's station the second time, he learned that Aaron was still under psychiatric watch but alert enough to talk. Donald stalked down the hallway through the chorus of beeps and chimes. He knocked on Aaron's door.

"Come in," responded a listless voice.

Aaron had been scrubbed clean of his usual professional polish. His chin was stubbly, his hair tousled, he wore a pastel hospital gown and a plastic wristband. There were no needles or medications or even plastic knives to be seen in the room. But a very faint light came into his dull eyes upon seeing Donald.

Donald took the chair next to the bed. "Hello, Aaron," he said softly.

"You don't need to talk so carefully," said the other. "I'm not going to try to strangle myself with the bedsheet. Or you, either."

Donald gave a small rueful smile. "Do you want to talk about it?"

"Which part? The part where the congregational president served me notice that I'd been terminated from my position due to 'conduct unbecoming a minister' and then said 'God bless' on his way out the door? The part where Missy told me she was taking the boys and moving back to Alabama and I could join them if I wanted? Or the part where I actually swallowed the pills and hoped I'd never wake up?"

"Why don't you choose," said Donald, still softly.

Aaron had been holding his gaze but at this turned his head and stared out the window. "I just don't know what this job is," he said at last. "If it was only a job, a job and nothing more, I could walk away from it. But it's been my whole life, as long as I can remember. I remember back the first time I really felt the love of God and was born again. I wanted to give my whole life to his service." He sighed. "I think—I think it started to go wrong right then. Everybody approved and applauded me for it, and I got hooked on that. Not on feeling God's love, but on other people's approval of me for feeling God's love." He turned back to Donald. "Looking back on it now, I figure it was all of five minutes between when I lived for God's approval only, and when I started living for man's approval. Can anyone ever have gone from being a God-pleaser to a man-pleaser faster than I did? Of course, I didn't notice at the time. You make people happy, your family and youth leaders and pastors and the whole church happy, and you think you're making God happy. They don't let you see the difference."

"Not till you're ordained," said Donald.

"Yeah," Aaron snorted. "Then they turn on you. They turn on you so fast. You toe the line and support the cause, or become public enemy number one."

"Persona non grata," said Donald. "I suppose that literally means 'a person without grace.'"

"*I* am a person without grace," said Aaron fiercely. His hands clutched at the rails on either side of his bed. "And why should I deserve any grace? I have served idols my whole adult life."

Donald said, "Grace abounds for idolaters, too."

"If this is grace," said Aaron, gesturing to the hospital room and somehow managing to conjure up his now-former church and bitterly disappointed wife and mean-spirited kids as well, "then I can do without."

Donald held silent, checking his impulse to correct and enlighten Aaron's doctrine of grace. At last he said, "I may be leaving my own church soon."

"Yeah? Why?"

"Well… they're driving me out. I think."

"What? But you're a good guy. You're no idolater."

Donald shrugged. "I have no particular conviction that my heart is idol-free. But a faction has turned on me. They're, well, they were our benefactors, in a way. People we thought were friends looking out for our best interests. But they turned on us—"

"Over what?" Aaron scooted in his bed to sit up straighter. He looked marginally happier. "Politics or abortion or gays or what?"

"No, actually, it's over the new columbarium. And whether we should have cremated our son."

"Oh." Aaron obviously only just remembered about Asher. "You're *kidding*. Over that?"

"Yep."

"Goddamn church people." Aaron leaned back again in the

bed and squinted at the news on the muted TV overhead. He smiled at Donald and said, "At least now that I'm not a preacher anymore, I can swear like I always wanted to."

"When I was in my initial state of shock over Asher, I tried drinking. Stupid, isn't it? But I literally thought, it's supposed to numb the pain, so why not give it a try? So I bought a couple cases of beer."

"So are you an alcoholic now?"

"No. I didn't like the flavor."

They chuckled a little. Aaron said, "You should've tried wine coolers. Not that I'd know, good Southern Baptist that I am. So what are you going to do? About your church, I mean."

"I don't know. I thought about contacting my bishop and putting in my papers to see if there was another call in the synod. At least that way we'd stay near Carmichael's family. But..."

"What?"

"I don't exactly respect the bishop, at this point, so asking for his help is odious, and it seems like this church debacle would follow me and my reputation anyway."

Aaron peered at him and said, "And also you don't want to give those bastards the satisfaction of driving you out."

"Well, no. But that hardly seems like the right thing to guide my decision, either. It can't be right to stay on if it tears the whole church apart."

"They drive you out over something like not cremating your kid, they *deserve* it," spat Aaron.

Donald shook his head. "You threw me off track there. Do you need to talk more about—what drove you to do it?"

Aaron seemed to shrivel a little, but he answered, "I couldn't keep it up anymore. And I couldn't see any other way out. I've been in this business more than a decade but I have no experience of doing it for the right reasons. But I don't have anything else, either. No skills or credentials for another job. And also I just, I just don't know myself any other way. Is there any Aaron that isn't a preacher? It's just a big empty hole where the person should be. So either I could keep on living a lie. Or I could become a zero." He met Donald's gaze. "That night, when I decided those were my only options, death seemed like the better choice. I convinced myself Missy would be better off without me anyway, without a husband who let her down, and the kids would find a better father."

"I'm sorry, Aaron," Donald breathed.

"Don't worry. I'm not gonna try it again. I must have known somehow not to take enough to actually die."

"I've noticed that people sometimes do desperate things when others won't let them act honestly. Or when they won't let themselves."

"Yeah. No more effective way of getting out of the ministry than attempting suicide."

"So are you going to move back to Alabama then?"

"Nothing to hold me here. We can move in with my folks, or hers, for now. I'll figure something out. But I gotta get out of the God business. How about you?" Aaron looked hopeful, as if Donald doing the same would ratify his own decision.

"No," said Donald gently. "That's not where I'm at. Look, Aaron, nobody's going to congratulate you for leaving the ministry. But it was getting congratulated in the first place that corrupted it for you. Walk away from it and please God. Don't worry about the others."

"They never tell you that walking away might be the most God-pleasing thing to do."

"There's a lot they don't tell you," said Donald.

∽

School started two days later. Donald and Carmichael had agreed that Saul was ready to ride the bus again. They packed up his bag with new pencils and crayons and a lunchbox containing a bologna sandwich, a cup of yogurt, and a real fruit roll-up, not the long-despised fruit leather from the Co-op. He was cheerful and excited.

Kitty approached the day in a mood foul and defiant. She withdrew in sullen silence when Carmichael insisted she tuck a little bag of maxi pads down at the bottom of her backpack. Then Carmichael tried to bring her out of her shell by asking if she wasn't excited to start switching classrooms now at the dawn of seventh grade. Kitty shrugged. Then how about starting a language? Most of the kids were taking Spanish because they heard it was easy. Kitty was one of the few opting for French, because Carmichael spoke it. Kitty mumbled, "They say Madame Rusnikov gives tons of homework," and impounded herself in her bedroom until it was time to walk Saul down to the main road to catch the school bus, and then hike over to the school by herself.

Once the kids were out of the house Donald said, "I'm going to try again to type up this letter to Gene," and Carmichael retreated to the sofa in the living room, determined to have a morning of relaxation as a reward for getting through the kids' summer vacation. Reward, but also excuse. All the pleasure had drained right out of her teaching, and now that there was no prospect of tenure, she couldn't bring herself to work on John Hector St. John, even knowing that a published dissertation would increase her chances of getting a position elsewhere. She should at least glance through the *Chronicle of Higher Education* for postings—however unlikely it was that she and Donald could again coordinate their employment—but instead she picked up the latest issue of *Gourmet* and wondered if she'd ever be able to afford lobster again.

An hour later the phone rang. "I'll get it," she called to Donald. "Hello?" she said into the receiver.

"Is this Mrs. Abney? This is Shibboleth Elementary," said the nasal voice at the other end.

"Oh, God, oh, God, what's wrong?" Carmichael babbled.

"Nothing, ma'am, nothing, please calm down," said the voice, alarmed at her reaction. "Nobody's been hurt. Nothing serious, don't worry."

"I'm sorry," Carmichael panted. "Did we forget to send in Saul's immunization record or something?"

"No, it's not that," said the voice, but it had a catch to it that kept Carmichael on the alert. "Here, I'll let you talk to Mrs. Delve directly."

She heard the phone changing hands. Mrs. Delve? She'd been Saul's first-grade teacher last year.

After the conventional formalities Mrs. Delve said, "Saul came to my classroom this morning instead of Mrs. Gomolka's."

"Oh," said Carmichael. How was that worth calling her about? "I'm sure he was just excited and got confused."

"No," said Mrs. Delve. "He came to my room on purpose."

"Well, maybe he's just reluctant to move on to second grade, you know, with all the losses of the past year. Why, won't he go to Mrs. Gomolka's room now?"

"No, he won't, but the reason why," and here Mrs. Delve paused for what felt to Carmichael like an eternity, "is that he says he's Asher. He says he's Asher Abney, just starting first grade."

"Oh, God," whispered Carmichael.

"I tried talking to him, Mrs. Abney, I really did. I told him that I knew he was Saul because he was in my class all last year, but he refuses to admit he's Saul and keeps saying he's Asher. I wouldn't have called you if I could talk him out of it, but he's disrupting the new children, and Mrs. Gomolka can't persuade him to come over to her classroom, either."

"I'll be right over," said Carmichael.

Donald came with her. At the office they were greeted by Mrs. Fitzsimmons, the elementary school principal.

"Where's Saul?" Carmichael demanded without preamble.

"We thought it best to let him rest in the nurse's office for now," said Mrs. Fitzsimmons. She led the way.

Saul was sitting in a molded plastic chair, swinging his legs and reading *Tintin and the Picaros*.

He looked surprised to see his parents but smiled widely

at them. "Hi, Mommy! Hi, Daddy! What are you doing at my school?"

Donald took the chair next to him and Carmichael knelt in front of him. "Saul," she began.

"You're silly, Mommy," said Saul. His voice was artificially high and cutesy. "Saul is in Mrs. Gomolka's class. I'm Asher. I went to Mrs. Delve's class but she was worried that I was sick so she told me to go to the nurse. I told the nurse I'm fine but she doesn't believe me."

Donald pulled Saul up on to his lap. "Sweetie," he said, "you know you're not Asher. You're Saul."

"You're silly like Mommy."

"You're Saul, and today Saul is starting second grade."

"Nuh-uh. I'm Asher and I'm starting first grade."

"Saul, that's enough," said Carmichael sharply.

All of a sudden Saul's cheerful countenance collapsed in on itself. "Don't talk mean to me, Mommy," he said, taking a huge breath that presaged sobs.

Carmichael felt like she was collapsing in on herself, too. She took Saul's little hands in her own. "Honey," she said, "honey, I know it's terrible without Asher. I know you miss him so much. I miss him, too. I know you want him back, but we can't, honey, we just can't..."

"But *I* am Asher. I'm here, Mommy, I'm here, why do you pretend like I'm not here?" The tears bulged and overflowed his eyes.

Carmichael looked at Donald. "Help," she whispered.

Donald wrapped his arms tighter around Saul and rested his chin on the top of his head. He rocked him a little. After awhile he said, "Do you know what I need right now?"

"What?" sniffled Saul.

"I need Saul," Donald said. "I need Saul because I can't have Asher anymore. I miss Asher so much, but I can't hold him and hug him anymore. So now that I can't have one of my sons, I really, really need the other one. I need my Saul more than anyone else in the world right now. It would make me so, so sad if I lost my Saul, too."

Saul trembled in Donald's arms but didn't say anything.

"Can you tell Saul for me," said Donald, "that his daddy really needs him to come back. It's OK if he comes all by himself, without Asher. God is taking good care of Asher right now. But I need my Saul back again. Can you please tell him to come back to his mommy and daddy?"

Saul kept quiet a minute, staring down at the floor, his hands curled tight inside Carmichael's. Then he said, "I think Saul is out on the playground. That's naughty because he should be in his classroom. Asher is always naughty but not Saul. I think if Asher goes and tells Saul it's time to come in and trade places, then Saul will be a good boy and go to his class like he's supposed to."

Donald glanced over at the nurse, who had been keeping a motionless vigil behind her desk. She gave a curt nod and said, "I'll take you to the playground."

Donald and Carmichael walked on either side of Saul, each holding one of his hands, down the long hallways that smelled of cheese and gravy and rubber. The nurse selected a key from her lanyard and popped open the door to the playground. "I'll wait for you here," she said.

The three Abneys took a few steps outside and then the adults stopped, uncertain. Saul was still holding their hands.

"Do you see him?" asked Donald.

Saul scanned the slide and swings and maypole. "There he is!" He pointed to the little carousel and dashed off toward it. Carmichael and Donald watched mutely as Saul grabbed one of the handles and ran to get the carousel spinning. He hopped aboard. With each revolution they could see him speaking to an invisible interlocutor.

When the carousel creaked to a halt he jumped off and tore back. "It's me! It's me, Saul!" he shouted at them. He flung himself at Donald in a frantic hug.

"Oh, Saul," Donald said, gripping him just as hard. "I'm so glad you came back."

Saul leaned out and said to Carmichael, "Asher still won't go to Mrs. Delve's class. She's gonna be sad. Can you tell her instead of me? I have to go to Mrs. Gomolka's classroom now."

"I'll be glad to," said Carmichael.

∽

In the adjacent building that housed the junior and senior high, Kitty was having a very different first day of school.

The excitement of starting seventh grade was just sufficient to overcome her reserve and contempt toward her classmates. She returned Jessica's shy "hello" and compared schedules with Jenny and pointed out a bathroom to Shannon who'd worked herself into a panic over not being able to find one. When the first warning bell rang, the four of them split up, Kitty and Jessica to one homeroom and Jenny and Shannon to another. Kitty watched the two girls retreat down the hall and enter a classroom behind Megan Moravsky. "At least we're not stuck with *her*," hissed Kitty. Jessica obediently agreed.

They made their way to their own homeroom, grabbed seats one in front of the other, and continued the obsessive review of their schedules until a boy walked into the room and turned the world upside down.

He was new this year. He had short black hair, a little wavy, and nice teeth behind his shy smile. He stood taller than most of the other boys in the seventh grade. By now the seats up front were the only ones left, so he sidled into a chair diagonally up one from Kitty. She had a perfect view of his profile. He was cute. He looked nice. He had to be smart. He didn't have any friends yet. He needed a friend for sure.

All at once Kitty realized that Jessica was talking to her. Stop staring, she admonished herself, and turned back to Jessica. But she didn't hear a word her friend said. She was torn between self-disgust at the uprush of emotion over a stupid boy, boys who ruin everything that is great about girls, and rationalizing that after all Marie loved Nutcracker and Jo did end up married to the professor, so it couldn't be *all* bad, could it?

The homeroom teacher stood up and summoned their attention. Kitty snapped around in her seat and tried not to stare at the profile of the very cute new boy.

Being an Abney, Kitty came up first on the attendance list. She raised her hand and announced a pert "Here!" that came out so loud the other seventh graders snickered. But the new boy who didn't have any friends yet turned to look at the voice coming from behind him. He made eye contact with Kitty and gave her a friendly half-smile.

By some miracle, his name came next. "Rob Adams."

"Here," he said timidly, half raising his hand.

Kitty Adams, she thought to herself. That doesn't sound so bad. I wouldn't even have to change my initials.

The teacher droned on through the attendance list, mispronouncing a not inconsiderable number of names. Then came the pledge of allegiance. Then announcements over the P.A. system. Kitty stared at the left side of Rob Adams's face, memorizing every detail.

Upon dismissal, everyone sprang up in a froth to make it to first period without earning a tardy on the very first day. Rob looked even more lost than the rest of them. Kitty steeled her nerves and sidled up to him. "Hi-I'm-Kitty-what's-your-first-class?" she said in a rush.

"Uh, hi," he said. "English." He kept staring at the schedule in his hand like it might speak to him and guide him to the classroom.

Kitty leaned in for a better look. Rob smelled like shampoo. "It's in room 210. That'll be upstairs. You better hurry."

"Oh. Thanks," he said. He gave her a sheepish smile. "I didn't know it was upstairs."

"All the two hundred classrooms are upstairs," she explained competently.

"OK. Um, thanks." He grabbed his backpack and trotted meekly off.

As she watched him go she recited in her mind, Kitty Adams Kitty Adams Kitty Adams Kitty Adams...

All through first period math she rebuked herself for not looking over the rest of Rob's schedule to see if they had any classes together. Instead she'd have to wait in agony till each new period to find out. Hope and disappointment cycled before her. Second period—no. Third period—no. Fourth period—no. She was so preoccupied wondering if she'd see Rob in the lunchroom that she completely forgot to tell Madame Rusnikov that she already knew some French because her mom was fluent and used to live in France. Instead Kitty mindlessly recited "bonjour" and "bonsoir" with the other kids who'd never heard a lick of French in their lives, until the bell rang and she could dash to the cafeteria to station herself for a good view.

But just as she exited the French classroom, the Spanish classroom across the way was letting out, and Kitty was struck like Lot's wife to see Rob Adams walking out right next to Megan Moravsky, the two of them chatting away as if they'd been friends their whole lives. Megan was smiling and simpering and tossing her head so her hairsprayed bangs bounced up and down. Kitty could tell she was wearing lip gloss, too. Rob was telling some story and Megan was laughing excessively. Kitty waited for him to glance over and notice her—he *should* notice her, after all, he'd met Kitty first, she'd helped him instead of just laughing stupidly at everything he said—but he never looked up. Before long Kitty realized that they were going to walk all the way to the cafeteria together.

The other kids from French class brushed past. Kitty stood still, her fingertips icy, her eyeballs riveted on the retreating forms of Rob and Megan, her insides feeling hard and heavy.

She followed the crowd surging toward the cafeteria. But Megan's a criminal, Kitty thought. The daughter of a criminal, anyway. It's dangerous for him to know her. He'll get sucked in before he knows what she's all about. I have to save him. I have to save him from her.

∼

"That was a thoroughly weak, lousy, and uninspired sermon, Donald," said Kezia cheerfully.

Donald smirked. "You've never been one to disguise your feelings."

"That's because I'm a savage!" She tore with her teeth at a chicken drumstick and grinned across the dinner table at Saul, who stared back in wordless wonder.

Kezia was Donald's second cousin, her own grandfather the younger brother of Donald's Grandfather Abney. Kezia's father, although technically a first cousin to Donald's dad, always got called Uncle Charlie by Donald and his siblings. Uncle Charlie had spent his working years as a missionary in the jungle of Peru, the same jungle where Kezia spent her childhood in alternation with lengthy stints at a boarding school for missionary offspring in Lima. To hear Kezia tell it, it was anyone's guess whether the tribes of the interior or the teachers at the school did more damage to the children's capacity to function in civilization once they reached their majority.

These days Kezia was living in Philadelphia with her second husband, Jacob. The first husband had been another dislocated missionary kid. They'd married young "for the dispensation to screw," as Kezia had once told Carmichael. The pleasure in that running its course as the two of them gradually realized they didn't like each other and their own selves even less, they accepted the shame of divorce as the lesser of two evils.

Kezia drifted through a decade of stereotypical self-destruction before committing to a course of Jungian psychotherapy in Philly, and "technically," she always said, "I didn't seduce my therapist because it was only one session with him before I knew I was utterly, hopelessly in love," so at the end of the session she set up an appointment with another therapist, marched back into the first therapist's office to ask him on a date, explaining, of course, that no professional ethics stood in their way. He told her to come back in thirty days if she was serious. She was, she did, and two years later they married, "much to the consternation of his mother, me not being one of tribe," as Kezia had told them at the reception party after their wedding. A rather tipsy Carmichael had in turn spilled the truth about herself, making Kezia one of fewer than a dozen people to know that she was Jewish before the infamous episode in the church basement. Kezia's offended mother-in-law had the good grace to expire shortly after the wedding, which took Jacob down another rabbit hole of Jungian analysis to cope with his feelings of betrayal of the Great Mother.

They were doing fine now, though, fabulous even, and by choice without any children to inflict their madness on. She was passing through Olutakli County en route to Syracuse for a conference on Spanish-language curriculum development. "And I wouldn't miss the chance to visit my favorite second cousin and his charming family."

"Is it true about the monkeys?" Kitty whispered.

"What do you mean, darling?" Kezia leaned in, her very white and very large teeth glittering in anticipation.

"About the tribes... that they... the women... you *know*," Kitty said. "I heard Daddy asking Uncle Charlie about it once but he wouldn't say anything. Is it true they do that?"

"*I've* done it," declared Kezia. "It's a rite of passage, when you turn sixteen, and you've developed nice large breasts..." She indicated her own, then glanced at Kitty's modest counterparts with a faint frown of disapproval. "You're young yet," she said kindly. "You take a monkey like so, holding it like a baby, and persuade it to suckle. The tribes believe it'll help the milk come in when you bear your firstborn."

"Is that *really* true?" persisted Kitty.

Kezia adopted a face of wounded integrity. "Would I make up something like that?"

"Mommy thinks you would."

"Well!" said Kezia, affecting offense, but she smiled hugely and returned to her attack on the chicken bones, sucking off every last bit of fat, skin, gristle, and cartilage.

Kitty seemed as alarmed by this as by the prospect of breastfeeding a monkey and asked, "What kind of food did you eat in the jungle?"

"Velveeta," Kezia responded promptly. "It survived the long shipment times. Also grubs. I learned that from the local kids. Like this." She plucked a grain of rice off her plate and held it up for Saul to regard, who had not moved or spoken all through dinner, mesmerized by Kezia like she was a snake. "About this size and color, still sweet, and they make a nice little pop in your mouth."

"I'm not hungry anymore, Mommy," moaned Saul.

"Did you know that they serve Amazonian jungle ants in some fancy restaurants now? It's true."

"Maybe we could save this for later, Kezia," said Carmichael.

Kezia looked at Saul's green face and apologized. "I'm not kidding when I say I'm a savage," she said. "I never did figure out what's OK to say when. That's why Jacob adores me so. He says it's like a direct window into the subconscious, living with me."

"I don't doubt it," said Carmichael, but she too was smiling.

"So let's get back to that lousy sermon you had the almighty gall to preach this morning," said Kezia. "You were raised better than that, young man."

Donald was far too fond of Kezia to take offense. "I thought you said you were an atheist now."

"I misspoke. Atheism requires a level of conviction I can't muster any more than for theism. Agnostic is the word for me."

"Like Bammy and Bampy!" Kitty cried.

"My parents," Carmichael explained to Kezia, and to Kitty, "I'm not quite sure that's the right word for them anymore."

"Atheist or agnostic or simply crippled Christian, I still

know a good sermon when I hear one, and *that*, dear cousin, was *not* a good sermon. I'm not sure *what* it was. Somewhere between a lecture and a sniveling apology. Who the hell do you think you are, *apologizing* to your congregation?"

"I'm no hellfire and brimstone preacher, Kezia, and no revivalist, either."

"Oh, God, I'm not talking about that. But you spent practically the whole sermon asking permission to be in the pulpit at all. It made me cringe. I may not believe in God, but I expect him and his ambassadors to assert their right to mess with me. Not tiptoe around me pathetically in the hopes I won't stomp on them." She demonstrated by jabbing her index finger into the pile of rice on her plate.

Saul imitated her action and cautiously put a single grain of rice into his mouth.

Kezia continued, "You did at least perk up when you gave Kitty her Bible. I liked that part."

"I'm starting confirmation class!" Kitty explained. "I'm the only kid in it this year, so it's just me and Daddy."

"What happens in confirmation class?"

"I study the Bible and the Catechism for two years, and then at the end I get a big party and people give me money."

"Well, that's not *exactly* the point..." Donald attempted to interject.

"Fabulous," said Kezia. "I hope you rake in hundreds. Is it too late for me to do confirmation, too? I might come back around to religion if enough money is involved."

After lunch Kezia hauled Donald outside, insisting he take her to pay her respects at Asher's grave and have a peek in the state forest. "I have a thing for dark and secret places," she explained. "It's very archetypal. Trying to make peace with my vagina, or something like that."

Donald omitted comment and led the way to the cemetery. Kezia subdued her usual ebullience, placing a respectful hand on Asher's tombstone and asking Donald to say a prayer. They held silence together for some time after. Then Kezia shook herself like a wet dog as she emerged from the unaccustomed reverence. Taking stock of her surroundings, she pointed with her chin to the adjacent monument. "And who has such a pedigree as to require a headstone of that size in a country church's cemetery?" she demanded with withering disapproval.

Donald explained about the Schickedanzes and, led along by Kezia's relentless nosiness, soon found himself unraveling the whole miserable story, the columbarium and Sandra's campaign to cremate Asher and Carmichael's rebuke about the ovens ("Ouch," said Kezia, followed by, "I have renewed respect for that woman. She's more than you deserve, Donald dearest"), the rumors about them leaving and the secret council meetings and the uselessness of the bishop and Carmichael losing her prospect of tenure and, ultimately, Donald losing his ability to preach.

By this point, they'd viewed the columbarium that started it all, retraced their steps through the meadow, and were pacing back and forth between the industrially regular rows of pine trees that blocked the sunlight overhead and left nothing but a litter of rust-red needles on the ground. "All of which is to say," Donald summarized, "I'm half-heartedly looking for another parish, and Carmichael for another teaching position, because either they're going to run us out of here or the congregation is going to split down the middle."

"And what about Asher? Are you just going to leave him here?"

"No, I suppose we'll have to figure out how to move him with us somewhere else. Though where else, we still don't know."

Kezia pulled at a loose strip of pine bark and watched ants and beetles tumble out. "Do you *want* to leave this place?"

"No. I'd have been perfectly happy to stay. Carmichael, too. But it hardly matters now."

"The thing is, it *does* matter." Kezia turned to face him,

hands on hips, glaring up at him through her John Lennon glasses. She was short, and her unruly brown hair was pinned up at random all over her head, but there was something indeed of a savage energy about her. Donald, despite towering over her, felt a little intimidated. "Are you a shepherd of these sheep or aren't you?"

"Well, yes, but if they won't consent to let me shepherd them..."

"Oh, bullshit."

"It isn't good for a congregation to be riven with conflict, least of all over the pastor."

"But this is not *that*. This is *wolves* overrunning your sheep, and you are just standing by and letting the wolves feast and devour. Is that what you are, Donald? A hired hand?"

"I know who should've been the preacher at church this morning," said Donald, trying to laugh it off, but Kezia only buzzed with irritation.

"For God's sake, man, I don't have to believe it to understand it, and the plain fact as you've just told me is that two wolves have been hiding out all this time in sheep's clothing and they intend to snatch and devour your sheep. Do you think they'll stop if you leave? Blood inflames the appetite, it doesn't quench it. They'll take out the next shepherd and who knows how many sheep in the process. Do you want that blood on your hands?"

"You're oversimplifying. They're not evil. I can't treat them like *they're* the bad guys and everyone else is nice and innocent."

"Look, this is not Judgment Day, and you are not God almighty. I'm not saying they're beyond redemption, or that the good guys aren't bad, too. Lord if I don't know that as well as anyone! But people have a choice whether they're gonna be wolves in this life or not, and no one's making that choice for them. I don't care if you wanna call it the devil or free will or something in between, but there *are* wolves, Donald." Kezia was drilling into him. "*I know about wolves.*"

Donald suddenly grasped that there were things about his cousin's past that he didn't know, things she had never told him, things that accounted for her bumpy path through life, not to mention her penchant for outrageous conversation.

"Kezia," he said, "I'm sorry. I didn't know."

"It's a topic best kept between me and my therapist," she trilled, relenting a little. "Which is why it was such a good idea to marry one." She flicked an ant with her finger and watched it soar aloft before dropping unseen amidst the pine needles. "Listen, Donald, all I'm saying is, take it from someone who knows. Don't play all naïve like everyone is sweetness and light. Don't pretend like you have to be that way 'cause you're a minister and you're supposed to see the best in everyone. That is not your job. Your job is to see the *worst* in everyone, so you can call them back from the brink before it's too late. And if they won't give up on their wolfery, then you gotta drive them out. For the sake of the sheep." She looked up at him with an appeal in her eyes that he could not remember seeing there before.

"But what if I'm to blame?"

"Your *kid* died, Donald!" she screeched at him. "Isn't the world harsh enough without the wolves taking advantage of your tragedy? So maybe you screwed up. So maybe you preached a string of shitty sermons. So what? *So what?* You're the shepherd. You protect those goddamn sheep!"

Her words struck Donald hard. The sheep are supposed to be God-blessed, not God-damned. But who was applying God's blessing to the sheep? No one. Donald had given up, given up too easily, drained of all his strength by his grief over Asher, skewered by a certainty about God that had no grace, no light, and no mercy in it, oversensitive to his own failures, frankly spooked by the wolves. And so his sheep were stripped of all blessing, lying naked to the gathering storm clouds of damnation, lured right into the waiting jaws of the wolf, like the gigantic wolf that swallowed up Mrs. Feuerlein's baby brother all those years ago. Instead of springing forward with a knife to slit open the wolf's belly and release the captives, Donald just patted the wolf on the head and wished it bon appétit. George and Jackie were carrying on heroically as sheepdogs, but they couldn't hold out forever. The wolves would devour them if they couldn't recruit them, as they'd recruited Al and Dale and Marilyn and Eunice and who knew how many others...

Donald felt something coming in to him, a kind of power.

It was not a nice feeling.

All right, Lord, he thought. I've lost sight of you as the wellspring of blessing and grace. All I can see anymore is your almighty judgment and terrible righteousness. But that's what's needed now.

If the wolves aren't condemned, then the sheep will be.

Not on my watch.

"Hey," said Kezia. She snapped her fingers in his face. "You went into some kind of trance there. Don't go all mystic on me. You need to get in there and fight."

"It's all right," Donald replied. "My loins have been girded."

"I've always thought you had nice loins," said Kezia. "You know, if it weren't for you being my cousin and all..." She laughed, yanked him by the elbow, and steered him back toward the house.

"Kezia," he said, "*is* it true about the monkeys?"

"You wouldn't believe the number of true things in this crazy world," she said. "You're such a babe in the woods. Donald darling, you haven't seen anything yet."

∽

Kitty decided she'd better gather intelligence before launching her campaign. For one thing, she had to make sure that Rob really was a nice boy, which was not to be assumed, given his evident susceptibility to Megan's hollow charms. Kitty was willing to give him the benefit of the doubt; after all, she'd been the new kid just four years earlier and knew that you couldn't tell right away who was decent and who wasn't. Loneliness would make you do strange things.

So she talked to him as assiduously as she dared in homeroom, and then again in fifth period social studies, the only other class they had together. And yes, thank goodness, he was nice, and also interesting. His family had just moved back to Olutakli County after a long spell in Minnesota.

This news delighted Kitty on two counts: first, Minnesota was right next door to North Dakota, where she herself had once lived, so they had something in common, and second, as she'd overheard from her father, there were lots of Lutherans in Minnesota, so maybe he was one, too, and could come to church. Though when she worked up the courage to ask, he blushed and replied, "Uh, actually, we're Catholic," which in turn made Kitty go white with horror at the prospect of Megan getting access to Rob on Sundays, too. But then he added, "We don't really go to mass ever, just on Christmas," which relieved Kitty on many levels.

It was hard to figure out if Rob had any other classes with Megan, given the four-minute scrum between classes, but as far as she could tell they had only Spanish together. Kitty felt more than one moment of unfilial resentment at her mother for speaking French instead of Spanish and wished she could've been more like crazy Kezia who grew up in Peru, though on reflection Kitty thought it was probably better not to have a mom who breastfed monkeys. Anyway, if Kitty was in Spanish class, she'd have to put up with Megan, too, and it was bad enough to be stuck with her in gym and science.

And so Kitty's every school day revolved around two poles: exerting all her powers of allure on Rob Adams during homeroom and social studies, and shooting out of French fast enough to spy on Megan and Rob exiting Spanish. Three weeks into the new school year, Kitty reached the depressing conclusion that she and Megan were just about neck and neck, a perfect draw, a terrible tie. Unless Kitty did something to pull ahead, they'd remain stuck in limbo. To be rendered an equal of Megan's in any respect was more than Kitty could bear.

On her walks to and from school, and as she lay in bed at night, Kitty considered her options. She indulged herself in envisioning the most egregious kind of attacks only because she knew she would never go so far in real life—humiliating episodes involving a faked blood stain on Megan's pants, or stealing her bra in gym class. Kitty wasn't sure if she was relieved or ashamed to realize she didn't have it in her to be quite so cruel.

Then she considered strategies of a more emotional and social kind. Suppose she gave it out that Megan was in love with dorky Shane Ferly. He was so weird and dumb he'd believe it, and that would put Megan in a wonderfully embarrassing position. But then Kitty realized she didn't want to make Shane's life any more miserable than it already was.

What if she took a more direct approach? She could spread the rumor that Megan liked Rob. Or she could write a note as if from Megan and stick it in his locker. Or—safer than trying to forge Megan's signature—she could write an anonymous note but leave enough clues in it that Rob would figure it out. Then Megan would *have* to deny it, and say that someone else did it and no of course she didn't like him, because it would be way too embarrassing to admit that she *did*, and then if Rob was in fact harboring any feelings for Megan he'd think she didn't have any feelings for him and so he'd give up and turn his full attention on Kitty and recognize how obviously superior she was to all the other girls in seventh grade...

Hmm. It was a good plan, but risky. The handwriting might be traced back to Kitty, or it could backfire entirely and lead to a profession of love between the two. What she really needed was to find some way to scare Rob off entirely, to make hanging out with Megan or liking her absolutely unthinkable. Kitty had to make him see how inherently repulsive a human being Megan was. That was the best bet. But how?

And then—the miracle happened. It could only be a miracle. It was unlooked for, unplanned, unexpected; a pure gift, right when she needed one.

At the tail end of September, Kitty and the other kids in social studies were scrambling to finish their current events assignments for the month. Mrs. Marino decided to give them the whole period and a big stack of newspapers to get it done, since this was after all the first month of school and they weren't used to the new rhythm of assignments yet. Kitty managed to insert herself in the work station next to Rob's. He was looking at the *Kuhsota Daily Register*'s sports section—a disappointing if unsurprising choice. She took the front section of *The New York Times* on the principle that it made her look impressive. There was an article about the aftermath of Hurricane Hugo, and another about the Soviets and chemical weapons. She paged through slowly, stalling so she could stay near Rob as long as possible, before choosing an article and going back to her seat to write it up.

Then she saw it. A federal trial underway at the Foley Square Courthouse in New York. Concerning financial crimes related to the 1987 stock market crash. Several defendants on the stand, including Richard Moravsky of Shibboleth, New York.

Kitty paused, breathed deeply. This was it. This had to be it. It was so clean, so simple. She didn't have to spread lies or forge notes. It was *news*, after all! Not even something she overheard her dad say. It was meant to be.

"Gosh," she said out loud.

Rob didn't respond, engrossed in news on the baseball playoffs.

She tried again, and louder. "Holy cow, I can't believe it. I wonder if…"

Rob looked up. "What?"

"Well, look at this," Kitty said in a shocked but innocent voice. "About this trial just starting."

Rob scanned the article. He said, "Oh yeah, I remember my dad talking about that when it happened, the stock market thing. It didn't seem like a big deal. He never mentioned it again."

"It was a *huge* deal!" Kitty said earnestly. "I mean, these men stole from people, and tricked and lied and covered their tracks."

"Yeah, but it's not like war, is it?" Rob said. He was clearly taken aback by Kitty's moral fervor.

"People lost their livelihoods," Kitty said sternly. Rob appeared chastened. But this was getting off track. Kitty pressed on, "That's not the part that surprises me. It's this. Look." She placed her finger below the names of the accused.

Rob dutifully observed. No reaction. "So?" he said.

"Richard Moravsky," she hissed.

"Oh, right. He lives here in Shibboleth!" Rob said brightly. "That's weird."

Good grief, he doesn't even know her last name, Kitty thought in exasperation. "Moravsky," Kitty repeated in a whisper. "That's the last name of one of the other kids in seventh grade. Maybe you know her—Megan?"

"Whoa, that's Megan's—who? her dad?"

"I think so."

"Her dad's on trial as a criminal?"

"Sure looks that way."

"Gosh. I had no idea."

"Well, obviously, she wouldn't talk about something like this. She wouldn't want other people to know the truth about her family."

"Yeah." Rob looked every bit as pale and dismayed as Kitty could have hoped.

"I mean, it makes you wonder. Monkey see, monkey do, right?"

"Huh. I better hold on to my lunch money, then," Rob said with a little laugh, but he was clearly disconcerted.

"It might be for the best," said Kitty gravely.

"All right, chatterboxes, break it up," called Mrs. Marino

across the room. "You've only got twenty minutes left to complete your assignments, and I'm not accepting them one minute later than the bell."

Kitty clutched the newspaper and scrambled back to her seat. It would be better to let Rob stew awhile. She flipped back to the article about the Soviets, thinking she could tell Bammy and Bampy about it because they talked about Soviets sometimes. She was so happy she hummed under her breath as she wrote out in precise cursive the who-what-when-where-why of the article. She slid it into the tray on Mrs. Marino's desk in good time.

When the bell rang she glided across the classroom, calculating it was better to leave Rob to his disturbing thoughts about Megan. Kitty was the first out the door and got the shock of her life.

There stood Rhea.

Rhea, in her chariot, flanked by her lions, her hard stony face set with grim judgment.

This was all wrong. None of Kitty's council ever came to school. None of her council was even left except for Rhea, and Kitty hadn't been out to visit her little cave in ages, because what was the point without the rest of them, and she'd never liked Rhea, never invited or welcomed her, but Rhea kept showing up anyway.

Kitty glanced behind her as the other kids poured out. None of them could see Rhea, that was obvious enough. But Kitty could. And Rhea could see Kitty. And Rhea was *not* pleased with Kitty.

She tried to play dumb. "What're you doing here?" she said in the quietest voice she could, without moving her lips.

Rhea stared. She had the stare to end all stares.

Kitty realized there was no point in pretending. "I didn't tell a lie and I didn't tell a secret," she muttered. "It was in the newspaper, after all."

Rhea was not impressed with Kitty's line of defense.

"It's for his own good," she pleaded. "It won't do *him* any good to get involved with her and her criminal family."

Still the relentless stare. It spoke its condemnation more eloquently than any words ever could.

"Well, you don't have to like it," said Kitty at last, brushing past the lions, the tips of their long tails faintly twitching.

She felt Rhea's cold hard stare follow her all the way down the hall.

CHAPTER SIXTEEN

October 1989

What is man when no longer connected with society;
or when he finds himself surrounded
by a convulsed and a half dissolved one?
He cannot live in solitude,
he must belong to some community
bound by some ties, however imperfect.

"Oh. Hi again, Lynn," said Donald after he opened the front door. "Come on in."

Lynn trotted in briskly, her professional lips pursed.

"Carmichael's not here right now. She has class on Monday mornings this semester."

"That's all right. You can share with her what I tell you today."

Donald gestured to the sofa and they took their seats. "I hope what you have to tell me is 'case closed.'"

Lynn kept her hands busy ferreting around in her purse and did not raise her eyes to meet his. "I'm afraid not," she said. "While no evidence has come in following the first call to CPS, earlier this week we got another call."

"I see," said Donald. "Same person? Same complaint?"

"I can't say anything about who made the report. All calls to CPS are strictly confidential. The complaint is the same, that the home is unsafe and places the children at risk of accidents." She paused uncomfortably and then added, "As happened last December."

"Surely this is the same as the last complaint. It's just someone out to sabotage us and our reputation."

Lynn gave an ambiguous twitch of her shoulder. "I can't comment on the motivation of the caller," she said in blatant contradiction to her parting remarks at the end of her previous visit. "At CPS we are legally obligated—"

"I know, I know," said Donald wearily. "Would you like to take a look around the house?"

"Thank you," said Lynn with a whisper of an apology behind the words.

Her examination was cursory at best. For Donald, the grime on the edge of the bathtub, the unemptied tub of scraps for the compost sitting open on the counter and attracting flies, and the pair of scissors splayed open on the floor of Saul's room filled him with dread and shame.

Lynn concluded her tour and took herself back to the front door.

"Can I show you around outside, too?" said Donald.

"I've already looked," she replied. "I see nothing to concern me. The case will remain open for sixty days."

"I know. And I presume another call will come just in time to prevent it from being closed."

Lynn shrugged. "I'm sorry," she said, and her high-heeled shoes clicked sharply down the steps as she walked away.

Donald retreated and stood in the middle of the house.

Now what?

Kezia's visit had done much to put the fire back in his bones. He still felt dead and lifeless preaching, but he knew now that it was OK to fight—that, in fact, it was necessary to fight. Not for the destruction but for the salvation of the sheep, and even, if the grace of God for enemies was true, possibly even for the salvation of the wolves. He heard the call, the charge, the blast on the shofar summoning him to battle. He was armed and ready.

He just had no idea what to do.

He and Carmichael spent hours talking it over. Apologies and demonstrations of humility backfired badly; that was clear enough. What was meant as a sign of strength toward reconciliation came across as a sign of weakness toward collusion. What he needed was something more like a backburn, fighting fire with fire and thereby putting the fire out. Trap the fowler in her own snare. Play dead, lure her out, then spring when she's least expecting it...

Donald pattered through the house aimlessly. He noticed a bulging can of tomato purée in the pantry and tossed it out, wondering if Lynn had noticed and would enter in their file, "Keeps food tainted with botulism on hand." Then he saw all the sharp edges on the empty cans in the bin that the children could easily cut themselves on, so he tied up the bag and took it outside and shoved it in the trunk of the car for the next time he drove past the recycling center. When he came back into the kitchen he noticed that some of the forks in the drying rack still had food crusted on them. Surely Lynn had noted the unsanitary nature of that, too. He scrubbed them and rinsed them and put them back in the rack.

"What am I humming?" he asked himself aloud, startled to realize he'd been doing so. He hummed some more, sought the words... ah.

> Joshua fought the battle of Jericho, Jericho, Jericho
> Joshua fought the battle of Jericho
> and the walls come a-tumblin' down.

Funny thought: Sandra was the one who led the singing that kicked off Sunday School each week, so she must have been the one who chose this song. She would have had no idea, of course, how Jericho was the neuralgic symbol of Donald's departure from his grandfather's ways, the grating uncertainty as to whether you could assert God's action in the world while undercutting stories that testified to his action, and whether a wall that did or possibly did not come a-tumblin' down had anything to do with whales or wolves, new creation or new covenant or new life early on a Sunday morning two millennia ago.

And here he was humming that song again...

The lyrics didn't get it quite right, of course. They made it sound like Joshua fought first and *then* the walls came a-tumblin' down. But the whole point was that Joshua didn't fight at all, at least not till later. This was the first big battle for the disputed territory of Canaan. The instructions from the Lord were intended to inspire faith but undermine certainty: just march around the city in circles for six days straight, blowing your trumpets all the while. That's it. No arrows over the parapets or poisoning the wells or battering down the gates. Just trumpets. On the seventh day they were allowed to shout. That would bring down the wall, and then they could do battle the old-fashioned way. Somehow the fanfare would break the enemy long before swords got involved.

If only it could have ended with the trumpets! Joshua must have been a thoroughly unpleasant person to be around. Traumatized by all the bloodshed, at the end of his life he must have been as jittery and unstable as a Vietnam vet. Maybe that accounted for his derisive snarl at the tribes' pledge of fidelity to serve the Lord God and him alone: "You *cannot* serve the Lord; for he is a holy God; he is a jealous God; he will not forgive your transgressions or your sins. You are witnesses against yourselves."

Terrible words. It would be nice to dismiss them, like so many of Donald's colleagues did, as the nasty spirit of the vengeful "Old Testament God," superseded and replaced by the hippie spirit of kindly Jesus. But "Jesus" was actually the same as "Joshua," the Hebrew name transmuted into Greek before undergoing a second transmutation into English. Jesus the unlikely warrior, who knows full well that the sheep of his flock are lying when they promise to serve him, who beholds them witness against themselves, who descends into hell with trumpet blast and pulls down its walls and routs the devil and all his empty promises...

"I've got it," Donald announced to the kitchen.

"I knew you'd get there in the end," said Grandfather Abney with a smile.

When Carmichael crested the driveway mid-afternoon, Donald was standing under a gigantic tent erected right in front of the entrance to the church, white and green streamers dangling down from its four corners. He was arranging and re-arranging chairs and a small table. She parked and joined him under the tent, blowing on her fingers. "Isn't it a bit chilly for an outdoor revival?"

"Yes," he agreed. "But the Spirit will warm us up."

"What exactly is going on here?"

"I haven't taken leave of my senses, if that's what you're wondering. I just finally figured out how to fight back."

"And this is it, huh?" She tilted her head to look up at the tent ceiling. "Where'd you get this?"

"Rented it from the county. They have a bunch for the fair they never use the rest of the year."

"With what money?"

"Most of my spending money for Germany."

"Ah."

"Could you help on the phone? I'll work from the church line and you can call from home."

"I suppose this will make sense soon?"

"Being sensible has only gotten us so far. It's time to try trumpets."

"I have no idea what you're talking about," said Carmichael. "But you are the least defeated-looking I've seen you in a long time, and that's good enough for me. Maybe this mad tent of yours will un-defeat me as well."

They divided the names in the church directory and set to work, though Donald skipped ahead to M and called up Dale Mayer first.

Dale was gruffly surprised to hear from the pastor, but Donald detected a note of relief, too. He inquired after Dale and Arlene's youngest son Kevin, in college at SUNY Kuhsota.

"What about him?" Dale asked.

"Do I remember right that he plays the trumpet?"

"Yeah. Idiot pastime. No one can make a living as a musician."

"Do you think he'd be up for a gig at church—and could he bring some other players along with him?"

"What're you brewing now?" Dale barked. "What's it gonna cost?"

"It's all out of my own pocket. But the congregation is in danger, Dale. You know it as well as I do. It's time to do something about it."

Dale's reply failed to mask his admiration for the sheer insanity of the pastor's plan. He promised to get in touch with Kevin and get him and some other guys over by evening, if possible

Kevin and company were no less intrigued than Dale and appeared just in time for dinner, which Carmichael managed to extend to feed them all. By seven it was dark. Donald recruited Kitty and Saul to help him unearth the church's supply of not-quite-finished altar candles, which would last till kingdom come, or at least the seven nights of a revival. The space under the tent flickered uncannily. Kevin and his three buddies lined up at the edge of the parking lot and, pointing their trumpets out over the valley, played to rouse the dead.

Only a handful of parishioners turned up that first night: Dale and Arlene, of course, and George and Ruth, and Hazel, and Bonnie, whose commute took her home through Shibboleth anyway. When the fanfare ended, Donald turned to the little crowd. He said it was no secret to anyone that the congregation was at risk of fracturing, and it was time to get serious about pleading before the throne of grace for the transformation of hearts and extension of the right hand of fellowship. He asked them to stand there and pray silently.

"What, no sermon?" George said.

"I don't think now's the time for talking," answered Donald.

"Me or anyone else, at least not out loud. Let's do our talking to and for God alone."

The parishioners looked around at each other uneasily, but Donald turned and knelt at the little table so he wasn't watching them. One by one they sat in the folding chairs, their eyes fell shut, their breathing evened out. Even Saul managed not to fidget.

It was cold enough that Donald didn't keep them long, but he encouraged them to come back the next night and persuade the other parishioners to come with them, too.

They did. The crowd swelled night by night, and even the weather cooperated with a well-timed Indian summer. Father Pat, Linda, Pieter, and Cathie among the local clergy turned up one night or another. So did Jerry from the Assemblies of God, who could grasp a thing like a revival, though when he discovered there was no preaching he let his disapproval be known and vanished again. Word that it was just silent prayer following a blast of trumpets drew out the tiny handful of Quakers, who endorsed the experiment as heartily as Jerry had poohpoohed it. But mainly it was the people of Mt. Moriah. On Friday and Saturday nights, the parking lot was as full of cars as at Christmas.

There were only four people who should have been there but weren't: Sandra, Alan, Eunice, and Marilyn. Their absence was noted and remarked upon, and as the days rolled by their absence articulated itself as a kind of self-condemnation. The whole point was to pray for the restoration of the fractured congregation, and gradually the other cantankerous partisans came around. Jackie was seen to put her arm around Hazel, who for some reason took to weeping during her silent prayers. A careful détente developed between Dale, Al, and George. Folks at the margins who had only the haziest sense of something amiss at church drew near, and the regulars greeted them without a whisper of reproach, or overstated welcome, either. Refusal to attend, on the part of the absent four, was as good as announcing that they desired no reconciliation at all. They wanted one thing only: to win. And they wanted to win by driving Pastor Donald and his family out.

The salvation of the wolves, Donald thought ruefully, is beyond the competence of this shepherd.

When he dismissed the assembly on Saturday night, he quoted from Joshua 3, "'Sanctify yourselves; for tomorrow the Lord will do wonders among you.'"

Then it was Sunday. Donald engaged the trumpeters to open and close the service inside the church, then to usher the congregation out into the tent for the final installment of the revival. It was again as full as Christmas and there was a heightened air of expectation. People were waiting for something to *happen*. Loitering in the sacristy before the service, wrapping the cincture around his waist, laying the green stole over his alb and feeling the weight of its embroidered cloth as never before, Donald was overtaken by a terrible qualm. This is exactly what didn't work for him, had never worked for him, about revivals. They pumped up yearning and anticipation but could never deliver the goods honestly. A facsimile of religious experience had to be served up, about as wholesome as a pie crust made from Crisco instead of butter, fake and possibly poisonous. Manufactured religious events trained people to seek substitutes and that was, after all, why so many ended up departing from the faith altogether. A revival had seemed like such a good idea a week ago, inspired even, nothing but prayer and trumpets. And for a time it had done good, ratifying and conjoining the body into one again while exposing the false brethren.

But now what? Marilyn, who had barely spoken him a word since her arrival that morning, was sawing away at the prelude. Donald espied Alan, Sandra, and Eunice alone together in a row, the space on either side of them the only empty seats in the house. What was Donald to do now? Shout like a battle-crazed Israelite? Tear around the church seven times in succession? Put his enemies to the sword? He wasn't even sure what he would preach. He'd prepared for the lectionary texts but that wasn't what anyone came to hear. And probably, once again, his words would fall flat. His words, and *not* the walls of Jericho.

Marilyn squeezed out the last reproachful note of her prelude. Donald marched solemnly from sacristy to sanctuary, bowed, issued a warm welcome. He made no comment on the size of the congregation or the past week's events, only announcing that there would be a final prayer session directly after the service. He gestured to the back of the church. Kevin and his fellow musicians let loose.

From his seat Donald could well imagine trumpets taking down, if not a fortified city of stone, then certainly a wooden clapboard church, without any divine intervention at all. Wow, what a blast. Some of the little kids stuck stagey fingers into their ears. Some of the old ladies seemed not to notice anything at all. The sound was tremendous, shattering, cleansing.

When the last reverberations died away, it felt like the whole church had been scrubbed top to bottom. Donald found he could go into the confession and forgiveness with new strength, and on through the kyrie and gloria and collect and lessons.

He read out from the pulpit the appointed gospel lesson about the nine ungrateful lepers and the single grateful one. The congregation responded with, "Praise to you, O Christ." They sat down and rustled in place and pinned their eyes upon Donald.

He felt the burden of expectation rush over him again. He had to decide now: either preach on the leper story as if it were any other Sunday, or name what was happening, what had been happening, and call them forth to what would and could happen if only…

No. He couldn't harangue them. And he couldn't engineer anything for them. He may have been the shepherd, but he was also a partisan sheep, and he could not abuse his office that way. Even Joshua knew it was the Lord's business to give the victory. Every attempt to steal it, even in the name of righteousness, was to court bitter defeat.

Donald stepped out of the pulpit. This itself was so unusual that the crowd thrilled. Donald almost laughed; the preachers of his youth couldn't be held to the pulpit for anything. He hitched up his alb a few inches and took the three steps down to the aisle. He was standing at their level.

"This has been my year of grief," he said. It surprised him; not at all what he intended to say. He paused and looked at Carmichael. She gave him the tiniest of nods. She was blazing toward him, filling him up with her strength, asking him to return the gift and strengthen her.

"My year of grief," he said again. This time he took in the rest of the congregation. They also nodded, very discreetly, and that was all right; Donald knew by now that Lutherans considered it the height of rudeness to react visibly to the pastor's sermon. He spoke of Asher. He recalled to them Asher's rambunctiousness, his affectionate nature and wild passions, the tragedy it was that all the qualities that made him so endearing had, it seemed, driven him outside and up the ladder on Christmas night. He talked about what it was like to have a black hole rip right through the heart of your family. The remorse and constant playing through of alternate schemes in your head, as if by reviewing all the possibilities you could unmake the past. The crushing realization time and time again that the past was the one thing that could never be altered. That grief was a good servant but a wicked master. The sense of betrayal at moving on and accepting life without Asher, but the unbearable cost of refusing to do so, for Kitty and Saul at least, if not for themselves. But also for themselves.

He looked to Carmichael, and she again confirmed that he was speaking the truth.

Then he said, "You were kind to us." He embraced the congregation with his eyes. "Not all of you said something. I could tell that some of you didn't know what to say. I'm sure some of you were asking in your hearts what kind of parents we could be to let this happen to our child. But when the shock wore off, you came around. You helped us out. In your own ways you bore this tragedy with us and accepted that sometimes the world is just a very hard place, and God is inexplicable to us all." Donald realized it was the first time he'd mentioned God so far. Right. Time to get back on track. He hadn't intended this personal of an address.

"My year of grief is not just about Asher, though," he continued. "Despite everything, we have been happy here. I have come to love you, as your pastor. Carmichael and I expected to stay on and raise our family here. We are so grateful for your care of us in this hard time. We want to stay with you. We want our children to stay with you. And we want to stay by Asher, the Asher as we know him now, sleeping in the cemetery just over there." He gestured, started to break; took a deep breath and righted himself. He felt Kitty's eyes on him, not sending strength but watching and testing. He could do this for her, and for Saul, too, even if for no one else. Help me, help me, give me the words, he prayed.

Then: "And yet, for all that, a division has ripped through the heart of our congregation." He felt the collective intake of breath. Why were they so shocked that he named it? They knew it as well as he did. "I have already had my family rent apart by death. It was terrible and tragic, but it was natural and neutral. Gravity just is. Gravity does what it does. Asher fell and the consequence was death. I hate it and I wish I could undo it, but it was not a poisoned death. It broke my heart in a thousand pieces, but the break was clean. But now…" He wobbled again and waited till he could steady his voice. "This division, in this church, this is not clean. This is not natural and neutral. This is not impersonal gravity, but personal animosity." He felt some of Grandfather Abney's rhetorical force flooding into him. He felt like one of the trumpets. "Some spirit at work in this church has taken Asher's death and twisted it. It has not left him at peace in his grave but used him like a thing, like a tool, to sow seeds of dissension."

A murmur now. Donald's glance sweeping over the pews told him it was mostly the less-than-regulars to whom this came as news. The council members and the every-Sunday folks sat still as statues.

"You wonder, who could be so cruel as to use my son's death to create a rift in the congregation? The answer is: no one. No one is that cruel. Maybe somewhere else in this fallen world, but not here."

At this, even the reticent Lutherans allowed the surprise to show on their faces.

"No one here ever intended evil. Very few people ever do. That's the domain of the devil. *He* intends evil. But most of the time he can't get at us on evil alone. We weren't made for that. We were made in God's image and we want what's good. But that's exactly where the devil does get at us—in wanting the good. In wanting to *be* good. That is the terrifying irony of the spiritual life. The more we desire God and the good, the less we can accept our failures to achieve either. The less we sin, the less willing we are to confess what sins remain and accept God's forgiveness. The closer we draw to righteousness, the less we can acknowledge even one speck of unrighteousness in ourselves. The better we are, the better we want to look. That's how the devil corrupts us, brothers and sisters. Not by our desire to do evil. By our desire to be good."

Now he was ready. He turned his eyes to Sandra and spoke as if to her alone. "When you lose your child, you lose all your illusions about yourself as a good person. In the eyes of the world, you're contaminated forever. How could a good person let that happen? And what I know now is what the gospel has been trying to tell me all along. *God's* goodness is what counts, not mine. God is so infinitely and unfairly gracious that he covers even a failed parent like me. God has deprived me of my ability to be right and good without him. And that is a gift. That is freedom. It's not a gift I ever would have asked for, but now that I have it, I thank God for it. So I say to you, too: you don't have to be good. You don't have to be right. You can relinquish your claims on both, because God's goodness is enough for you. It covers all your failings and false steps and misguided notions and self-delusions and everything. Everything! You can give it all to God, and God will take it. God will bear it away. In Christ he already has. We are free," and here Donald turned away from Sandra and addressed the whole congregation again, "and in that freedom we can be a church together again."

He stopped. He didn't say "amen" and consequently nobody was quite sure if he was done. There was one lone clap of the hands, followed by a titter from the teenage girls. Then there was an unnatural silence as everyone tried to avoid the slightest movement, unsure as to what would come next.

"We're going to skip ahead to the peace," Donald said suddenly. "And we're going to take all the time we need. Let's try and have everybody shake hands with everybody else. The peace of the Lord be with you always!"

"And also with you," chimed in the congregation, relieved to be back on script. All at once a groundswell of chatter, almost hilarity, overtook the quiet space. Handshakes extended to pats on the back and hugs. There were unguarded smiles. Soon the buzz of "peace be with you" was nearly as loud as the trumpets.

Donald retreated to his seat behind the lectern and stared into space. A few people ventured up to peace him but most, as if by common consent, left him to recover. Once he dared to glance sideways toward Sandra. She, Alan, and Eunice were the only ones who hadn't stood up. They extended hands to people around them and forced smiles, but that was it. Donald felt the wind go out of him. It hadn't worked. The olive branch only hardened them further. That was not what he intended.

The service proceeded without further incident or drama. The three hostile parties received communion from him without eye contact. Marilyn actually waved him away, as if she couldn't stop playing communion hymns for even a second. After the benediction, the trumpeters led the congregants out the door and under the tent. It felt like something of an anticlimax, but the leavened mood of the congregation carried the hour. The final silent prayers felt alive and agile, launched up to heaven as if by slingshot. Eunice had driven off right away, and though Alan and Sandra lingered at the far edge of the crowd through the prayer time, the moment it ended they fled, too. Donald gave Marilyn plenty of time to clear out before returning to the sacristy to disrobe.

Carmichael was waiting for him at the pantry door. "That was good," she said. She looked happy. "I felt a lot of walls come a-tumblin' down at that speech of yours. Or sermon. I'm not sure exactly what it was. But it was exactly what we needed."

"Some of the walls came down," said Donald. "Not all of them."

"No," said Carmichael. "Not all of them."

"I'm not sure some walls will ever fall. I'm not sure I like falling at all."

"You sound like Dr. Seuss," laughed Carmichael. "Come on in and have some lunch."

∼

On the night of the parent-teacher conference, Carmichael learned two items of interest. The first was that, every single morning, Saul stopped by Mrs. Delve's classroom to inform her with regret that Asher wouldn't make it to school today, to which she would invariably reply, "Well, thanks for letting me know," and then he'd trot on over to Mrs. Gomolka's class for a full day of being himself. Under the circumstances, Carmichael reflected, this was probably the best they could hope for.

But the second item was the one that really surprised her. As she cycled through the seven-minute meetings with one teacher after another—quite a change from the lulling peace of sitting in a single elementary school classroom—Carmichael learned that her daughter was utterly disengaged at school. She turned her homework in and did fine on tests, better than fine even, but she was listless and distracted.

Carmichael cleared her throat and tried to explain that their family had suffered a tragedy, but before she could get the words out, all the teachers interrupted politely, indicated in oblique terms that they already knew, and explained that Kitty had not started the school year so vacant. It'd been going on only the past two or three weeks. It could of course be that, you know, from last year. But maybe it was something else entirely. A real shame, because Kitty had great potential.

Carmichael told Donald when she got home that night. His face displayed alarm, not at the possibilities of grief, but at the emotional world of an almost thirteen-year-old girl, well beyond his ken or competence. "I'll handle it," Carmichael said, trying not to giggle at her husband's rising panic. "Only I don't know quite what it is I've got to handle."

That was Thursday. On Friday morning Saul was already finished with his Cheerios before Carmichael realized that Kitty wasn't out of bed yet.

She stomped upstairs in irritation and shook the covers beneath which Kitty lay. No response. She peeled back the lilac-covered layers. Kitty's eyes were squinched shut, her arms clutched tight around her stuffed wolf Virginia.

"All right, what's going on?" Carmichael said, sitting down on the bed next to her.

Kitty mumbled, "I feel bad. I don't want to go to school today."

Carmichael felt her forehead. "You don't have a fever. Do you have a cold?" Shake of the head. "Upset stomach?"

"Maybe."

"What does 'maybe' mean? Either you do or you don't."

"I just feel yucky all over. I don't want to go to school."

Carmichael regarded her awhile, Kitty's hair splayed madly

around her head. When the silence dragged on uncomfortably long, Kitty popped one eye open to look at her mother.

"Well? Do I have to go?"

"First you have to tell me what's really going on. Your teachers last night said you started off the school year fine, but now you're completely disengaged in class."

Kitty looked away with her one open eye. After a pause she said, "I'm sad about Asher."

"I know you're sad about Asher, but that isn't what's changed in the past couple of weeks."

"I'm sad that we might have to move away because Mrs. Forrad has been so mean to you and Daddy."

"That is far from settled. And I don't think that's it, either. Look, honey, I was a girl your age once, too. I know that things pile up inside that we don't want to tell our parents. I think I would have been a lot better off if I'd told my mom more stuff. And if she had told me more stuff, for that matter." She stroked Kitty's bare arm. "C'mon, honey, tell me what's really going on."

It was like inviting a hurricane to her embrace. Instantly Kitty was wailing and spewing snot and unleashing a flood of incomprehensible words. She flung herself against Carmichael, who almost fell off the bed with the force of it. For a good long while she just held Kitty and let her sob it all out. When she settled down again, Carmichael called to Donald to get Saul to the school bus. Then she shut the door, sat on the floor next to the bed, and said, "Let's start over again, because I didn't understand a word you said."

After no inconsiderable number of questions for clarification, doublings-back, and imaginative inference, Carmichael ascertained the following facts. First, that Kitty had a despairing crush on a boy named Rob. Second, that Megan Moravsky deliberately told Rob about Asher and made it sound like it happened because they were a terrible family. Third, that afterwards Rob stopped talking to Kitty completely. Fourth, that even after achieving her evil purpose, Megan kept on spreading vile talk about Kitty, including that she had a crush on Shane Ferly, still played with dolls, didn't know who Paula Abdul was, and thought "acid-washed" had something to do with drugs. And so, even though officially Kitty didn't care what other stupid kids thought of her, the cloud of shame that surrounded her was so immense that she just couldn't face going to school anymore. Not to mention the fact that Rhea (Carmichael supposed this to be another classmate) was always following her around and wouldn't leave her alone. So maybe, Kitty said, she could just take a month off, like back in January.

After an initial surge of mama-bear rage on behalf of her cub, Carmichael remembered that Megan was also a girl with a mom, though possibly by now not a dad, which triggered the memory of Kitty's betrayal of the Moravsky family secret, which led to, "Why would Megan tell Rob about Asher at all?"

Kitty raised damp and doleful eyes to Carmichael. "Because she likes him, too," came the dead response.

"Well, I gathered that. But it seems... a bit extreme, as a way to put him off you. Are you sure there isn't some other reason for it?"

Kitty flopped back down on the bed, pulled the covers halfway over her face, and turned to the wall. "She's just evil," came the whispered explanation.

Carmichael peeled back the blanket. "Are you sure she wasn't thinking, 'Turnabout's fair play'?"

Kitty snuffled.

It took a good deal more prodding before Carmichael ferreted out the missing parts of the story. How Kitty started it, again, with the newspaper article about Megan's dad, prompting Megan's retaliation and the all-out war of slander and shame that ensued between them, to the point that the entire seventh grade was taking sides—a sizable majority choosing the Megan camp because she was rich and pretty and because crime was cooler than death, as Kitty saw it. The only silver lining to the whole debacle was that Rob wasn't talking to either of them anymore, so at least Megan hadn't won *him*, too.

"Please please please don't make me go to school, Mommy. I hate it. I hate it. Everyone stares at me again, like they did in February. It's not fair. It's so not fair that a horrible accident happened to us and it makes people think there's something wrong with us, but Megan's dad actually *did* something wrong and people just think it's exciting."

"But Kitty, you really were pretty hard on Megan..."

She only dove under her covers again and seized up, refusing to soften to her mother's touch.

Carmichael went downstairs and relayed the story to Donald, who if anything looked more alarmed than before. "Can you stay home with her this morning? I just have a midterm to administer at eleven and then I can get back in time for a late lunch."

"Sure, that's fine. Do I... do you want me to talk to her?"

"Not necessarily. But what I'm thinking is, I know how these things can take on a life of their own if not interrupted, and maybe what Kitty needs is kind of a reset. I haven't been down to see my folks in ages, so since I've got all of next week off for fall break, how about I take her down there for the week? Her grades are fine, so I don't think the time away from school will hurt her, and it might do her a world of good."

"If you think so," said Donald, still helpless in the face of female distress.

"Will you be all right on your own for a week with Saul?"

"Saul's emotions I understand."

"*Do* you?"

"Well... no. But I misunderstand them less than Kitty's."

Donald drove them over to Kuhsota on Sunday afternoon to catch the bus. Waiting in the parking lot, he and Carmichael did the usual post-church breakdown. It had gone well, or so it seemed. The Forrads, Eunice, and Marilyn still appeared to be conspiring but they'd lost their wider support, the rest of the council being demonstratively warm toward the pastor and his family. Dale in particular kept talking about his boy Kevin playing trumpets at the nightly prayer services and what a thing that ever was. Jackie actually winked at Donald on her way out of church and said, "You'll see, we got 'em on the run now."

"I wish you a peaceful week in our absence, then," said Carmichael.

"And I wish the two of you an exciting one in New York."

"Bring me a present!" cried Saul. "And one for Asher. Except he can't open it. You could bring *me* his present, and then I'd have two," he added slyly.

Bammy and Bampy couldn't have been more excited to have a visit from "our country girls," as Frank put it. There were fresh bagels every morning, and a different flavor of cream cheese to try with them every morning, too. Kitty got to run around Carl Schurz Park in broad daylight while other kids trooped to and from school. They positively binged on museums. They saw mummies at the Met and pears awaiting harvest on espaliered limbs at the Cloisters and, at the Museum of Natural History, the gigantic blue whale that had terrorized Kitty in nightmares after she first saw it at the age of four.

One night they ate at a Chinese restaurant where the waitress wore red silk and the food didn't taste anything like the takeout place next to the Grand Union in Shibboleth. Kitty extracted not one but *two* chocolate elephant heads out of her grandmother from the pastry shop in Yorkville. She couldn't even count the number of egg creams Bampy treated her to.

After a tour of the Central Park Zoo and homage paid at the statue of Alice, Carmichael assessed that her daughter had been sufficiently reset to afford a final day of less frantic activity before returning home on Saturday.

Kitty was still asleep on Friday morning when Carmichael sat down with her parents to fabulously fragrant coffee and bagels with chicken liver pâté. The slanted autumn sun filtered in delicately through the broad windows of their brownstone, lighting up the canopy of the trees frosted with red and yellow. It was familiar and strange, homey and someone else's life at the same time. I shouldn't wait so long between visits again, Carmichael thought.

And yet, oddly, reconnecting with her parents' life—and the alternate life of her own that it represented—made Carmichael homesick for Shibboleth. I can't believe I really want to stay there. But I do. And not only for Asher.

A word Donald liked to use floated into her mind: call. I have a *call* to Shibboleth. Not like his pastoral call, but no less real for that. I can't let them take it from me. Only God can take it from me.

She paused over her coffee. Does that mean I believe in God again? She considered a moment, then dismissed the question. There was a time, when faith was newer, that she could pose the question to herself and give a straightforward answer. That, apparently, was in the past now. These days conviction came at her sideways, as in this impulse that no one could take her call from her but God alone, who presumably would have to exist in order to issue or retract it at all.

Judith and Frank were engrossed in the papers and their breakfasts when Carmichael looked up and said, "It's Friday. Why don't we go to a synagogue tonight? It would be a nice thing to do on our last day here."

If she had proposed screaming "Anarchy!" while running stark naked down Amsterdam Avenue, Carmichael could not have startled her parents more. Judith's bagel flipped out of her hand and landed liver-side down on the Persian carpet below.

"Why would you want to do *that*?" Frank said.

"Why wouldn't you?" countered Carmichael.

"I don't even know where one is. Or what time the services start. Or if you can go if you're not a member or something."

"You have a phone book, don't you? I'm sure we can find out."

Judith surfaced after scrubbing the carpet free of pâté. "You don't need to offer to do this for us, honey. It's fine. Let's do something more exciting for Kitty on her last night here."

"This sounds pretty exciting to me. And Kitty's never been to a synagogue. Well, for that matter, neither have I. And we *are* Jews, aren't we? Of course they'll let us in."

"I just don't know," Judith wavered.

"Is it because of the Soviet thing? Do you think you somehow don't have a right to be there?"

"You always have such a way of putting things." Judith ducked down again.

"Yes, Mom, I do. Please leave the carpet be for a second. This matters to me. Dad?" He was engrossed in the crossword again and looked up with obvious reluctance. "Come on. A year ago you were excited to reconnect to our family heritage. So what if your parents did what they did? This is *us*, now. 'The gifts and calling of God are irrevocable,' as a famous Jew once said."

"Which Jew was that?" said Frank.

"Saint Paul."

"Oh." Frank looked down at his crossword again, and Judith blushed.

"For heaven's sake," said Carmichael. "Come on. Show me these letters and papers and things you've been going through."

That at least got them moving. Frank brought a couple of boxes out to the living room. Carmichael looked at the fine paper covered with a foreign script written in blue ink obviously dipped from a well. Judith pulled out two much-creased forms, the paper soft from the passage of years, identical English print on both but with different handwritten answers. Carmichael read the entries aloud. "'Juudit Lazikin.' 'Prants Bam.' Wait—this is you!"

"It's the papers we got when we came into the United States for the first time."

"Your name is—"

"Juudit, originally. The J is pronounced like a Y in English."

"And Dad, 'Prants' is Frank?"

"That's right."

"I feel completely unnerved to realize that all this time you've had other names, and I never knew."

Frank shrugged. "That's what immigrants do. They strip off the past. Even I didn't realize how much my folks had to strip off and leave behind."

This led to the documents from the Soviet Union with their harsh Cyrillic typeface and defiant hammer-and-sickle insignia. Carmichael shook her head in wonder. "I guess there's no denying it, is there?"

"See, the thing is," Frank said, and Carmichael could tell he was making an effort to say what needed to be said, "Estonia is still under Soviet occupation. My parents got out, we got out, but Soviet occupation is what they wanted and worked for. All this time later, forty years later, the country is still under the Soviet thumb. Even this singing revolution of theirs has done no good. My folks helped to make it happen—your mom's, too. I know it's crazy, but somehow I feel responsible for it, and there's no way to make up for it. I've never been, you know, I've never been religious. I don't know how it got into you, because your mother and I sure did nothing to encourage it. I'm just…" He trailed off.

Carmichael waited. Judith was watching him intently. She didn't seem to know what he was going to say, either.

Finally he said, "I'm a man with no past."

"And I'm a woman with too many futures," Carmichael replied. "It fits, somehow. No past means too many futures."

"What do you mean, honey?" said Judith.

"Nothing. Just constant questions about what kind of life I could have. And now that I know which one I want, I'm not sure I'll be allowed to have it. But Dad, look, you don't have to go on without a past. Or you either, Mom. That's what this is all about, isn't it? Going through these papers and talking about being Jews. You have a right to your own past. It doesn't matter how dark and strange and messed up it is. I bet you go back into anyone's past and it won't take more than three generations to find something bizarre and unhappy. So what? That's the human condition. Let's do this. Let's find a synagogue and go to it. Let's take it back for you. For all of us. For Kitty and Saul."

"For Asher," Judith murmured.

"Won't you feel uncomfortable in a synagogue," said Frank, "with you being, you know, a Christian now?"

"I'm both."

"Is that allowed?"

"It just *is*."

"All right," said Frank. "It's all right by me if it's all right by you, Juudit." He smiled at her. "What do you say?"

Judith took a deep breath. "I say all right."

∽

Kitty was shaken out of her museum hangover by a hysterically cheerful grandmother, who ordered her to leap out of bed and swallow a bagel whole because they had to rush right out the door. "Why?" Kitty moaned.

"Because the service starts at nine!"

"What service? Are we going to church?"

"No, it's a synagogue service. Come on, get dressed and put on something nice!"

Kitty's moan turned into a groan. When Carmichael came into the guest room to change into a dress, Kitty whined, "What are we going to a synagogue for? And why do we have to go right *now*?"

"I just called and found out today is a holiday and there's a special service at nine. If we wait till tonight it'll just be an ordinary Sabbath service."

"Why can't we wait till the ordinary one tonight? 'Remember the Sabbath day and keep it holy,'" she quoted from the Small Catechism. She'd worked on memorizing it for confirmation class during the long bus ride down to the City.

"Well, it just seemed exciting that today is a holiday."

"What holiday?"

"Actually... I don't remember. It's not something famous like Passover, which is in the spring, anyway. I can't remember what the lady on the phone said. We'll find out when we get there."

"But wait, Mommy, I don't understand why we're going to a synagogue. I don't want to go."

"We're Jews, and we've never been to a synagogue. It'll be interesting."

"I still love Jesus," said Kitty stubbornly.

"So do I. You don't have to stop."

"Do *they* think that?"

"I don't know what they think, but we won't bring it up. We're just going to watch. They do share more than half the Bible with us, after all."

Kitty flung herself out of the twin bed and reached under it for her backpack. "I'm going to bring my Bible with me. The *whole* Bible."

"Honey..."

"You can't stop me."

Carmichael eyed her, seemed to bite back several comments, and finally said, "OK. Just bring it your backpack. There's no need to be extremely obvious about it."

Despite the rush they arrived fifteen minutes late. "A gute kvitl!" beamed a woman in a bright white blazer and skirt.

"Likewise," said Bampy uncertainly.

The woman handed each of them a bound bouquet of green leaves on long stalks. "Your lulavim," she explained.

Kitty said, "It's like on Palm Sunday." The woman gave her a confused look but reached into another box and pulled out four lemons, handing them around, too.

"And here's your etrog," she explained.

Bammy looked bewildered and a little frightened. "Do you use these at every service?" she asked in a faint little voice.

The woman laughed. "No, no, it's special for Sukkoth. Today's the last day! It's very special, you'll see. Go on ahead and find a seat." She opened one of the large double doors and waved them in, then tapped Bampy on the arm and discreetly placed something in his hand. It turned out to be a yarmulke.

He got a funny look on his face, said, "Here goes nothing," and plopped it on his bald spot.

Kitty felt as small and frightened as her grandmother. The room was huge—much bigger than Mt. Moriah, or even the Methodist church in Shibboleth. Instead of one aisle down the middle it had two. There was an upper balcony on three sides; above the balcony, stained glass in geometric patterns; and at the far end, a huge round window with a gigantic star of David. On the floor beneath the star of David stood what appeared to be an altar and a pulpit on a raised dais, just like you'd see in a church. Except of course there wasn't any cross or Jesus anywhere.

But it wasn't even the size or the familiar-unfamiliarity of the place that unnerved Kitty. It was the people. The place was packed, despite it being a Friday morning, and all the people were in costume. Both men and women were wrapped in white shawls with dark stripes down the side. All the congregants held up their lulavim, which fluttered faintly. It was like walking through a portal into a foreign country.

Kitty trailed after her mother and grandparents to a pew in the back. One of the people at worship caught her staring and she dropped her eyes, burning red in shame. She shoved over to the end of the pew to get as far away from the action as possible. She dug out her Bible and clutched it in her lap, daring someone to look around and see her holding it and know who she was really. But it didn't take long to realize that her family wasn't going to be any help at all. They were totally engrossed in the service already, prayers and chanting and stuff like that. At one point Carmichael leaned over to advise Kitty that the reading was from Numbers and she could look it up in her

Bible, but by the time she found it the reading was already over and done with, and they were on to more prayers.

Then the air in the room changed. There was a kind of excitement brewing. Kitty felt tense and wary. She looked up at the man standing behind the pulpit up front. He was dressed in a white robe exactly like the acolyte's gown she wore at Mt. Moriah. He explained how, at every morning service during this week of Sukkoth, they'd marched with their lulavim and etrog and prayed a hoshana but today, on the great and final day of Hoshana Rabbah, the congregation would rise and march not just one time but *seven* times around the Torah scroll, praying all seven hoshanot as they walked, holding their lulavim high.

"Mommy," whispered Kitty, leaning across Bammy and Bampy, "I think this really is Palm Sunday. Do Jews have Palm Sunday, too? Look at these bundles they gave us, there are palm branches inside them, and they're tied up with palms in a knot like when we make palm crosses. Don't you think that's what this is?"

"Well," Carmichael said doubtfully, "I don't see how it could be. It's not like Jews would celebrate Jesus' triumphal march into Jerusalem." The man in the white robe was saying something more about the hoshanot, and Carmichael paused to listen. She clutched at the printed program that came with the lulavim and etrog and flipped it over. "Hoshana Rabbah," she read aloud. "The Great Hosanna. 'Hoshana' and 'hosanna' are the same word…"

"Like we sing at church!" Kitty said in an obtrusively loud whisper. "'Hosanna in the highest!'"

The man up front was still talking. This time Kitty tuned in, too. He talked about the hoshanot as prayers for salvation but also prayers for rain because, in the land of Israel, Sukkoth marked the beginning of the rainy season. Since all life depends on water falling to the earth, later on in the service they would beat their lulavim five times against the ground till the leaves fell off, and the sound would remind them of rainfall. "As for why we march around the sefer Torah seven times today instead of just once," he continued, ==the origin of many of our traditions is lost in the mists of time, but probably it's to align our prayers with those of Joshua at Jericho.=="

Kitty heard a weird noise pop out of her mother.

The man up front pulled out a funny-looking horn, like it was a literal horn off an animal's head, and blew into it. "Seven days Joshua and the warriors of Israel marched around the city of Jericho, blowing the shofar," he continued. "And on the seventh day, the Lord God, blessed be He, gave them the victory, and the walls of Jericho fell, securing the victory for God's chosen people in the promised land." He blew again. Some other people up front pulled scrolls out of cylindrical containers and laid them on the altar. All at once the congregation was on its feet and spilling into the aisles, lulavim raised high.

Kitty looked back at her mother, who seemed to be in trance. "Mommy," she hissed. "It's like that song we sang in Sunday School."

She nodded. "Wait till I tell Donald," she breathed.

"So I guess it's not Palm Sunday. I guess they have a holiday about Jericho and how the walls came a-tumblin' down."

"I guess so," murmured Carmichael. She shook her head and looked at her parents and Kitty. "Well? Shall we join them?"

Bammy gave a firm nod. "Yes. I'm ready."

"Me too," said Bampy.

"Not me," declared Kitty.

Carmichael gave her a look of surprise. "Why not?"

"I don't want to. It's weird. I've never done it before. It's too much like Palm Sunday. They might find out about us and think we're cheating." She had at least ten more objections ready to hand, but Carmichael cut across them with, "That's fine. I'm not going to force you. But I think you'll feel much more self-conscious staying put while everyone else is marching."

The three adults slid out of the pew and joined the procession, which was boisterous and dramatic. "Hoshana!" the congregation cried in response to a soloist chanting a prayer. Kitty quickly realized that indeed only a few people were staying in place, mothers with babies and, from the looks of it, a few other recalcitrant youths. If she stared at the crowd, they would definitely stare back at her. Obviously her Bible was the only way out of the awkwardness.

I'll find the Jericho story, she told herself. She flipped through till she found the book of Joshua, and then flipped through Joshua till she found Jericho in chapter six. She read it through, trying to focus her mind on the words and not on the tumult of "Hoshana!" all around. When she finished she heard a voice chant, "Send help for Moriah, the site of your temple, joy of the earth, perfection of beauty—Zion, place of the holy of holies. Help us now."

Yes, help Mt. Moriah, said Kitty under her breath. Help us not to have to leave. Help Daddy and Mommy figure it out so we can stay by Asher.

And again the crowd: "Hoshana!"

Hey, I was praying, thought Kitty. She said her mealtime and bedtime prayers, and no end of church prayers, but a spontaneous prayer seemed special and impressive and fitting for a confirmand. She sat up taller and prouder in her pew. The section on the Lord's Prayer in her Catechism said that God wanted us to talk to him like to a loving Father. And so she had. That was pretty cool. She should try it again. What else should she pray for?

Well, Saul, obviously. God bless Saul. She considered praying for Asher and decided against it; she was pretty sure she'd heard her dad say you didn't have to pray for dead people because God was already taking care of them. She prayed for Bammy and Bampy, then Meemaw and Papaw, and all of her aunts and uncles and cousins. Jessica, Jenny, and Shannon. Rob Adams for sure.

Megan?

Of course, you were *supposed* to pray for your enemies.

Jesus said that all the time. But then, Jesus also taught us to pray "deliver us from evil." And Megan was up to her neck in evil, trained in evil from her youth. Kitty should pray for Rob to be delivered from the evil of Megan, and that would be for Megan's own good too, wouldn't it, if she was no longer able to lure more people into evil? Maybe it would even help Megan repent. Kitty visualized the black cross on Megan's forehead on Ash Wednesday. Megan's downfall was a good thing to pray for, for sure.

Dear God, please stop Megan from being so evil and doing evil to other people. Help me to win against her so she can't harm anyone else. Amen.

"Hoshana!" bellowed the worshipers. Bammy and Bampy were passing by just then and waved their lulavim at Kitty. She nodded and dropped her eyes back to her open Bible. They fell on the opposite side of the page, at the tail end of chapter five.

She read, "When Joshua was by Jericho, he lifted up his eyes and looked, and behold, a man stood before him with his drawn sword in his hand; and Joshua went to him and said to him, 'Are you for us, or for our adversaries?' And he said, 'No.'"

No!

Kitty stared transfixed at the page. The words ran together and the description of the man with his drawn sword turned into an image of him, the image into a figure that spiraled up out of the paper, and the figure into Jesus: Jesus ablaze like the burning bush, his eyes boring into hers, his sword pointed at her heart, while all around the unseeing crowd kept shouting "Hoshana!" and waving their palms.

But *they* were not the traitors, like the crowd on Palm Sunday. *Kitty* was the traitor. She had to be a traitor if she could call up a Jesus of such fury.

The prayer against Megan ricocheted through Kitty's brain and forced her to paraphrase Joshua's question, "Are you for me or for my adversary?"

To which Jesus responded: *No!*

Then he collapsed back into the page, which righted itself into words again.

"Honey, are you OK?" Carmichael plopped down next to Kitty. She'd been smiling hugely till she saw Kitty's shell-shocked face. "Are you really that uncomfortable here? Should we go now? I think we've seen the most exciting part."

Kitty shook her head a tiny bit and screwed her eyes up tight to keep the tears from spilling out. She shoved her face into Carmichael's shoulder and whispered, "I was really mean to Megan."

"Oh! Oh, well." She hugged Kitty. "I'm glad you've realized that. I hope you can set things right. Things can't *always* be set right, as you've seen in this past year. But sometimes they can." She stroked Kitty's hair. "May I ask what brought this on just now?"

Kitty felt around for her Bible and slapped it onto Carmichael's lap. In the process it flipped over a page, but Kitty didn't see. Carmichael picked it up with her free hand and read. After awhile she said softly, as the normal prayers had resumed, "This part in chapter seven, about Achan and his dishonest gain? *That* did it?"

"No," said Kitty crossly, pulling back to examine the source of the error. "You're on the wrong page."

Bampy joined them. "Hey girls, I think we're going to beat these branches on the ground for rain now. Do you want to join in?"

"Do you, sweetie?" Carmichael said.

Kitty wiped her eyes. "OK," she said and followed her mother into the aisle.

∼

"I told Daddy we'd wait for him inside here," said Carmichael as she led Kitty on the short walk from the bus station to the campus center at SUNY Kuhsota. Kitty yawned and trotted obediently after, having slept most of the trip up from the City.

They sat down in the lobby of gray concrete and innocuous brass busts of college notables. Kitty curled up on a bench and dozed off again. Carmichael paced to stretch her legs after the long ride. A few minutes later she heard someone call her name.

She turned to look. "Oh, hi, Tanisha. How've you been?" They exchanged pleasantries. "So, what've you been up to this fall? Are you teaching here now?"

"Ha! I wish," said Tanisha. "No, I'm just temping at the admissions office. Hopefully I can get my foot in the door, but no guarantees."

"Wait, but," stammered Carmichael, "you dropped the lit course, so I just assumed you had a better offer somewhere else."

"Dropped?" said Tanisha. She tugged on a long braid. "I didn't drop that class. I was informed I wasn't needed."

Carmichael's eyebrows surged together. "That—that is not what we were told. We were told you withdrew."

"I *definitely* didn't do that," Tanisha countered. "I was told you decided you wanted to teach the lit class after all."

"What, me specifically?"

"Yeah, you. And since you're on the staff you got first dibs."

"I definitely didn't do *that*," said Carmichael. "I wanted to teach an elective instead. It was promised to me, originally."

The two women gazed at each other.

Tanisha leaned in. "That man is up to something," she said conspiratorially. "You know who I mean. I never did trust him any further than I could throw him."

"Can't argue with you there," said Carmichael. "Sorry you got tangled up in this. Good seeing you."

Donald pulled in a couple minutes later. After loading their bags and sleepy daughter into the backseat, Saul relentlessly poking at both, they took their places in the front seat.

Carmichael said, "Do you remember what happens *after* the battle of Jericho?"

"Uh..." Donald stalled.

"Money. A guy named Achan takes what isn't his. And Joshua finds out."

"Oh. Right. Why exactly are you bringing this up?"

"It means something," said Carmichael. "I'm not sure how just yet. But it does. It does."

CHAPTER SEVENTEEN

November 1989

*Who knows what revolutions
Russia and America may one day bring about;
we are perhaps nearer neighbors than we imagine.*

The week bridging October and November galloped by in a holiday spirit. Reformation Sunday marked the return of the church festivals after the long dry spell of Pentecost. The congregation belted out "A Mighty Fortress" like it was their national anthem, and Donald indulged in an outsized discourse on justification by faith. Even Marilyn had to concede it was interesting, despite going on for a shocking twenty-eight minutes.

The next day Kitty turned a regrettable thirteen, but she did not on that account refuse the black forest torte that Carmichael made every year for her birthday.

The day after *that* was real Reformation Day, better known to the unwashed masses as Halloween. Kitty wore a dirndl borrowed from Mrs. Kipfmueller, in honor of her dad's upcoming trip to Germany, and took great offense that she was continually mistaken for Louisa from *The Sound of Music*. Saul went as Batman, along with every other boy in Shibboleth between the ages of four and eleven.

There was a brief lull in the festivities during the second half of the week, sufficient for Donald to collect gifts for his German hosts and pack them; also sufficient for Carmichael to spend too much time with the papers and the evening news, tracking the aftermath of the massive demonstration in Leipzig on the thirty-first. She talked about it and around it until on Saturday she blurted out, "Are you sure it's *safe* for you to go to Germany right now?"

Donald ceased his attempt to fold several pairs of blue jeans as tightly as possible into the last free corner of his suitcase. "I'm not sure about anything, least of all safety," he said. "Haven't we learned that better than anyone?"

Carmichael's head drooped. "True," she murmured.

He hugged her. "I'm sorry. That came off a bit harsh. You don't want me to make a promise I can't keep, do you? I don't know for sure it's safe. But I think it's extremely unlikely that anything bad will happen to me. Those governments are out to get their own, not create an international incident with an American clergyman."

"I know, I know. It's just—it seems like things are really heating up over there."

"Your dad started talking about the protests in Estonia more than a year ago, and nothing's come of them."

"True. I'm sorry. I'm being irrational."

He smiled. "I don't mind you being a bit irrational about me. It means you want me to come home again."

She smiled back. "Maybe I should be more worried about a lady comrade seducing your heart and mind for the revolution." She threw a pillow at his head and then went to find the gum and earplugs to pack in his train case.

Next day All Saints' came around again. It was an exceptionally unpleasant morning, even for November, chilly with a steady rain falling, and the service in the cemetery lacked the previous year's novelty. Hearing Asher's name alone on the roster of the dead of the past year put the congregation in a somber mood. After the service everyone wished Donald safe travels, they'd be praying for him and looking out for Carmichael and the kids, come back soon and don't end up in a communist prison. George slipped a wad of cash into the pocket of Donald's alb when he wasn't looking, and Al alluded mysteriously to a conversation they'd be having upon his return, which, Donald deduced after some puzzling, was not going to be about firing him or forcing his resignation, but paying for his trip after all.

In the afternoon Donald drove over to see Mrs. Feuerlein, who'd stayed away from the service on account of the rotten weather, to pick up a package to bring to Fritz—not that Donald was sure he could fit anything else in his luggage at this point. Fortunately it amounted to only a card, a packet of old family letters of some historical interest, a bag of chocolate chips with a recipe for cookies translated into German, and a needlepoint for the baby's room. "Lenchen is pregnant again," Mrs. Feuerlein explained proudly. "I am so happy, it vas terrible for zhem to lose zhe first baby."

"Oh, I didn't know that. That's wonderful."

Mrs. Feuerlein nodded and pushed a cup of rose hip tea on Donald. He needed the vitamin C to stay healthy on that long flight full of stale air.

"That reminds me," he said, "I've meant to ask you ever since Fritz was here but it kept slipping my mind. He told me a wild story about a wolf and your little brother—"

"Gotthilf! Ja."

"Right. 'God helps.' But what I'm wondering is—I mean, it can't be true, can it?"

"Vhat do you mean, it can't be true? I vas zhere, I saw it vith my own eyes."

"You really did see it, then. It's not just family legend."

"I vas already twelve years old, old enough to know zhe difference between imagination and reality. It vas in Russia, zhe only holiday ve ever had as a family. And pounce! Zhis volf, he creeps up and svallows my baby bruzher whole. And our host, zhis Herr Reiswig, he snatches up his knife and slices zhat volf right open and out tumbles Gotthilf, bloody and crying for sure, but alive."

"Unbelievable."

"Believe it! It is true." She took a sip of her own tea with an air of assurance and joy that, Donald had found in his time as pastor, accrued only to the elderly who had lived well and fully.

"Tell me, Sabine," he said, serious. "You've lived a long time. You've seen a lot. There are wonders, to be sure, like the rescue of your little brother, and other things besides. More than the imagination or the news let us believe sometimes. But there are also impossible tragedies, failures of the wonder to arrive and change the situation, like Fritz and Lenchen's first child, the one they wanted to name Gotthilf..."

"Or your own little vun," said Mrs. Feuerlein tenderly.

"Yes," Donald managed to say. He took a moment to collect himself. "Are they all just accidents? The good as well as the bad? I could resign myself to a meaningless universe on account of the bad. But the good seems harder to account for, somehow."

"I do not know zhe mind of God." She closed her eyes a moment, looking like a sage or a hermit awaiting an oracle. "I lost everyzhing to come to zhis country, my family and my homeland and my language. I am not sorry. It gave me a husband long after I lost hope for vun. It has been a good life here. But it cost me somezhing. I don't know vhy my homeland has had to suffer all zhese years, and I vonder vhy it was given to me to escape vhen zhey did not."

"No one ever deserves escape, do they? It's always and only a gift."

"You know zhat part of Yob—" it took Donald a moment to work out that she was referring to the book of Job "—vhere he says, Shall ve receive good at zhe hand of God and shall ve not receive evil? But for me, it vas zhe opposite. Zhe question vas never about receiving zhe evil. I expected zhe evil. Vhat always troubled me vas receiving zhe good. Especially vhen zhe good vas not given out evenly to ozhers."

"Shall we receive evil at the hand of God but refuse to receive the good?" he paraphrased for her. "Is that what you mean?"

"Ja. Ve believe evil is real vhen ve see it. Ve trust zhat it is not lying to us. But ve do not trust zhe good. Ve fear zhat it is a fairy tale."

"But you actually saw a fairy tale yourself. You saw Little Red Riding Hood happen!"

She chuckled. "So, I have learned to take zhe good if God is so kind as to give it. I do not refuse it. You, too, Pastor. You must accept zhe good zhat God gives you and trust it, not only zhe evil and zhe pain he has put on you."

"Well, I'll try to take it if he gives it. But I don't think I dare ask him for it still. At this point, I'm just glad to do someone else a good turn. I hope this visit will be a blessing for Fritz, as his was for me."

"I have a good feeling about zhis trip," said Mrs. Feuerlein. "Now, let an old voman take her nap. And come see me vhen you get home."

∼

It was Donald's first time out of the United States, which cast a marvelous glow over every stage of a journey that otherwise would have been nothing but anxiety and exhaustion. After kisses and blessings on Kitty and Saul on their way to school Monday morning, Donald and Carmichael drove up to Albany together. They had lunch and then drove on to the airport, four hours in advance of boarding just for the commuter flight to JFK, but since he was checking all the way through to Frankfurt he didn't want to take any chances. Besides, they were both too nervous to loiter at home. As it was, the line was short and he was supplied with boarding pass and baggage claim checks within half an hour. Carmichael left then to be sure to get home before the children did. It was a long hug before they parted. "Come home in one piece," she said as she let him go.

"It's just two weeks," he said, trying to counter her emotion with his reason, knowing full well it would drive her crazy. "You were away longer when you took that cabin in Grand Forks to finish your dissertation."

"It's not the amount of time, it's what you're headed into," she said. "I can't take another shock. I can't lose anyone else."

"You won't," he said firmly, and some of his conviction seemed to pass over to her.

The first short flight was succeeded by a confused passage through the sprawl of JFK: the guts of the ceiling hanging open and exposing the network of pipes and wires; signage that contradicted itself; large Indian families in bright colors and expressionless Japanese businessmen in muted ones. Donald eventually got his bearings and went through security and passport control, found his gate, couldn't sit still, bought a *New York Times* and a very unsatisfactory egg salad sandwich. The headlines gave him pause. The top one read, "As Berlin Wall Totters Symbolically, Europeans Brace for Economic Impact." Despite the provocative headline, the article said only that East Germans were taking advantage of a loophole to travel into Czechoslovakia and then on to West Germany. A diplomat commented that he didn't think the wall would come down at all unless Krenz decided to stop using "repressive measures," whatever that meant. Presumably shooting defectors. Fritz's parish wasn't far from Czechoslovakia, Donald recalled. Maybe they would see the streams of people crossing the border.

Well past sundown the flight boarded and Donald found himself in the middle of the middle bank of seats, with neither window nor aisle at hand; he rued his lack of travel savvy. During a meal to make him think back to the egg salad sandwich with longing, small screens dropped down from the aisle ceiling and showed "Ghostbusters 2." Afterwards the lights dimmed and the screens showed the flight path over Gander, Newfoundland, and on to the North Atlantic. Despite cramped quarters and crooked neck, Donald fell into a relieved sleep.

The plane touched down in Frankfurt late the next morning. Donald's bleary eyes flew open at his first encounter with Europe, with Germany, with the sheer fact of being on foreign soil. Hearing another language on the loudspeaker delighted him, as did the slightly different proportions of the doorways and hallways, the shape of the electrical outlets, the air of efficient restraint, the subdued advertisements. He collected his suitcases at baggage claim like it was Christmas and almost regretted that he had "nothing to declare," if only for the experience of the thing. On the other side of passport control he changed dollars into deutschmarks and made his first purchase, a fat pretzel with gigantic salt crystals. Only when he finished eating it did he realize it was indistinguishable from the kind you got from a cart in Manhattan. Still. It was his first *German* pretzel.

A crisp young woman in a dark blue uniform at the information desk directed him—in flawless English—to the office that handled transfers to West Berlin. He joined a line of likewise squint-eyed overnight travelers, and at noon they all boarded a bus. The driver promised a travel time of approximately eight hours but warned that it would depend on border delays when they crossed into East Germany and then again when they crossed into West Berlin.

This time Donald had more than enough window. When he wasn't dozing off involuntarily he stared at the gray countryside, no doubt slightly less charming at the beginning of winter than it was in high summer, but he fell instantly in love with the little villages and their red-tile roofs and tall steeples. He understood the enchantment that had befallen Carmichael during her semester in France years before.

At the first border they idled a good long while. Young men with machine guns slung about their persons mounted the bus and took their time examining the papers of each and every passenger, passport and visa and letter of intent and letter of invitation. They were asked in rote English or French or Spanish how much money they were carrying, why they wanted to visit Berlin, if they would visit the East during their stay. It seemed all the other passengers were staying in West Berlin only; Donald feared his onward passage would incite suspicion.

He wondered if he should've worn his clerical shirt, or if that would have made matters worse. As it turned out, the guards were pleased that he was proceeding eastward, and even made a kind of example of him to the other passengers, whose capitalist blindness prevented them from taking advantage of proximity to the worker's paradise. It sounded like a speech they'd been instructed to recite whenever opportunity afforded. One of the guards stayed on the bus as it pulled through the layers of gates and guns and barbed wire. Apparently his job was to guarantee that the bus didn't stop again till it got to Berlin.

That was mid-afternoon. Donald spent the rest of the daylight hours mentally veering between the thrill of seeing signs for towns of great Lutheran significance—Eisenach where Luther hid at the Wartburg castle; Erfurt where he went to university and joined the Augustinian order; Leipzig of the famous debate and, just a few days earlier, the massive rally that Carmichael had been following obsessively; and after that, wonder of wonders, Wittenberg itself—that thrill, on the one hand, and the equally felt horror at the landscape of communism, on the other. The gray of the fields and hillsides was nothing compared to the gray of the towns and cities, the factories and quarries, the marching lines of soulless apartment buildings, although these last were only barely gray anymore, most of them tarnished and blackened with age or possibly soot. Weren't environmentalists among those protesting the regime?

In the end, the trip didn't take much longer than promised. The passage into West Berlin was easy—the guard hopping off the bus just before it crossed—and all at once the lights and colors of capitalism switched back on, normalcy restored. At the bus station another crisp young woman in uniform directed him to his hotel next door. At the restaurant on the ground floor Donald ordered a plate of sausages with strong mustard and, on the principle of cultural openness, a pale bitter beer. He managed half of it, crawled upstairs, and fell effortlessly into a long night's sleep.

At nine the next morning a specially commissioned taxi picked him up at the hotel to take him the final stage into East Berlin. Fritz had promised to be waiting on the other side of the Bornholmer Straße checkpoint. At this point, with no other means of communication, Donald could only hope it would be so. His nervous tension mounted as the taxi made its way through the cheerful neighborhoods of West Berlin. Even the blackletter typography on the bakeries and shop windows couldn't quite lift the pall of anxiety. Nor did it help that the driver—who, like all Germans, apparently, spoke perfect English—remarked jovially, "You have picked an exciting time to visit East Berlin!" but shook his head all the same.

"What do you mean?"

"Do you not read the newspaper?" asked the driver with surprise. "On Saturday there was a big march on the east side, thousands of people. They said they must have the right to travel to all places at all times. So the DDR promised a new law for travel. But when the law came out on Monday, it was not new and different. It was just the same, no freedom to travel. So the people marched again in Leipzig—you know about last week in Leipzig, yes?"

This time Donald could say that he knew.

"The DDR newspapers say there were fifty thousand people in Leipzig on Monday, but I have a friend who lives there. He says it was five hundred thousand."

"Half a million people?" asked Donald incredulously.

"Yes, that is so," said the driver.

"Is it… Do you think…" Donald didn't even know what question he wanted to formulate.

The driver shrugged and smiled into the rearview mirror. "Who knows? It is interesting."

Donald lapsed into silence the rest of the way to the checkpoint. The floodlights were switched off since it was morning, but he could see them stretching up high. More walls, more wire, more guns, also dogs, and a long stretch of empty road passing over a curvaceous bridge surmounting train tracks below. It wasn't busy at all. The driver pulled up to the diplomatic line and stopped. A blasé guard approached, seeming to know the driver by sight. He took all of Donald's documents and vanished. The minutes stretched on endlessly. At last he returned, handed back the papers, and indicated that Donald could get out. The driver got out, too, and opened the trunk to retrieve the suitcases. He shook Donald's hand. "Good luck," he said, and then drove off again, leaving Donald stranded not metaphorically but literally in a no-man's land. The guard made a cursory inspection of the luggage, then swept an indifferent hand eastward. Donald settled his satchel on his shoulders, grabbed the two suitcases, and strode toward East Berlin, wondering if he'd ever come out again.

All fears subsided the moment he heard a voice bellow, "My friennnd!" Fritz came running, waving his hands with frantic enthusiasm, and crashed right into Donald. "You are here! You are here! I am so glad! My friend, my friend!" He crushed Donald with a hug and then seized the suitcases as if he were stealing them, swinging around and shooting back in the direction he'd come.

"Let me take one of them," Donald panted after him.

"No, two make me the balance," Fritz said. "Lenchen! I have him!" he shouted.

Donald looked up and saw a pretty, smiling woman with strawberry blonde hair and a discreetly pregnant belly. They were introduced and, after Lenchen apologized for not speaking English, she launched into a series of detailed inquiries about his trip in precise and grammatical English. By the time he had answered to the couple's satisfaction they reached a boxy putty-colored car. "My friend, this is a Wartburg 353!" Fritz announced, as if introducing Donald to the car. "Named for Luther's castle, yes?" He stowed the suitcases and then slapped the trunk shut like it was a horse's rear. "Na ja, there is much to explain," he announced.

The first item of business was the astounding fact of their having a car to pick him up in at all. It was not theirs. Although they'd been on the waiting list for three years, even a relatively non-persecuted pastor could not expect any advantage in procuring an automobile. The Wartburg belonged to Lenchen's cousin Petra, a journalist in Berlin. Further, as it turned out, this cousin lent them not only her car but also her apartment, because she had gone to Warsaw for a few days to report on the meeting between the Polish and West German governments.

So, Fritz and Lenchen thought, since it was some three hundred kilometers from Berlin to their village of Zschopdorf (Donald didn't have the time or mental capacity to compute the distance in miles, but it seemed fairly far), they'd spend a couple of days in the capital first. "We will arrive in time for the Peace Decade to start on the twelfth, but," Fritz said, with an uncharacteristically apologetic tone creeping into his voice, "to tell you the truth, my friend, I am not quite sure it will happen this year."

Out of this flood of information a still jet-lagged Donald struggled to extract a modicum of meaning. "You mean the ten days of prayer? But that's what I came for, isn't it?"

"Yes, yes, and I am sorry about that," said Fritz, tucking Donald into the passenger seat and then rushing around to take the wheel. "I did not want to write and tell you, in case you decided not to come. There is still much good you can do on your visit, and much you will learn. But at the moment is everything quite strange. We try not to hope for too much."

"But we hope!" cried Lenchen from the backseat.

They drove off. Fritz apologized that there was not much to see on the way to Petra's apartment in Marzahn, but in the afternoon they could have a look around the city. "At minimum we will bring you to the Brandenburger Tor," he said. "This was left for us in the East. It is the most famous sight that we have."

"Except the wall," objected Lenchen.

Donald peered out the window at boulevards wide though

relatively empty, at least by New York standards. "What's that?" he asked, pointing to his right. "It looks like something from 'The Jetsons'—I mean, like something in science fiction."

"Fernsehturm," said Fritz efficiently.

"Television tower," translated Lenchen.

Marzahn proved to be a labyrinth of grim gray high-rises. Donald expressed cautious pity that cousin Petra was stuck in such a place. Lenchen explained with a laugh that it was a sign of how privileged Petra was to get such a nice new apartment in Berlin, and all to herself. "I do not ask her what she does in her work, to win such an apartment," she added. "Just like she does not ask me and Fritz what we do with the church to work against…"

Fritz cleared his throat uproariously. He pointed with a finger at the dashboard. "It is also a very nice car that she has," he commented.

Donald looked over at Fritz in puzzlement, and back to Lenchen. Then the penny dropped. Successful journalist Petra's car might be bugged. It gave Donald a weird thrill.

Their caution must extend to the apartment, Fritz explained in a hurried whisper as they moved between Petra's parking spot and the front door of the building. Donald nevertheless found plenty else to occupy his attention, first and foremost that in a twenty-story building the elevator was out of order. Several workmen clustered in front of it on the ground floor, though the fact that they were smoking and (judging by the powerful odor as they walked past) even drinking in the morning did not offer much hope for a quick repair. Luckily Petra lived on the sixth floor. Lenchen denied any difficulty in mounting the stairs and kept up with them handily. She attributed her good health to the produce of their own and their parishioners' gardens, as well as a steady diet of cake.

Donald expected an enormous, lavish, and aristocratic dwelling after Fritz and Lenchen's admiring forecast. And perhaps, relatively speaking, it was, but at first all Donald could see was how thin and fragile the furniture looked, as if the blond wood veneer was ready to peel and pop off at any second. His second impression was the contrast between the gray exterior of East Berlin and the riot of obnoxious color within. The curtains in each room were garish and bright: Warholesque poppies in the living room, navy blue and purple dots in the bedroom, wavy yellow lines in the kitchen. The countertops were pink, the sofa orange. Only the plain gray carpet that covered every floor, and the dark wooden (though also veneered) wall unit holding an ancient television and the complete works of Jules Verne, expressed any restraint.

After an extended battle over who would sleep where—Fritz absolutely insisting that Donald take the only bed, Donald counter-insisting that pregnant Lenchen should take it and he was more than happy to curl up on the orange sofa—the American gifts were liberated from the overstuffed suitcases. Fritz was extremely pleased about the jeans, Lenchen about the chocolate chips and recipe since she had only heard about but never tasted the wondrous ambrosia from abroad. They had a lunch of rye bread with slices of ham, something like salami, and bland white cheese, plus a selection of pickles, then headed out for an afternoon of sightseeing. Donald was struck chiefly by the sheer massive scale of the communist-erected buildings, broader than they were tall. He nearly choked at the sight of Lenin's bust on the side of one of them.

Dusk was falling by the time they reached the Brandenburg Gate. The plaza in front was vast and empty, just a few people milling about, guards too, of course, but the place would have been forbidding enough without the human patrol. Through the Gate's tall columns Donald could see the wall on the other side.

"It's strange," he said. "I passed through the wall this morning, but somehow I didn't feel it. The whole travel experience was so exciting and draining, and I was anxious about making all my connections and meeting up with you. But now, somehow, looking at it here—it seems so absolute. Like reaching the end of the earth, where the waters fall over into the abyss."

"I am told," said Fritz, "that on the west side stands a sign before the wall that says, 'Sie verlassen jetzt West Berlin.' It means, 'Now you leave West Berlin.' I think that this is funny, that they inform you with such a sign. There is no doubt that you leave West Berlin when you come so near the wall!"

"The gate looks like an invitation to pass through and see the other side. But it's a locked door, not a gate at all."

"Twenty-eight years has it stood here," said Lenchen. "The wall is older than I."

Between the sobering sight of the wall and Donald's jet lag reasserting itself, they decided to call it a night, stopping only for a Ketwurst on the way home.

Thursday passed in similar leisurely fashion. They traveled by bus to the far end of Karl-Marx-Allee and walked its length toward the center, stopping off for a bite at Café Moskau, Donald bemused by the regime's slavish adoration of the Soviet Union. Fritz shrugged dismissively at what everyone knew to be propaganda. In the afternoon they explored several museums, Fritz assuring Donald that he need not regret his inability to comprehend the socialistically-inflected German.

Their last stop was the Berlinerdom, which was, Fritz informed his visitor, the largest Protestant church in all of Germany. After they left, Donald said, "Am I allowed to hate it?"

Fritz snorted. "Ja, of course," he said. "It was built by Kaiser Wilhelm, in order to make himself the ruler of the church. Then your country bombed it. Then the DDR built it again without the crosses. It is an interesting monument. But it is not a church."

"Agreed," said Donald. He glanced at Lenchen, seated on the stone steps out front and rubbing her swollen feet. "Let's call it a day, shall we? I don't think I'm the only one who's tired."

"Ah, wonderful," said Fritz. "There is a good football match on the television tonight. I did not want to take away from your time in Berlin, but I am glad to see the match."

Back in Petra's apartment, Lenchen assembled a dinner of tomato soup with potatoes, pickles, and hot dogs—"It's Soljanka, the only thing the Soviets gave us that we actually like," she explained—and afterwards Prasselkuchen, a thin cake topped with jam and streusel, so flaky that after a single bite Donald turned into a snowman of shattered crumbs and apologized at length to the absent Petra.

They settled in to watch the football match, which Donald discovered in fact to be a soccer match, and furthermore to be broadcast on a West German station. "Oh, right, I remember now you told us last March that you can get Western media here, despite... everything."

"Ja, of course, all over the DDR we can. Only in the valley of the clueless they know nothing of the West!" He laughed and explained about a region near Dresden where Western television and radio signals didn't reach, and how the rest of the country accordingly laughed at those people's trusting belief in the regime's version of events. "Even in our small village we know better."

At twenty minutes to eleven Donald, barely able to keep his eyes open, was relieved to see that the game was finally over. He hadn't wanted to ask to go bed, since the TV was in the living room and he didn't want to be maneuvered into the only bed after all. Lenchen had long since passed out in a chair upholstered in coarse celadon fabric. Fritz thanked Donald for his patience and started pulling linens and blankets out of the broad cupboard adjacent to the TV. As he reached to shut if off, he visibly started. His finger halted halfway to the switch.

"What?" said Donald.

Fritz stared on, unresponsive. A news anchor was speaking.

"Fritz?"

"Lenchen, Lenchen, wach auf!" he said in a low and urgent voice.

She awoke at once. "Was ist los?"

"Is everything OK? Has something bad happened?" Donald said.

Fritz sat down with a thump on the coffee table and kept staring at the screen. Lenchen's mouth actually dropped open.

"Tell me what's happening," Donald pleaded. Carmichael will never forgive me, he thought frantically.

"It is not bad," said Fritz, coming out of his stupor. "It is unbelievable."

"The borders are open," said Lenchen. "All of them."

"What?" said Donald, dumbfounded.

"It cannot be true," said Fritz.

Lenchen waved at the anchorman. "He had not invented such a story," she said. "It had been too dangerous. He says that this night the DDR announced the opening of the borders."

"No visa? One can go through? Any person for any reason?" Fritz shook his head. "I have dreamed crazy dreams, but this is too crazy to believe."

Lenchen hefted herself to her feet. "Let us find out," she said. "The news says that the checkpoints are right now open. People already go through. Let us go and see."

Fritz stared at her. "Now you are the crazy one."

A rapid-fire exchange in German ensued, but Donald could catch the sense of it well enough. Lenchen wanted to go to one of the checkpoints and see for herself, while Fritz worried for her safety, the baby's safety, and not least of all the American's safety.

Evidently reaching an impasse, Lenchen reverted to English. "We do not know if this will last," she said to Donald. "Probably it is some trick to send the protestors out of the DDR. Then they will again close the border. But I never have been in the West, not one time. Not one visit to West Berlin. It is maybe the only chance for our baby to go in the West. I want to go walk in West Berlin. One day I will tell our child about it."

It was the first time Donald had ever seen Fritz look worried about anything. He and Lenchen alike tried to draw Donald to their side of the argument. He refrained, not sure himself what he wanted, torn between curiosity and fear. "I'll do whatever you decide," he said, and discreetly took himself to the bathroom to let them finish their debate in privacy.

When he reemerged, Lenchen was already in her coat and hat and was struggling into her shoes. Fritz gave him a funny smile. "We go," he said. "Woman is the stronger. That is why the snake had to speak to her first, because she could convince the man to eat the apple, but never could the man convince the woman."

Lenchen stuck her tongue out at him.

Given the late hour and the distance, they decided to risk taking Petra's car. Fritz and Lenchen (this time in the front seat, at Donald's insistence) continued to chatter in high-energy German at one another. The most immediate question was which border crossing to try. "Isn't Checkpoint Charlie the most famous?" Donald asked.

"Ja, but it is in the south part of the city, on the other side of Unter den Linden. I think we should go back to Bornholmer Straße. It is the nearest." Lenchen agreed.

Despite the cold they kept their windows cracked open. They heard action before they saw it, a low rumble in the distance that could have been either cheerful or baleful.

Then they turned a corner and Fritz slammed on the brakes in sheer astonishment.

The streets and sidewalks were full of people; absolutely, unbelievably full. A narrow line of cars slunk between the crowds at a snail's pace. It might be hours before they reached the border at that rate. After further consultation the three of them decided to park on a residential side street and continue by foot.

"It is a party," said Fritz as they neared the crowd. There was shouting, laughter, and an apparently infinite supply of bottles being passed around and slurped up by the rejoicing masses.

"What are they singing?" asked Donald. "Is it your national anthem or something?"

"You joke, my friend!" cried Fritz. "It is your American, David Hasselhoff."

"You mean like Knight Rider?" asked Donald incredulously.

"Ja, this fall his song 'Looking for Freedom' has been very popular in the west. Here also, but we hear it only on West German radio. The DDR does not allow it. So, the people sing it instead."

Fritz wrapped a tight arm around Lenchen to protect her from the crush of the crowd, and Donald moved in as close as he could on her other side. As they surged forward, Fritz and Lenchen asked around for news of what was happening. Most people didn't know how or why; they'd just heard from someone by phone or on the streets that all the borders were open. At last one middle-aged man overheard the question and shouted over the rumble of rejoicing, "Schabowski said it himself! There was a live news conference today. He said all travel to the west is permitted, including through Berlin, effective right away!"

Fritz translated for Donald, then said back to the man, "But why? Why the change?"

The man shrugged happily. "Does it matter?"

"I wonder only how long it will last," Fritz said to Lenchen and Donald.

They pushed on, declining the exuberant offers of beer and knockoff champagne from their neighbors. The sinuous bridge at the checkpoint loomed ever closer. Someone was swinging a black, red, and gold flag. Fritz pointed it out to Donald and noted that it lacked the communist symbol in the middle. "It is the flag of the West, not the East," he said.

"Will they really let us through?" Lenchen shouted to the people around them.

"The crowd wouldn't keep moving forward if they didn't," someone answered.

"How many people are here, do you think?" Donald asked.

"Ten thousand?" Fritz guessed.

"More," said Lenchen categorically and joined in the communal singing of "Looking for Freedom."

They approached a blank-faced tower and someone filming nearby. The crowd was moving fast now; they had to run to keep up. They reached the spot where Fritz had met Donald just the morning before, and then got to where the taxi had let Donald out, and then, swarming around the slowly moving cars and sailing right past the border guards who were unarmed and nodding at the very people they had only hours earlier been obligated to contain and, if necessary, shoot, the three of them completed their passage across the bridge.

Lenchen planted her feet on the road and lifted her arms to the night sky. "I am in the West!" she shrieked. She patted her belly and murmured to it in exulting German. A couple of passersby grinned at her and shot off a spray of champagne in a dazzling shower over her head. She laughed, grabbed Fritz by one hand and Donald by the other, and tugged them into West Berlin.

∼

"Finish up," said Carmichael vaguely. Without Donald around, she found herself acquiescing to Kitty and Saul's tastes in dinner, settling for a harmless pot of spaghetti and meatballs. Saul had insisted on eating his inside a buttered slice of bread to make a meatball sandwich, complete with pasta topping. Kitty spent an inordinate amount of time trying to master the trick of twirling the spaghetti around her fork without it all unraveling before it reached her mouth.

"Is there dessert?" Saul asked through a mouthful of starch.

"Not tonight," said Carmichael.

"Aw," said Saul.

She whisked her own plate and the serving dish away before the children even finished and got to work on the dishes. Donald had warned her that he didn't know if or when he'd be able to call, but to assume that no news was good news. Easier to believe of someone who hasn't gone behind the iron curtain, thought Carmichael. She breathed long and slowly and prayed with the fervent attention that only fear could induce. He's fine, he's fine, he's fine, she told herself over and over.

Kitty brought in her and Saul's dishes.

"Homework?" said Carmichael curtly.

"Just spelling and a math worksheet."

"All right, you settle down at the dining table and get Saul to bring out his homework, too. Wait—take the washcloth and wipe it down first."

Saul intently coloring, Kitty scoffing at the easiness of the week's vocabulary, Carmichael caught herself hovering. "I'm going to watch the news," she said. The children didn't even register her announcement. She stepped over to switch on the TV and sat in Donald's easy chair, imagining that he was hugging her.

Two commercials and then Tom Brokaw appeared, not in his usual position at the NBC news desk but outside somewhere, at night, high up above a crowd, in—

Oh, my God, thought Carmichael.

In Berlin!

"What you see behind me is a celebration," the newscaster said from the screen. "As announced today by the East German government for the first time since the wall was erected in 1961, people will be able to move through freely."

Carmichael screamed.

"What is it? What is it, Mommy?" Saul came tearing over and Kitty was quick behind him.

"Did something bad happen?" Kitty demanded.

"No! I mean, I don't think so! Look, look, it's the Berlin Wall, it's open." Tears streamed down her face.

"Berlin? Is Daddy OK?"

"I'm sure he is. This is good news, not bad news. Oh, my God, I don't believe it. I never would have believed it."

Homework abandoned, Kitty and Saul both found perches on Carmichael's lap and there they stayed, watching the rippling crowd beyond and below Tom Brokaw. People apparently from the East pranced along the top of the wall like acrobats, holding umbrellas as water poured down on top of them.

"Does it rain only on the East Berlin side?" Kitty asked.

"That's not rain. It looks like they've turned a fire hydrant on them. Though I don't know why, if the borders are open. Maybe they just don't want them climbing over the wall instead of going through the checkpoints."

At seven the phone rang. It was Frank. "Did you see, did you see?" he shouted down the line.

"I did, Dad, I saw it, we all saw it!"

"Do you realize what this means? If the wall opens up, it means that Gorbachev isn't going to do anything to stop it. And that means the Estonians will win, too, they will, they will, nothing can stop them anymore. Their songs will bring that iron curtain down after all!"

"Open borders are one thing, but do you really think they'll tear the wall down?"

"What's the point of having a wall if people can move across it freely? You wait and see, honey, you wait and see. That wall is gonna come down."

Once she was off the phone, Carmichael grabbed Saul and Kitty's hands and danced in a circle with them. "You two, remember this day! Remember it always! This is the biggest day you have ever lived through, maybe the biggest day you will ever live to see. The wall is coming down!"

Saul started, and Kitty joined in:

Then the lamb ram sheep horns began to blow
The trumpets began to sound
Joshua commanded the children to shout
and the walls come a-tumblin' down.

Saul shouted, and then they were all shouting. They danced all over the house, singing at the top of their lungs and pretending to blow "lamb ram sheep horns."

At last, exhausted, they tumbled to the floor of the living room. Kitty said, "Do you think Daddy's there? Do you think he'll get to see any of it?"

"I doubt it," replied Carmichael. "I don't think Pastor Fritz and his wife live anywhere near Berlin, and he arrived yesterday morning already. Too bad, though. It would have been neat for him to see it."

∼

Even as Carmichael spoke those words to their children in Shibboleth, Donald along with Fritz, Lenchen, and some uncountable number of East Germans—and some uncountable number of equally jubilant West Germans, too—were approaching the Brandenburg Gate, and from the west side, no less. Even Fritz hadn't seen it from that direction before.

"There's the sign," Fritz pointed out, laughing. "My friend, I am so happy to see this sign with my own eyes. It is the proof that I am in the West."

Lenchen accepted a cup of water from a grinning West German and a stack of sweet rolls. After thanking the benefactor she held one out to Donald. "Rosinenschnecke," she said. "What is that, Fritz?"

He thought a moment. "Raisin snail," he said.

Donald laughed at the unappetizing name, and at the sheer unbelievable wonder of the scene around him. "Look, there's a news anchor up on that cherry picker," he said. "I wonder who it is."

"Probably someone from the ARD. That is the West German news station. Come, let us go closer to the wall."

They slid through the crowd without trouble. The wall came ever closer into focus. "It's covered with graffiti," Donald observed.

"It is a good question," shouted Fritz over the noise of the masses, "who hated the wall more, the East Berliners or the West Berliners."

"Fritz, what day is it?" Lenchen said.

"Thursday. Well, no, it is now Friday."

"No, what day of the month?"

"The ninth. No, the tenth. I am confused because it is so late."

"The *ninth*, Fritz! The ninth of November!"

"Ach, mein Gott!" Someone nearby heard them, and Fritz and Lenchen conferred at length with a few others. At last Fritz turned back to Donald to explain. "The ninth of November is no good day in German history," he said. "It is the day that Adolf Hitler made his victory in the beer hall. It is the day that he sent his men to attack the Jews—we call it Kristallnacht."

"I know about that."

"Dear God! Will this be the ninth of November like the others? Is this the beginning of a terrible war?"

All at once one of the other people standing nearby pivoted on his heel and shoved something into Donald's hands.

"What is it?" he said.

"Ein Stück der Mauer," said the man.

"A piece of the wall," translated Lenchen.

Donald stared down at it. It had a fragment of bright color from the graffiti; otherwise, it was gray and shedding dusty debris all over his clothes. Fritz and Lenchen stared, too. Then they looked up and realized what was happening. People were attacking the wall. Some had hammers or chisels. Others had nothing more than a ballpoint pen. A kind of frenzy seized them. Donald tuned in to a chant beating the air around them. "What are they saying?"

"Die Mauer muss weg," repeated Lenchen after a pause. "The wall must—away. That is not good English," she apologized with a smile.

"Down with the wall," proposed Donald.

Fritz looked around. "And no one stops them," he commented. "The wall will not survive. Look at these people. Nothing can stop them."

Then Donald—feeling utterly ridiculous, without any right to his emotion, being after all a purely accidental American swept up in the night's events—Donald wept, tears pouring out of him like one of the water cannons on the east side of the wall, grinning as he wept, rocking his chunk of wall like it was a baby. "I see it now, I see," he sobbed. "Walls come down. They come a-tumblin' down. Thank you, Lord."

Fritz and Lenchen chimed in unison, "Amen!"

Then Fritz reached into his pocket and pulled out a Swiss army knife. "It is not really Swiss," he demurred. "Just a cheap DDR knife. But it works. We can take turns. Come, my friend."

And they advanced to join the happy throng tearing down the wall.

~

This time when the phone rang Kitty grabbed it. "It's Meemaw!" she shouted as she handed the receiver over to Carmichael.

"Are you watching the news?" Dot screeched through the wires.

"We're two hours behind you," said Carmichael, "but we saw it two hours ago on NBC. It's crazy, isn't it?"

"Did you see Donald?" she shouted back.

"Donald? No. What do you mean?"

"We just saw him! Me and Jimmy both! He's there, he's there!"

"You can't be serious," said Carmichael in a faint voice.

"He was standing back aways behind Tom Brokaw, we both saw him, he was smiling and holding up a piece of stone or something. He's there, honey, he's a part of it!"

"Oh, God," said Carmichael. "Do you think it's safe?"

"Well, they're not going to do anything with Tom Brokaw right there filming the whole thing," Dot said stoutly. There was not a modicum of fear in her tone, which was so unusual as to bolster Carmichael. "Don't you worry, honey. It's a miracle. God don't let people down when he does miracles."

After Carmichael got off the phone and told the children, Kitty asked, "Can we watch too? Maybe we'll see Daddy!"

"Well, the news isn't on anymore. I think they're doing a live broadcast each time it turns six-thirty in a new time zone. But they won't show it here again. Anyway, it's time for you two to get into bed."

They protested and stalled more than usual, but by nine they were both tucked in, bedroom doors shut. Carmichael wandered back down to the living room in a daze.

"I can't just sit here and do nothing," she announced to nobody. She looked at the clock again, even though she knew the time. "It's too late to call anyone."

The phone rang again. It was Al Beck, wanting to know if Pastor Donald was all right. She told him she thought so, had no reason to think otherwise, but she didn't repeat Dot and Jimmy's belief that they'd seen him on the news—that seemed a bit too much like wishful thinking to be true. Al said he'd let the congregation know so she wasn't flooded with phone calls.

She thanked him, but after hanging up she wished she *was* flooded with phone calls after all. She dialed up her parents and they hashed it out, Frank speculating wildly about what this would mean for Estonia, Judith adding that maybe, just maybe, if it all worked out and Estonia were free again, it would be worth trying to track down their long-lost relatives. But the Berlin Wall was one thing, the Soviet Union releasing a captive republic or reversing its communist course was quite another. They'd just have to wait and see. One miracle at a time was plenty.

"It reminded me of Hoshana Rabbah," said Judith. "Do you remember how the leader said it was to commemorate Joshua and his men bringing down the walls of Jericho?"

"Yes, Mom, I remember that *very* well."

"Don't you think that what's going on in Berlin is something like that?"

"Grant it, God," intoned Carmichael.

When they got off the phone it was ten. The house was intolerably quiet, except for the occasional spit of an ember from the woodstove in the living room. Carmichael sorely missed Donald's care of the parsonage's moody heating.

Then, once more, the phone rang.

She leapt and got it before the second ring. "Hello, hello?"

There was a crackle and hiss on the line, the sound of unintelligible parties at some impossible distance consulting nasally, then static, then, "Carmichael! It's me, it's Donald!"

"Oh, my God, where are you?"

"I'm fine, I'm fine! Have you seen the news? Are they telling you about it in America?"

"Yes! It was on NBC, we saw it, your parents just called and said they saw *you* there, is it true, were you there?"

"I was, I was, I was! Not right when it started—" and he recounted the evening, though Carmichael could only extract the occasional detail on account of the terrible connection and Donald's extravagant happiness causing him to jump around from one thing to the next.

Eventually she figured out that he'd joined the flood into West Berlin and it was entirely possible that he'd been caught for a moment on TV.

"Are you still there now?" she bawled back into the phone.

"No, we hitchhiked back to the same checkpoint we came through—" moving on too quickly for Carmichael to object to his hitchhiking, though of all the potentialities for danger that evening, catching a ride with a happy stranger was surely the least of them "—and then we had to find the car and now we're back in Lenchen's cousin's apartment, so I have to get off the phone now, she didn't actually give us permission to make phone calls and there's a chance the line is bugged—"

"Bugged?!"

"But I don't think any of that is going to matter now. That wall is coming down!"

"A-tumblin' down," Carmichael shouted back. "The children and I were singing it all evening."

There was a fast goodbye and more static and a click.

Carmichael smiled at the receiver as she set it back in place. "You may talk about the king of Gideon," she sang softly. "You may talk about the men of Saul. But there's none like good old Donald at the battle of the Berlin Wall."

∼

They spent one more day in Berlin. The whole city was in a festive mood. For all the people who had turned out in the night, most of the city's population either didn't hear or didn't believe a word of it. But by midday on the tenth, there was no denying that the entire world order had been flipped upside down. There were rumors, as yet unverified, that the whole thing had been a mistake; that the government hadn't intended any of what transpired, as evidenced by one last half-hearted attempt to require visas and impose waiting periods before exiting. But no one paid any attention to that. The border guards let cars and pedestrians through without question or delay, and the mood was such that even if they'd tried to stop the hordes it wouldn't have worked. By early afternoon day-trippers were already returning with overstuffed shopping bags from the West. There was no way to guess how many people left the east with no intention of ever returning.

Donald, Fritz, and Lenchen strolled all day along the length of the wall, between checkpoints, next to hitherto unimportant stretches, back and forth in front of the Brandenburg Gate. Everywhere they went people were on the wall, climbing the wall, attacking the wall. This time they had more than penknives and screwdrivers. Mallets and pickaxes and sledgehammers were hard at work. There was gray dust everywhere, but every cough it induced was like expelling a long, long sickness.

On the morning of the eleventh—which Fritz did not fail to note was Martin Luther's baptism day—they took Petra's car for a last look at the wall before catching their noon train south. Even with all that had happened, they weren't prepared for what they saw: bulldozers of East German make and model assaulting the very boundary of their existence. The three of them got out of the car and watched agog like kindergarteners as huge chunks crumbled and fell to the earth.

When they returned to the apartment to park the car and pick up their luggage, they found Petra just returned from Poland. She gave Lenchen a rueful smile. "The greatest news story of my life," she said, "and I missed it."

"I don't think the interesting news stories are going to stop any time soon," said Lenchen consolingly.

Petra shook her head. "There's a lesson in it. I went chasing after the news to try to get ahead. And then you, who have never cared about getting ahead, were right on hand when it happened. I used to wonder how you could be happy, Lenchen. But I think you made the better choice."

Lenchen clasped Petra's hands. "Come see us soon," she said. "You won't get in trouble for it now. I think Fritz and I can tell you some things that will be very popular news stories."

While the extraordinary turn of events colored everything that followed, Donald embraced the more modest joys and wonders in the week and a half that remained to him. Parish life at the St. Lukas-Kirche in Zschopdorf was even more vibrant than he expected from Fritz's loving account of the solidarity among believers in an unfriendly regime. Donald couldn't help but feel the occasional twinge of envy when he thought back to the last half-year at Mt. Moriah. He goggled at the church's twelfth-century edifice, the Reformation-era altarpiece ("copied from a Cranach," Fritz told him proudly), and the eighteenth-century death memorials of aristocratic patrons, though he couldn't deny that the building wasn't exactly useful for Sunday School or committee meetings, and already in November it was deathly cold. He sampled a staggering array of cakes and was invited to tour tamped-down winter gardens and hibernating orchards. One day Fritz borrowed a Trabant from a parishioner and drove Donald to Wittenberg—dreary, demoralized, and in disrepair, but Wittenberg all the same. Donald's heart all but stopped at the sight of the Castle Church where Luther had nailed the Ninety-Five Theses. "Hard to do on a metal door," Donald observed.

"It is not the original door. Pilgrims came and took the wood of the door away, like we have seen the people do to the wall in Berlin. Soon there was no more door. They replaced it with metal, so that the people could not steal it."

"Holy relics for Protestants," laughed Donald.

"Ja, something like that," agreed Fritz.

"I'll be content with my piece of the wall."

Of course, everywhere they went they had to repeat the story of being right there on the night the borders opened, though Donald kept quiet as the East Germans speculated about the possibility of German reunification, whether it signaled a change for the Soviet Union, and above all what it would mean for the church.

The second Sunday of Donald's trip, after preaching at the morning service, he and Lenchen had a long farewell with promises to visit again someday. Fritz accompanied him on his northward train and then all the way to the hotel in West Berlin.

"You know, Fritz," said Donald, "I remember some of my parishioners asking you if you didn't want to stay in America, or at least emigrate if you had the chance, and you said no, you wanted to stay with your people, despite all the disadvantages. At the time I thought it was noble of you, but maybe not the best choice for your future or your family. But now—it's incredible! You're going to be part of rebuilding your church. Your whole nation, even. What a gift."

Fritz smiled and nodded. "That is true. But I am not so

idealistic. We will be happy about the freedom for two weeks. Maybe one month. Then we will begin to fight. There will be many problems. Most of my people, you have seen them, they are very old. They know no other way, and they are too old to change themselves. It will be hard for them. If we again join to West Germany, all the young people will leave us and go there. Yes, it will be better. But it will be hard."

"Don't be over-optimistic now," Donald laughed.

"Come, come, my friend, you have said that it is like the walls of Jericho. Victory—but then all goes wrong. It is the whole history of the world."

"We choose the Lord, say the people—but then Joshua tells them, you cannot choose, you cannot serve the Lord."

"Genau. But that is OK. We still have the victory. It is real. It is only not the last victory. We do not set all our hope on a victory that comes before the last victory."

Donald said thoughtfully, "That's true. And in more ways than one."

Fritz enfolded Donald in one of his famous bear hugs. "I will miss you, my friend," he said. "Come again and see me one day."

"I will," said Donald.

CHAPTER EIGHTEEN

November 1989

*Place mankind where you will,
they must always have adverse circumstances
to struggle with;
from nature, accidents, constitution;
from seasons, from that great combination of mischances
which perpetually lead us to new diseases, to poverty.
Who knows but I may meet in this new situation,
some accident from whence may spring up
new sources of unexpected prosperity?
Who can be presumptuous enough to predict all the good?
Who can foresee all the evils,
which strew the paths of our lives?*

When Megan was absent from school on Monday, Kitty didn't think much of it. In November everyone started getting colds and that's probably all it was. No further thought about Megan's Tuesday absence, either. On Wednesday Kitty wondered if maybe she had the flu. By Thursday Kitty wasn't the only one who had noticed or was talking about it. The rumors floated to her ears. People were saying that Megan's dad was in jail, this time to stay.

Kitty raced up the hill to the parsonage after school, rummaged around in the paper recycling bin, and yanked out *The Kuhsota Daily Register* and *The New York Times*. Both covered the outcome of the trial. Richard Moravsky was one of several convicted; his sentence was three and a half years at the Federal Correctional Institution in Otisville. An op-ed in the *Register* expressed dismay that once again lower-ranked managers like

Moravsky and his co-defendants were left to take the rap for the real scoundrels higher up the food chain.

Kitty folded up the papers and sat back on her heels. She remembered with a twinge how gleeful she'd felt at Father Pat's mention to her dad about Megan's dad, and how she'd put the information to evil use at once. And then, again, how she showed that other newspaper article to Rob Adams, convincing herself it was OK because it wasn't a secret, and anyway Rob had to be warned about her. And then how Rhea started stalking her right afterwards, never saying anything, just watching with those scary marble eyes of hers. Apparently Rhea's chariot didn't fly as far as New York City, because during the visit to Bammy and Bampy's there'd been no sign of her. Though maybe if she'd been along, Jesus himself wouldn't have had to come out of Kitty's confirmation Bible to thunder his judgment upon her.

The funny thing was, right after it happened, and she admitted to her mom how mean she'd been to Megan, a soft, light, gentle feeling filled up her body, all the way out to her toes and fingers and ears. She'd almost floated out of the pew, though when it came time to pummel the ground with the lulavim she'd gone for it with a ferocious intensity. It really did sound like rainfall. Then when she got back to her seat, she picked up her Bible and hugged it and had the crazy feeling it was hugging her back. She didn't see Jesus again, but she was pretty sure he wasn't mad at her anymore.

Rhea was another matter, though. It was a weird thing that Megan had scared off so many of Kitty's council members but even she couldn't do a thing to get rid of Rhea, the only one who was left. And also the only one Kitty would have been perfectly happy to do without. She might even thank Megan if she managed to scare off Rhea.

On Friday Megan was absent again, and at school everyone was talking openly about her jailbird dad. No one actually understood what he was guilty of, except that it wasn't violent, and still the luster of money and New York City and the stock market papered over some of the recriminations. But not enough. Kitty couldn't blame Megan for staying away.

Kitty found herself thinking about Megan all day Saturday. The next week was a short week of school, because of Thanksgiving. Maybe she'd stay away again so people would forget about her dad. But school kids never forgot anything. They'd zip right back to it the week after Thanksgiving.

The church service the next day went horribly slow. Donald wasn't getting home till late on Monday, so this was the second Sunday in a row with the fantastically aged retired pastor who lived in Acernus and had to be driven in by his sixty-something son. He crept through the liturgy and preached so quietly that no one could hear a word he said. The only good thing about it was that Kitty overheard some of the grown-ups saying how happy they'd be when Pastor Donald got home.

Afterwards Kitty intercepted Mrs. Kipfmueller in the parking lot. She explained what she needed to do. Mrs. Kipfmueller said she saw no reason why not, she'd just have a quick word with Kitty's mother. Once they sorted it out, Kitty spent the afternoon hard at work under Mrs. Kipfmueller's direction.

The next morning Carmichael, as agreed, drove Kitty and the enormous Tupperware flats over to the school, Saul saying he'd rather ride the bus as usual. Kitty insisted that they park off to the side with a good vantage point of the sidewalk leading to the building. That was because she knew Megan didn't take the bus either but walked from her fancy Greek revival house on Spruce Street. The minutes dawdled by and Kitty fidgeted endlessly in the front seat, keeping her head low and peering over the edge of the window like a seriously unskilled spy.

"It's eight twenty-one," Carmichael pointed out. "Either you missed her or she's not coming."

"I didn't miss her, we've been here twenty minutes, and even if her mom drove her they'd have to come past us here."

"She's probably not coming at all, then."

"But if she *is* coming, she'll wait till the last second so she doesn't have to talk to people in the hallway before homeroom. Or anyway, that's what *I'd* do."

"Kitty..." droned Carmichael, twiddling the key in the ignition.

"There she is!" Kitty screeched. She pointed in the distance. Megan was still a few minutes' walk away. "Quick, quick, drive me right up to the front!"

Feeling like a bandit in reverse, Kitty clutched the side of the door as Carmichael whipped around and stopped in front of the entrance on the far right side of the school, closest to the junior high wing.

"Thanks, Mommy," Kitty called and banged the door shut with her foot, wobbling up the steps and through the door under the weight of the stack of Tupperware in front and her book bag in back. As arranged the night before by phone, she deposited one container with Jenny Ulster in her and Megan's homeroom and took the other to her own.

"Wow, what's that?" said Rob Adams with wide eyes.

"Yeah, what *is* that?" said Jessica into Kitty's ear, leaning forward from her seat to get a better look.

Right in sequence, their homeroom teacher Mr. Alvin chimed in, with a tone of polite interest that reserved the right to confiscate, "What've you got there, Kitty?"

She peeled off the lid to display twenty-four yellow cupcakes, capped with very dark chocolate frosting, and on each, in careful white cursive icing, *Welcome back, Megan!*

Kitty stood up and announced to the homeroom, "Megan Moravsky was out all last week so I made these to welcome her back."

"But Megan is in Miss Vansittart's class," said Mr. Alvin. This elicited a titter from the students, as it was widely speculated that Mr. Alvin and Miss Vansittart harbored feelings for one another, chiefly because they were the only single teachers on the whole junior high staff.

"Yes, I know," said Kitty, trying not to sound impatient at the imputed stupidity. "I brought cupcakes over to her homeroom, too."

"Well," said Mr. Alvin at a loss.

"Megan has been having a hard time lately," Kitty pressed on while she still had the floor. "I should know about having a hard time."

She paused while the sluggish brains of the seventh grade caught up with her insinuation. She could almost see the light of comprehension flicker on in each pair of eyes. Oh, right. Kitty. Dead brother.

"So I thought these would cheer her up, and make everyone glad to have her back again."

It was hard to say if the kids got the point, since the smell of the chocolate was wafting through the classroom and riveting all attention. Mr. Alvin granted his dispensation for Kitty to distribute her treats. Jessica helped, and soon the chatter resumed its normal volume accompanied by grateful smacking of the lips to enjoy every last bit of frosting.

It wasn't a day for gym, and for once Kitty couldn't bear to hang around after French and surveil the Spanish class's exit. She pretended to have cramps during lunch so she could eat her food in the nurse's office, then miraculously recovered in time for fifth period social studies, but ended up ignoring Rob in her anxiety over sixth period science when she would actually confront Megan in the flesh.

Megan was obviously on the alert. They locked eyes on arrival and then looked away. Kitty didn't take in a single word about paramecia or cilia or diatoms or any of it. When the forty-one minutes were up, she didn't know what to do. Should she wait for Megan to leave first? Then she noticed that Megan was packing up really, really slowly. She let everyone else get out ahead of her. That meant she probably wanted to talk to Kitty. Kitty packed up slowly, too, and timed her advance to the door just as the last person left.

She wasn't sure what to say so she just shot a glance at Megan.

Megan was waiting for it. "Thanks," she said, barely above a whisper. "For the cupcakes."

"You're welcome," said Kitty automatically. She looked at Megan carefully. Her eyes looked tired. Even her freckles looked tired.

Megan seemed to try to say several different things that all died en route to her lips. Finally she gestured into the hallway and said, "Miss Vansittart still has the container. She said she'd hang on to it till you get the chance to pick it up."

"Oh. Good. OK. Thanks," Kitty babbled.

"The frosting was really good," Megan squeezed out.

"Yeah, Mrs. Kipfmueller doesn't use cocoa powder, she uses this kind of chocolate bar that doesn't have any sugar in it."

"Like for diabetics?"

"No, like for baking."

"Oh." Then Megan said, "Um, I gotta get to English," and hoisted her fat science textbook.

"Yeah, I gotta go, too."

They left with out goodbyes or smiles.

Over dinner Kitty relayed the day's events in excruciating detail to Carmichael, who was not very attentive, anticipating the car due to pull up the driveway at any moment. She'd had a college meeting she couldn't miss, she told Kitty, so she'd asked Mr. Pohl to pick Donald up at the airport instead. Kitty was excited to see him again, too, but wished her mom would pay just a *little* more attention. She repeated three times over the nice things Miss Vansittart said to her when she retrieved the Tupperware. Even Saul got frustrated enough to shout, "Mommy! Listen to Kitty!"

At that Carmichael focused enough to say, "Well, that was a very nice thing you did."

"It looked like everyone was being friendly to her today," Kitty said. "I'm only in one class with her, plus gym every other day but not today, so I couldn't see for myself, but Jessica said she didn't sit alone at lunch and there was always someone talking to her in the hallway."

"I'm kind of surprised it worked," said Carmichael. "I mean, to be honest, I didn't want to stop you because you seemed so intent on it, but I kind of thought you were drawing attention to yourself, not to her."

"I got the idea from *Charlotte's Web*," said Kitty.

"'SOME PIG'!" spewed Saul through a mouthful of salad that was more ranch dressing than lettuce.

"Exactly," said Kitty. "I could never figure out in that story why everyone got so excited about Wilbur instead of Charlotte, because obviously it's the spider who's amazing, not the pig. But it worked. So I thought I'd do the same for Megan."

"Megan's a pig!" shouted Saul.

"Yeah, but she's *some* pig," corrected Kitty.

Then the pantry door burst open and seconds later they were climbing all over a very tired, very happy, very welcome Donald.

∽

The next morning, once the kids were off to school and the adults had the opportunity to reacquaint themselves in private, Donald and Carmichael drove over to New Zutphen for breakfast so he could relay the extraordinary events of the previous two weeks. That took them through the morning and a late lunch at home, and then, still energetic despite the jet lag, Donald suggested they may as well keep going and take the collected jars and cans and newspapers to the recycling center, whereupon Carmichael remembered that they had to pick up their turkey at the farm in New Aksum. It was only after they returned home and were rearranging the shelves in the fridge so that the turkey would fit that Donald wound up his narrative.

For all the enthusiasm of his extraordinary story, Carmichael detected at once the slightly hurt feeling behind his next comment: "I have to say I was pretty surprised to see George waiting at the airport for me last night instead of you."

Carmichael finished packing green beans and mushrooms around the turkey and was relieved that the fridge door shut without protest. "I know, I'm sorry. Of course, there was no way to let you know about the change of plans."

"Something came up?"

"Yes. I would've told you sooner, but you haven't let me get a word in edgewise." She gave him a little smirk.

That got his attention. "What's happened?" he said, as if realizing that just because, oh, the Berlin Wall fell, that didn't mean nothing else was going on in the rest of the world.

"You remember how I asked you about Achan and his theft, right after Jericho?" Donald looked puzzled. "Oh, well, I did, right when you picked me and Kitty up from our trip to New York." He nodded vaguely and she went on, "And how Tanisha told me that she didn't decline the lit class but was told she wasn't needed because *I* wanted to teach the class?"

"Oh, right. So?"

"Well, it wasn't much to go on, but it was something. After you left, I had a frankly clandestine meeting with Tobias Gooch Teylow and told him about it—about Tanisha, not the story in Joshua, of course—and asked if he thought there could be anything in it. And then *he* said that his request for funding for a professional conference had been declined on what he took to be spurious grounds, but since he knew that Alan had it out for him, he didn't think anything more of it. But then he said, maybe the real issue was that there wasn't any money for it at all, even though there should be."

"Like some kind of fund for faculty perks?"

"Exactly. There is one, or there's supposed to be one. So anyway, Tobias and I agreed to spend the next couple days quietly ferreting out of the others in the humanities department whether they had run up against any surprising refusals of funding… and *everyone* had. But no one had ever said anything about it, because they were all nervous about looking bad in front of the others. All the declines of funding were phrased as if the request was spurious or unjustified, or that the faculty member's output didn't merit college support. You can imagine that no one exactly wanted to advertise that fact."

"But what does it mean exactly, other than Alan being highhanded and stingy?" Donald asked. He reached into a cupboard and pulled out a box of Halloren Kugeln he'd brought back with him, extracted a chocolate-covered sphere, and handed it to Carmichael.

"It means," said Carmichael, accepting the candy with a glint of grim satisfaction, "that our dear professor Alan Forrad has been misappropriating funds."

Donald's Kugel fell out of his mouth. He caught it just in time. "*What?*"

"He's always been buddy-buddy with Dean Stanhope, so he must have managed to persuade him never to look too closely at the books, assuring him he'd take care of it. Since deans are perpetually overworked, I guess he was perfectly happy to trust Alan."

"Did you get proof?"

"Ultimately, yes, but it was pretty awkward in the interim. Once Tobias and I were convinced that something was amiss, we met with Stanhope privately and told him our suspicions. Needless to say, he didn't want to hear it, and Alan had obviously convinced him that Tobias was a doddering old fool not worth taking seriously. But he couldn't very well refuse to investigate once we laid out our case, and we got him to admit he hadn't been inspecting the humanities department's books for some time—years, I suspect. So he asked us to sit tight and wait while he looked into it. Tobias and I both expected him to drop it, but I guess the thought that he might've had the wool pulled over his eyes by someone he trusted galvanized him into action. A week later he summoned us to look over copies of faculty requests for funding, and sure enough every single one of them was denied. And then he showed us records from the business office—and the humanities account is just barely in the black. Disbursed in various ways, but nothing corresponds to faculty requests."

"So what happened to the money?"

"Looks like Alan just took it."

"He just—embezzled it? People *do* that?"

"You are such a naïf," Carmichael laughed.

"Don't go French on me now," he joked back. "But what I don't get is, why? I mean, he doesn't have a bad salary, I assume, and it's not *that* expensive to live here."

"I don't know for sure, it's not like he told us outright, but—"

"Wait, you've gone to Alan with this already?"

"That's why I couldn't pick you up at the airport last night. Stanhope, Tobias, and I had a meeting with him at two and I couldn't exactly miss it."

"And you've been holding it in all this time?"

"Well, I think the fall of the Berlin Wall takes precedence over a minor case of financial malfeasance at a tiny state college, don't you?"

Donald shook his head in wonder and popped the escaped Kugel back into his mouth.

"Yeah, so we met with him yesterday afternoon. I think the second he saw me and Tobias in there with the dean he knew the jig was up. He scowled but he didn't deny anything. Stanhope was beside himself, enraged and hurt and shocked and everything. Tobias looked unbelievably smug, though I think he had a right to that. I tried to keep as neutral as possible."

"But it wasn't easy."

"No," Carmichael confessed. "I was pretty happy to witness his downfall."

"So now what?"

"Well, Stanhope told Alan he had twenty-four hours to tender his resignation, but he gave it immediately."

"Just like that?"

"There was no denying the obvious. I don't know what he's going to do now. He's not gonna get another position in academia, that's for sure."

"How terrible," said Donald.

"Good Lord, you can't actually be *sorry* for them after all they've put us through?"

"Well…" said Donald feebly. "I guess I still don't get why he did it at all."

"He didn't say, though the dean asked him over and over, but I have a guess. Didn't it ever occur to you that it was kind of strange that Sandra didn't work? She's always gone on about her volunteer work on the board of Hope for Olutakli, so I guess I thought—or she led me to think—that they had so much money she didn't have to. But either she wouldn't work, or couldn't find a job, or maybe, and this is what I honestly think, she wanted the prestige of volunteering and being a benefactor without the slog of actually working or the comedown of receiving pay for it. You know, you said it yourself in that sermon or speech or whatever it was you gave on the last day of the trumpet revival. It's not wanting to do evil, but wanting to be good, that gets us in the end. I think she wanted to look exceptionally, extraordinarily good and generous. But they just couldn't afford it."

"They do have an awfully nice house," Donald remarked.

"I know, don't they? The furniture and books and art on the walls and all that. It's kind of a showpiece. I liked it because it reminded me of the City. I suppose that's why I fell for them, in a way. But it was all a sham. I bet Alan took the money because they were in debt, or to finance Sandra's expensive tastes and refusal to work."

"Poor man," clucked Donald.

Carmichael snorted. "Don't kid yourself. He was a willing infidel. I bet he liked the status of having a wife who didn't work and could do all that volunteer stuff. Heck, he was all about being a benefactor to me, promising me my own special electives and tenure way ahead of schedule. They were on the same page, morally."

"Thus saith the Lord," Donald teased. "I guess they'll be leaving Shibboleth, then."

"Probably."

"Then they'll take Alan's mother out of her niche and carry her with them. And the columbarium will be totally empty."

"I suppose. But haven't you grasped the greater significance of all this?"

"What?"

"*We can stay*," Carmichael declared. "Alan has no more say over my future at the college. They'll leave the church, too. The tide was already turning against them, but without them even Eunice and Marilyn won't be able to hold out much longer. Everyone at church the other day kept saying how excited they were to see you when you got back and hear all about your trip. And I'm pretty sure CPS won't be getting any more calls about us. We've done it. We've won."

"You're right." They hugged and Donald kissed her hair. "I can't say I'm thrilled about the way it all fell out in the end, though."

"You're too nice," Carmichael said, muffled through his shoulder. "But I *can* say that I am actually grateful that all this happened."

He pulled back a bit to look at her face. "Really? I wasn't expecting that. How so?"

"The anger was a ballast for my grief," she said. "Sadness just drags you down. Anger gives you a reason to live. I sure wouldn't have chosen it, but what I say is, thank God for good enemies."

"Good enemies," Donald echoed. "If only they hadn't needed so badly to be good."

~

Two days later Mt. Moriah hosted the ecumenical Thanksgiving service.

Al Beck showed up early waving a letter of resignation from the Forrads, wondering what he was supposed to do with it, because he'd never known anyone to submit such a letter to the church before. Donald told him to file it and not worry about it unless they asked for a letter of transfer to another congregation. Al added that he'd seen a for-sale sign up in front of the Forrads' house. Jackie appeared just then, three reluctantly scrubbed and dressed-up sons in tow, and insisted that Donald give her a high-five of victory. He did, but only because no one else was around to see it.

Before long the other local clergy filtered in to get their bearings and do a quick run-through of the service. Once that was over, Pieter from Second Reformed sidled up to Donald and said, "You sly bastard, foisting Eunice back on me again."

"What?" Donald replied in genuine astonishment.

Pieter looked surprised at his surprise. "Didn't she tell you to your face? Well, I sure got an earful. All sorts of dark insinuations about your driving good and innocent people out of the church, and how she wasn't going to wait around for the axe to fall on *her* neck, too."

"I—it wasn't—good Lord!"

Pieter laughed and clapped him on the back. "I know. I mean, I *don't* know, but I don't want to know, and I don't care. I understand how these things go. I'm just jealous that you're free of her again."

Hazel and Dale manifested quietly, one at a time, to welcome Donald home and, in so many words, apologize for their defection, Dale by chucking two gallons of maple syrup at him with the gruff comment, "You won't get this nowhere else for free so maybe it'll make you wanna stay," and Hazel by fluttering, crying a little, and asking if there was anything she could do to ease the difficulty of the upcoming anniversary of dear little Asher's passing. Donald comforted her and then said he really had to get into his alb and she bustled out of the sacristy, apologetic all over again.

Marilyn showed up alarmingly late for the service. She beckoned him into the sacristy and launched into a long and extremely vague speech that may have been an apology, ending with the bright announcement that she would not be withdrawing her membership from Mt. Moriah after all.

"Oh," said Donald. "I hadn't realized you were contemplating leaving."

Marilyn looked offended that Donald hadn't realized just how narrowly he'd escaped losing her. She said, "Well, in the end I realized how important my role is here, and it would be wrong to leave the church without any organist at all. It's the right thing to do, staying on. I expect I'll stay on till the day I die."

"Oh," said Donald again, this time more like a sigh. "Well, God be praised."

The church was packed to the walls, people sitting in folding chairs along the outer aisles and standing in the narthex, no doubt because word had gotten round, not least of all in *The Kuhsota Daily Register*, that a local pastor had been present at the tremendous events in Berlin a few weeks earlier. The fact that, even as they spoke, huge demonstrations were taking place daily in Czechoslovakia made it even more exciting. After changing his mind half a dozen times, Donald displayed his holy relic—the chunk of the wall that had been placed in his hands—on a table off to the side of the pulpit. He did his best to baptize it by preaching on, of course, the battle of Jericho. And if the crowd behaved more like an audience than a congregation, well, so be it. Donald could hardly deny that he enjoyed their gasps, their laughs, and by the end even their tears of assent to the proposition that God almighty does indeed bring down even the most forbidding of walls.

As Donald pronounced the final "Amen" he noticed, in the back pew, a nodding, beaming Mrs. Feuerlein. Next to her sat Grandfather Abney. He grinned at Donald and gave him a thumb's up. Then he put his arm around Mrs. Feuerlein and they left the church together.

It was only after the turkey feast at home was finished that Donald got a phone call, informing him that Sabine Feuerlein had died peacefully in her sleep early that morning.

∽

On the Saturday after Thanksgiving, Carmichael paid a visit to the Co-op. It was empty inside except for Rachel, who came bounding out to greet her.

They sat down together at one of the tiny wobbly tables over a lemon-ginger infusion ("you need this now that the days are getting so short") and pumpkin muffins. Carmichael brought Rachel up to date, more or less, on recent events, with the concluding assurance that whatever the cook at Tiny's or anyone else might think, the Abneys were very definitely *not* moving away from Shibboleth.

When she was getting ready to leave, Carmichael plucked up her courage and asked Rachel if she and Todd would like to come over to dinner next Friday.

Rachel lit up. "A dinner party!" she exclaimed. "I haven't been to one in ages. But wait—is it allowed for me to come to a church house?"

"A parsonage," Carmichael supplied.

"Oh, is that what it's called? I mean, is it OK with me being a Jew and all?"

"*I'm* a Jew," said Carmichael.

"But you're also a Christian. Maybe I'm disqualified."

"Then my parents would be, too. Of course you're allowed! I'd allow you even if you weren't. Our other dinner guests aren't any religion at all—my colleague Tobias Gooch Teylow and his wife Prudence."

"What names," breathed Rachel admiringly.

Carmichael told her the time and Rachel volunteered to bring a couple bottles of sulfite-free red wine. She waved cheerily before slipping into the back room.

At the door Carmichael looked back at the tiny table. It was crowded with her alternate selves, so many of them that they were sitting on each other's laps, blending like transparencies on a projector screen.

Jewish Carmichael arose and grabbed the hand of her nearest neighbor. That one followed, grabbing another hand, and so they came, an interlocking chain of Carmichaels, kicking and striding right toward the flesh-and-blood one as if in rhythm to a secret Hava Nagila pounding in their ears. Jewish Carmichael looked into bodily Carmichael's eyes, smiled, stepped inside her, and vanished from sight. Then the next, and another, and another.

Right in the middle of them came Rachel weeping. She, too, looked Carmichael in the eyes, without a smile, without a dance, and Carmichael felt something like a cold splash as the weeping woman stepped inside her chest.

The rest of the Carmichaels sprang in after her, one after another, until the very last one, the warm, silly, suntanned California Carmichael, who gave her a spirited tap on the cheek and dove in.

They were gone.

And yet, Carmichael thought, as the chimes on the door jangled behind her, they're still here. No longer alien, but aligned. At home. One.

~

Mrs. Feuerlein's funeral took place after church on Sunday afternoon. As no snow had yet fallen, congregation and coffin alike could proceed directly from the church to the waiting grave in the cemetery.

Saul had been extremely upset when he learned that Mrs.

Feuerlein was going to be buried on the far side of Mr. Feuerlein instead of right next to Asher.

"Asher is so lonely," he declared, tears streaming out of his eyes. "He needs someone to keep him company."

Donald was already over at church so Carmichael, at a loss, held him close and said, "Asher has the angels to keep him company."

"Angels are *boring*," Saul shot back.

He was irritable and moody all through the morning service and picked at his lunch, even though it was grilled cheese and tomato soup, his favorite. During the funeral service he would not keep quiet, pestering Carmichael and Kitty with questions about rocket ships and dinosaurs or rehearsing the plots of his favorite episodes of "Inspector Gadget." When the pallbearers carried Mrs. Feuerlein's coffin out of the church, Saul just about yanked Carmichael's arm out of its socket in his eagerness to be the first to follow.

They trod across the crunchy frostbitten grass to the perfect rectangle in the dark earth. Ray Jansen and the rest of his staff from the funeral home were on hand to help the pallbearers lower the coffin into place. Donald stood at the headstone, where the names of both Gerhard Feuerlein and Sabine née Hartmann Feuerlein had already long since been engraved, along with her year of birth but not, as yet, her year of death. The prayers unspooled in their lyrical solace, promises tasted but not yet triumphant, glimpses of a hope so tremendous that perhaps, after all, more than a glimmer would unseat the reason and disqualify the soul for the task of living. Donald related the tale of Mrs. Feuerlein's remarkable brother Gotthilf, survivor of the insides of a wolf, and her parting charge to him before he left for Germany to accept the good from the hand of the Lord and not only the bad. The congregation nodded its assent to her wisdom. Donald invited them to toss a handful of dirt onto her coffin.

But before Donald could demonstrate how to do it, Saul

burst free of Carmichael and, instead of flinging dirt on the coffin, flung himself.

"Saul!" Carmichael screamed.

"I want to go with her!" Saul wailed. "I want to go with her and see Asher!"

Before Carmichael or Donald could even move, George Pohl dropped to the ground and slithered into the narrow margin between the dirt wall of the grave and the shiny wood of the coffin. He tugged Saul free from his prone posture on top of the coffin lid and wrapped his arms around the struggling boy.

"Nope, nope, nope," he said into the top of Saul's head. "We lost your brother. We aren't gonna lose you, too."

"I don't want to be here," Saul sobbed. "I want to go where Asher is."

Dale caught up and sat himself down, legs dangling into the grave, and nodded for George to hand Saul over. The boy became inert, dead weight, and it took effort to make the transfer. Dale arranged Saul on his lap while George, awkwardly, braced himself against the coffin to eject himself up onto the grass.

"Now look it here," said Dale to Saul. "Don'tcha remember how you and me made your brother's nice soft grave over there?"

Saul nodded listlessly.

"We put him there and he's gone to sleep and he's not gonna wake up for a real long time. I know it's hard because he was your brother and you shared everything with him."

"Not everything," whispered Saul. "I didn't share my teddy bear with him and he didn't share his doggy with me."

"Well, it's kinda like that. You don't get to share the grave with him. You gotta let him stay there, and you gotta stay here with us."

Saul gave another little heave of despair.

Carmichael finally came out of her trance and, mindlessly issuing thanks to Dale and George, scooped Saul up into her arms. She held him and rocked him and told him how much she needed him to stay and live and be with her and Daddy and Kitty. Kitty took hold of his shoe and squeezed it. Donald signaled to the mourners to commence with the dirt and joined his family, kissing the back of Saul's hot head.

Al came by and whispered, "You can go home if you want to now, Pastor. Ray and I will take it from here."

Donald nodded and escorted the other three back to the parsonage.

When Saul's tears dried, Kitty set to work distracting him with a game of Connect Four. After he lost interest, she tried Hungry Hungry Hippos, and that did the trick for awhile. Carmichael put together an early supper of scrambled eggs on toast made from a misshapen loaf of challah she'd attempted on Friday. They watched the news and learned that the whole communist party leadership in Czechoslovakia had resigned two days earlier, almost a million people were still demonstrating in Prague, and what was left of the government agreed to meet with a playwright named Vaclav Havel, who was the head of the dissident movement. "I know you don't understand, but you should try to remember this, Saul," Carmichael said to him, curled up in a tight ball on her lap. "This is good and exciting and happy news. If it keeps up, we might even have a chance to find our family in Estonia. Bammy and Bampy's cousins still live there somewhere. Maybe we can visit them someday. I bet they have kids your age."

Saul gave a tiny nod but didn't unfurl from his bundle.

When the news was over he said he was tired and wanted to go to bed. Donald and Carmichael exchanged looks—Saul had never been known to retire voluntarily before—but agreed, taking lavish time over his bath and teeth. Donald read him three bedtime stories. Carmichael sang a lullaby. Kitty brought him her stuffed wolf and slid it under the covers next to him.

"It's the wolf that swallowed up Mrs. Feuerlein's little brother," said Saul. "Maybe he swallowed up Asher, too. Maybe Asher is inside his tummy." He poked at the spot.

"Virginia's a she, not a he," said Kitty. She gave Saul a fast hard peck on the cheek and took herself early to bed, too.

Carmichael and Donald found themselves staring at each other from opposite ends of the sofa, the only sound the pops and cracks from the woodstove.

At last Carmichael said what they were both thinking. "Is Saul ever going to be OK?"

A log rumbled and turned over inside the stove, causing Donald to look at it. He turned back to Carmichael. "I don't know," he said heavily.

She nodded. Then, "Oh, God, I'm dreading next month. I don't know how we'll ever celebrate Christmas again, but I know this first one will be the absolute worst."

"And then Asher's birthday a week later."

"Yeah. You know, there are times I think I just can't go on another day hurting like this. But every time I notice I'm *not* hurting, I feel like a traitor."

"I do, too. But we saw today the cost of being ruled by that. It's one thing for parents to grieve and get stuck on their grief. But it's something else for a seven-year-old boy to get stuck on it so much that he gives up on his own life. We can't let that happen, no matter what."

"No," she breathed. "Then we'd lose them both. And that would certainly be worse. But reassure me, please—he's going to come out of this at some point, isn't he? He's not going to go on like this forever?"

Donald reflected. "He might," he said. "I think we have to accept that he might. I think if we're going to get through this, we have to decide that we'll surround him with love and strength because that's what we do. Not because we know when or if it will fix him."

"So you're saying it could go on forever." Carmichael felt her chest heave with a rising sob and stifled it.

"Some situations go on a long time. But that doesn't mean forever. Sometimes walls do come down."

"*That* wall took forty years to come down! Do you think Saul will be stuck in his grief for forty years?"

Donald reached out and took her hand. "I don't know anything," he said. "I just know that he is our living son, and we'll live with him, even if he's shut up inside his own walls. We can pass in and out. We can tell him about the world outside. Someday, when he's ready, he'll tear them down himself and come out."

"Are you sure?"

"No. I'm not sure," he said. "But I hope and I trust. And I know it's happened before. That will have to be enough for us."

"It is enough," said Carmichael.

∼

Megan seemed to be back to normal again. She was bossy in gym class, playing offense in soccer and screaming directions at the other girls. She had friends around her at lunch. She came out of Spanish class talking to Rob again, but then Kitty was talking to Rob again, too, so that didn't mean much.

In science class she would give Kitty a curt little nod, not saying anything friendly, but somehow communicating that maybe possibly they didn't have to be enemies anymore.

For all of which reasons Kitty just couldn't understand why Rhea wouldn't leave her alone already. She dogged Kitty's steps from one class to the next, loomed like a greedy shadow behind doors, and glared out from between her lions, who seemed ready to pounce at any minute.

Rhea didn't talk to Kitty at school, not a single word. But she didn't go away, either. After another week of her hauntings, Kitty realized that if she didn't figure out fast what Rhea was up to, she'd lose her mind.

So, heading home from school across the first snowfall, Kitty leaped and skidded and looked back to make sure Rhea was following. She'd heard somewhere that you should never run away from a predator because it triggers their chase instinct—but that was exactly what Kitty wanted. When she got to the parsonage, she poked her head through the pantry door and shouted, "Daddy, I'm home but I'm gonna stay outside and play," even though it was a lie. She kicked through the powder of snow out to the east edge of the meadow, past the ropy gray arms of the lilac tree. She glanced back. Rhea was coming straight at her.

Kitty dropped to her bottom and wiggled her way down to the mouth of the cave. The sight of it used to fill her with excitement and intrigue, her own private place that no one else knew about, where her council members came and talked to her only. But now it reminded her of the eggshells leftover after you made a cake, empty and useless. The cave was smaller than she remembered. She couldn't fit inside without her neck being tilted in an uncomfortable position. She scooted back out to the front lip of the cave and let her legs dangle over the slope.

Rhea turned the corner and faced her.

"You didn't ever figure it out," Kitty accused. It felt good to turn the tables on her persecutor. "You promised you'd work on it, but you never even tried to stop me from growing up. And everything happened just like I was afraid of. I turned into a liar and did bad things. But it's *your* fault, not mine. You let me down!"

Rhea broke her long silence. "There is only one way not to grow up," she said. "I told you so at the beginning."

"Well, maybe that's what I should have done instead!" Kitty snarled.

"There is already enough death in your family," said Rhea.

Kitty felt like she'd been smacked, and hard. Rhea was exactly what most adults weren't. She never made anything easier or nicer. She never lied. But Kitty wasn't going to be refuted so easily. "Maybe I should have died instead of Asher, then! Then I wouldn't have turned into what I turned into."

"That is not for you to choose!" Rhea hurled the words at her like each one was a lightning bolt. Kitty trembled all over.

Rhea had never been so terrifying. She was growing bigger, too, blocking out the sky that shone dimly between the tree limbs behind her. "You may not choose death. You have been given life. You are to grow into it."

Kitty was sniffling, scared, but another part of her was surging angry. "Yeah, but look at me!" she made herself retort. "I've been rotten. I'm turning corrupt like everyone else. I could have stayed cute and innocent like Asher. Who even knows what I'll end up doing? What if I grow up to be like Mrs. Onderdonk? Or worse, like Mrs. Forrad? It would be better not to grow up at all. Even if it meant..." She couldn't quite bring herself to say it.

Rhea began to vibrate and glow, like molten metal was flowing through her veins. She leaned in close to Kitty's face. Her voice dropped to a whisper, but the whisper was even more frightening than the lightning-bolt shout. "Do you insist on playing at death? If you do, I will give you a taste of it."

"Wait, what—" Kitty cried, but before she could get another word out, Rhea seized her by the hair and dragged her forward. Kitty toppled off the lip of the cave and all at once she was falling—

falling—

through the blackberry canes, which though wintry still tore at her with their little spines, ripping at her coat and corduroys, scratching her face and hands, but that was nothing compared to the terror of rolling down the hill out of control, thumping painfully against jagged rocks, and she tucked in her knees and wrapped her arms around her head and hoped she wouldn't get knocked unconscious and how much longer could it go on—

Whump.

She stopped rolling. She didn't uncurl for a minute, just lay there, feeling wicked bruises rising on her back and elbows. When she was sure that the earth was solid beneath her, she stretched out her arms and legs experimentally and opened her eyes.

Rhea was standing right over her. She looked fine. She must

have hovered down on her chariot.

"I fell," said Kitty.

"And yet you live," said Rhea.

Kitty sat up. She looked around at the thicket of trees and the dead leaves and the steep slopes rising on either side of her.

"I'm in the saddle," she said. "I fell all the way down!"

She heaved herself up to her feet and scanned overhead to figure out where she'd come from. The skids in the leaves and broken blackberry canes pointed the way.

"Holy cow, that's a long ways up." She rubbed at her sore spots. She looked over at Rhea. "Will I be able to climb back up again?"

"You can," said Rhea. "It will be hard. But you can."

Kitty thought for a moment before speaking again. "Will you help me?"

She expected a lecture or a scolding or another discourse on death. But Rhea said simply, "Yes."

It *was* hard climbing up again. The blackberry bushes were the only plants growing on the rock face and their roots were too shallow to give Kitty a reliable handhold, even if she could ignore the spines piercing her hands. There were enough jagged edges sticking out for her to grab and hoist herself up one toehold a time. She thought how strange it was that the very rocks that smacked and bruised her on the way down were the ones aiding her climb back up again. Twice she slipped and slid a few feet down before she could catch herself. It started to snow and that made her hands slippery and stiff. Rhea did not lift or carry or push Kitty up. But she stayed right behind her the whole way.

At last Kitty reached the top, flung her chest over the edge, and saw once again the lonely soulless cave right in front of her. She braced herself for one last heave of her legs, and then she was safe at the meadow's edge. She crawled over to the lilac tree and flipped on her back. Snowflakes fluttered down and settled on her eyelids.

She felt a warm hand on her forehead.

She opened her eyes. It was Rhea. Her stare had softened. She wasn't exactly smiling, but she wasn't boiling with fury, either. Her hand was sending some kind of electric honey into Kitty's brain.

"Live," said Rhea.

"But what if I—" Kitty tried to ask.

"You will. Live anyway."

Kitty thought she should feel terrible about it, but Rhea's warm hand made it tolerable somehow.

Rhea straightened up to her full awesome height. She snapped her fingers and the lions whooshed in with the chariot.

Kitty asked, "Are you leaving? For good?"

"Yes. For good," said Rhea.

The chariot leapt into the air and was gone.

Kitty flipped over again and pushed herself to her feet. Her elbows and back hurt really bad. She took baby steps toward the house.

Asher fell, and he didn't live.

I fell, and I did live.

It isn't fair.

But it *is*.

Live anyway, Rhea had said.

Kitty leaned a hand against the parsonage. Now her right ankle was starting to ache. She must have sprained it.

I'm gonna end up telling more lies, she thought. I'm gonna do more rotten things.

And still Rhea's charge resounded through her head: Live anyway.

Daddy is living. He's extra alive now since he got back from Germany. He wasn't ever this alive, even before Asher died. Mommy comes and goes, but mostly she wants to live. Only when the sadness gets the better of her she starts to give up. But then she finds something to get mad at and she comes back to life again.

And Saul?

Poor Saul. Saul wants to give up and be with Asher. Rhea was right to make fun of me for playing at wanting to die, because I don't want to really, not like Saul does.

She reached the steps up to the pantry door and sat down on them and discovered yet another bruise on her rear end.

Since I'm going to live anyway, she thought, I'll live for Mommy and Daddy. And for Jesus. And all four grandparents, and Jessica and Jenny, and Mrs. Kipfmueller, and Rob. I guess even for Megan. Especially for Saul.

She heard the scuffle of feet on gravel. A second later Saul appeared around the corner of the house, trudging along under the weight of his backpack.

"Kitty!" he cried. She always got home from school first, but she never waited outside for him. He smiled to see her there. A deep, real smile.

Kitty gripped the railing and levered herself up. "Come on inside," she said. "I'll make cocoa and we can drink it while we play Operation."

"Cool!" shouted Saul. He dashed up to her, then watched curiously as she hopped up the steps on her left foot. "What happened?"

"Do I ever have a story to tell you!" Kitty said as she opened the door for him. "You just won't believe it."

FOR A DEEPER DIVE

Curious to learn more about the names, details, hidden themes, symbolic meanings, and creative process behind this novel? Check out the *Palimpsest Guide to A-Tumblin' Down*, available exclusively from Thornbush Press. And while you're there, pick up the dessert section of the Mt. Moriah Lutheran Church cookbook, featuring Carmichael Abney's apple crisp, Ruth Pohl's kranzkuchen, Arlene Mayer's maple-walnut spirals, and more!

www.thornbushpress.com/product/atumblindown

ACKNOWLEDGEMENTS

Gratitude is due first of all to those who answered questions and offered the inspiration that gave me the gumption to pursue this sprawling novel.

Thanks, then, to Hans Kasch and Thomas Böhmert for their insights into life in the DDR.

Thanks to Andy Johnson for his expertise on burial practices.

Thanks to Gracia Grindal for answering questions about Norwegian-American Lutherans.

Thanks to Chris Smith for coaching my Queens accent for the audiobook.

Thanks to Adam Richardson of the Writer's Detective Bureau for answering a few questions about police matters.

Thanks to Ellen I. Hinlicky and Paul R. Hinlicky for answering questions about social work and academic politics.

Thanks to Carrie Frederick Frost for sending me (all the way from Washingon state to Tokyo) a print copy of *In This House of Brede* by Rumer Godden, which proved a key source of inspiration for presenting literarily the minute interactions of a close-knit community.

And thanks to Mary Elise Sarotte for having written the outstanding book *The Collapse: The Accidental Opening of the Berlin Wall*, without which this novel could not have been written.

Any errors in the telling of this story are entirely my own!

The second round of gratitude goes to the beta readers of this novel in its various stages. My heartfelt thanks to Ellen I. Hinlicky, Katie Langston, Anneli Horner Matheson, Matthew and Cindy Musteric, and Andrew L. Wilson.

Third, great thanks to all the wonderful readers who subscribed to the serialization of this book over the summer and fall of 2022: Carrie Frederick Frost, Richard Graham, Natalie Hall, Stewart Herman, Ellen I. Hinlicky, Brett Jenkins, Joey Knatterud, Melinda Knatterud, Katie Langston, Angela May,

Allison Zbicz Michael, Mark Michael, Sarah Oba, Ricky Phillips, Jan Powers, Micah Prochaska, Amy Ross, Sarah Rossiter, Dawn Smith, James Smith, Nicole Smith, Anna Stevenson, Charles St-Onge, John Wilson, Roger Wilson, and Virginia Wilson.

Last but not least, gratitude is due the good people of Immanuel Lutheran Church in Delhi, New York. Everything that is good and worthy about Mt. Moriah Lutheran Church and the town of Shibboleth, New York, has been inspired by both. All the sins and failings depicted herein are the work of my imagination upon the aggregate experience of both myself and of many other pastors and laypeople I have known.

SARAH HINLICKY WILSON

is the Founder of Thornbush Press.

She serves as Associate Pastor at
Tokyo Lutheran Church in Japan,
where she lives with her husband and son.

She co-hosts the podcast
"Queen of the Sciences:
Conversations between a Theologian
and Her Dad" with Paul R. Hinlicky.

Sign up for her quarterly e-newsletter
"Theology & a Recipe"
and learn more about her other books at:

www.sarahhinlickywilson.com
and
www.thornbushpress.com

- Her mom sitting shiva
- Kitty's council

Made in the USA
Middletown, DE
03 June 2024